Water:
Selkies, Sirens, & Sea Monsters

Edited by
Rhonda Parrish

Water:
Selkies, Sirens, & Sea Monsters

Edited by
Rhonda Parrish

TYCHE BOOKS LTD.

Published by Tyche Books Ltd.
Calgary, Alberta, Canada
www.TycheBooks.com

Cover Art by Ashley Walters
Cover Layout by Indigo Chick Designs
Interior Layout by Ryah Deines
Editorial by Rhonda Parrish

First Tyche Books Ltd Edition 2020
Print ISBN: 978-1-989407-27-1
Ebook ISBN: 978-1-989407-28-8

This book was funded in part by a grant from the Alberta Media Fund.

For Jo

Table of Contents

Introduction

Rhonda Parrish

I'M NOT SURE if I'm ready for this to be over, to be honest. I always procrastinate when it comes time to write an Introduction because I struggle with them (which may be why they always end up more like an "Editor's Note" than an "Introduction"), but for this one the procrastination levels were epic. And I think, in part, it's because this is the fourth and final book for this anthology series. And I'm going to be quite sad to see it end.

But it's ending on a really high note.

I'm biased, of course, and not just because I'm the editor, but also because water is without question my absolute favourite element. When I was very young, if I was being fussy or annoying, my mother used to fill up the kitchen sink and plonk me down in it and let me splash and play. It never failed to calm me down. And that relationship with water remains to this day, all these many years later. The sharp smell of chlorinated water always makes me smile, as does the scent of the ocean. And both call to me.

That connection to the water makes me understand the yearning of selkies and the beckoning power of sirens.

When the publisher and I decided to put a selkie in mid-transformation on the cover, I don't think either of us realized how perfect a cover that would be for this collection, but it is. Perfect, I mean. Not because there is a preponderance of selkie stories here—there aren't. Really, there are only a few pure selkie stories and poems within these pages, but there are a lot of transformational ones.

Which really fits with the water theme. Even single drops of water, over time, can erode away stone—shifting and transforming it—and large bodies of water take no time at all to change landscapes. Or people.

Water shifts to take the shape of whatever contains it, so how can it be surprising that those things it contains also transform?

In some of these stories water *is* the siren, the shapeshifter, the monster. In others it's less a character and more a setting. Or a force. Or a mystery.

What kind of wonders might oceans and swamps, lakes and rivers contain? What kind of creatures? What kind of magic?

The stories and poems in this collection don't have all the answers to that question, but they do pose a variety of intriguing possibilities.

Rhonda
Edmonton, Alberta
1/28/21

The Diviner

Catherine MacLeod

MELLY TOOK THE lid off the stock pot and drew a slow breath. The broth was dark and fragrant, just beginning to boil. She stirred in salt and rosemary as the phone rang.

The caller ID said *Shay Lumber*. Her husband said, "I'm bringing Gary and the new guy home for supper."

"There's a new guy?" Parsley, bay leaf, lemon zest.

"Archie Dennis retired last week."

Chives, pepper, roofing nails. "When will you be home?"

"We'll be there by six." It was five-thirty.

There was a soft *crack* as her wooden spoon splintered. "No problem."

(Rule: The correct answer was *always* "No problem.")

He said, "Good," and hung up. Jon Shay wasn't the kind of man who asked if you needed anything from the store. Melly liked the company tradition of inviting the new hire to supper, but she'd learned early in the marriage to keep ingredients for a fast meal on hand.

She put a pot of water on to boil. She had spaghetti, homemade sauce, and Parmesan. She had garlic bread, green peppers, and the sure knowledge that Jon's brother Gary would eat bruschetta until he passed out. There was orange sherbet if they wanted dessert, and a half-dozen beer in the fridge.

She set the stock pot in the sink, added a broken locket, and stirred the broth with Jon's hammer. One more deep sniff. A drop of blood slid out of her nose.

Perfect.

THE NEW GUY'S name was Christopher Graham. He said, "This is for you," and held out a small potted plant. Three mauve flowers on long stems swayed gently with the motion.

"They're beautiful."

"To be honest, I don't know what they are."

"Cyclamen," she said. "They're a kind of African violet."

"Thank you for having me to dinner, Mrs. Shay."

"Everyone calls me Melly." She kissed her husband's cheek and said, "Supper's ready, dear. Gary, will you take in the beer, please?"

When they'd gone into the dining room, she hung up their coats. She plucked a hair from Gary's collar and dropped it in the cooling broth, then took the pasta to the table.

Jon said, "Chris lives just a mile up the road, by the bridge."

"You're renting the old Winston place? Have you met your neighbours yet?"

"I met Bob Lyle."

"Did he warn you about the Miller house burning down?"

"No."

Jon said, "He usually starts talking about it in August. You saw that old hulk of a house between your place and here, right? It's sagged like that for the last eighty years. Every Halloween Bob worries that teenagers will torch it. But it's so rickety the craziest of them wouldn't go in there. And it's full of rats." He grinned as Melly shuddered. "My wife doesn't like rats."

Melly shook her head, embarrassed. She hated them *almost* as much as Jon did, but would never say so.

(Rule: Don't embarrass the husband, even in jest.)

"I hope you'll like Kemper's Bend," she said.

"I'm sure I will. I came from a place like this, called Andersville." Chris looked down at his plate. "It's not really there anymore. I worked at the mill there, too. But it burned down a couple of years ago, and that was it for half the town."

"And the other half?" she asked.

"A company called *Whycorp Gas and Oil* found natural gas. You know about hydraulic fracturing?"

"Fracking," she said faintly.

"Yeah. They said there wouldn't be any damage to our wells, but there was. They brought us bottled water for a while, but then they stopped."

Jon said, "No one told you?"

"What?"

"*Whycorp*'s been here for almost a year."

It was the first time Melly had ever actually seen the colour drain from someone's face. She almost reached out to take Chris's hand, then caught herself—she barely knew him, and Jon wouldn't like it.

Gary said, "Can I get seconds, Mel?"

"Sure."

He was clueless as ever, she thought, but at least he'd changed the subject. He rattled on about Jon's new truck, Jon's new generator, and Jon's new big-screen TV. When the conversation moved on to work and hockey, Chris joined in politely but was sparing with his opinions.

Definitely a small-town boy, she thought. (Rule: The new boy speaks only when spoken to.)

Gary said, "That was delicious, Mel."

"Thanks."

"Could you give Charlene the recipe?"

"I don't have one," she admitted. "I just cook by feel. You know—pinch of this, dash of that. Mostly it turns out okay."

"Too bad Charlene can't do that."

She doesn't have time because she's too busy icing her latest black eye, Melly thought. *And it wouldn't matter if I had a recipe because you don't want her talking to anyone. And stop calling me Mel, you ass.*

Chris rose when she did and picked up his plate. She said, "Guests don't do that. And you have a movie to watch."

"I do?"

"You do," Jon said. "I got *Batman*. The original, with Michael Keaton."

She cleared the table as they went into the den, then checked the pot in the sink. She opened three more beers, poured a spoonful of broth into one, and dumped a bag of pretzels into a bowl.

"Should we wait for your wife?" she heard Chris ask.

"No, she likes those black-and-white movies on the late show. She's not into masked vigilantes."

"Ha!" she said, handing Gary the doctored beer. "For all you know I could have a secret identity of my own."

"Yeah, right—The Diviner, finding new wells and vanishing into the night."

Melly laughed along with the men. Movie music cued up as she left.

She strained the stock into a half-dozen plastic bottles, labelled them neatly—*Agony-in-Waiting*—and carried them into her pantry. She lined them up on the shelf with *Non-Fatal Paralysis, This-is-War,* and *Get-Over-It.*

Jon was wrong: she did like *Batman,* and she knew a bit about vigilantes. The Diviner wasn't the most dashing alias, but it was what most people in the Bend called her. Most of them had seen her pacing a construction site, carrying a willow branch they were half-convinced she didn't need. They'd seen her go still, feeling for deep-running water. She was never sure if it pulled her toward it, or if she pulled it up, but when she felt the branch start to tug, she said, "Dig here." She'd never been wrong.

She washed and dried Jon's hammer and put it back where he'd left it. Tonight's potion was a concentrated mix; Gary would shatter every bone in his hand the next time he hit his wife. He'd smash his feet if he kicked her. And if he bit her it was going to be all kinds of ugly.

Melly studied her reflection in the kitchen window as she washed the dishes. She had on her *homebody* smile, the look of a devoted and compassionate wife.

Jon was wrong about that, too. She knew all about masks.

THE NEXT MORNING'S brew was a gift for Emma Reese, excruciatingly respectable widow and town gossip. Her house was across the street from both the laundromat and the coffee shop, giving her a good view of the town's comings and goings. Her gossip was getting nastier, and Melly had become her favourite subject: "She's too good to go to church like the rest of us. She thinks all water is holy."

Melly knew Emma was probably just lonely, but there were

better ways of getting attention. *And I dowsed your well, remember?*

Melly mixed a batch of *Silence-or-Else*: one part wood rot, one part horse manure, one part common dirt, and a lot of peppermint, stirred with a very sharp knife and chilled.

A few cheerful words to Emma in the coffee shop, a little misdirection, and the potion was in her cup. From now on any malicious lies would burn her tongue like a mouthful of wasps. The pain would fade to a three-alarm chili burn after an hour and be gone an hour after that. Melly doubted she'd ever realize what caused it. No doctor ever would.

"Did you hear what happened to Ivy Patterson?" Emma asked. "Somebody threw a rock through her bedroom window last night."

"What? Who?"

"Probably a jealous wife," Emma said, and clapped a hand over her mouth. Melly checked another job off her mental to-do list.

The next time she saw Ivy in the grocery store she said, "I heard about your window. Are you okay?"

"No." Ivy's hands shook as she paid her bill. "Angela Mackie threw the rock. I can't prove it, but I know. I started dating Shaun last week."

"But she dumped him a year ago."

"Yeah, I thought it would be okay. But as soon as another woman wanted him, she was interested again. She hasn't mellowed, you know?"

Melly did. Twenty years after graduation Angela was still known for her dark beauty and spiteful temper—and her appetite for chocolate and other women's men.

Ivy said, "I'm scared."

Melly drove her home. Ivy's cat was dead on the doorstep. Melly called Shaun and the police, and discreetly collected a claw from the cat and bits of the broken window before they arrived.

"Tomorrow is Angela's birthday," Shaun said. "This must be a present to herself."

When she told Jon about it that night, he said, "That's crazy, even for Angela. Smashing the window, you'd expect that from her. But killing the cat is a whole different kettle of fish."

Interesting way of putting it, Melly thought, and started her potion with a fish chowder. She simmered a cup of the milky broth with the cat's claw, slivers of glass, and a capful of vanilla. She strained it, then added sugar, cocoa, and butter. After a night in the fridge the fudge would be silky and tempting.

She'd wrap it in waxed paper and leave it in Angela's mailbox with a birthday card signed, *You know who.* It would leave Angela terrified of going anywhere near Ivy, or anything that belonged to her. Which, for now at least, included Shaun.

Melly served the rest of the chowder for supper. Jon wiped his bowl out with a slice of bread and said, "You're a damned fine cook, Mel."

She was. The first thing she'd ever learned in her mother's kitchen was, "Cook with intent. Know exactly what you want to make. Your intentions are as much an ingredient as the salt."

Melly had understood that immediately, though not on a level her mother would have recognized. She doubted her mother would have approved of some of the things Melly had intended in her kitchen. But she was pleased that Melly had taken on a share of her workload, and equally pleased by Jonathan Shay's growing interest in her daughter. The oldest son of the mill-owner, and a little too handsome, he was considered a good catch.

Melly hadn't expected him to come calling, but apparently a good batch of biscuits was a powerful draw.

His interest in her had cooled over the years, but familiarity would do that, she thought. Familiarity and a potion in his coffee every morning for a month. It hadn't made him lose interest in other women, but she was fine with that—maybe some of *them* liked it rough.

Still, she thought he was fond of her in his own way, even if that way called for caution on her part. She kept his house clean and his clothes well-mended; she fed him well and flirted with him in public.

And kept her mask firmly in place.

JON WAS A rarity among the Shay men, though. As long as her work was done and appearances were maintained, he didn't mind if Melly had a social life.

(Unspoken rule: Don't enjoy it too much.)

It consisted mainly of having a library card and going for

coffee after doing the laundry. She repeated most of the news she thought would interest him, but not all. It would be unseemly to be too well-informed. She thought he wouldn't want her knowing as much about fracking as she did.

She'd read hundreds of articles about it, but the look on Chris Graham's face when he'd heard about *Whycorp* had told her more than any of them.

The sight of two *Whycorp* employees in the library just rubbed her nose in it.

"Who are they?" Chris asked.

"*Whycorp* researchers. I've seen them using the computers here before. Maybe low-ranking minions don't get their own laptops."

A group of little kids skipped between them clutching Doctor Seuss books. Members of the local book club chattered in the corner. Angela Mackie stalked past with a new murder mystery, wearing a heavy gold cuff bracelet and a smug expression. Melly guessed both were probably courtesy of a new boyfriend. She hoped the book wasn't research.

"This is a pretty town," Chris said. "It's too bad."

"Don't count us out yet."

He shrugged. "Some people will fight back. Most won't. It's too easy to look away and believe things will work out somehow. They won't understand what they're up against until it has its teeth in their throats."

"Where did the rest of your family go?"

"There's only me left."

"I'm sorry." She glanced at the book in his hand. "Peter Straub?"

"Yeah, I've always liked the scary stuff." Melly passed him a book from the shelf behind her. "Lovecraft? I've never read him."

"He bumps in the night like you wouldn't believe."

"Where's Jon?"

"Out in the parking lot. It's our Saturday morning ritual—I buy groceries and get new books, and he complains to his friends about having to wait for me."

"I'll go say hello, then."

Melly checked out her books. The *Whycorp* men were still there. They thought the town didn't know what it was up against.

She whispered, "Neither do you."

HER SATURDAY NIGHT mask was made of lipstick and mascara. She donned it after braiding her hair, and wore it with new jeans, a silk shirt, and the silver earrings Jon had given her for Christmas.

The local tavern was the go-to place for date night in the Bend. Melly chatted with the wives of the mill workers, nursed a glass of Chardonnay, and, when the band started a ballad she recognized, interrupted Jon's dart game with his friends.

"Sorry, guys, I like this song. You can have him back when I'm done with him."

There was a chorus of hoots as she led him onto the dance floor. Jon rolled his eyes and grinned back at them. Melly danced a little closer than necessary, knowing it would be commented on later.

He said, "There's Chris." She looked over to where Chris had taken Jon's place in the game. He glanced at her, as if he'd known exactly where she was, then turned away.

"Shouldn't you tell him what a hustler Gary is?" she asked.

"Don't think so. Some things a man has to learn for himself."

THE NEXT MORNING Jon said, "This might be your last hiking day."

Melly said, "You're right." Partly because he was, and partly because he liked hearing it.

"I'll pick you up around one."

"No problem."

The maple leaves looked as if King Midas had gone on a bender. In another day or two they'd fall all at once, and the sky would fade from this joyful blue to a mauvish-grey. The fall rains would be hard and steady. Jon parked the truck a quarter-mile past Bob Lyle's house, and Melly got out, dragging her backpack with her.

When he was gone, she stepped over the smallest of the *No Trespassing* signs and pulled an oversized garbage bag out of the culvert. She hefted it over her shoulder and headed into the woods.

On Sundays she hiked the mountains while Jon visited friends. She'd been tramping the woods since she was old enough to go out alone. She'd been tramping *these* woods since the sign for *Whycorp Gas and Oil* had been staked at the corner of the property.

It would take time for them to set their drills, she knew. They were probably still looking for underground mapping data. If the research showed the hoped-for results, they'd find a suitable site and drill a test well.

Each stage of exploration required a specific permit; obtaining each one could take up to six months. But *Whycorp* was patient. They'd move in eventually.

Melly smiled as a bluejay sailed overhead. A deer stepped out of the brush and looked at her, unconcerned. Except for a few ATV enthusiasts, and teenagers looking for a place to party, hardly anyone ever came up here. Which made it perfect for *Whycorp*. She'd read the literature until she almost had it memorized—they couldn't drill within one hundred metres of any building, road, power line, or water well, unless they could prove the operation wouldn't cause any damage. The mountain was hell-and-gone away from pretty much everything.

She'd accidentally found her first well here when she was fourteen. She remembered walking behind her parents, swinging a green branch, and yelping as it suddenly tried to yank itself out of her hand.

Her father yelled, "Let go before you get hurt!"

Too late. The branch shot three feet and jabbed into the ground, leaving her with a palm full of splinters. She still had scars, but what she remembered most was her parents whispering, "Water witch."

She didn't know what that was. Apparently, it was her. She checked out books on dowsing, and stole library books on witchcraft, not wanting anyone to ask questions. No one commented when she started divining, but she thought it best to keep quiet about what else she'd taught herself.

It was basically just more cooking with intent.

From the mountain she could see almost all of the Bend, a place where church still summoned the faithful and yard sales were an event. And the best thing Charlene Shay could say about her marriage was that she'd never needed stitches.

Best friends in high school, they might've spoken one hundred words to each other since graduation, half on the day they'd married the Shay brothers in a double ceremony, the rest at their mother-in-law's funeral the week before. They'd stood together watching their husbands work the crowd, Charlene's eye makeup not quite hiding the bruise.

Melly whispered, "What happened?"

Charlene rummaged in her pocket and found the locket Gary had given her as a wedding present. "I broke the chain," she said sadly. They turned as Gary approached, and Melly saw the red weal across the back of Charlene's neck.

"What are you girls talking about?" he said pleasantly.

"I was just asking how your dad's getting along," Melly said.

"He's coping," Gary said, and squeezed Charlene's hand. She dropped the locket. As he led her away, Melly heard him growl, "What did you tell her?"

Melly collected the locket and went to pay her respects. "I'm sorry, Bert. This must be an awful shock for you."

"She knew her heart would give out if she didn't slow down. She got what she asked for."

And if I had to live with you, I'd ask for it, too.

Melly turned her back on the view and went to a spruce with a red ribbon on its lowest branch, marking where she'd ended her last hike. She took a plastic bottle from the garbage bag and opened it, a tiny sound escaping, like distant thunder. She swung her arm in a wide arc, splashing the potion. Water always travelled. By now it would have carried her brew over almost every inch of *Whycorp* property.

She called the recipe *Cease-and-Desist*.

She'd watered the property every Sunday since the *Whycorp* sign had gone up. Soon she'd have their land magicked and the edges sealed. And her teeth in their throat.

"THERE THEY GO," Bob Lyle said. A black half-ton with the *Whycorp* logo on the door rolled past the coffee shop. His fingers twitched as if itching to make the sign of the evil eye. Like most people in the Bend, he was worried about the damage fracking could do to their wells.

Melly had heard the conversation so many times she knew it by heart, but she kept collecting ingredients for the next batch of potion: cinnamon crumbs sprayed from cursing mouths, napkins crumpled in anger. She gathered words and wants and anxiety the same way she scraped paint from their roadside protest signs—carefully. *Whycorp* didn't understand care, and it never hurt to confuse the enemy.

"Have you heard about the reward?" Grace Tanton asked. "On November first they're going to start offering one thousand dollars to anyone who reports a trespasser on their land. Melly, don't you still hike up there?"

"Sure. It's one of the prettiest places around."

"Of course," Bob grumbled. "That's why they're ruining it."

Melly shrugged. "I guess I'll get one more look at the view before Halloween." She'd have to—somebody *would* report her for that much money.

Grace said, "Bob, did you ever find out who your grandfather sold that land to?"

"Nope. He's been dead a year and I'm still sorting his papers. Half the ones I expected to find are gone. Could be he burned them. I should've kept a closer eye on him—if he was tottery enough to fall and split his head open, maybe he shouldn't have been handling his own money." Bob scrubbed his hand over his face. "I found the price of the land marked in his bank book, but not the property transfer. So, no, I don't know who leased the land to *Whycorp.*"

Melly drained her mug and said, "See you later, guys. I have to put my wash on the line."

Bob said, "Yeah, I heard it's supposed to rain tomorrow."

Somehow the conversation always came back to water.

THE RULES OF conduct in a small town mostly boiled down to *Live and let live.* The rules of marriage, Melly thought, were harder to understand. *Love, honour, and obey* was a minefield. When she'd married Jon, she'd been too young to know how dangerous some words were.

The words she'd been thinking lately were nothing she'd share with her husband.

She considered them as she made a new batch of *Cease-and-Desist,* throwing in tear-stained napkins, chewed fingernails, hair pulled out in frustration, and a cup of dirt from the mountain. She murmured them as she folded the laundry and cooked a casserole for supper. Sighed them as she watered her plants and caught herself caressing the cyclamen.

Chris Graham had blind-sided her. He'd changed everything,

simply by speaking to her politely. By treating her as something more than an appendage. By reminding her that it was easy to look the other way and believe things would just work themselves out.

It was easy to look away with a mask obstructing her vision. She could still tell herself Jon was the pick of the Shay men, but that wasn't saying much. He'd never raised his hand to her, but she'd spent half her life making sure he didn't have a reason to and knowing *he* would decide what might be considered a reason.

He was the first man she'd dated who'd seemed steady. She'd wanted to stay in town after her parents' deaths but hadn't been inclined to stay by herself. She'd been glad to settle down with him, not realizing she'd just settled.

Jon had slowly cracked her open, and she'd let him.

He paid the biggest bills—property tax, truck payments—and kept the bank book in his desk. She paid the small bills—lights, phone, groceries—and ended up with pocket change. And she'd never thought much about it.

But now she thought of her father yelling, "Let go before you get hurt!"

She remembered the moment she'd almost covered Chris's hand with hers. If Jon hadn't been there, would he have twined his fingers through hers? She wasn't imagining the attraction between them. It wasn't love, couldn't be on such short acquaintance, she knew. But it was . . . interesting.

She bottled the potion and caught rainwater for another batch. She had a week to save the town.

She wondered how long she had to save herself.

THE NEXT SATURDAY Chris wasn't in the library. Melly had the groceries and cold beer in the truck before Jon got restless. He stopped for gas on the way home. As he filled an extra can for the generator, he said, "There won't be many more days like this."

"You're right."

"Supposed to rain tomorrow."

"I heard."

"Well, I have things to do this afternoon. You want to go hiking?"

A break in their routine was rare; and, she realized suddenly, kindness from Jon sent a chill down her spine. He was up to something. But she couldn't pass up the chance.

"I'd love to. Thanks."

"I'll pick you up around five."

"No problem."

Melly lugged two bags up the mountain and finished watering *Whycorp*'s property, then slogged back to the road. She sat on her heels and pondered Jon's sudden generosity.

Jon and Kemper's Bend: she couldn't leave either without pain. But she had to go. Her desire to bury *Whycorp* was growing by the hour.

The wind died down. Melly knew how it felt. She and the mountain were both holding their breaths, waiting to see if an assault could be averted.

She couldn't think of fracking as anything else. *Whycorp*'s people would drill a hole straight down, then a horizontal branch, then send down a bundle of small shrapnel and light explosives. The bomb would open thousands of small perforations. Thousands of tiny wounds. They'd pump in millions of gallons of water to crack the shale, allowing the gas inside to rise under its own pressure.

She could picture this quiet road overrun with trucks. She thought of their water and air being contaminated and knew why Chris was afraid.

On the way home, Jon said, "Tired?"

She was. "No, I'm good."

It wasn't until the supper dishes were done that she realized how absurd the question had been. In all the time she'd known him he'd never asked her that. Right—he'd suggested she go hiking so she'd be too tired to go to the tavern. He had plans that didn't include her.

"Jon, would you mind if I stayed home tonight?"

"Are you sick?"

He was laying it on thick, she thought. "No, but I guess I *am* a little tired. I'll just curl up with my new book."

"I won't be too late," he said.

"No problem."

DOING LAUNDRY ON Sunday was another break in the routine, but the house didn't need any more cleaning and she wanted to get out of it. "Are you going out?" she asked.

"I'm going to Blaine's for truck parts."

"Will you drop me off at the laundromat?" He carried her laundry bag out to the truck. She shuddered behind his back.

Chris said, "I didn't think anyone else would be here at this hour."

"Neither did I. It's a ghost town out there."

"I'm a little worried about offending good folk on their way to church."

"We'll be gone by the time church takes in."

He said, "I'm sorry I missed you at the library. I looked for you at the tavern last night." She glanced up quickly. "Don't worry. I didn't ask anyone where you were."

More dangerous words, she thought. They both knew what he was saying, and that neither of them would repeat it to anyone.

(A rule about breaking the rules: The person who can get you in the most trouble could end up in more trouble themselves.)

He asked, "What kind of name is Melly?"

"Short for Melissa. It's kind of a fancy name for a small-town girl. No one uses it. I would've if I'd ever left town, though."

"Ever think about it?"

"I used to. There were places I wanted to see. Venice was my first choice." A city built on 117 islands: even her dreams had been about water. "What about you?"

"Part of me wanted to leave town. Most of me figured I wouldn't. But some nights I'd head for the county line in my dad's car, hoping the cops weren't around. I'd pretend I was leaving, and then I'd slow down and do a U-turn, because where would I go?" He checked his dryer, paid more quarters. "I'd like to see London, but I've never had any desire to *live* in a city."

"Have you read the Lovecraft yet?"

He grimaced. "It's the reason I'm up so early."

Melly fished coins from her purse and tossed it onto her washer. And realized as she threw it that it would knock her laundry bag behind the machine. She couldn't grab it in time.

"Chris, can you help me?"

"Sure." He leaned over her and snagged it with his fingertips. His breath was warm on the back of her neck. She shifted her hips slightly. He settled into the curves of her body. They pressed together for a single breath.

He pulled away. She took the bag. She thought he was crazy,

kissing her like that. Anyone could've walked in on them. It was against all the rules.

But so was kissing him back.

JON SAID, "I'M going out."

"Will you be home for supper?"

"I don't know. Keep something warm."

"No problem."

Melly remembered she'd left the tote bag with her laundry soap in the truck. As Jon got in, she reached behind the passenger seat and groped for the handle. She picked up a gold cuff bracelet. She shoved it in the bag and waited to feel a sense of betrayal. She didn't. At least it explained why Jon said he was buying parts for a new truck.

Angela would consider a prosperous business-owner a good catch, and, of course, she wanted what belonged to someone else. Being with such a beautiful and spirited woman would make Jon look good, too. As he had with his truck, Jon was trading up for a faster model.

Melly was willing to fight for the water, the town, Charlene, and, at long last, herself. But this would be too hard a battle for something she didn't want anymore.

She waved goodbye and strolled into the woods. It felt good to walk away from the house. She could smell rain coming. It started just as the Miller house came into view, and she sprinted for the back wall. It wasn't much shelter, but better than nothing. She palmed the wet off her face and whirled as a hand fell on her shoulder.

Chris said, "Sorry, it's just me." She eased through the door behind him. "I came out for a jog and got caught in the rain."

"No one ever comes in here."

He swept part of the floor with his jacket and sat down beside her. "Melissa, I—what?"

"There are r-rats over there."

He drifted a rusty nail across the room, scattering them. "We're all right." He put his arms around her. He kissed her back.

Part of her was disgusted that she wanted to make love here. Most of her thought tenderness was a revelation. Finally, she didn't even mind the rats watching.

SHE KNEW WHAT would happen if Jon found out.

(Rule: He can, you can't.)

"I've already eaten," he said that evening. She put the beef stew in the fridge. "I've got some calls to make." He retreated to his office and closed the door.

She listened to the rain on the roof, hard and steady. Chris had said, "I'm leaving. I know what's coming, and I can't watch it again."

She'd wrestled her wet clothes back on. "I'll miss you."

"Not if you come with me."

She nodded slowly. She wasn't inclined to leave town by herself. It would be nice to have company for a while.

She said, "Where would we go?"

"I don't know. Venice? When can you leave?"

Whycorp was done here. The town would be okay. "Anytime."

"I'll pick you up at eight tomorrow morning."

HE DIDN'T. TUESDAY morning, she thought about going to his house, but there was the danger of someone seeing her and calling Jon. She thought of phoning him, but worried about leaving her number on his caller ID. In small towns someone was always watching.

She put *Get-Over-It* in Jon's scrambled eggs, hoping to slow him down long enough for her to find Chris. But Wednesday morning, when he poured her a cup of coffee for the first time in their marriage, she knew her time was up.

She said, "Thanks, dear. See you tonight."

She watched him from the kitchen window. Just before he got in the truck, he looked back and gave her a little wave.

Whatever was coming was going to be bad.

She was at the coffee shop by eight. She'd barely sat down before chatter was coming at her from all sides. Someone had broken into Gary's house this morning and beaten him to a pulp. Both his hands and one of his feet were smashed, and his teeth and jaw broken. The police didn't have any leads. Charlene was in shock.

The reps from *Whycorp* were putting up the new *No Trespassing* signs today instead of tomorrow, and how was that for trick-or-treat?

Angela Mackie had been seen buying rifle shells.

And Grace had been talking to a friend at the mill. It was too bad Jon had to fire the new guy, but the mill had lost one of its regular customers recently, and times were tough.

Melly was out the door.

There it was, she thought. When you stopped looking away you could see the pieces falling into place. If the mill had suffered a setback, how could Jon afford a new truck and a gold bracelet?

Going into Jon's office for the first time felt like break-and-enter. She found the documents in his desk drawer, under his *Batman* DVD. Gunther Lyle's signature was on the bill of sale for the mountainside property. She wondered what *Whycorp* had found out when, and where Jon might've heard about it.

She thought about Gunther's head cracked open and his papers missing.

Jon's leasing agreement was printed on *Whycorp* stationery. The receipt for the bracelet was tucked in his bank book. There was still a tidy sum in his account. She wondered if he'd known Angela was terrorizing Ivy, and thought he probably had.

He must have enjoyed knowing he was the richest man in town, even knowing that soon there might not be a town to be rich *in*.

It was 9:00. Melly willed her hands to stop shaking. There was still time to do what needed doing, but not if she let herself fall apart.

She approached Chris's house from the back, out of sight of the road. His truck was there. The back door was unlocked. There was a packed suitcase by the kitchen table, and one of his shoes by the fridge. A chair had been overturned. She made herself walk upstairs. His wallet and keys were on the nightstand beside the Lovecraft. She put them in her pocket.

There was only one other place she knew to look for him. He was there. The rats had been at him.

Later, she told herself. She could cry later. She took a scrap of his shirt, a fragment of broken skull, a soft ball of brown-and-grey fur.

She wondered if Jon had planned to dump her here, too.

She started her potion with all the *Non-Fatal Paralysis* in the pantry, then added the rest of the *Agony-in-Waiting* and *This is War*. Tears dripped into the pot as she added the scraps from the old house. Her wedding ring made a little *plop*. She bit down on her lip and bled into the pot, then left it to simmer as she emptied the rest of her potion bottles down the sink.

Not that anyone would know what they were, but she didn't want to leave weapons lying around.

She went to the sunporch to get the cyclamen. It was on the floor, roots torn, pot smashed. She scooped it into another pot and set it in the driveway with her backpack.

There was only one way Jon could've found out. Someone had been watching the laundromat and realized she was in there alone with Chris. Someone who just couldn't resist saying to Jon, "Oh, by the way . . ." Emma Reese's mouth would burn if she lied, not if she told a malicious truth. Jon would wonder why Melly hadn't mentioned seeing Chris herself. Apparently cause for suspicion was all it took to set him off.

(Rule: Unspoken words are dangerous, too.)

She carried the stock pot out into the porch, locked up behind herself, and threw the potion hard against the door. It sloshed high up the walls and made a wonderful mess on the floor. Jon's first steps into the porch would exhaust him, but maybe he'd get in the house before collapsing. The fall might split his head, his lips, his chin. Something. The potion would deactivate after enough had been absorbed to do the job. Jon would still be conscious but unable to move when the rats came. The potion would call them. They'd feasted on Chris and would've absorbed his fear of *Whycorp*; they weren't likely to spare the man who'd invited the monster in.

Jon would know how it felt to have teeth in his throat.

For a moment Melly wondered if she should feel some sympathy for him—with Bert for a father, neither he nor Gary had ever had much chance of growing up sane.

The moment passed. She shrugged into her backpack, took the cyclamen and the spare gas can, and headed for the Miller house. It was raining again.

She splashed gas across the floor. It would burn through, dropping Chris into the cellar. The rest of the house would collapse on top of him. She looked at what was left of him. There was no one to miss him but her.

She struck a match and ran as the rats came flooding out.

She took Chris's truck. One more stop to make.

The new *No Trespassing* sign was up. The *Whycorp* truck was parked in the turning lane. The two minions in their company jackets were arguing beside it, poking at their cell phones. Melly rolled down the window. "Trouble?"

"Our truck quit, and our phones have stopped working."

Melly drove on. They could walk to a garage to get a tow truck, but it wouldn't help. Eventually they might get around to borrowing a couple of plough horses. No machine would work on the mountain now—trucks, ATVs, computers, drilling equipment, all dead. The potion was working. The water was fighting back. If they still wanted to frack the mountain, they'd have to find a way to do it by hand.

Whycorp would move on now, not realizing they had a nemesis. Not knowing she was contemplating possibilities.

She'd never been sure if the water drew her toward it, or if she pulled it toward her, but she thought it was time to figure it out. She wondered if she could pull rain from the sky or turn back floods.

She wondered if she'd forget Chris someday, and didn't think so.

Once, she would've thought Halloween was a strange time to take off a mask. Now it suited her fine. (Rule: No more damn rules.) She checked for cops at the county line and hit the gas.

The Diviner vanished into the night.

Hidden Depths

Kevin Cockle

EXT; AFTERNOON; SEASIDE

COLIN PORTER SITS on a rocky shoal overlooking the Pacific Ocean. He's young, late twenties, though sporting the lines and demeanour of an older man. Blandly handsome; a little on the sombre side; dressed in jeans and a cable-knit fisherman's sweater. Rolex Submariner on his wrist brings to mind the slogan: "At home on the ocean's floor, or in the boardroom."

We hear the lapping of water nearby, and the crashing of surf in the distance. Colin stares out to the horizon with an expression of . . . what? Depression? Contemplation? It's not exactly clear what he might be feeling or thinking. We pause on his self-absorption long enough that the reader begins to wonder about motivation.

Suddenly A MERMAID flops halfway out of the water onto a nearby rock. Her tail is hard to see clearly: either the shadow of it is there beneath the surface, or she's being generated by the water itself somehow. Long, dark green hair matted wet about her neck; strategically placed shells at her chest. She grins broadly, looking expectantly at Colin, knowing he must see her, waiting for his acknowledgment.

Slowly, Colin takes his head in hands.

COLIN
Not another Mermaid. For Christ's sake.

MERMAID
Hi!

COLIN
(Looking at her now) Hey. Listen, I'm good. I don't need saving.

MERMAID
Sure you do!

COLIN
No, seriously, I'm fine. But thank-you, you know, for showing up. It's very thoughtful.

MERMAID
(Kindly, patiently) I wouldn't be here if you didn't need saving. You have to know that. Why don't we talk about it?

COLIN
(Standing in irritation) Aw, now see? I'm fine, or at least I was fine. Don't you people know that it makes humans miserable when you ask them about whatever's bothering them?

MERMAID
I know it makes them miserable when nobody asks.

COLIN
Yeah, well, not me. I am actually fine.

MERMAID
Do you have a name?

COLIN
(Looks at her in exasperation, then resigns to his fate, resuming his seat.) Colin.

MERMAID
Colin.

COLIN
And you are?

MERMAID
Marina

COLIN
Figures.

Marina nods. It does kind of figure.

MARINA
So, Colin, what do you do?

COLIN
(Chuckles at the banality of the question, even coming from a
sea creature.) Well, I'm in P.R.—public relations.

MARINA
Oh, well there it is then. That was easy.

COLIN
The hell are you talking about?

MARINA
Your problem. You're anxious because you have an imaginary
job, and the stress of basing your day to day existence on
something so ephemeral is eating you alive. I saved a bunch of
finance guys a couple years ago, so I'm sort of an expert on this.

COLIN
(Incredulous.) *You* are telling *me* that I have an imaginary job?

MARINA
Well?

COLIN
That isn't the problem.

MARINA
Ah-ha! So there IS a problem!

COLIN
(Standing in reflex at having committed such an amateurish mistake) No. Listen. There is no problem. At least no problems that everybody else doesn't have, and certainly no problems big enough to require help from the catch of the day!

MARINA
(Smiling reproachfully) Now, now—don't get testy.

COLIN
"Testy"? What are you, my grandmother?

MARINA
(Patting the rock) Come on. Come and sit down. Let's not get off on the wrong fluke here. Please?

Reluctantly, Colin resumes his seat.

MARINA
Okay. So you don't think it's your job?

COLIN
It's not my job. I mean, sometimes, I do think about it—what you said—but it's not really that big a deal. I could do other things.

MARINA
Well, how about your life in general? Are you married?

COLIN
No.

MARINA
AAAAAhhhh . . . (revving up like she's on to something.)

COLIN

Gimme a break—nobody's married these days.

MARINA

Oh. Is there someone though? Maybe I'm here because you're
lonely?

COLIN

No, there's someone. Actually, we're just down for the day
visiting her folks, so . . . there's someone.

MARINA

And you thought, what? "Guess I've done all the visiting I'm
going to do today, see you later, I'm off to the beach"?

COLIN

(Smirking in spite of himself) Yeah, something like that. I'm not
much of a . . . whatever. Small talker.

MARINA

You know Colin, I don't think you've been entirely honest with
me about this last bit.

COLIN

What do you mean?

MARINA

There really isn't anybody, is there? You just drove down for
the day by yourself for a few hours of melancholia by the sea.
That's okay, that's what it's here for.

COLIN

(Pissed again) What . . . ? Where do you . . . ? There is so a
girl—Penny Baxter—I've been seeing her for three months, and
it's good, not great, but really good, and it's good enough!
Jesus!

MARINA

I'm sorry!

COLIN
Well you shouldn't be so damn presumptuous.

MARINA
No, I mean I feel sorry for you. I don't believe in any Penny
Baxter, as plausible as the name sounds, especially for making it
up on the spot like that. Imaginary job, imaginary girl . . . this is
bad.

Colin is stupefied, gesturing incoherently—how can he answer
her contention? Suddenly, we hear a voice off-screen: PENNY.

PENNY (O.S.)
Colin? Co-lin?

COLIN
(Triumphant leer at the mermaid) AH-HA!

Marina appears crestfallen.

COLIN
Penny! Over here! C'mere—I want you to meet someone.

Colin clambers over slippery rocks to PENNY, an outdoorsy
sort with a bright-eyed, friendly mien, and who appears to be a
few years Colin's senior. Colin takes her by the hand and guides
her back to Marina.

COLIN CONT.
Penny, this is Marina. Marina, THIS is Penny. In the flesh.
Q.E.D.!

PENNY
(Reaches down to shake hands with Marina) Ooh, is this one of
those mermaids? You certainly seem to attract your fair share
of these, Colin.

COLIN
No shit.

MARINA

We were just discussing that, Penny. Would you care to join us?
The truth is, I think I'm going to need some help on this one.

PENNY

Ooh—fun! (She eagerly sits, gesturing for Colin to do likewise.)

COLIN

Okay, look . . . this is sort of becoming an inquisition or
intervention or something, and it's starting to make me a little
uncomfortable. I don't know what to tell you. Either of you. I'm
not unhappy. The weight of the world is not resting upon my
shoulders. I must just have one of those faces.

PENNY

(Laughing) You do have one of those faces, that's true!

MARINA

But I don't think that's it. Unless you're unhappy because you
don't have any problems—no "real" problems. That's messed
up, boy.

COLIN

You know, the law doesn't even recognize mermaids. We could
spear-gun you, and it would be like a free month's supply of
smoked bass!

MARINA

Bass! (She's aghast: Colin has no idea how bass are perceived in
the aquatic context)

COLIN

(With emphasis) Largemouth!

PENNY

(Laughing out loud) Oh! That's funny!

Marina begins to cry. In the distance, the breakers seem to get
louder, the waves bigger. Penny is immediately mortified, Colin

chagrined. Penny touches Marina's shoulder in a tentative gesture of apology as Colin sits. Collecting herself, Marina speaks, eyes flashing at Colin.

MARINA

You know . . . you're the meanest of anyone I've saved, do you know that? You are, and I can't understand why. One night, I felt a man who needed me and I went, and it turned out to be Claus von Bulow. I didn't like him, but he was drowning. One night, even Claus von Bulow was drowning, so I saved him, and he wasn't mean at all.

The thing is, most of the people I save are bad, or go on to be bad after I save them, but you . . . you're not like that. But still. You're the only one who's ever tried to hurt me.

COLIN

(Dejected, confused. Penny puts an arm around his shoulders as he speaks.) Look, I'm really, truly sorry. I didn't mean to hurt you.

MARINA
You called me a bass!

COLIN

I was kidding! I said we should shoot you with a spear gun too, but I didn't mean it.

MARINA

Oh, well, I guess that makes everything all right then.

COLIN

No, no it doesn't. I've never believed that. Listen . . . I think you'd like to believe that my world is artificial and that yours is like some kind of natural fail-safe clock, but I don't think that's right. Mountain goats occasionally slip and break their necks. Monkeys miss tree limbs. I mean, you guys probably make mistakes too. I'll bet the odd ghost gets the wrong house sometimes, and probably even the odd mermaid swallows a mouthful of water the wrong way . . . you know what I'm saying?

MARINA

(Smiling sadly) I know what you're trying to say. I really don't think it works that way. Not for us.

COLIN

Oh, so you're perfect?

MARINA

No. Sometimes they drown anyway. Like right now. I'm not saving you.

A long pause as Colin gathers his thoughts.

COLIN

Does Penny have to hear this?

MARINA

I think so.

COLIN

I'm not going to be able to put my finger on it, you realize.

MARINA

You don't have to. Not directly on it, anyway.

COLIN

All right. There's a, an Atwood poem about mermaids, only . . . those mermaids trick the sailors into the water so that they drown. And the sailors are happy to go because they think that they are rescuing the mermaids from this island or rock or something. And the mermaids make them feel that way; they make the sailors feel that they are the only men who can save them.

MARINA

But that's Atwood! She's mean!

COLIN

No she's not. Because the mermaids really are trapped and . . . I see an awful lot of mermaids. And I'm afraid, that's all. What if it's a trick?

MARINA

(Compassionate smile) So that's it. Fear. It always is of course, but there are so many different kinds. No wonder it was so hard—that's a complicated little loop you've got going there.

Marina leans forward, kissing Colin on the cheek; looks at him to make sure the magic is registering.

MARINA CONT.

Well it's not a trick. Not this time.

Marina smiles again, and for just a moment, the Disney façade wavers, revealing the needle teeth of an eel; the pitiless, ancient eyes of a Coelacanth. Then she slides beneath the waves without a ripple, and is gone.

Penny reaches for Colin's hand, leaning into him.

PENNY

I didn't know you read poetry.

COLIN

I've never read Atwood in my life, but if anyone were going to write a poem like that it'd be her, so I figured I'd be okay.

PENNY

Still. That was weirdly nice of you.

COLIN

I have hidden depths.

PENNY

Can't believe you're worse than Bulow, though.

COLIN

Shut up.

Colin kisses the top of Penny's head, and there they sit, watching the great green waves roll in, listening to the gulls above. Waiting by a sea of possibilities, just in case.

Creatures of Water and Salt

Greta Starling

it was one of those summer romances
her the lifeguard everyone wanted cpr from
him the swimmer everyone wanted lessons from
somehow always arriving before the beach opened

on the last day after everyone left
he climbed up the lifeguard stand
"i want to taste your lips," he said
so she kissed him right there
he tasted like salt and longing

she picked up her towel, ready to leave
and he said "wait," said "you're still dry"
"how can you watch this all day and not swim?"
she laughed because she thought that every day
and they jumped off the pier hand in hand

when she surfaced, she saw no boy
only a horse as chestnut as his hair
when he surfaced, he saw no girl
only a seal as gray as her towel
"oh," she bubbled; "oh," he neighed

they climbed back up the ladder
her towel separating from her skin
his mane shortening to tousled hair
"you can't drown a selkie," she said
and she expected him to run or swim away

"i could take that towel of yours,"
he said, "throw you in without it"
"i passed the lifeguard test in human form
but yes, the towel is my cloak"
she shook it out and it turned to sealskin

"you can't drown a selkie," she said,
"and i can't seduce a capaill uisce
so i suppose we're at an impasse"
he reared his head in laughter
"i think you could seduce a capaill uisce"

so she kissed him again
he tasted like salt and longing
this time for her, not her blood
she tasted like salt and happiness
for a water creature who wouldn't deny her

the water she loved

After Ariel

Elise Forier Edie

MARIE FOUND THE monster under the 59th Street Fishin' Pier.

The night before, a storm had whipped Ocean City to tatters. Ropes banged on the flagpole outside her house. Waves from the bay crashed over the lawn. All night, Marie thought she heard someone screaming outside. Her mother said it was just the wind, go to sleep, Marie. But in her room, by candlelight, Marie felt the back of her neck shiver. It sounded like someone was out there, lonely and afraid. She stared at the candle flame until every time she shut her eyes, a ghost light burned in the middle of her forehead. And the screaming went on.

Next morning, the sun shone like nothing had happened. Marie ran on the beach, alternating sprints and jogs like her track coach had taught her. The curling waves were scary, glass-green and high as houses. Storm flotsam lay everywhere, covered in flies: smelly piles of seaweed, dead fish, shells, logs, a couple of shoes, and hundreds of glutinous jellyfish, arranged in slimy swirls. High above, clouds of ravenous seagulls swooped and shrieked.

Marie finished her run at 59th Street and cooled off in the Fishin' Pier's long shadow. Rickety wood pilings staggered drunkenly into the ocean. The bait shack, perched on planks, looked poised to tumble into the waves. A sign had been knocked askew. It said, "FOURTH OF JULY KIDS DERBY HERE! For Rent: Pole's, Net's, Bucket's For Sale: Bait, Ice Cream."

Marie sat underneath, on a pile of rocks. This had been her secret place since third grade, when she had spent a whole summer pretending to be Ariel, the Disney mermaid. She would arrange herself on barnacle-studded stones, legs in a sort of tail shape, pretending the arcade at the Boardwalk was a palace, and Prince Eric waited in a sailboat for her with the dolphins, beyond the waves. Marie had crooned the movie's soundtrack, acted out all the parts. She had combed her hair, and wished it foamed around her shoulders like Ariel's cartoon tresses. The planks above thumped hollowly whenever anyone walked on them; and the pilings thrummed if ocean waves smashed especially hard. No one ever found her. It was her own private sea grotto. And even though she didn't pretend to be Ariel anymore, Marie still liked to go there.

Now, the huge waves chased each other through the lattice of pilings and sent hissing rivulets into the rocks. Marie sat exulting, her sweat cooling, heartbeat slowing. When she curled her back against a barnacle-sharpened rock, she heard a low moan, barely audible underneath the seething of the sea. She craned her neck and at first couldn't figure out what she saw. It lay among the rocks, big and barely breathing. She thought, "pink nylon bag;" she thought, "spiny blowfish;" she thought, "hairless dog." Then her brain put it all together, and she knew what she was seeing, and she screamed and screamed, and so did the thing she was looking at, and its mouth was wide and stuffed with awful, slime-covered teeth, like a shark's.

MARIE RAN AWAY and collapsed on the sand, a few yards away, skin crawling. Her mind raced in circles. No way she had seen it! But she had. But that thing couldn't be real! Right? She'd seen a dead dolphin, or a shark. No, no, but it wasn't any of those! Her father was a marine biologist at the Chesapeake Bay Conservation Centre. Marie knew what sharks and dolphins looked like. This thing, this creature had arms—it had arms, and fins on its head, and trailing tentacles, and gills—it was pink, and brown, and fat—no it wasn't—yes it was—and no way, no way, no way, no way, no way—

After a while, she staggered back to her feet and tiptoed under the pier, chest clenched from being so scared. A cold breeze wafted from the grotto, bringing with it the smell of fish and blood. Her spine prickled. She told herself, chicken, chicken; she told herself, come on, if it's a mutant, albino dolphin, don't you want to save it?

Marie braced her hands on the rocks, folding her lips over her teeth to keep from screaming. She peeked.

Oh, God. It was definitely a monster. Either that, or some poor deformed sea creature, maybe washed down from the Hope Creek Nuclear Power Station. Marie's knees buckled, but she pressed her palms into the barnacles and made herself look.

It had the shiny black eyes of a seal, and a seal's blubbery body, ending in a smooth, speckled tail. Instead of flippers, flabby pink arms sprouted. Instead of a seal's cute, doglike face, humanoid features, smashed ugly and flat, gaped at the planks above. Everything was dominated by an awful, awful mouth, as wide as its face, and lined with jagged teeth. Marie stared and took shaky breaths. The thing's torso rose and fell in tandem with hers. A gash in its side, crusted and black on the edges, gaped and oozed blood. Something was wrong with one of its hands—appendages? Pseudopods? Whatever you called them—it looked mangled and bloody, probably broken.

A part of Marie's mind said, "Mermaid. Actual, frigging mermaid-monster-thing. Washed by the storm onto the beach. Wow."

Another part focused on the creature's wounds and said, "Must have banged itself good on the rocks in the storm last night. It looks really hurt."

But the loudest part of her mind just bleated, "Ew! Ew! Ew! Ew! Ew!" over and over again, like a berserk fire alarm.

FOOTSTEPS THRUMMED ABOVE—a couple of kids galloping to the bait shack. These were followed by the more sedate rhythms of parents or grandparents, strolling behind. Fine sand filtered down, along with splinters of sunshine. The monster averted its head, so flakes wouldn't fly in its shiny eyes. It caught sight of Marie again. It didn't scream this time. It just looked at her and she looked back. Long whiskers, or tentacles grabbed at the air around its face. Marie shuddered as the thing shifted feebly and a gout of thick blood burbled from the wound in its side. She could see fat, white and glistening in the peeled back layers of skin.

Behind her, the waves teased just out of reach. The tide was receding. No water would swirl back in the grotto for hours and hours.

The monster looked away. More footsteps rumbled above.

Marie rested on her heels and thought.

It was Fourth of July weekend. Kids, grown-ups, by the hundreds, by the thousands probably, would crowd on the pier in a couple of hours. The annual Kids Fishin' Derby would begin, a bloody affair of dangling nightcrawlers, bludgeoned perch, sunburned shoulders. Wooden planks would be smeared with blood and melted popsicles. The WBEC radio disc jockeys would set up a flapping tarp and blast music over the Boardwalk. How soon before someone else found the monster pinned here? And then what?

Marie had vivid memories from when she was ten years old, of her dad trying to fend off bystanders who wanted to poke and pet a terrified dolphin. It had been mired in mud on a cold, February day, washed up by a winter storm. Dad kept yelling, "Please. This is a wild animal." But people kept darting in, shouting like the seagulls. One woman wanted to sing to it. A guy brought a flensing knife to butcher it. Another man brought his kids and got really pissed when her father told him they couldn't just hug the dolphin and play with it.

A reporter had snapped pictures, too. Marie and her dad had been on the front page of the *Coastal Dispatch*. "Scientist fights to save beached dolphin," the caption read, and there Marie was, clear as day, dark head bent next to her father's, the terrified animal between them, everyone else just rain slickers in the background.

Dad would know what to do to help the monster. He had been living a hundred miles away in Annapolis with his new girlfriend Greta since March, but Marie was pretty sure a mermaid would bring him home. Greta was twenty-three, taught sailing, and had a butterfly tattooed on her ankle. But a mermaid was a mermaid, right?

"Hold on," Marie said to the monster. "I'll get help."

BEFORE LEAVING, SHE collected seaweed in disgusting armfuls and piled it, wet and dry, on the rocks. A discarded plastic sack made a kind of glove, which Marie used to pick up jellyfish. These she arranged on the rocks too, hoping to provide a painful deterrent for any curious children. The monster hissed and bared its horrifying teeth as she worked but Marie kept her distance and averted her eyes. Then she dashed home as fast as she could.

Marie found her mom ransacking the kitchen. Her boyfriend Gus was there and a teenaged boy, someone new.

"Are the phones still out?" she asked.

"Hello to you, too." Gus was carrying a cardboard box out to the garage. He wasn't smiling or joking. He was being a dick, like always. Marie resisted the urge to give him the finger.

Mom said, "Hi, honey. How was your run? This is Jessie." She indicated the blond boy by her side. "He's Gus's nephew, visiting for the summer. Right, Jess?"

The boy nodded. Almost everything about him drooped, from his long blond hair to the laces of his black Converse sneakers. Only his eyes roved, gaze crawling all over Marie's chest and thighs. She crossed her arms.

"We're going to Gus's place today," Mom went on. "He has a generator, so there's electricity. I guess no one knows when they'll get the power back on. Could be a couple days, even."

"Uncle Gus is always prepared." Jessie smirked. A clump of acne, blooming on the corner of his mouth, moved while he talked.

"We're organizing and heading over." Mom had piled five different frozen pizzas on the green-flecked Formica counter and indicated a gallon of milk at her elbow, and a bag of squishy-looking Costco popsicles. "I don't want our food to go bad. So, we're loading Gus's truck with everything in the freezer."

Without electricity, the kitchen was strangely quiet, no refrigerator hum, no air conditioning kicking on. Marie could hear her throat click as she swallowed. "What about the phones?"

"I think they're still out too, hon."

"Can I borrow your cell phone to call Dad?"

"What do you want to call him for?"

"I found something under the pier at 59th. An animal in trouble."

Mom shook her head. "Honey, leave it alone. It's Fourth of July weekend and the roads are a mess. Even if you get a hold of your father, he probably won't come down. The bridge will be a disaster."

It's a mermaid, Marie wanted to say, but Jessie was there. "It might be important."

"And it might be dead by noon, too. Let it go, sweetheart."

"Mom." Marie glanced at Jessie again. He had cocked his head to one side and caressed his lips with a fingertip, while he looked speculatively at the swell of her hips. He wasn't even trying to hide it. He glanced at her face and smiled. "Can I just call Dad to tell him about it? Please? Maybe someone else from the Bay Centre will want to come down and see."

Her mother dug around in her dungarees and passed Marie her iPhone with a shake of her head. "We're leaving in a few minutes, honey, so hurry."

"Chop chop," Gus added, returning from the garage. His khakis were crisp, his polo collar popped. Marie could taste his aftershave wafting around him, chemicals and pine.

"I won't be long." She squeezed by Jessie and dashed up the steps to her second-floor bedroom.

Gus yelled after her. "Uh. We could use some help with the food, Marie."

She shut the door to her room. She called her dad, heart pounding. He didn't pick up. She didn't know what kind of message to leave on his voice mail. "I found a mermaid," sounded stupid, like something a kid would say. "I need to talk to you," sounded better, but not urgent enough. Finally, she just said, "I found something on the beach and I need your help. Dad, please." She texted him, too. She also called his office at the Bay Centre. But the phone there just beeped at her, probably because it wasn't working.

Marie bit her lip. Should she guard the mermaid and keep it alive while she waited for her father?

She knew Dad would totally want to drive over Bay Bridge, even in Fourth of July traffic, once he realized the magnitude of Marie's discovery. And she should definitely try to guard it from other people. She racked her brain. Could she feed it? What would it eat? Did it need to be kept wet, like a dolphin, or would it be okay drying out, like a seal? She had trouble thinking straight. Part of her was simply dizzy with wonder—it was all real! She had found something truly amazing! Her dad would totally shit when he saw it! Then he would hug her to death and they'd be on television together!

But another part of her was terrified. What did she know about it? What did anyone? How could she really help it? What if it died? And what if someone else discovered it while she was dithering here in her room?

She tried consulting her computer, but the Wi-Fi was dead. She looked frantically around, at her stuffed animals, her track and field ribbons, her old books: Oz, Baby-Sitters Club, Hank the Cowdog, Fairytales.

She plucked the fairytales off a shelf.

"Marie! We're leaving," Gus called up the steps. "Hurry up."

She opened her bedroom door. "I'll ride my bike down to the house later," she yelled. "I want to take a shower and stuff."

"I need my cell phone back," her mother chimed in.

Marie padded down the hall, pausing at the top of the steps. Mom and Gus stood framed by the front door. Gus's arms were crossed, his brow beetled, crew cut bristling. Mom just looked tired. That's all she ever looked, since Marie's dad had taken off, tired and sad.

"Can I have it a little longer?" Marie asked. "Please? I'll give it back, I promise. I just haven't reached Dad, yet."

"Marie, your mother asked for her phone. Don't make her ask again." Gus glowered.

"It's okay." Mom patted his arm. "You keep it for a little longer. Just . . ." She gave a hurt, little smile. "Don't be mad if your dad doesn't answer, all right? He's . . . it's a holiday, honey. So don't expect much, okay?"

"Thanks, Mom." Marie waved at Gus's deepening frown. "See you later, Gus."

She flew back to her room. She could hear them talking behind her. Gus said, "You can't keep giving in like this. She walks all over you. She didn't even help us load the truck."

Mom said, "She's fourteen and her parents are getting divorced. Talk to me about it more when you have kids, Gus."

Marie shut her bedroom door. She leafed through the book of fairytales.

Hans Christian Andersen offered no practical advice about the care and feeding of actual mermaids. So, she pictured the monster's jagged, sharp-looking teeth and decided it must be a predator. She thought of the arms, grabbing at stuff and cramming food in the creature's mouth. There were some old crab traps in the garage. They were a little rickety and rusted, but still usable. Mom kept rotten chicken necks in the freezer for bait and Marie discovered these were nicely thawed, thanks to the storm. Marie slid the gooey blobs into the wire traps and, gagging slightly at the smell, lowered them by rope into the bay behind her house. The sun-drenched water glimmered, still choppy from the storm. She hoped a few hungry crabs might have taken refuge by the sea wall.

They had, too. After showering in tepid water, Marie dragged up three medium sized blues in the traps. One was a female, so she threw her back in the bay. The males she tossed in a deep plastic bucket. They stalked around the bottom, feet scrabbling, claws upraised, tough and scared.

"Sorry, guys," she whispered.

Before heading back to the Fishin' Pier, she checked the cell phone. No word from her dad. Marie texted him that she was heading to 59th Street, that she would meet him there, that he should come quickly. Then, after scratching her head a little over how to get the plastic bucket all the way to the Boardwalk on her bike without spilling the crabs, she crammed it in a large canvas rucksack. The bag had shoulder straps and looked ridiculous, swelling on her back like a huge hump. But it left her hands free to steer her bike. She set off, wobbly but staying upright, feeling important, feeling like she mattered.

A light breeze bathed her face while she pedalled. The power outage had shut down traffic lights on Route One. Clerks at roadside ice cream parlours lined the sidewalks in their colourful aprons (pink for Sherbet Scoop, green for Giovanni's), giving away cones and sundaes to passersby. A couple of good Samaritans directed traffic on the really busy intersections, old guys in hunting vests, with cheap straw hats on their heads. A line of people snaked out of a dark Clover Leaf grocery store, the electronic doors propped open with milk crates.

On the sand to Marie's left, where the waves pounded, a few

kites soared. Some brave souls even jumped and swam in the giant waves, looking tiny as sandpipers. She could hear the surf crash, even amidst the roar of car engines.

As she coasted over the little bridge by the Royal Farms Gas Station, keeping well on the shoulder, a car slowed behind her and honked. Startled, she weaved into the grass, almost toppling. She managed to stop and turn, awkward because of the huge rucksack. Jessie waved from behind the wheel of Gus's bright red Hennessey Velociraptor.

He opened the door and stood so he could call to her. "Need a ride?"

"I'm not going to Gus's." Cars inched by them.

"So? I'll take you wherever you want. Hop in."

For a second, Marie was tempted. She was alone after all, and not sure she was up to the job of saving a mermaid. But Jessie licked his lips and ogled her T-shirt, where the knapsack straps had pulled it tight. So, she just said, "Nah. I'm okay."

"Well, where are you going? So I can tell your mom?"

"She knows." Marie waved and pulled into traffic. The line of cars was long and slow. Jessie wouldn't be able to follow her in the shiny, red truck.

MARIE'S BREASTS WERE new. So were her hips. They had both ballooned suddenly in the past year and had totally messed up her track and field scores. Before, Marie had been making steady progress on the triple jump, once even hitting a 38, amazing for a middle schooler. But her new high school body had a different centre of gravity. Her jump didn't work anymore. Nothing worked. This spring, she hadn't even qualified for Girls State. That's when her coach had looked her over, frowned, and said maybe she should think about cross country.

No one in her family liked her new body, either. Her dad had stopped touching her. Just a few years ago, she had still slept on his chest, when she was sick or scared, her cheek pressed warm and safe against his beating heart. Now he hugged her like some old lady would, holding her away and kind of patting her back. And her mom had started dropping stinging little comments. "Really? You're wearing those shorts?" and "God, Marie, could your pants be any tighter?"

Gus's comments were less direct, but somehow pervier. "In

other countries, your mom and I would be marrying you off right now. Think about that." His eyes, on her ass, had been focused, laser-like.

Marie tried to imagine telling her mom about how Jessie looked at her, all hot and horny. That Gus did too, sometimes. That her dad avoided her, probably because she reminded him of his girlfriend Greta, now. And how that the whole thing made her want to sink into the floor and die.

But Marie was pretty sure her mother would just say something like, "Well, what do you expect, honey, when you're wearing shorts like that?"

It was no use reminding her mom that she herself had bought Marie's track uniform. The striped Lycra shorts she wore for training were required for school meets. They were approved by the booster club. How was it her fault they hugged her butt?

MARIE SAW ACTIVITY under the pier as she approached from the road and her body tensed. Drawing closer, she saw a small collection of people had gathered. She could tell they were mostly boys, because they wore no shirts. She could also tell they were doing something awful, because they shouted and keened in shrill, exultant voices. She ditched her bike by a dune and started running, forgetting to be careful of the crabs banging around in the plastic bucket on her back. Her feet dug so hard in the sand, it sprayed up behind her, while the bucket jounced and bobbled.

"Hey!" she called, as she drew closer. "Hey, get away from there!"

It wasn't as bad as it could be. There were only a handful of boys, and she could see no parents, or TV cameras. The jellyfish barrier had done its work, and so the little creeps were mostly scrambling on the rocks near the edge of her grotto. Still, some of them had long sticks, and were trying to poke at the monster. One boy had collected what small missiles he could—shells, stones, all too light, Marie thought, to do much damage, but dangerous and stupid, anyway.

"This is a marine protected area," she said, as they turned to look at her. "You can't climb on these rocks."

This was complete bullshit. No marine protected area would be next to a boardwalk and have a big tourist pier right over it. But Marie was counting on the boys' ignorance. Stifling her panting, quelling the shaking in her voice, she borrowed language from half-remembered conversations with her dad and went on. "You're trespassing on government land. Any animals here are under the protection of the Federal Fish and Wildlife Department. Stand aside."

Most of the boys fell back, dropping their stones and sticks. But one tow-headed kid refused to give ground. "There's a sick shark," he told her. His eyes glistened with excitement and he clutched a long, whip-like branch in his hand.

"Not a shark," she said. "An injured sea lion. And it shouldn't be disturbed." Sea lions lived in California, but again she counted on the boy not knowing that. It had been her experience that most tourists were idiots when it came to wildlife. They thought opossums were kitties and that blowfish were good eating.

"Who are you?" the boy asked. He whipped the branch back and forth.

"I'm a licensed volunteer." Marie amazed herself as lie after lie jumped from her lips. "I'm here to protect the sea lion until the veterinarian comes. Now get out. This animal isn't a toy; it's an endangered species."

The blond boy looked sceptical. Marie was taller than he, but she was still only a few years older, and dressed in her blue Stephen Decauter High track shorts and a tight white T-shirt. There was nothing official about her, except the language she used.

"We found it first." He pouted.

"No. It was found while scientists were surveying the beach this morning."

"Well, where are they now?"

"Putting together a rescue operation. I told you, this animal is under state protection. Now leave."

Marie loomed over him. He glowered. Then he whipped his stick one last time and stood aside. The other boys followed suit. Hoping she looked tough and hard, she started scrambling up the rocks.

"There's jellyfish," one of the other boys said.

"I know. You get used to them," she said, stifling a cry as a dead sea nettle stung her hand. It was like fire on her fingers.

When she turned to look back at them, palm still smarting, they weren't watching her anymore. They had huddled in a clump and spoke in low voices that she couldn't hear above the roar of the ocean.

She turned her back and clambered to the mermaid, ducking down out of the wind.

Between the rocks, the air was warm and peaceful and smelled of old shells and seaweed. The mermaid didn't hiss or show its teeth. It didn't move or wiggle or threaten. Its horrible mouth hung slack. For a second, Marie thought it might have died, and her chest clutched. But then its torso rose in a gasp and she sighed in relief.

She shrugged off the rucksack. One of the crabs had died on the journey. Another stalked around its broken claw. Dammit. Her eyes stung a little as she plucked out the dead crab. She set it aside on a boulder, its white belly pathetic, its legs slack and spread, starlike. She grabbed the live one out of the bucket, and being mindful of its claws, dropped it on the creature's chest.

She hoped the mermaid would use its uninjured arm to pluck at the crab and eat it. But the creature didn't respond, not to the crab or to her. It just took another hitching breath while the crab scrambled away. Marie grabbed at it and threw it back on the monster. Again, the monster ignored it.

"Come on!" she urged. "You need your strength!"

But the mermaid just lay there and the crab gamely scrabbled off.

Marie wondered if the creature's skin needed to be bathed in seawater. She picked up the bucket and started clumsily back over the rocks to fill it. The boulders by the shore were slippery with seaweed and she had to tread carefully.

Something struck the side of her face, hard and brightly startling.

"Ouch!" She was more surprised that hurt. But she slipped and scraped her thigh while the bucket bounced down on the sand. "Shit!" She felt stinging heat and looked over to see the blond boy stooping down to fire another missile.

"What are you—" But she couldn't even finish before another rock banged on her teeth. Her skull rang. Tears bloomed in her eyes. "Stop it!"

"I found it first." His friends had all scattered, but he stood defiant, his skinny fists clenched. "It's mine."

"The fuck it is!" Her lip stung and her head rang. Without

thinking, Marie grabbed up a large stick and leapt. The anger in her was white hot and pulsing. The kid cowered, but Marie thwacked him on the shoulder anyway. When he cried out, she hit him again, this time on the ass. "How do you like it?"

"Don't! Ow!"

"Hurts, huh? Fuck you, you little brat." She smacked him across the back. Splinters flew from the stick and a big red stripe appeared on his golden skin. "She doesn't belong to you! Get out of here." She felt a kind of horror, mixed with glee, fiery and heavy, all at once. Her eyes stung with tears. But she was happy too, beating this horrible boy. It felt good. She raised the stick for another blow.

He turned and ran. She watched him go, breathing hard. "She's not a shark, you dumbass!"

She went back to the mermaid. It did not care if she cried, so Marie did. Her whole body heaved. Her sobs sounded like screams in her ears and the aching hole in her chest was so big, even the sea would never fill it.

THE MERMAID DIDN'T respond when she dumped a bucketful of seawater on her a while later. A couple of seagulls flapped close, so Marie banged on the rocks with her stick until they flew away. She checked the cell phone. Sometime in the last hour, she had managed to crack the glass. Her mom would be pissed. And her father still hadn't called.

Marie figured he might be on his way to her. But he also might be just having sex with Greta, his phone forgotten, his old life forgotten.

In the end, Marie made a kind of nest for herself among the rocks, like she had when she was little. She crooned "Part of Your World," while surf pounded in the background. She rested her back against a boulder and propped her feet on another one. Dried white bird shit had dripped down in a white cascade. The dead crab still lay where she left it, belly turned to the dock above. Marie closed her eyes and listened to the surf and the pilings thrumming, as people walked back and forth, back and forth, reeling in fish and killing them.

She had remembered to bring food for the mermaid, but not for herself. She thought about hiking to the Boardwalk to get a hotdog. She could buy a cold lemonade there, too. She could also call *The Maryland Coast Dispatch* and ask them to send someone to the 59th Street Pier for the story of a lifetime. She could take a picture of the mermaid right now and email it to the Huffington Post, or CNN. Post it on Instagram, it would probably go viral by sundown. She should do it. People would want to know there were real mermaids. Scientists would want to study this one. It was ugly, but it was magical.

Time passed. Marie just sat and stared at the bird shit until she fell asleep.

THE PHONE BUZZED in her hand and she woke with a start. The sun had moved way behind her. It burnished the ocean and tinged the clouds with fire. Marie stared at the phone's display. It said Gus was calling. She answered.

"Honey, are you all right?" Her mother's voice sounded worried.

"I fell asleep."

"Where?"

"Under the pier. I'm sorry."

The mermaid looked dead, really dead. It wasn't moving. Its eyes had gone cloudy white. Marie felt her throat swell. "It's dead, Mom. I think it's dead and Daddy never called."

Pause. "Well. He's awful busy, honey."

"With what?" Marie's nose was running and she wiped at the slime impatiently. "Why doesn't he come see me anymore?"

". . . You'll have to ask him." Her mom's throat sounded tight. She added, "What if we come and get you, babe?"

Marie squinted at the ocean. The sun made it so bright, it hurt her eyes. "Yeah."

"We're having a cookout. Gus got crabs."

"I'll meet you by the pier."

"I'm sorry it died. What was it? A dolphin?"

Marie looked at the mess on the rocks, the gaping mouth, now ringed with flies. A tiny white crab inched over the creature's tail. Marie flicked it away. "I don't know." She added, "It's nothing."

"We'll be right there." Mom hung up.

BY THE TIME Jessie found her, the sea was much higher and the sun had almost set. A cold wind whipped at the red, white and blue flags decorating the pier. The mermaid had begun to stink.

Marie stood away from it, on top of the rocks, balanced like a ballerina. She was throwing dead jellyfish back into the sea, her hands white and red from all their stinging.

"Hey," Jessie said.

She turned. "My mom didn't come?"

"She's dealing with dinner. They sent me."

Marie nodded and tossed another dead blob. "Can we stop and get a lemonade? I'm thirsty."

"We can stop and get whatever you want."

They hiked up to the Boardwalk and bought a lemonade from an Eastern European exchange student in a bright yellow hat. The lemonade was ice cold and soothed her parched throat. The electricity must have been restored while she slept, because around them, arcades beeped and bonged; music blasted from shitty clothing stores; a whole pack of fat kids pounded into the Laser Tag building. Under the neon, Jessie's face looked orange and then green.

He had parked the shiny red truck in the public lot, still pretty full at this hour. Jessie loaded her bike in the back. Marie climbed inside, sucking on the lemonade.

Jessie started the engine. "How old are you?"

"Almost fifteen."

"Sophomore next year?"

"Yeah. You?"

"I flunked my senior year at Choate. My parents think Uncle Gus is going to straighten me out."

"Will he?"

"Who knows? I'm a problem child." Jessie sounded pleased.

He pulled into traffic, heading north. The sun sank lower behind him. Big hotels up ahead reflected bronze light in their windows.

"What were you doing down there at the beach all day?"

"Trying to save some kind of animal. I think it was a new species, but it died."

"New species. Really?"

Marie shrugged. "The ocean's big. It's got a lot of things in it that no one's ever seen. Maybe I saw one today. I don't know. It doesn't matter. It's dead." She swallowed the lump in her throat.

Jessie drove by a gas station. "You get high, Marie?"

She didn't. She never had. She was an athlete. She was a good girl. She tried hard. She always had.

Her lips moved. "Yeah. I get high all the time." The lie came easily, like the ones at the pier about the Fish and Wildlife Department. She thought of those boys. She thought of smacking the blond one hard with a stick.

Jessie lit up a hand rolled cigarette and passed it over. Marie took it between her fingers, resting her feet on the dashboard. She stared at the car's plastic ceiling. Gus kept his truck nice. Her dad never did. He was careless and his Jeep was always sandy and smelly, rubber masks and fins rattling in the back with a tackle box. Still, when she was a girl, crossing the Bay Bridge with him, top down, it had always felt like flying. At night especially, when the bridge lit up like a fairytale castle, the ropes of star-like bulbs swooping over dark water had seemed magical and dangerous.

Jessie said, "Man. I thought this summer was gonna suck. But you're here. So, things are looking up, huh?"

Marie put the joint to her lips and sucked. The smoke hurt her chest and stung her eyes. She blinked hard, managed to hold the smoke in like she'd seen other kids do at parties, and then let it out slowly. Would smoking weed screw up her cross country times? Did it matter? Probably not.

Jessie grinned. The sun had slipped behind his shoulder. Marie passed him the joint, letting her head fall back against the seat.

To her right, the ocean still pounded. Up ahead, the road stretched into the night.

in the bog where
we are walking cautiously

Kate Shannon

all hail the swamp witch
and the opossum that lingers between her teeth
the graceless wreckage that pools from her sullen fingers
the small and oft-crooked lair of her roosting
where she roasts children and their little toes
over her fire pit of most sinister doom
& cackles
& cackles

all hail the swamp witch
and her wasteland,
how fertile soil turns beneath her wicked feet
and how empty be her shaking arms in the night
clasping nothing and the sulphurous air;
sometimes, a skull that looks like her skull sits in her palms
& stares
& stares

all hail the swamp witch
and her innocence that was drowned beneath the milkweed
how her body twisted and fought under their hands
wild is the magic that gathers in her waterlogged lungs
twisted still is her sleeping body when it does sleep
other nights, she waits for them in her viscera
& screams
& screams

Blazing Stars

Sara Rauch

EARLY THAT SUMMER, the pirate reappeared at the Blue Whale and Ella scented trouble. Or maybe it was the unmistakable brine of octopus—boiled, she'd guess, bought by a well-meaning nearby merchant wanting to fancify their menu without any knowledge of what to do with all those tentacles. Grilling was better, she would have said. Heaps of hot sauce help too.

A good-looking man-boy, the pirate, not young so much as never grown up, plenty of swagger and sword, with a bullish septum piercing and a pink carnation tucked in his corduroy blazer lapel. That carnation was the trouble. It meant a romantic streak, a temperament drawn to declarations of undying love. Nothing she needed. She was happy with her quiet life. A tiny house off a dirt road, the flying fish—er, birds—come to warble each morning, walking to and from work (legs! how perfect they were!), scooping ice cream for passers-thru and locals alike.

Standing in her kiosk, she watched the traffic flow. The solidity of the shock-absorbent mat beneath her feet, her toenails painted a pearly pink inside the comfortable clogs she'd bought when she was promoted to head scooper. People approached her, usually pleasant because who isn't about a triple-scoop of Fudge Ripple, and once satisfied, moved on. Sometimes a tourist might ask where she was from, assuming she was a college girl working a summer job, and she used to say, Down under, but they'd puzzled over her lack of accent until she did a little research and changed her answer to Here and there. People didn't seem bothered by that, most of them believing such a past to be full of glamourous adventure, and maybe the truth wouldn't have changed their minds.

I SET MY sore brown eyes on her one bright afternoon the week my mother went over yonder. Her last words: *There's more for you here.* Well, how I was supposed to gather her meaning, I wasn't sure. All I could see was hightailing it back to the seas, no more reason binding me to land. Till I saw Ella, that is. Didn't know her name the day she stopped me bolt upright in my tracks. She was handing out a banana split, with that smile. That smile made me reach for my sunglasses only to remember that I'd lost them and neglected to plunder a new pair. Nothing in Catoosa sparkled or glared like the sea. Till Ella, anyway. She was sinuous as seagrass, stunning as an anemone.

I didn't say hello that day, nor any of the days—long, full of small talk and paperwork and condolences—that followed and I went back to sea as planned at the end of summer. But I couldn't shake the ice cream girl from my mind. So when we came back through the Gulf the next spring, I signed off and jumped a steamer north, back to the small town where I'd grown up, back to the family home I hadn't had the heart to put on the market. Back to her, or to the hope of her, that I'd find her again handing out sundaes.

There she was, aged not a day. Her hair a lustrous amber, piled on top of her head and secured beneath the little paper cap all the scoopers had to wear. I didn't know what I would do until I stood right in front of her and she said, a little loudly, as if I hadn't heard her the first time and maybe I hadn't: Sir? What flavour would you like? Sir?

Well, I've never been one for ice cream, but I found my tongue: Sweet cream, with red hots.

Did she gaze at me a little long before preparing my outlandish order? Did her hand linger when I took the cone? The person behind me *ahem-ed.* I bowed, and got out of there as fast as I could and only later realized I hadn't paid, coins still jangling in my pocket.

ELLA RECOGNIZED AN omen when she saw one. Whether good or bad, she didn't yet know, but given her contract and the electric current that jolted through her when the pirate's fingers brushed hers over the waffle cone, she'd wager bad.

She'd chosen Catoosa because it was the second farthest inland seaport in the States. (Duluth had proven much too cold.) A pirate was not part of the plan—she wasn't allowed to be too far from open water, just in case, but what kind of pirate summers in Oklahoma? This rabble-rousing, sword-and-swagger man-boy belonged on a ship, or at the very least on the Cape, or the pier in Santa Monica, or guzzling a Singapore Sling somewhere in Tahiti.

When her shift ended, she balanced her drawer with a few dollars from her tips and wished the Blue Whale goodnight before walking home to a can of sardines and Gose brewed with free range sea water (marred only slightly by the coriander). After eating and tidying up her kitchenette, she sat on a lawn chair in the yard humming. She couldn't sing, given the rules of her agreement, but whatever the pirate had activated with his touch reverberated through her like a conch horn's growl. She had to voice it somehow. Eventually she climbed up to the loft and turned out the lights. Despite the thick mattress and heavy comforters, she tossed and turned all night, listening to the peepers, adrift on tides of worry.

'COURSE I'D GONE and forgot to pay. You don't pay for anything on a ship, not with cash anyways. So I went back the next afternoon and ordered yet another Sweet Cream with Red Hots, and she assessed me before scooping, not unkind in any way, but wary.

This time I put the money on the dinged aluminium counter while she had her back turned, double what I owed and then some. At the register, she shuffled some bills and reached for the quarters but all's I choked out was, You keep the change.

Well she looked as alarmed by that as if I'd sung the declaration I'd been practicing—*I've searched the seven seas for you*—so I backed away, boot heels tap-tapping, watching her watch me, eyes as turquoise as the Caribbean. Eventually I bumped into someone who said *Excuse me* in the most aggravated tone and I had to break our stare to apologize.

I've had my share of booty, but Love? At home I consulted my mother's leather-bound library which informed me mostly that love was tragic—a name echoing across a moor, a dagger brandished by missed communication, turning a moment too soon and losing it all. Why risk it? I posed to the empty halls, and the ice cream girl's face floated before me in answer.

Maybe I'd clean up the place, invite her 'round. Cook her a nice dinner. Prove my normalcy. Never mind all that sad, forbidden stuff. Never mind that I hadn't been a landlubber since my teen years, and those years were long behind me. We'd have a nice place in the country, a big front porch to rock away the sweet summer nights, cold lemonade in tall glasses, and maybe a brood rough-housing in the front yard.

AT THE END of the week, Ella crossed the breakers and ventured into dialogue. She didn't want to. She told herself not to. The tingle in her hands had taken over her whole body, a tsunami she had no desire to ride. The Love Rule was the one rule she'd figured it wouldn't be hard to obey.

She said: I'm sorry, we're out of red hots.

It was true—before the pirate, no one ever got red hots—they weren't on the reorder radar.

He looked down at his worn leather boots, and she thought he might leave and she teetered between happy and sad. She'd assumed her emotions would be more solid on dry land, but they taunted her with the same slippery waves.

Then he looked up and took a deep breath and said, Change is good. Butter cream with toffee, I reckon.

My favourite, she said before she could stop her tongue. Damn the red hots, look what she'd done.

Maybe I can buy you one, some time, the pirate said with a laugh.

Maybe, she said, turning away to scoop.

When she turned back, he had his phone out, fingers poised over the screen. He said, I don't know your name.

Not so shy after all. She held the cone while she told him, reciting the number she'd worked hard to memorize after obtaining the blasted plastic contraption in the bright-white store in the mall.

I'll call you, he said, sliding the phone back into his pants, and taking the cone from her hand, cheersed her. His smile, a mess of crooked teeth, unleashed seahorses in her stomach.

Crab shite, she cursed softly, ignoring the next customer's curious look.

I KNOW THE rules, or at least, I researched the rules—how long to wait to text, what to say to charm her, where to wine and dine her—like you could run falling in love the way you do a business. I'm a pirate, through to my core. I called her that night.

HE ARRIVED AT her tiny house on a red ten-speed. What was that phrase she'd read in one of the musty books she dug up at library sales—*A woman needs a man like a . . .* ? She almost laughed. But this wasn't funny. His face shone so earnest in the dusk as he nudged down the kickstand, pulled a bouquet of daisies from the crate bungee-corded over the back tire.

What was she doing, tempting fate this way? Didn't the summer grass tickle her bare feet in the most pleasurable way? Didn't she like stretching her calves and hamstrings after a double shift? Didn't she love nights spent reading, poring over pictures of this new world, no one wondering when dinner would be ready?

She'd pricked her finger with a new piece of sea glass and signed the sea witch's long sheet of kelp: no kissing, no singing, no history. She said yes to it all. And she was content. She had no intention of returning. She had a stack of books waiting to be read, she had zucchini and tomatoes flowering in her garden. Land suited her.

But look what land had done: gone and brought her this handsome, confounding stranger. A pirate, of all men. Oh, that swagger.

Worse, too, was that being with the pirate felt good, felt better than walking, running, dancing. By the end of the first date, when he hugged her goodnight, something in her body crested and it was if she was floating, suspended in the air, full of light. No, she didn't want to go back, though nor did she want to give him up, and so despite what was at stake, she bargained she could control it. Even if only for a few more dates. But the flattery of gladiolas, the flutter of his eyelashes against her cheek, his big, rough hand holding hers, the salty, homey scent of his skin . . .

Well, it was hard.

Three kiss-less dates would surely dissuade him, she thought. She was charming, she knew, but not enough to keep a grown man hooked with no promise of fulfilment. Here, as under the sea, there was a rhythm to these things and she was bucking it. Besides, soon the summer would end and he'd head back to his boat, she was sure of it. That was his life, the one *he'd* chosen.

She hadn't expected someone quite so rough around the edges to be such a gentleman. Each night he hugged her, and held her hand, and asked to see her again.

The night of their fourth date, she smoothed cocoa butter over her freshly shaven legs, slipped into an ivory crochet dress, and fastened back her tresses with the abalone comb she'd brought with her. She'd never worn it—there was nothing like it on land, and she hated to draw attention—but she thought it might work like a talisman, a reminder of the life she'd walked (or was it swam?) away from. If she'd walked away from everything she'd once known, she could walk away from a pirate.

Right?

Wouldn't her sisters gloat if Ella was bound home because she kissed a human? She remembered Marisel's words, as she outlined the rules of the agreement: *Love is too* easy, *she drawled. You'll have to earn your oxygen some other way.* The last thing Ella wanted was to be another lovelorn diva haunting the grottos half-crazed with loss, not even for the pirate, no matter how her heart beat otherwise.

By our third date I'd fairly confirmed my suspicions—I mean, who else has a jacuzzi hot tub installed alongside their 300-square-foot house?—and her accepting another invitation really meant something. From what I knew of legend and lore, we were courting disaster. Still, I'd gone to the Salvation Army and dug up an old ditsy quilt, had stopped off at Lindeman's for a loaf of day-old bread, gathered lilies from the house's overgrown back garden. I couldn't help myself—it was seemingly impossible, but I didn't want to give her up.

Everything in my body lit when she was near, a yearning I'd only known on ships, ploughing through the waves toward that endless horizon and the implacable heavens. I didn't know how to breach the barrier, to broach the topic, of what had been lost for her gains and what she'd have to give up for the blaze dancing between us. I had a few books in my possession—sea myths and tales from the deep, that kind of thing—but they were ancient, and seemingly out of date, because she still had her voice, even if I'd never heard her sing. I needed something more current, so I paid a visit to the occultist in Tulsa who charged me a full treasure chest and spun a long, elaborate tale of independence and strength, abandon and hope, finally revealing the loophole I'd have to gamble on. It was a delicate business, not my specialty, but for Ella I'd do anything to pull it off.

HE ARRIVED AGAIN on the bicycle, and blushed at the sight of her dress. This old thing, she said, in mock modesty, and they laughed. But seriously, he said. You're too pretty to risk the bicycle. Let's walk.

Where could they go, she wondered, within walking distance? They headed away from town along the shaded country road, turning off at a trail marker most would have missed. The path was flat and clear and opened out onto a crescent of sand and cattail-ringed pond. You've never been here? he asked.

This explains the peepers, she said.

We used to have parties here, long time ago, he said.

She sat on the quilt he'd lain out and looked at the dark water. There was only the faint lap of ripples licking the shore and the rustle of the pirate behind her, unpacking the crate: baguette, dented tin of caviar, two cans of Er Boquerón, fresh radishes, and a lemon. The last, she'd told him, was one of her unexpected favourite tastes. How earnest he was, how willing to please her. She pushed away the thought of how his face would fall when she delivered the "let's-just-be-friends" monologue she'd practiced in the mirror.

He settled next to her and cracked the beer, cut into the lemon with a paring knife and offered her a thick wedge. She took it and bit—she loved the shocking brightness, almost like sunshine between her teeth. The caviar, despite the dent, was miraculous, a swirl of silk on her tongue. Longing—or was it nostalgia?— bubbled in her.

Do you know that old ballad, the one where the pirate falls overboard? He hummed a bit of melody, keeping his eyes carefully on the pond.

It was as if the beer had gone straight to her head. I don't—I can't—sing, she stammered.

Ah, so modest, he said. I bet you have a beautiful voice. But I just want to know if you know the story.

Yes, she knew the story, knew it well. The hum she'd perfected on land was but a shade of the full contralto she possessed amid the waves. She'd been renowned. She'd sung that ballad in enclaves and caves filled with captive merfolx, gathered accolades around her like a cloak until all of a sudden they tightened like a noose. She saw her fame would ebb, and she'd end up married off to some pleasant-enough merman who'd claim they were equals while expecting her to take care of the babies. Her sisters all insisted they loved their lives, but Ella was too shrewd not to notice the puckered mouths and averted eyes, the faint air of resignation.

Even her fame wasn't enough capital to avoid being trapped by that same fate. She went to visit Marisel only to see what her options were. The sea witch—far more beautiful than the rumours led you to believe—listened closely to Ella's fears, her dark locks bobbing as she nodded along to Ella's list. *You know the stakes?* Ella nodded, though she didn't really. Did anyone? She knew she'd have to give up everything she'd ever known, but that seemed a small price to pay to live on her own terms. As Marisel ticked off the complete list of terms, Ella daydreamed of life on land: pants! sun! freedom! Nowhere in the vision that had guided her to the very edge of the Verdigris did she imagine a pirate.

He hummed a few more bars. A heartbreaker, that tune, he said.

She wanted to get away from the conversation, but didn't know how. She twisted the cloth napkin on her lap. This is delicious, she said. Really thoughtful. And decadent. But I have to tell you something—

He cocked his head and assessed her. She realized then that his eyes were the colour of wakame. Never before had anyone seemed to stare so deeply into her—Was it her soul? She was supposed to have one now, gained along with her legs, but was never clear if the novel buoyancy she felt on land was from this mortal gain or if it was more practical than that: oxygen filling lungs, standing upright, walking, dancing.

I really like you, she started, but I'm not like you.

I know what you are, the pirate said.

Inside her, what felt like a stone plummeted. She hadn't paid enough attention to the contract before signing—she'd been enchanted, headstrong as always—and though she knew she was forbidden from kissing, and singing, and speaking her secret, she had no idea if someone else figuring it out was grounds for return.

How? she asked, rubbing her thighs.

How would it happen? Would her skin turn to scales? Would she wake up bobbing in the dark waves? Would Marisel arrive and bundle her off under cover of night?

I did my research, he said. I have an idea. A proposal of sorts.

No, she said. You shouldn't—

He reached for her hand. His was dry, and warm. Ella, listen—

I don't think you understand.

But I do.

This is dangerous, she said. For both of us. Impossible.

I think I know a way, he said. If you'll trust me.

The stone inside her dropped even further; surely this was a declaration of love, the very worst transgression she could commit. The air grew close, suffocating her. She pulled her hand from his and stood, unsteadily. Impossible, she repeated. I made my choice.

Before he could say any more, she turned and fled into the woods. Branches whipped at her cheeks and she stumbled over roots. Eventually she found her tiny house. Her feet in their pretty leather sandals were scratched and bleeding.

I DIDN'T GO after her. 'Course not. She needed her space, to think things through—least that's what I figured anyway. Give it a few days, I told myself, as I paced the family house. To distract myself, I built a towering pile of junk in the backyard and set it afire. I had already called an antiques dealer, who'd pulled up in a twenty-foot truck and hauled away the more valuable pieces. A realtor had come through and appraised the property. The price she listed seemed fair. *Good bones*, she said. *But it'll need work.* Well, don't we all, I thought as I signed the seller's agreement. If Ella didn't accept my proposal, I'd have the money to captain my own ship. But if she did, we wouldn't need cash at all. To be safe, I'd called a lawyer and drew up a will, sending the proceeds of the sale to Catoosa's Historical Society, under condition that they take my mother's books and make room for our story.

SHE CLEANED AND bandaged her feet, taking extra care with the antibacterial ointment, and then she made a cup of tea and settled in to her fate. The little cuckoo clock read 11:30 and though she had no real reason to support her hunch, she figured midnight to be the right hour for the transformation to occur. Should she get to the river? No, she decided, sipping the chamomile. If she was going to have to go back, then Marisel would have to come get her. Stubborn to a fault she knew but she wasn't going to just give in. The pirate's sun-beaten face floated before her and she whooshed away the apparition with a wave of her hand. It was her own fault, really. Four dates. The abalone comb. She dove headfirst into choppy waters and what did she expect? Surely not the calm she'd long ago convinced herself she wanted. The clock ticked closer to the hour. She set down her half-full teacup in its pretty floral saucer and stood. Though her feet hurt, she paced the small living room, trying to take everything in: the Berber wool rug, the smooth grain of the fold-up maple table where she ate meals, the high trill of grasshoppers outside her open windows, the bright pink lilies wafting their heady scent. She would miss her bed, the coffee percolating on the double burner stove, the walk to and from work, the dazzle of chocolate sauce and those fake red cherries. All the books she hadn't gotten to. Magazines. Maps. Talk radio. Thunderstorms. Soil. Spoons. Kitchen whisks. The sun's first rays.

At 11:59, she sat down in her chair and closed her eyes.

The pirate.

She held her tears. One last breath. Two. Three.

PIRATES GET A bad rap for being wild marauders, hard drinking, grizzled, and ill-suited for the day-to-day. I never really understood that—it takes a lot of practice, a lot of patience, a lot of care to keep a ship afloat.

I'd planned to give her a week, really let her mull things through. But once the embers of the last pile of junk began to fade, I couldn't wait any longer. I packed and paced over the creaky pine planks, anxious for her answer.

AS SHE SCOOPED ice cream at the Blue Whale the next afternoon, she ran through her reasons: *loss of autonomy, her tiny house, love was for fools, oxygen, her sisters' "I told you so's," lemons, toes* . . . She'd woken cramped and sore in her chair and like a mother with a newborn baby, the first thing she'd done was count her toes. All accounted for. But beneath all the reasons she could count to stay, something else nagged her. It was like a fly hitting the kiosk window, desperate to get out.

The pirate.

Loving him would ruin everything. *Loving him.* The words, once exhumed, clamoured all the harder. It was an exercise in futility to try to escape them.

Her scoops were extra big all afternoon, unwieldy. Her boss asked if everything was okay. Yes, yes, she assured him. Everything was fine.

When she finally hung up her smock and pushed out the back door, there was the pirate, leaning against his bicycle against a vast oak. She often sat under that tree to eat lunch, and pressed her back against its crackled grey bark, enjoying the roughness through her thin t-shirt. She counted the plinks of acorns as they fell and whispered to the squirrels who nattered in the branches. The ice cream stand's door was whooshing shut behind her. For a moment, time stood still, and she did not know which direction she would step. Forward or back, safety or unknown, old self or new.

An acorn flew from the sky and landed at her feet. She looked up to see the squirrel, standing in a crook, shaking its fists. The squirrel tossed another acorn. It landed square on the pirate's tricorne, bouncing off with comic effect. The pirate glanced around, and then, seeing where her eyes focused, tilted his head up and laughed. His laugh was like the buried treasure of a shipwreck—strange, weathered, eternal. In the bicycle's rear basket she noticed an unruly profusion of blazing star. She thought then of the song he'd hummed, the ballad that had made her famous, of the final, inscrutable lines, and understood then what his proposal must be. If she said yes, it'd be something new altogether—neither land nor sea—for both of them.

She stepped toward him and would have kissed him, but he placed a finger on her lips and said, We have to do this just right or it won't work. He helped her climb onto the bicycle before climbing on himself.

Where to? she asked. She thought of her tiny house, standing alone in the woods as dusk settled. The ivory linen curtains. The collection of river stones on the sill. The Summertime tea cup drying in the dish rack. She hoped someone would find the place and treat it well.

To the river, he said. South, and then—

He raised his hands around her in a gesture of release. The sky burned pink as coral, stitched with stratus clouds lacy as sea foam.

You ready?

She never knew if she was, but she placed her hands over his on the curved metal bars, and said, As I'll ever be.

There's Something in the Water

Katie Marie

NO ONE EVER got rich and famous by writing for an agricultural magazine.

However, one could pay the bills. Which, back when I had accepted the permanent staff writer position was all I was going for. Working freelance had been cool and all, a lot of freedom but the stress of a non-guaranteed income hadn't been worth it. The months where I sold enough were great, the months where I didn't quite manage to meant eating nothing but instant noodles and turning the heating off to save money.

I remind myself of those cold and hungry days as my train pulls up to the tiny and battered-looking station and a feeling of dread fills me. I shuffle onto the single platform. The only visible sign has arrows pointing left saying trains facing that way are going to whatever passed for a city in this part of the country and trains going right are heading to the next village.

"Hey!" I ignore the first call, but the second gets my attention. I turn to see a burly chap who looks like how a child might describe a farmer, like someone playing dress-up rather than an actual farmer. "You from the magazine?"

"How can you tell?" I say, moving my bag into my other hand to shake his offered hand.

"Most people round this way are carrying feed sacks, not laptops." He offers me a big smile, showing too-white teeth that were so straight they had to be cosmetically altered. "I'm Finn McGuinness, I thought I'd come to meet you here as getting a taxi into town is out of the question."

"Oh," I frown. "In that case, I appreciate your help."

"Cars just out this way," I follow Finn off the platform and down to his car. Finn's car is more what I expected from a farmer; there are tools on the back seat, dog fur everywhere, and said dog yapping happily as we approach and clamber in. I make a mental note to get my coat cleaned when I got home.

"So," Finn says as we pull away from the shed pretending to be a train station. "What got you writing for the quarterly of all things? You don't look the farming type."

"My dad was a farmer. You don't exactly give off the lifelong farmer vibe yourself." Finn snorts at my accusation.

"Yeah, I moved out this way a few months back when my granddad died. He left me everything, so I figured why not. I was only an average financial advisor, why not see if I can be an above-average farmer."

"That's certainly a career change," I mutter. Finn nods.

"Hell, yeah it was," he laughs. "But I'm loving it. Getting back to my family roots."

"You've certainly landed on your feet with a farm here. We've been trying for years to interview a landowner round this way, but no one would ever speak to us."

"Yeah, the old boys are a bit set in their ways, they think telling the world our secret will break the good luck."

"And is that all it is, good luck?"

"No way," Finn says smiling widely. "There's a lot more going on here than luck, and I plan to share it with the world. But you're going to have to wait until tomorrow. Don't worry though, it's worth the wait."

The car pulls into the town, though calling it a town is generous. It is a street, a single shop/pub, a couple of houses and a small church. I have a room booked at the pub, and I have to admit the idea of a decent dinner and a long sleep before starting work tomorrow certainly sounds good.

As we get out of the car, I am unsurprised to see curtains twitching in the few houses. I am prepared for a chilly reception.

I hadn't exaggerated when I told Finn we'd been trying for years to speak to one of the locals here. Their refusals were rarely polite.

"Don't let it bother you," Finn says when he notices me looking. "As I said, the folks around this way take their privacy to a ridiculous level. Just keep your head down and the worst they'll do is glare a bit."

I look down the street, the church is nestled at the end of the road. It is similar enough to every church I've ever seen, but the great statue out front marks it as not being from any faith I know. I can't understand exactly what I am looking at. It is sort of humanoid, two arms, two legs, but the head looks more like a lamprey eel than a man.

"Uhh, yeah when a town is this isolated, they can have some weird ideas," Finn mumbles as if embarrassed.

"You're telling me," I mutter. Glancing up at the pub, I notice it doesn't have a name but the image on the sign is an eel.

"Come on, let's get you settled."

Getting me settled involves Finn talking to the landlord while I try to ignore the array of unpleasant looks I'm getting from the few local patrons. The looks get more venomous the longer I stand there, and I can feel myself shrinking under the obvious hate. By the time Finn convinces the landlord to hand over the keys to my room, I am surprised that the others in the bar aren't spitting at me.

The room I am given is small, the furniture old, but it seems clean enough and smells of fabric softener and old wood. Not the worst place I'd ever stayed despite the cold welcome.

"You'll forgive the boys," Finn says. "They're not used to, or too keen on company. Very tight-knit community you see."

"Yeah, I saw," I mutter. "Don't worry, I don't require their hospitality. Just so long as they restrict themselves to dirty looks and muttering, I'll live."

"There's a good chap," Finn claps me on the back. "If that's the case then, fancy a spot of dinner?"

"I'm not hungry, I think I'll turn in early and meet you at the farm tomorrow morning." Finn's face drops a little at my rejection, and I remember that he is relatively new to this community too. His grandfather might have been a lifelong resident, but Finn only moved out here two years ago. I wonder if the locals have warmed to him yet or if he is still an outsider? Does he crave my lukewarm company? Regardless, I have been travelling all day and am exhausted. I want to crawl into the small old bed and sleep for a week. I certainly don't fancy sitting in the bar for dinner feeling the glares on my back.

"Oh, ok," Finn says, his smile coming back quickly. "I'll see you in the morning then, I'll cook breakfast, bright and early."

Bright and early indeed, I think the next morning as I head up the single road out to Finn's farm. It is a grey drizzly day, with the kind of rain that soaks into you and leaves you cold for hours.

Finn's farm is about two miles out of town, so it's not a long walk, but by the time I reach it my already dark mood is undeniably foul. Finn sees my approach and jogs out to meet me, the little dog yapping at his heels. His cheerful demeanour instantly makes my mood worse.

"Hey, hey," he says, slowing his jog as he reaches me. "You're soaked through, come inside, I got some food on and we'll get you dry."

His house is modest and warm, and with my long coat drying over a radiator and a warm towel to dry my hair and face I do feel better. My bad mood all but evaporates when Finn puts a plate of breakfast in front of me, eggs, sausages, tomatoes, and potatoes. I positively inhale the food. It is amazing, full of flavour and something I can't put my finger on, but it makes me happy.

"Good, right?" Finn grins when I put my knife and fork down, and I nod. "I'm a terrible cook, but nothing spoils food grown and raised on this farm."

"I've heard the rumours, and tried the produce you lot ship out," I nod in agreement. "Hence why my editor has been fighting to get me down here. He wants to know your secret."

"You know what the expected yield is on a farm this size?" Finn says, but gives me no time to answer. "About a third of what I consistently produce."

"I am aware," I nod. "As I said, we want to know."

"The secret yeah," Finn says. "Well, the old boys here aren't happy about it. If it was up to them the secret would stay here and no one would ever know."

"I'm grateful to you," I smile.

"I have no experience," Finn says. "Of farming, I mean. I came here as a boy, spent some of my summers with my granddad, but

I don't know shit about farming, not really. Yet a little bit of help from the old boys and boom, this place is chucking out food. I've never had to buy a pesticide, never rotated my crop, nothing. Can you imagine what it would be like if we could do this all over the country? Hell, we'd solve world hunger, put a massive dent in climate change and all that good shit."

"If what you say is true," I start.

"Course it's true!" Finn all but yells. "And those bastards want to keep it to themselves. Not on my watch, no sir." He stands, puts the cleared plates in the sink. "Right, come on, I got to show you this thing before anything else happens."

"Anything else?" I say and stand. Suddenly, my head spins and my legs give out from under me. I crumple to the floor in a heap.

"Holy shit, you all right?" Finn helps me back into the chair.

"Yeah," I mutter taking a few deep breaths to try and steady myself. "Just didn't sleep well last night."

"The old boys give you trouble?"

"In a way, maybe," I say. Taking the glass of water Finn produces. "There was a lot of noise, yelling and whatnot outside in the street. It was really strange, I looked out the window to see what was going on and there was a group of people, a fair few given the size of the town, down by the church all yelling at the statue thing."

"Ahh yeah," Finn says. "Well, this is a pretty isolated community, and they have strange ways."

"You keep saying that," I say and stand again, pleased when my head doesn't spin this time. "I'm fine now."

"Good, we'll head out then, but you give me a shout if you want to rest or something." I nod and follow Finn back outside. The rain has stopped—it is still dull but at least it's dry.

"Earlier you said before anything else happens," I say as we head towards the edge of the farm.

"Yeah," Finn says walking a little in front of me. "The old boys were here last night, and they didn't just make a lot of noise." He points to one of the large storage sheds as we pass it, the word "Traitor" has been painted along the front. As we walk around, I see that the entire other side of the building is gone save for some scorched remains.

"They burnt down your property!" I snap.

"Yup. Don't worry, there was nothing in there—I was clearing it out and they knew that, they were just sending a message."

"That's one hell of a message," I say. "You call the police?"

"Nah, no point. It's just the boys and they won't hurt anything else. They just want me to know how mad they are at me."

"You sound very calm for someone whose property is being destroyed because he's talking to a journalist," I say.

"Most people who want to hurt you, they don't target the one place you've cleared out. If they wanted to hurt me, they'd have burned the house, or the livestock shed. Not this empty thing. It was about to fall down as it was. Really, they did me a favour."

"Some favour," I say, following as Finn leads me past the boundary of his farm and out across some scrubland into a small wood. "Where are we going?"

"I suppose I should tell you now," Finn says. "Sorry for all the cloak and dagger nonsense, I just I don't express myself as well as I'd like in words, and I figured it would be better to show you."

"Well?" I prompt when he doesn't continue.

"It's the water," Finn says. "The reason everything grows so well and so easily here, there's something in the water."

"The water?" I raise an eyebrow.

"Yeah, all the water in the town and surrounding farms comes from the spring in these woods, and anything you water with it . . . well, you had breakfast this morning."

"Do you put steroids in it or something?"

"Hell no," Finn sounds outraged as he continues to lead me through the woods. "It's always been here, the town records mention it being the reason people settled here, and the church records . . . well, they talk a lot of hokum about gods and devils, but they talk even more about this spring. People worshipped the damn thing and I can see why."

He stops talking as we emerge into a clearing. Finn's spring is more like a small lake—too big to be a pond but I can see the far side easily enough. I could probably swim it if I had to and I'm not a great swimmer. At the near side of the lake, there are rocks, and from out of them bubbles the water.

"They pump it down to the town?" I say, gesturing to a large, ancient-looking pipe. Finn nods.

"Been doing it since the town settled here. The church nuts think there's a god in the spring, but I'm no nut. I just know there's something special about this water, and we need to get it scientifically tested, find out what it is, reproduce it, and send it out to the world."

"You own the land?" I can't help but ask.

"No," Finn says. "No one does. It's in the town charter that the spring is common land, public, everyone who lives here has a right to the water."

"Well, I'm no scientist," I say. "I can't test it for anything."

"But you can write the article, people will listen."

"No one will listen." The voice of a woman makes both Finn and I jump. I turn and see her coming out from the trees. She is small and frail-looking, like she's been ill for a long time. Her stomach is grossly distended, like someone pregnant with triplets.

"Hello, Clara," Finn mutters. "Does Martin know you're out here?"

"No one will listen to you," Clara says. She comes closer and I can see her eyes are cloudy. "No one. We will protect what is ours, you won't take him away."

"Ain't no one taking anyone away," Finn says, putting a hand on her shoulder. She shrugs him off and, to my surprise, starts weeping.

"You will, you're trying to," she weeps. "And the men are too weak to stop you, they should have burned you."

"Hey," I say. "There's no need for that talk, no one is taking anything away."

"You're trying to take him," Clara screams and shoves past us, surprisingly strong for someone who looks so frail. She puts her back to the lake and glares at us. "I will protect you, Lord, I won't let them have you."

"I'm sorry," Finn says to me.

"Don't worry," I say. "It's obvious she's not well."

"I am alive!" Clara screeches at me. "I was to die and in his infinite grace, I was spared and preserved. I drank of the water and I live, man's illness could not kill me, I live in his grace."

"Clara," Finn steps forward, his hands out, palms facing her. "Come on now, let's get you home, you need to rest."

"No!" she yells and pulls out a small knife. "I'll kill you before I let you take him."

"Is there someone we can call?" I ask.

"No," another voice says, and again I jump. I was so focused on Clara that I hadn't heard anyone else approach, but when I turn there are two dozen people behind us.

"Martin!" Clara calls.

"Hello, Finn," Martin says. He is a giant of a man, bigger than Finn by several inches and broader. He looks like a man who's spent every daylight hour doing manual labour.

"Hi, Martin," Finn's voice shakes. "I'm sorry, I didn't know Clara was following us. I'd have taken her back myself if I'd known."

"I know, Finn." Martin nods. "You're a good sort, at least we all thought you were."

"Come on, Martin, you know I'm not hurting anything. What we have here is a gift, a real natural gift. We could help so many people, we could save hundreds of lives."

"Don't care about hundreds of lives," Martin says. "I care about this town."

"The town will benefit from this!" Finn says. "Can you imagine the kind of medical care you could get for Clara if we did this?"

"She's fine," Martin says.

"The hell she is!" Finn snaps. "She's riddled with tumours. Water can't cure that!"

"I live in his grace," Clara says yet again. I hear a splash and look to see her step backward into the water.

"Clara, get out of there, people drink that," Martin says firmly. Clara does not obey and takes another step backwards.

"He calls to me." She is weeping again as she speaks. "Tells me to leave you, tells me to go to him, to live with him in the water."

"Clara, sweetheart, come out of the water," Martin has lost his anger and sounds soft, concerned. He doesn't want Clara in the water.

"No, I have to go," she says. "He came to me, told me I had run out of time, I had to go to him, or he'd take away his grace from me."

"Clara," Martin stops at the edge of the water. Clara is just out of arms' reach, and he sounds very worried, his voice is shaking as he says her name. "Please, sweet thing, come back." Clara shakes her head.

"Why doesn't he just go and get her?" I whisper to Finn. Finn shakes his head.

"Come on," Martin says, and Clara takes a slow step towards

him. "Come on faster, love, there's not much time."

Looking past her, I see a shadow in the water. There is something in there with her, something big.

"What the hell is that?" I gasp just as the shadow reaches Clara and she disappears under the water. "How the fuck did she just disappear!" I yell. "She wasn't even in past her knees."

"He came," Martin collapses on the shore. "He took my Clara." A man from the group steps forward and puts a hand on Martin's shoulder.

"She's with God now," he says. "In his grace."

"In his grace," the group behind us echo the words.

"What the hell just happened?" I look at Finn, he is white as a sheet and trembling. His expression is one of dawning horror and I wonder if mine is the same.

"You see now, Finn," Martin says, his voice flat. "Do you believe now?"

"The water is sacred, his gift to us. He is a benevolent god, he asks for little and gives us much," the man next to Martin says proudly.

"There's a big fish in the lake," I say to myself. "A really big fish."

"It's not a fish," Finn says. "Holy shit, it's real."

"He grants us life and plenty," the man next to Martin says, and the crowd echo him. "He gives us all, and in return we protect him." Again, his words are echoed. "We grant him sanctuary from the poisons and toxins of man's world, we provide him food and any payment he requests for his gifts."

"I shouldn't have brought you here," Finn says to me. His face is pale, his words are slurred like he's going into shock. "I'm sorry, pastor. I shouldn't have done this."

"I'm glad you see sense," the pastor says. "Unfortunately, it has already been done. You have placed him at great risk, not only bringing a stranger here but one who can speak to so many."

"It's just an agricultural magazine," I mutter, feeling suddenly vulnerable now that Finn seems to be siding with the town.

"How was I to know!" Finn shouts. "It sounded crazy and you showed me no proof."

"You should have had faith," Martin stands up, his gait is unsteady as he walks towards Finn. "We all have faith; you should have listened to us." His big hand closes on Finn's shoulder and he shoves. Finn stumbles forwards the few feet into the water. Instantly, Finn tries to run out, but Martin and the pastor block him. I don't understand his panic, the water is only lapping at his ankles, there is no way a fish the size of the shadow I'd seen could get to him in such shallow water.

"An offering, Lord," the pastor calls. "Come and partake of our gift, grant us your grace that we might be eternally blessed." The shadow reappears on the lake where Clara had disappeared, and Finn yowls like a child, terrified beyond all reason. He tries once again to escape but is pushed back in by Martin.

The shadow darts back and forth as if frustrated and then something rises up out of it. It is huge, towering over all of us despite the shallow depth of the water, and I struggle to make sense of what I am seeing.

It is dark, mottled green and black, and it smells like everything wrong with the ocean all merged together.

It reminds me of the statue that stands in front of the church, but that was vaguely human, and this is no man.

It has a long eel-like tail in place of legs and though its torso might be humanoid its arms do not end in hands but split into three overly long webbed digits. Where a head should be is a long tentacle-like appendage.

The creature lashes in the open air, and Finn screeches. The head-tentacle splits down the middle revealing row upon row of needle teeth and the creature lunges forward, its entire head latching onto Finn. There is a brief moment of thrashing before Finn disappears into the lake.

I gawp, slack-jawed. "You killed him," I whisper foolishly when the water stills

"He is not dead, he will live forever in our Lord's grace," the pastor says.

"But you won't," Martin says. "Finn was good people, stupid but good. He deserved his fate, just like my Clara did."

"As do you," the pastor says to me. "The harvest will be good this season." He nods to Martin, who smiles at me and advances. I back away but bump into one of the men behind me. He takes a strong grip on my shoulders, steers me toward the lake, and pushes.

The Witch's Diary: Adventures in Hut-sitting

Rebecca Brae

Pandias, Blood Moon 20, 205

HESTER DIGITALIS WISHBONE has arrived!

What a beautiful valley. The forest is dark and foreboding, and the log hut is quaint, but charming (and not in a magickal lure-unsuspecting-hut-sitters-to-their-death kind of way). The Fates are smiling on me. One more job and some extra coin before I head back to Grimoire College. After a summer of minding the Cesspools of Crimoneera, this is an amazing break. I owe Professor Bloodroot a tankard for recommending me.

The place was difficult to locate by air, even with directions. Trees overhang the clearing and only the topmost section of the hut's steeple peeks out. I feel very safe, cocooned by ancient trees and a ring of towering mountains. Small clearings and streams dot the valley, and a lake sits at its heart, so deep in its centre that the water appears black. From above it looks like a giant watchful eye.

Babs (as she insists I call her) met me at the gate. A waist-high fence surrounds her yard, a feature that wasn't of immediate note, but upon closer inspection I realized it was composed of old axes and leg and arm bones. The gate itself is fascinating. Some talented artist has arranged a collection of bones into a raven sculpture with splayed wings. A human skull serves as the chest piece and delicate hand bones make up the bird's head and beak. I suspect the fence is the embodied answer to how this forest is so ancient and healthy. Babs must be a very effective protector.

She even looks like part of the forest. Twigs and leaves entangle her hair, moss blankets her shoulders and acts as anchor to the lichen draping down her back like a lacy cloak. Mushrooms sprout from her pockets. Clouds of mostly congenial bees buzz around her and every so often a squirrel runs up to hide nuts in her hair. Her feet are bare and whenever she stops, she burrows them into the dirt so it's easy to imagine her toes sprouting roots and searching out water. She doesn't just have wrinkles—a great landscape of canyons dominates her face, and I swear I heard her eyeballs creaking. She is old, perhaps old enough to be the original protector of this wood, but age does not slow her down. She's undoubtedly the most Elder of any Elder witches I've met.

We got chatting and I found out that she's vacationing at a secluded beach on the west coast because she wants a "spot of fun in the sun." How cute is that? An old friend of hers, a sea hag that she had a fling with long ago, invited her out. She's beyond excited. I hope she has a wonderful time and doesn't let her anxiety about leaving her hut spoil her fun. She calls it Pasha and talks about it as a mother would her child. She made me promise to keep a close eye on it, saying, "Don't let Pasha get away from you" as she petted the doorframe.

I will take extra care to keep it clean, of course, but it does make me wonder what kind of trouble she expects. I suppose it's not so strange to care about a place. I've never settled down long enough to have the opportunity.

Pasha the hut is cosy. Cabinets of every size and shape cover the back and west walls, all locked or belted shut with leather straps. A large fireplace and cauldron dominate the east wall. A worn rug, small table, and two comfortable chairs sit by the hearth (she must occasionally have guests). Every kind of herb, tool, trinket, and charm I've ever heard of, and several I haven't, hang from the ceiling. I can't step in any direction without banging my head on a mug or getting a mummified chicken foot caught in my hair (Babs is shorter than me). I'll have to tie my hair back and remember to crouch. A loft bedroom overhangs half of the main floor and a trap door in the roof leads to the steeple. I left exploring that to another sun.

Babs showed me which cabinets housed common supplies, like the washbowl, towels, bedding, etc. I'll try to remember the locations, but there's so many cupboards that I'm sure I won't.

She also seemed very concerned that I familiarize myself with the area. I told her I don't often get lost, having a witchy sense of direction and a trusty broom, but that didn't impress her and before leaving, she took me on a tour of the valley in her flying mortar and pestle!

I hesitantly joined her in the bowl, and she took off like a bolt shot from a crossbow, steering with the pestle. My neck is still aching. The mortar was wobbly at first, but the faster we flew, the smoother the ride was. Not my preferred mode of travel, but I see the utility if you have a lot of baggage (my broom bags hold little in comparison).

We flew around her bee farms and walked through her impressive mead-making operation. She topped the tour off by flying halfway up a mountain called Krov' Drevnikh to a system of caves where she ages and stores her mead. Poisonous, bright red mineral veins line the main tunnels. She advised me not to even touch them. What a fantastic use of natural defences.

I have never tasted so many delicious concoctions. Her favourite recipes are her "Elemental Meads" and I wholeheartedly agree. They are inspired creations. Fire is a spicy, intense drink. Earth has woody undertones and a lingering aura of rich amber. Air is smoky, yet sweet. Water is refreshing and light with a subtle hint of lily. And Spirit, ah Spirit. It is as ethereal as its namesake, changing with the moods of the drinker. Sometimes it is tart and hits the tongue with a lightning bolt of flavour, and other times it is as mild and velvety as the honey it was made from. Spirit bottles are marked with blackened corks to set them apart because the brew has interesting side effects. Babs muttered something about hallucinations and random bodily sensations.

She selected a Spirit bottle for me and packed one as a gift for her friend. I can attest to its potency. I only had the smallest of sips during the tasting and, while it's possible I've grown snakes as hair, I'm pretty sure it's just the mead. At least I hope it is.

I like this witch. I wish we could spend more time together, but I don't think that's likely. Although her vacation plans suggest she enjoys getting out and being with people on occasion, I'm sure she's a hermit by choice. Can't blame her. Most people aren't worth the energy it takes to hex them.

Tydias, Blood Moon 23, 205

I WAS UNABLE to make a diary entry last sun because I couldn't find my diary, or my anything. On the plus side, I figured out why this job pays so well.

I went for a walk to explore the valley (on a Moondias . . . I should have known better) and ended up spending the rest of the sun looking for the bloody hut. Don't get me wrong. *I* was not lost. *It* was lost. I made my way back to the clearing, only to find the fence encircling an empty patch of dirt and flattened grass. No Pasha.

The fence was intact, so there hadn't been an explosive catastrophe, and I did a quick dispelling which confirmed the hut was not invisible. The only strangeness was a giant footprint in a patch of soft earth made by a three-toed beast. It was concerning. Was there a hut-stealing monster on the loose? Surely, Babs would have mentioned that.

A more thorough investigation uncovered some trees with broken branches, quite high up. The disturbed foliage formed a rough trail leading away from the clearing.

After contemplating the bone fence, I decided monster hunting was less scary than Babs and followed the trail. Every so often, I came across another footprint or caught sight of something moving in the distance. A few times, I came near enough to hear it crunching through the undergrowth, but the bugger was fast and it always managed to elude me.

Of all the times to go out without my broom! I made a promise to never do that again and sealed the deal with magick. I set up a reoccurring spell. Every time I leave my abode (whatever and wherever that might be) without my broom, a fish will materialize and slap me in the face. I am *not* making this mistake again.

I came close enough to the beast to confirm that either something with chicken legs was wearing the hut like a snail would a shell, or the hut itself had sprouted legs. I didn't much care which it was. Either way, catching up was difficult. After several close calls, I began to suspect it was playing a game of hide-and-seek. One time, I found it crouched behind a tree. It was a large tree, but still . . . I crept to within a few arms' lengths, but it sprung up and took off again.

Eventually, I wised up and asked the local flora for help tracking it. Most were forthcoming, a few were unpleasant (brambles are prickly at the best of times, but no one can claim they weren't given fair warning), and one was downright dodgy. My Dendronic Principals prof. warned us to be careful with birch trees. Now I know why. They lie, just for the fun of it. And when one starts talking, they all do. It's more tedious than being cornered at a party by a flock of tittering nobles.

Dusk had fallen by the time I managed to corral the hut-beast in a cove by the lake. It was reluctant to go anywhere near the water. Maybe it's afraid of the lake, or water in general? Who knows? All I really cared about was that it was mercifully unwilling to trample me to get away. As soon as the hut realized it was caught, it started spinning in place. I think it was a tantrum. Very childish. I ended up sitting down to wait it out. Not a terrible solution. Believe me, I needed the rest.

I was cold, exhausted, and not at all amused by its shenanigans. The damn thing had run through one of Babs' bee farms. Its stomping riled up all the hives and I was now lumpier than an award-winning toad. And here I thought our class pilgrimage to Hekate's temple through the Underworld had been challenging.

The hut-beast eventually tired and squatted on the pebble shore as far from me as it could get without being in the water. Every time I moved closer, it flinched and hopped away. Sometimes, one of its toes would touch the lake by accident, and it leapt back, blowing a puff of smoke from its chimney.

I wanted to scream at the hut-beast. Instead, I did the mature thing and talked to it in a calm tone. I honestly don't know where I summoned that up from. The hut settled as I related stories about my friends at college. It shuffled closer whenever I lowered my voice, so I spoke quieter and quieter, luring it in, until it was close enough that I could grab the door handle.

It jumped up as soon as I moved, but I had already opened the door. I didn't know if I was diving into an angry beast's maw or the hut's interior, but at that moment, I didn't care. I'd sleep somewhere, whether in a monster's belly or on a pine and moss mattress. I am happy to report that it was a regular hut inside.

I wish Babs had been more specific in her warning to not let Pasha get away. I thought she meant to keep the place clean, not that the damn thing might actually run off. Yesh.

The eventide was a rough ride. I now understand why the cupboards are all lashed shut and the furniture is bolted to the floor. I did a lot of bouncing and sliding around as the hut charged through the forest. It finally stopped in another clearing with a similar bone fence to the first, only this gate sports a wolf sculpture. I wonder how many fences there are.

I fully expect the hut to pull another runner the moment I step foot outside, but we'll have to work something out because I desperately want to do more exploring. I'm stiff and sore so going anywhere this sun holds no appeal. Luckily, I found enough herbs hanging about to make a salve to relieve my bee stings. Mead took care of the rest.

There is only one unopened bottle of mead left in the hut. When that soldier falls, things will be truly dire. I'm saving it for next sun—something to fortify me for the supply run and subsequent hut search.

Wendias, Blood Moon 24, 205

MEAD ACQUIRED. HUT found. Disaster averted.

Freydias, Blood Moon 26, 205

THIS WAS AN unintentionally exhilarating sun.

The sky was clear and the air brisk as I set out this morn to replenish the herbs I used from the hut in my bee salve. I also wanted to see if I could hunt down some spell components to augment my own supplies. There is a stunning array of flora and fauna in the valley and I've only seen a small fraction of it.

Everything was smooth flying until just before dusk when I

happened across a woman collecting mushrooms. She was a delicate-featured, dark-haired creature who moved with the grace of a hawk dancing in the winds. As soon as she saw me, she darted behind a tree.

I didn't question her jumpiness. I've often felt the urge to secret myself away in remote regions and ply my craft as a hermit. There are only so many side-long glances, whispers, and sneers a witch can endure before she breaks out the evil cackle and lays waste to the supposed "civilized" world.

I went about my business, smiling whenever I caught sight of her. She soon warmed and we exchanged names and pleasantries. Mei knew of Babs and was happy that the hard-working witch was finally taking a vacation.

My new friend possessed a vast knowledge of local flora and fauna. We spent an enjoyable time wandering and discussing various properties of the plants we found. She brought me to a glade carpeted with knee-high shrubs bursting with buds. As the moon rose and its light caressed the tight blue petals, star-shaped flowers unfurled and released a sweet-smelling intoxicant. The scent was apparently irresistible to fairies so we only stayed long enough to admire the beauty and fill a small vial with stamens. Fairies are dangerous pricks.

Our conversation was so engaging that I lost all track of time, and it wasn't until my stomach rumbled that the late hour became apparent. As an apology for diverting her attention from mushroom picking, I invited her back to the hut for supper.

Pasha nervously shifted from foot to foot and refused to sit as we approached the clearing. Fortunately, the hut was worn out enough from our early morn game of hide-and-seek that it didn't try to run, but we still had to climb a rope ladder to get to the porch.

I explained to Mei that Pasha was afraid of water and probably apprehensive of the dark clouds blowing in. A towering ring of trees surrounded the hut's clearing of choice this eventide. Their branches were thick with leaves and arched overhead, providing ample shelter.

I set about preparing a stew with the root vegetables we harvested on our walk. A rich, oaky Earth mead made a lovely base for the broth, and we polished off what was left of the bottle while waiting for the cauldron to bubble.

Mei was enchanted by the drink and broke out an endless repertoire of dirty jokes after a few tankards. Her laugh rang out like a thousand tinkling bells. It sounded suspiciously Fae, but I dismissed the worry as she had made her dislike of the fiends obvious in our hasty exodus from the moonflower glade.

After we ate supper and settled by the fire, I had a sudden thought and climbed up to the bedroom to dig out a root I found on the previous sun's excursion. I was reasonably certain it was a soul's lament bulb, but wanted to make sure and figured my companion would know. I was just coming down the ladder when I saw Mei reaching into a high cupboard in the kitchen.

At first, I thought she was looking for another bottle of mead, but she pulled out an iridescent bridle and stared at it with such intensity that it could not have been an accidental find. The bridle was easily large enough to fit a huge draft horse and the ends dragged on the floor as she held it up. What it was made of, I don't know. It seemed a perfect union of starlight and water. Watching the soft rainbow luminosity flow through it was mesmerizing. Mei clutched it to her chest as if it were a long-lost love.

I jumped down the last few rungs of ladder and startled her. There was a flash of guilt in her eyes before she schooled her expression into innocent shock. We stood facing each other until I broke the silence, asking her to hand the bridle over.

She clapped a hand over her mouth to stifle the nervous giggle which burst out. Her gaze darted around the hut and she suddenly shape-shifted into a large foxlike creature with pure white fur and three bushy tails. Before I could act, she leapt out of an open window with the bridle in her mouth. I would have followed, but the hut was standing and it was too far a fall for me. I grabbed my broom and dove out the door in time to see her scamper into the trees.

I flew over the treetops, straining to catch sight of the faint glow of the bridle and flashes of white fur amongst the foliage. Behind me, Pasha stomped through the forest in hot pursuit. For the hut to take an interest, I surmised the bridle must be an item of some import. The situation was doubly grim as Babs was due back next eventide.

Flying proved problematic. I had imbibed a bit too liberally and was so focused on watching the forest floor that I occasionally forgot to avoid trees. I lost track of Mei after one spectacular entanglement with a fir tree and had to search the area on foot to pick up her trail. With the help of some cooperative rabbits (after I explained who my quarry was), I eventually found a large, stone-framed hole tucked into the side of a hill. It looked to be a perfect fit for my erstwhile guest. As I drew near, my adversary leapt out and tried to run. Luckily, Pasha was there.

The hut sidestepped and stomped one of its great chicken feet down on her tails. The bridle was in her mouth and I snatched it away as she yipped in surprise. Its iridescent straps were cool to the touch and, although solid, moved against my skin like a stream of water.

Mei wisely stilled. Her lips curled as she glared at Pasha's foot. I advised her to hold her temper because there was another foot where that one came from.

She changed back to human form, conveniently freeing herself, and pleaded with me to let her keep the bridle. She only needed it for a short time and promised to return it at sunrise.

Yeah, right. I had already been taken in by her once. She obviously planned the whole caper, otherwise how would she have known to look for the bridle in the hut?

I quickly searched her den to confirm that she hadn't stolen anything else from Babs. It was nicely appointed, with a blanket- and pillow-strewn sleeping nest, shelves carved from the rock, and thick rugs lining the floor. There was a neat pile of hand sewn toys to one side of the sleeping area.

When I returned, I found her trying to free her hair from under Pasha's foot. There must have been another attempted escape while I was inside. She stopped struggling and burst into tears as I approached.

I steeled myself. She had stolen something I was responsible for and caused me considerable trouble and minor injuries. I was in no mood.

And then she started talking. I tried to block out Mei's words, but couldn't. There was an earnestness that refused to be ignored. Once I heard her true story, I allowed myself to feel a connection again, just a faint strand of the web that joins each and every one of us.

Her kit had been stolen by a fearsome kelpie that lived in the lake at the centre of the valley. It tricked her child onto its back before she could warn him. She raced to the water, but the waves had already swallowed them, and she nearly drowned trying to follow.

The bridle was her only hope. With it, she could call the kelpie and order it to return her kit . . . if it hadn't already eaten him. Her eyes flooded with terror—a soul-consuming dread felt by all caregivers of the young, I'm sure.

I didn't trust her, but I couldn't turn my back on her or the youngling. I agreed to see her plan through with the express understanding that I would remain in sole possession of the bridle at all times. I made her pluck a tuft of fur from her tails before we left. With that, I could easily cast a location spell to find her again if she tried anything nefarious.

We flew to the rocky lakeshore on my broom and Pasha followed from the ground.

It soon became clear that Mei didn't know *how* to call the kelpie, only that it was possible. She screamed at the lake, venting her anger and pain. She started in human form, but her tails came out as frustration rose and when her desperate gaze met mine, her teeth had sharpened to points.

For lack of a better idea, I waded in and dipped the bridle in the water. After swishing it about for a while, the moon-kissed waves in the centre of the lake began to swirl and quicken, until the ribbons of light disappeared into a deepening whirlpool.

I jumped back as a dappled, storm-grey mare charged to shore on waves born of no wind. The beast stood before us, hide twitching, eyes like coloured galaxies eddying in the blackness of space. It was at once beautiful and powerful and utterly terrifying.

I held my ground. I wasn't certain I knew any spells powerful enough to fend off a creature such as this, but I felt in my bones that running was not a survivable option.

Holding the kelpie's gaze, I summoned my best don't-mess-with-the-witch-voice and ordered it to bring the kit it had stolen to shore, unharmed.

It tossed its head and let out a grating cry somewhere between a whinny and growl, never once breaking eye contact with me. The silvered mane frothed about its neck. Excitement shivered along its hide.

I sighed, looking between the bridle and the beast, knowing

what had to be done and yet fighting the knowledge. What else did one do with a bridle?

I swear the kelpie smiled as I slipped the harness around its snout. All I could see was teeth, serrated and murderous. The beast lowered its head, allowing me to hook the top strap over its ears, and then casually snapped at my leg. Luckily, my spell component pouch was in the way. From how quickly it spat it out, I'm guessing liquefied lizard toes and hwriupt dung balls were not to its liking. *(NOTE: Get new spell component pouch.)*

I tossed the reins over its head and caught them against its neck. The kelpie's hide was slick and cool, covered with something more like jellyfish tendrils than fur. One eye rolled around to watch me as I stood beside it, one foot on the beach, one in the water.

Riding a kelpie down to its underwater lair was about the last thing I ever wanted to do, but Babs had entrusted Pasha and all its contents to me. It was my choice to help Mei, so this was my responsibility.

The kelpie shifted restlessly, nodding its head to test my hold on the reins until I gave them a stern jerk to prevent the beast from dragging me all the way into the water. I called an air elemental and wrapped the sprite around my head, hoping its air would last longer than the kelpie's desire to drown me.

Holding the reins with one hand, I grasped the kelpie's mane with my other, intending to pull myself onto its back. The kelpie interpreted the slight loosening of the reins as its cue to go.

It turned and dove into the lake. I barely kept my grip as water surged around me, dragging at my robes. And then, we were underwater and I was stretched out, flying above the kelpie's back. Down and down we went to depths as black and cold as a winter's night. I could see nothing, not even my cantankerous mount. A great weight pressed on me from all sides. I held my breath as much as I could, only breathing when my lungs felt like splitting, and then only in short gulps so I would not exhaust my air elemental too soon.

Just when my fingers grew so numb I doubted my ability to hold on, we surfaced in a cavern. Thick, knobby columns of white stone hung from the ceiling. Some barely touched the water's surface and others descended to the bottom. Luminescent blue dots glowed on the ceiling in an impossible starscape. From each point of light, thin lines of suspended droplets extended down and waved in the slight breeze of our arrival. They looked like strung beads, beautiful and innocuous, which is how I knew to stay well away from them. The cave would have been lovely if not for a heavy stench of decay.

The water was mostly shallow, barely rising past the kelpie's first leg joint as it strode forward. I elected to stay astride, unsure of my ability to pull myself back up.

My resentful steed slipped on something that shattered under its weight. I took a closer look and saw that the floor was littered with remains, both animal and human. Here and there, mounds of bones and skulls rose above the water creating little islands. I suddenly gained a greater appreciation for my broom riding lessons and the hard-won balance they had developed.

Muffled whimpers came from one corner. There, a young boy no more than five season cycles old sat huddled on a thin stone shelf. His legs were pulled tight to his chest so that no part of him touched the water. A group of the blue lights had gathered over him, their dangling filaments stretching down almost to his head. He seemed oblivious to the grasping peril.

The boy's cries became panicked as we approached. I don't think he noticed me until I warned him not to stand on the shelf and asked him to come closer so I could lift him up. He remained motionless, lost in shock and fear. No amount of assurances or gentle persuasion enticed him to move. Finally, I presented the tuft of fur from his mother's tail as proof that she had sent me to rescue him. His button nose twitched and he unclamped his arms from around his legs.

The kelpie edged forward. Drool trailed from its mouth and mingled with the fetid water below. I pulled the reins to direct my mount's rear at the boy, thinking it safer than the toothy end. The kelpie danced in place and jerked its head, trying to shake my hold. It bucked and there was a reverberating thud as a hoof chipped a chunk of stone off the shelf.

The near miss spurred the boy into action. He jumped into the water and grabbed the fur from me. While he was distracted, holding it to his nose, I seized his arm and hefted him onto my lap.

The kelpie skittered sideways in a bid to unbalance us, but I clamped my legs around its body. Its next trick was to try unseating me by rubbing against the wall. I stubbornly held on and jerked the reins toward the pool we had entered through.

The kelpie snarled and ground its teeth, then surged into a gallop and plunged headlong into the deep. I managed to pull the boy up high enough to include him in my air elemental's bubble just as he gasped from the onslaught of cold. He inhaled a partial mouthful of water but coughed it up. I clung to the reins and mane with only one hand now, asking the Goddess to help guide our way to the surface. Quickly.

It was not quick. We moved in darkness for so long I began to wish we were back in the deadly cavern. The air in our bubble thinned until I wasn't sure whether the blackness was the water or looming unconsciousness.

A thin ribbon of white rippled in the darkness ahead. It grew into a sheet and finally we broke the surface into blessed air and moonlight. I released the air elemental and it drifted away as we lay on the kelpie's back, frozen and waterlogged, but thankfully alive.

Mei let out an excited bark when she saw us and her kit returned the call.

My wily mount stopped just shy of the water's edge and whipped its head around as Mei came alongside. Its open maw snapped at her, missed thanks to her agility, and tried a second time.

I gave the temperamental beast a sharp swat on the nose with the ends of the reins while its head was turned. It reared and the boy slid off into his mother's arms. Mei leapt from the water and sprinted for the treeline. I think she called out a thank-you before they went full fox and disappeared into the forest, but I'm not sure.

I would have been less miffed if she hadn't left me to deal with the nightmare kelpie alone. It wasn't looking any friendlier as it snorted and pawed at the rocky bottom, glaring with eyes now blazing red. Nobody likes losing a meal, but kelpies apparently take it harder than most. And I still had to get the damn bridle off.

Leaning forward, I hooked a finger around the top strap just behind its ears. The kelpie must have felt my weight shift because it dipped its head, tipping me off balance. I landed awkwardly in the water, too close to its teeth, and scrambled back to the beach with the bridle in my hand. Thankfully, there was no bit, so there was nothing for the kelpie to bite onto. I'm sure I would not have won that tug-of-war.

Then it started raining. Not a nice, gentle mist. Nooo. This was a full-on downpour obscuring everything more than a few arm's length away. I couldn't even see the kelpie's ass-end.

It was also about this time that the last dregs of mead in my system deserted me and the full terrifying weight of what was standing before me crashed down like a brick house in a tornado.

The kelpie's eyes narrowed as rain drenched the once dry beach, extending its domain. It stepped forward, nostrils flaring. I shooed it back. It glared and pawed, and took another step. I tried again, holding the bridle up as I commanded it to return to its lair. It paused, watching, but did not retreat.

I needed more. I conjured the image of our Goddess Hekate's wolf form in my mind. My component pouch was long gone, so I pulled a few of my own hairs out, scooped up a water elemental that was playing in a puddle, and whispered the spell into my palm, draping the wolf illusion over me like a robe. When I was done setting the glamour, I pulled power from the storm to make it visible and used what was left to amplify my voice.

"Do not test me. Return to your lair and pester us no more or this lake will run red with your blood. Be gone!" My words boomed over the driving rain.

The beast reared and bared its teeth. For a moment, I believed it was about to stomp the life out of me and suck my bones dry. To my everlasting relief, the kelpie instead charged back into the lake. Its tail cracked like thunder as it hit the surface and disappeared.

I waited until the water calmed (as much as I could see) before dropping the glamour and backing toward Pasha, who was nervously hopping between the edge of the forest and the beach. I dared not turn my back on the lake. The hut stilled long enough for me to back in. It says a lot about Pasha's loyalty that it endured the dreaded rain to stay close. Beautiful Pasha, I owe you a riotous game of hide-and-seek!

Once I was inside, the hut took off and I bounced around until I could grab a chair leg and strap myself in (I'd found the handy buckled straps under the seat cushions that morn). At this point my body was completely numb—a small boon.

There was a lot of cleaning up to do after. Our supper bowls and spoons had been out, not to mention the half-full cauldron of stew. It's a good thing Babs's bowls and tankards are all carved hardwood. It's also fortuitous that Pasha possesses some kind of protection against fire. Logs from the fireplace were rolling about, but nothing was even singed except the bottom of my robe.

Before heading to bed, I carefully placed the bridle back in its cupboard. I hope. It was one of the open ones in the bank of cupboards Mei was searching. In any case, it's probably close enough that Babs will think she misremembered where she last put it. I'm not going to mention this little snafu to her. Some things are better left unsaid. This is surely one of them.

Pandias, Blood Moon 27, 205

BEFORE DAWN THIS morn, I climbed onto Pasha's roof to a comfortable spot where I could straddle the ridge (for stability in case the hut decided to move) and lean my back against the warmed chimney. Little storms of glow-wyrms flitted about, cavorting in the dying darkness among the trees. They flowed like rivers through the valley following the meandering lines of magickal energy that lace the area. It was beautiful and so very peaceful. A welcome and stark contrast to the terror of last sun.

I didn't dare stray far from Pasha, so I spent my remaining time reading some herbal companions I found in a cupboard, interspersed with less energetic games of hide-and-seek than the hut was accustomed to. And I never once set out without my trusty broom either! The cold fish I received in the face a few suns ago was indeed an effective reminder. The scent lingers. Score one for hexing yourself, I guess.

Whenever we weren't playing together, Pasha kept jumping up, spinning around, and then sitting back down, blowing an impatient huff of smoke from its chimney. I think it sensed that Babs was coming home. It's quite a sweet companion. Babs is a lucky witch.

During one of our short forays, I discovered a section of forest where the ground heaves as though the earth itself is breathing. I lay down, matching my breaths to its rhythm, among trees so ancient that hundreds of season cycles would pass them by as easily as a gust of wind through their leaves. I have never felt so grounded. Despite the Kelpie misadventure, I will be sad to leave.

Babs arrived in the early eventide. The old witch had a wonderful vacation and was so full of stories that she invited me to stay for supper. We spent a good portion of the night chatting. Doris the sea hag, who Babs has rekindled a relationship with, rescued a baby kraken from some ill-fated sailors, and they had a wild time keeping the little scamp out of trouble. It didn't sound as though they tried overly hard. In at least one instance, her girlfriend set the kraken loose to scare a group of picnickers away from her favourite cove. It may or may not have eaten one of them. Babs was vague on that point, though she did come back with a new bag of bones.

She was pleased that Pasha and I had gotten along so well and gifted me two bottles of mead as thanks (along with the hut-sitting fee). She also tried her best to convince me to cave-sit for Doris, who is planning to visit the valley this winter, but I had to decline her generous offer. It will be a good long time before I feel up to another hut-sitting job.

It was the wee hours before I secured my broom bags and set out for Aestradorra, back to the college grind. What a grand adventure this has been! I can't wait to tell my friends. They're never going to believe I rode a kelpie.

ADDENDUM: It just occurred to me that the kelpie may have been Babs's familiar. I didn't see her with any other potential familiars, and the fact that it lives in her valley and she had the bridle are telling. Here's hoping it doesn't carry a grudge about the loss of a meal!

Siren's Song

Colleen Anderson

We are
    salty summer slumbers and sand in your shorts
        illicit lusts upon the beach, and

We are
    scampi, tuna steaks and calamari
        fugu, fish fingers and shark fin soup, and

We are
    mysteries netted and dreams devoured
        human half a delicacy, cries a piquant extra, and

We were

Sarah McKenzie

L. T. Waterson

THE SUNLIGHT SPARKLING on the tops of the waves was the first thing to catch her eye when she stepped out of the hotel lobby. The smell of salt carried on the breeze tickled her nose and she breathed deeply. She had missed the smell of the ocean almost as much as she missed the feel of the water enclosing her body. The name she had inscribed in the hotel register was Sarah McKenzie, a name given to her by the man who had called himself her husband, and one she didn't intend to use any more.

He had been entranced from the first, the gleam in his eyes when he'd seen her had told her there was unlikely to be an escape this time, and that had been ten years ago. Then just a month ago he promised her an anniversary to remember, a trip back to The Grand Atlantic Hotel, and the chance of escape.

She had done her best to hide her elation, merely glancing up from her novel and then back again when he announced the news. Outwardly, she presented a calm demeanour, but in her deepest heart she had been overjoyed. It was hard not to dance as she carried out the domestic chores that her husband thought she should perform. Soon she would be free.

Clive McKenzie was dying, something she was aware of a long time before he was. He was a man with a heart condition, and despite everything, she had almost grown to love him but for love to truly flourish it has to have space and freedom, and she had had none of those.

She had left him in room 202, stretched out on the bed, dead at fifty-two from a heart attack. No blame would attach to her but nevertheless she had to get away.

The breeze turned into a wind that whipped around her, blowing her thin skirt up around her legs. Stepping carefully on the path, her feet clad in lightweight shoes, easily discarded, she walked towards a set of steps leading down to the hotel's rose garden, cold and barren now in the winter months. Beyond that was a cliff and beyond that the ocean. The sound of the waves crashing on the shore made her heart beat faster, *so close, so close*, the words echoed in her head.

She picked her way down the steps quickly. A desperate need to see the waves filled her, to touch the water once more, to feel it close around her and over her, better than any lover's embrace would ever be.

Even hurrying she moved like a dancer, lithe and sinuous, although the heavy dark coat that she carried threw her balance off.

"Mrs. McKenzie!" The voice rang out behind her, the wind bringing it forcefully to her, and she knew it could only be one of the hotel staff, perhaps they had already found the body. She turned her head back towards the voice but in so doing missed her footing on the bottom step and fell.

Sharp pain shot up her leg and brought tears to her eyes. *She had been so close.* A minute ticked past although she barely noticed. Doing her best to staunch the falling tears she struggled to rise but unable to put weight on her injured leg she could do no more than flail hopelessly on the ground.

"Are you all right?" A young man with wide innocent brown eyes and a shaggy mop of blond hair, peered down at her from the top of the steps, *was he the owner of the voice she had heard?*

"I'm fine." She squinted briefly up at him and wiped at her face to hide the tears before turning her attention back to her own situation. In the fall she had let go of the dark coat and it was there, only a little way from her. If she stretched she might be able to reach it.

"Let me help you." The young man, with one hand on the

guard rail, leapt down the few steps that for her had proved so treacherous. "Those steps can be a bit slippery this time of year. Are you hurt?"

He was attractive of course and there were perhaps worse fates.

"I'm fine," she repeated her earlier words in a monotone and watched, expressionless, as with his other hand the man scooped up her coat from the ground. Now that freedom had been snatched away she allowed herself to be pulled to her feet.

He smiled at her, a smile she had seen before. "Let me help you back to the hotel." He wound an arm around her waist and supported her as she limped back up the steps that should have provided her with a route to freedom. "I'm Mark by the way."

"Sarah," she said in a low voice, "I'm Sarah McKenzie."

At the top of the steps she halted, looking back longingly towards the waves, before allowing herself to be led back into the hotel.

Midnight Man versus Carrie Cthulhu

Chadwick Ginther

I STEPPED OFF the Ghost Docks and onto the sodden riverbank, a knight on a lonely moor, an Argonaut at sea, a superhero fighting an unknown villain.

The Midnight Man.

Protector of Mort Cheval from the denizens of dread—only I wasn't in my home city. I wasn't *anywhere*. The mist parted without the sky lightening. If anything it grew darker. Closer. Smothering. No sun or moon above, but I could still see under the red-stained sky. Wind roared and I felt nothing. A bell toned, low and resonant over the water like a heartbeat; two short rings followed by a long sustain. Hearing that bell was a bad omen; one meaning I'd been summoned to die.

Like all the others.

I didn't know where I was, but I knew what I'd see when the mist cleared. A boat. *The River Queen.*

Her boat.

She didn't have a name. None I could find. I assumed all who received her dreams gave her their own name, and those names died with them.

I called her Carrie Cthulhu.

There were things even necromancers feared. Things Beyond them. Things as inexorable as gravity. As the tide. Things that hunted them as they hunted humanity. I've fought necromancers, vampires, ghouls, and ghosts, and I've put them all back in the ground, but I hadn't been able to fight the Ghost Docks' pull.

I hadn't thought of my grad night in years. It was one surreal thing lost in a sea of them. Everyone said Ron had been drunk. Fell in the river and drowned. He wasn't alone anymore.

The rumours said Carrie Cthulhu's dreams found us before we died. *She* found us before we died. And now, her dreams had found me: a sea carved the continent in two again, as it had been in an earlier time of monsters. She was a glacier scraping the world clean. Within, her bones glinted like moonlight on water, and wreathed in shifting shadows despite their prison. A goddess at the heart of a new sea, or an old sea reborn. The rest of my grad class hadn't come back from their voyages to her domain. I would.

Superheroes always come back.

I'd stick out in my outfit were anyone alive here to notice. Black leather jacket with luminescent double Ms on the shoulders, red-tinted Grave Sight goggles to see what was hidden from the living, ball-and-chain bombs to lock spirits into their flesh, and twin Colt Model 1911s loaded with tombstone bullets to put them in the ground. I had other gear in my car, but the Docks' pull prevented me from loading up. People would say it was a mad thing to put on a costume and fight evil but to me it wasn't a costume, it was a uniform. The Fight was real, even if most folk found more comfort ignoring the truth than confronting it.

The last mist burned away, exposing *The River Queen*, simultaneously new as the day it was christened and entirely consumed by rust and decay; a time-twisted double image. The boat had settled, canted slightly towards the riverbank, going nowhere, and ferrying only the soon-to-be-dead.

The River Queen hadn't always been Carrie Cthulhu's territory. Once the paddlewheel craft had chauffeured innumerable grad classes and socials into drunken oblivion. For over fifty years, it, and boats like it, had carried millions of passengers along the Red River—even Pierre Trudeau and Colonel Sanders had been in on the action. Business slowly died after the flooding in the '90s and then abruptly after Carrie Cthulhu found us. The boat had been grounded for over ten years in the Real, sitting like a curse. A warning.

A trap.

I wondered if the flooding was what had woken Carrie Cthulhu—a memory of what was, what could be, not a river prison, but an inland sea. Whatever had first rung her bell, she was awake, and *The River Queen* was the eye in her storm.

There wouldn't be a ten year reunion for the four graduates from my class who remained alive. Four. From a class of one hundred. They'd all walked the same walk I'd just finished, I was certain of it.

Almost a hundred dead.

I'd taken over the family business—undertaking, not monster hunting—and buried my share of them. I hadn't been close with any, and as a mortician's son, I knew better than most: people die. Even the young. Especially the young, sometimes. Those whose bodies were found were interred. The bodies were always found in water, and the deep doesn't release its secrets easily. Far more simply . . . disappeared. Drownings. Suicides. A couple "clear" murders and animal attacks. Before long, the numbers became too many to ignore. When people spoke of us at all, they brought up the "grad curse." Whispered at why, but did nothing. They knew nothing of the Fight.

Water slapped the abandoned boat's hull. Mosquitoes buzzed and crickets sang. Their noises blurred together, making my skin crawl. The bell rang, louder this time, its twinned sound came from within the boat.

Footsteps jerked me from my reverie. I whirled, guns drawn. I recognized them; two women and a man, each walked their own Ghost Dock. Jenn, Sean, and Teri. Mort Cheval's only other grad curse survivors. I lowered my weapons, even if I only holstered one pistol. I'd expected to face her alone. Best I could figure, the other witnesses had all died alone. Carrie Cthulhu must've been getting impatient.

My old classmates stepped tentatively onto the river bank; regarded each other, then me. The Ghost Docks receded into the mists behind them. No way home. No way out. While I recognized them all, they didn't know me at a glance. None were dressed the way you'd expect for Southern Manitoba, but then neither was I.

Jenn, who'd had an East Coast lilt in her voice when we'd sat next to each other in English; a Maritimer who'd been landlocked for too long, it only snuck out when she talked of "home," or when she got excited or drunk, was dressed for an anime convention. Sean looked like an expensive suit stuffed with bullshit and weasels. His suit's fabric stretched as if trying to contain a professional wrestler, not the skinny, mouthy prick I remembered from the volleyball team. Teri was slender; a brunette with eyes that had seen too much. Her suit flattered her more than Sean's did him. Slim-fitting and solid black. Her hair was long now, she'd sported a buzz cut in school. Didn't know her well. Didn't know any of them well, now or then, only that none had stayed in Mort Cheval.

Sean recognized me first, despite my uniform. "Tom? Old Tommy Tombstone? I thought you killed your parents. Shouldn't you be in prison?"

"I didn't kill them." I growled out the words. Ten years on, and Sean still irritated me. *They were already dead when I shot them.*

"You were never this . . . theatrical, back in school," Jenn said, inferring my identity from Sean's insult. "You were so quiet then."

"Yeah," Sean added. "Quiet like a serial killer."

I'd been quieter then—anything to avoid notice. That'd only drawn *more* notice back in the day, and so I'd leaned into the macabre the way only a mortician's son could. You could say it'd become a habit.

Sean snorted. "Looks like you still read comic books."

"*I* read comic books," Teri said, a "fuck you," clearly implied.

"The thing that summoned us is there." I gestured at the boat, ignoring the sniping. I didn't have much hope of getting myself back to the Real, let alone all of us. But I had to try. "The way out must be there too."

"What, exactly, brought us here?" Jenn asked.

"You know." The river gurgled slowly by. "You all saw her too. I call her Carrie Cthulhu."

Sean jabbed me in shoulder. "Never heard of her."

I shoved his hand away. "Probably because she's killed everyone who'd ever seen her. *Sean.*"

"You're still nuts."

"I've been trying to forget her for the last ten years," Teri said, her words barely a whisper.

"We were drunk." Jenn looked out over the river. "None of us know what we really saw."

"Believing that won't help." Nobody responded. "Call shit a shovel, it still won't help you dig. *I* know what we saw. Do you have any idea how unlikely it is that our *entire graduating class* would be dead within ten years?"

"Wait, everybody?" Teri asked.

"Except us."

Teri considered the weight of the revelation. "How?"

"Monsters are real."

Sean snorted. "Monsters are real? *That's* why you're dressed like an idiot?"

I imagined the others had moved away from Mort Cheval, and any reminders, even if only subconsciously. Carrie Cthulhu lived on in their dreams and nightmares, lurked in their depths, waiting to emerge. I hadn't forgotten, but I had no room in my nightmares for her. Until recently. Now I had to end her. Or I was dead. And I wouldn't be alone. The bell tolled, louder again. I winced. The others did too.

When the bell's tone was down to a low sustain, Jenn let out a long sigh. "You think our answers—our 'truth'—are on the boat."

"And our way out?" Teri asked.

"Wait here if you want." I tried to smile reassuringly. "Not knowing hasn't saved anyone yet."

Teri shuddered. "I don't wanna know."

"Then good luck."

I clambered up the riverbank and jumped onto the boat's upper deck. They'd follow me or they wouldn't. Must and rot mixed with the river's wet scent, stronger here than on the banks. The deck creaked under every step. No matter which way I faced, it felt as if I were trying to keep myself from tumbling into the water. Graffiti, fire remnants, drug and booze paraphernalia, remnants of many nights' country drinking back in the Real were more obvious in their reflection here. All on the open deck though, as if whoever'd come here knew better than to venture deeper.

I held my hand out. Jenn took it first, Teri followed. Sean refused, and almost bounced off the rail and into the river. He glowered, red-faced, daring us to say anything.

"Where do we go now?"

I gestured at the stairs. "To where it began."

THE FISH FLIES coating the boat deck were thick enough you'd need a shovel to clear them. They reeked. Dead eyes stared over mouthless faces.

Something skittered away from my glowing double Ms; the others turned the flashlight apps on their otherwise useless phones to scan the deck. Whatever it'd been had left no trail through the swamp of fish fly carcasses.

"What was that?"

Sean snorted. "Your imagination?"

I didn't look back at him. "That would be worse."

The only way downstairs was through the bugs. The bell rang, louder again than it'd sounded from shore. Loud enough the boat shuddered, and we all clutched the railing. I lightly brushed the dead bugs aside with my boots, making a path for the others.

"*Ewwww.* I *hate* fish flies!" Teri covered her mouth. "They're so gross."

"They can't hurt you." Sean rolled his eyes, and stomped after me with no care for the path; his boots crunched over carcasses, squishing stinking, slippery guts out from between the treads. "They don't bite."

The background noise of river insects intensified. Fish flies flipped and flopped, wings sputtering. White carapaces split, and living bugs oozed out. The bugs shook their wings and took to the air. They swarmed Teri. She swatted them, but the cloud shifted from her strikes and clung to her flailing limbs.

"Holy shit!" Sean screamed.

"Do something!" Teri shrieked. "Somebody do something!"

Jenn backed away, striking the railing so violently she almost pitched over.

Teri, enveloped, slapped her arms but wherever she crushed the bugs, she attracted more. Her screams became a gurgle.

My guns were useless. They'd only kill Teri.

Ball-and-chain bombs bonded spirits to flesh. Might work. Lock whatever animated them into something we could kill.

I hurled the bomb—a hollowed eggshell—and the silvery powder inside coated Teri and the flies, but it didn't lock the fish flies into their bodies, it bonded Teri's spirit into their flesh.

I saw her bleed away in a thousand-thousand little streams. The insects stared at us with mouthless human faces—Teri's face—eyes weeping. They flew away and fell onto the water in the outline of a woman's body. Spines crested the water and an unseen beast feasted until only a few scattered flies remained, drifting on the current.

I wanted to be sick. I'd as good as killed her.

"Nice job, numbnuts," Sean muttered. "Glad we have a *hero* to keep us safe."

"Can't hurt you," Jenn swatted Sean. "Jesus Christ."

"I should throw you in after her." His asinine bulldozing through the trap had put Teri in danger. I'd have to live with my share of the blame but he didn't seem to care. Sean shrank from my glower. His puffy suit deflated as he looked away. I pressed a Colt to him. "You're lucky I can only give you a quieter end. One you don't deserve."

A bloody outline of Teri's body stained the deck, invisible amid the rust other than its slick sheen. Beyond that, our way was clear.

WE FOLLOWED THE bell downstairs to the lower deck, where our graduation party had been ten years ago. Its double ring sounded twice; the boat's respondent shudder pitched us against the wall. The door to the ballroom clung, creaking, by one hinge.

Ten years since I'd been onboard.

The stars were bright that night, and far from the city, seemed all the brighter. The arm of the Milky Way stretched across the sky, a starry river mirroring the muddy Red we sailed. And then the stars were *gone*.

The boat lurched to a stop, we all tumbled to the floor. Tables dumped their wine glasses, people fell over. Barefoot dancers shredded hands and feet on a beer-and-sweat-slicked dance floor. The creaking ship sounded loud as a tornado as the engine struggled to get us clear and moving again. I don't remember the words that came over the intercom, but "Nautical Disaster" had been playing; Gord Downie's warble transitioning the song from slow to fast when the impact occurred.

Out of that blackness, from the void where there'd been sky, oozed a snake. It was as if the creature had swallowed the stars like mice, and all she left behind was red. The serpent's body split, forming legs. Split again, and arms stretched. Again and again, its singular head became many. I watched it happen, fascinated and unnerved in equal measure. In a blink, the monster was gone and the stars returned. The DJ started The Hip again, but the song couldn't hide the cries of, "Man overboard!"

Our classmate, Ron. The first of us to die.

It was as if nothing had disturbed the room in the last ten years except the elements. The floors were slick with muck, though broken glass still littered the floor. Graduation decorations, faded, rotted, but still hanging—if only by a whisper—hinted at our New Orleans-themed party.

The bell tolled, *bong-bong*, three times now, and my ears popped with pressure, as if we were deep beneath an unknown ocean's waves. This simple boat had become an assault on reality. A palpable wrongness saturated its walls. You could rub it between your fingers. A visible stink—almost blinding in my Grave Sight goggles. The hairs on my neck stood up, and my mouth went dry. My cheek twitched uncontrollably. Jenn stooped to grab a broken chair leg. I didn't blame her wanting a weapon in hand.

I hadn't brought enough for the whole class.

The floor hissed like air escaping a tire. Jenn shone her phone flashlight toward the noise, illuminating a Gordian knot of snakes, undulating, scales creaking over one another, their hisses loud as a thunderclap. Manitoba wasn't home to any poisonous snakes, but I also wasn't about to test that *here*. There was something wrong with their heads. They didn't look right. They had almost human faces. No . . . They had *exactly* human faces.

Sean's face.

Sean inched closer, entranced. When we were kids, he'd kept a couple pet snakes. Loved them. He should've had better sense than this.

Smiling dreamily, he knelt to get a better look. "They're beautiful."

He *would* admire his own stupid face. I grabbed his collar. "Do *not* touch that fucking snake. You saw what happened to Teri."

What he'd *caused* to happen to Teri.

"Yeah, yeah," he said, standing and taking a step back. "I saw her first. Your . . . Carrie Cthulhu. I call—called—her something else. *God.*"

I spun him around to face me. "What do you mean?"

"I saw her. And I gave her what she wanted." Sean clutched at his jacket. He rippled under the fabric. "A sacrifice."

"*You* pushed Ron?"

"He was my friend. But she was *so* hungry."

He popped his jacket buttons. In my Grave Sight, his ribcage was hollow. No human meat, instead it was full to spilling with snakes. He hissed and lunged.

Guns out, fun's out.

I fired, unthinking. The reports echoed in call and response to the ringing bell, thunderous inside the ballroom. Accuracy didn't matter here. I couldn't hear, or think, over our mingled screams. Pain. Fear. Anger. I wasn't sure which was more foolish, bringing guns to a snake fight or snakes to a gun fight. Tombstone bullets kill dead things dead, but the way Sean's snakes ate shells, "dead" was as good as "alive." Carrie Cthulhu had more snakes than I had bullets. I squeezed off a couple more shots anyway.

Jenn scrambled behind me, stomping and swiping as she fled. A snake wrapped around Sean's neck and dragged his body into the mass. The snake held me in its gaze. It was impossibly long— as if it stretched into infinity. Safe distance was no longer safe. I fired until my clips emptied. Reloaded. Fired until all the snakes inside Sean were still. His last gasp lingered for a moment, as if he'd expected the serpents to save him, and he fell.

The remaining snakes cored their way through Sean's body, shredding the rest of his meat, until only a scramble of flesh and scales and bone remained. Floating amongst the shit and refuse like a flat pink turd, was a human face. I stared impassively. I've seen fucked up shit in my time. This wasn't the worst. Bad, yes, but not the worst. And Sean—whatever he'd been turned into— had this, and more coming.

Jenn burped out a garbled, "I think I'm gonna be sick."

"Hello, Midnight Man. Hello, Midnight Man," the snakes said, as if singing in the round, until I couldn't make out my own name. Their tide receded, melting away, leaving me panting, Colts smoking.

The last snake said, face slick with blood as it slithered away, "See you inside, Midnight Man."

My name echoed in time with the latest ringing of the damned bell.

When the sound subsided, Jenn asked, "Why'd they call you Midnight Man?"

"You've never heard of Midnight Man?" She shook her head. I was both pleased and disappointed. "It's the name I use when I fight monsters . . . it's . . . me."

Jenn put her hand on my shoulder. "I know I'm going to die someday, Midnight Man, but I don't want to die *here*."

I was glad she'd used the name. Choosing it had given me hope when I'd first joined the Fight. I'd wanted it to mean hope for others when things crept out of the night.

The boat lurched. Metal squealed, and wood creaked. Jenn fell into me, knocking me to the floor.

"What the hell was that?"

We both paused as if separately trying to assess.

Unsteadily, I stood and helped her up. "We're moving."

"What?"

"Impossible. This shit-heap's been stuck for ten years, and *now* it breaks free?"

"We're definitely moving."

"Maybe we could use a lifeboat?" Jenn said. "Get off of here?"

"Maybe." I had no idea if they were still river-worthy, where we'd take it, or if we'd be a bigger target in a smaller boat. "We're headed for Winnipeg."

Out in the wild, in the dark, with fear churning our hearts like a storm surge, it was impossible to discern how quickly we drifted. I'd suffered through a lifetime of impossible already. More frightening than the impossible: the definite result once this tub of snakes got to a city.

Our class had merely been an appetizer.

BEHIND US, THE undulating wake in the river grew closer. It was unsettling, seeing the boat move while its paddle wheel remained dead. Something breached the surface, slithering in the shadows, visible, but unrecognizable. Water droplets splashed up, as if we watched a casino fountain show in miniature, filling the river, bank to bank. A low, resonant hum filled the air. I sucked a breath between clenched teeth.

"She's coming."

The river exploded behind us, a towering column of water, and when the water fell, *she* was there. Blocking the red sky, I saw her—the monster that had grounded us on grad night. Carrie Cthulhu. Seeing her, I knew I'd come back to this boat to die. And death was close.

She stepped out of the river, water raining from her foot; muck slopped with loud slaps onto the roof, ringing like thunder. Her foot landed on the boat. Jenn dragged me back, as I watched, transfixed. Rusted metal squealed as the roof deck crushed lower, pancaking the upper deck and crushing the DJ booth.

The boat sat deeper in the river, water slopped into the ballroom, but we kept moving toward the city.

A lifeboat tumbled free from its moorings, stayed tethered to *The River Queen* for a moment, and snapped free, drifting away from us, taking our last hope of escape with it.

In my Grave Sight she blazed—an atom bomb next to the matchstick of the sky—like some unnamed spawn of Jörmungandr. A Leviathan. Not a monster. A god.

Snakes rained from the ceiling, falling into the boat in a torrent, all eyeing us with a merciless reptilian gaze. They slithered together, forming a mockery of a human form, using Sean's meatless, bloody skeleton as the frame. Carrie Cthulhu's body in miniature loomed over us, back flat against the ballroom's ceiling.

With her many mouths, she said, "I. Am. The. One. Who. Sleeps. And. Would. Wake."

She moved like a hagfish, all cartilage, twisting in impossible ways. She smiled, and inside each mouth was another mouth, rasping maws designed to shear meat away from a corpse. Her tongue split, weeping blood. Another fanged maw gaped. The floor groaned with each undulating step the avatar took toward us, and I worried it would give way under her weight.

Water slopped in faster, but we still drifted.

I counted my breaths, trying to calm myself while I waited for her to kill us. Each intake of air loud as a turbine, each exhale a scream, my heart thundered. She was too great for this ruin—prison or home—too great for our world. No perceived limitations of our reality would stop her.

The bell tolled with her every step, shaking the boat. Shaking us to our cores.

Paint peeled, as if trying to escape the sound. Rust and rivets dropped like hail. The last of the decorations sank into the muck.

Tombstone bullets slapped into her with wet thuds—I didn't remember drawing—but only river muck leaked out from between the writhing snakes. She paid wounds no heed.

I fired my Colts until they clicked dry. Her vastness remained astride the river while she faced us in the ballroom.

She was there.

And here.

A pulse between the two flashed in my Grave Sight like a strobe timed to the bell.

I whispered the name I'd given her, and it immediately felt small. *I* felt small for even uttering it. Carrie Cthulhu's shifting gaze would not leave me. I was grateful for that, at least. Keep her occupied with me, not Jenn. She took a step toward me, and was in my face faster than a wave breaking. Her maw bobbed from shoulder to shoulder as she canted her neck opposite of whichever leg moved forward. She stopped before me. Thousands of forked serpent tongues tasted the air around me. Tasting *me*. Rancid breath billowed from the maw, a well of fish left to rot.

She wanted to drive me mad.

Madder.

I'd been a little bit mad since the necromancer murdered my parents. Stole their funeral home. Stole their lives. Stole their deaths. Mad enough to drive him away. To put my parents to rest. Mad enough to come here. To believe I could win.

Once, giving up would've been inconceivable. Never a care, never a wayward glance over my shoulder wondering if this the right thing to do. *Righteousness* had never been something I'd felt a dearth of. I *knew* I was right. I knew my heading was true. Stay the course, even if I didn't know where it would take me. Another lie. I drifted toward death. Always to death.

"You. Are. Already. Claimed. A. Pity." Each snake spoke one word. "Doom. Tastes. So. Sweet. Can. Taste. It. So. Heavy. Upon. You."

"That's just death." The retort made me feel smaller than

saying her name.

"No. Death. For. You. Not. For. A. Long. Time." The flickering snake tongues made a chuckling sound. "Leave. Her. I'll. Leave. You. To. Fate."

Trying to process her speech left me with a fire in my temples, and blood trickling from my nose and the lips I'd bitten to stop my screaming. She turned to Jenn, as if leaving the choice to me. Her maw widened and the gurgle of the river outside became surf crashing. A monstrous skeletal hand lashed from the gaping mouth like a frog's tongue, flashing in the moonlight. Jenn jumped in between. The hand dragged her into the black.

The maw gaped. Waiting. Human lives mattering was an esoteric concept. I didn't want any of them claimed by the Fight. Individually speaking, one shouldn't matter anymore than another. Maybe I could still get home. One escape might be enough. But Jenn had tried to save me.

I dove in.

DROWNING IS SUPPOSED to be a peaceful way to go. I'd never believed it. I'd seen enough death, *caused* enough death, to know there's always terror, always fear, no matter how you go. I'm just not used to feeling it anymore. Instead, I was sodden. Cold. Breathless. As if I'd gone swimming the day after the ice had left the lake.

Shapes whirled like riptides, coalescing in moments in the sea foam, then destroyed. I saw myself in the images, and the future where my fate was claimed. Vision or not, I knew it for truth. My parents' killer. The one necromancer I hadn't put back in the ground. Yet. And behind him, a cackling nightmare. The one responsible for him. For me. She waited for the future Carrie Cthulhu found so fucking amusing. A life burying the dead, not avenging them. Serving my enemies, not putting them in the ground. Mourners wept until their tears flooded me. Black. Salty. Crushing. Colder than the ocean's bottom.

I couldn't fight her. She was the sublime, I was a tank firing at Godzilla. An asteroid against the vastness of the universe. If I died here, Jenn would die. And unknown, countless others more beyond her. I couldn't kill Carrie Cthulhu, but survival might foil her design. I had to believe it would. Believing I could save someone else would allow me to save myself.

Somehow.

The tears were purer than the blackness of Carrie Cthulhu's ocean. I embraced them. My fate couldn't be worse than her victory. The blackness lightened. I saw the surface. I fought.

I WASHED UP on an empty beach littered with grey shale instead of sand, wanting to die and not wholly unconvinced I hadn't. My throat burned as if a bubble of bile had popped down it. I felt like a shattered vase, haphazardly glued back together, but not cured, ready to crumple with the hint of a breeze. The stones cut through my leather, and I seeped blood onto them. For once, I welcomed the blood. If I bled, I lived.

Only a whale bone tent stood out from the shale. It loomed, cyclopean and weird, in an unnatural spur, as if the sea had receded only in that spot, for it to be erected.

"You alive?" Jenn asked.

I looked from her to sky to sea to tent. "I think so. You?"

She shrugged. "Part of me hopes so, the rest hopes not."

"Yeah." I pushed myself to my feet with a groan. "That's pretty typical."

"What now?"

I gestured at the tent. "After you."

"After *you*. You're the one with the guns."

For all the good they'd done us.

Bloated drowned souls with fish-pecked eyes watched from the water's edge, waves passing through their forms. The spirits were arranged in the same order as our class photo, with only a few gaps left to fill. Notably *mine*. The faces were changed beyond recognition. Sean and Teri looked fresher, if not better. Both were puzzles with their pieces cut in the shapes of snakes and fish flies, seams glowing red.

"They're all here," Jenn said. "They're really all dead."

Standing still gave no respite here, and the dead were no comfort. We walked across the shale, trailing blood, socks squelching in our boots, for an interminable distance, while the hut never grew closer. Our classmates' spirits followed us, witnesses to our end, or, with the gang all here, marching along to their own final dooms. When our feet were ready to fall off, and we'd walk no more, the hut appeared right in front of us. We stood, chilled and chattering in its shadow. There was no door.

The bones were bleached by a sun I couldn't find in the sky. An elongated ribcage, wider at the front, formed the hut's structure. Segments of tail plugged the gaps between the ribs, wrapping round, and plunging into and out of the shale. Finger bones—the hand that'd snatched Jenn, and larger than me here— formed a steeple shape at the hut's widest end. There was no sign of a skull.

"These are *her* bones," I said, certain it was true. She'd lived once, died once, and yet both conditions were still true.

Inside the bones, I saw something red, and glistening. Flensed skins covered bone on the inside, but the only meat and blood within belonged to Carrie Cthulhu's victims. Our dead classmates drifted through the bones, under the steepled fingers, and into the hut. The bell rang once as each entered.

"An entrance, but no door," I murmured.

"How do *we* get in?" Jenn asked.

I wasn't sure I wanted to enter, even if our answers were inside. My boot knife scratched off the bones and meat as if I were trying to shave slivers off stone. I tucked the blade away and hefted a piece of shale, wincing as it sliced through my gloves. It'd cut me through my leathers, maybe it'd cut through whatever lined the hut. It was a thing from her time. A thing older than any steel. I sawed an opening in a gap between the bones and squeezed inside, emerging blood-slick.

A bell—*the* bell—hung from an elongated reptilian skull at the centre of the hut. Carrie Cthulhu's skull. Whatever had killed her in the time before time, must've built this hut from her bones. Maybe it'd celebrated its victory too soon. While she was in our world, she wasn't here but when she consumes us all she can feed in the Real.

A city to start.

Then the continent.

Then the world.

The bell's clapper was a heart; as it beat, the bell rang. The sound drove us to our knees. My Grave Sight followed the pulse, a visible thing, rippling in the air like a pebble dropped in pool. The pulse matched the one between Carrie Cthulhu and her avatar, only it extended triangularly. Two of us, and Carrie Cthulhu herself. It had to mean something.

I grabbed the heart; I needed both hands to move it, and

ripped it from the bell. Its weight almost bore me to the ground. It touched the edge of the bell as I sank. The ringing stopped. The last sustain hung in the air. Mist filled the farthest, narrower side of the hut.

The Ghost Docks came.

The fog suffused everything. The docks stretched ahead forever into the mist. Behind me, the hut was gone. The beach was gone. The river. The boat. Even Carrie Cthulhu. At the end of the dock was home.

The bell's sustained note diminished. The heartbeat tried to push us back, but there was no sound with it separated from the bell. If we didn't make it home before the last tone ended, we wouldn't.

"Let's go!"

We ran.

A river of time pushed us backward on the Ghost Dock as we raced the dying bell home. Churning water splashed the dock trying to wash us off the path.

The heart wanted us back. Wanted to consume us.

Our classmates' spirits followed us, we were the moon to their tide. As long as we pushed against the current, they came too. The further we walked, the lighter the heart felt, the less Carrie Cthulhu's gravity dragged, and the more indistinct they became, as if the water washed them to wherever they were meant to end up. Free from here.

Free from her.

At the end of the docks the heart had shrunk in my hand, becoming a tiny black pebble. We stepped off the dock and onto a very different beach. Finally, the heart disappeared, sand blowing in the wind. The bell tone ended. We wouldn't hear it again.

Carrie Cthulhu would sleep. Until she woke again—and wake she would. And this would start all over, even if humanity wasn't around to see it.

Jenn wasn't in her anime outfit anymore, now she wore a sundress and bolero jacket. Her hair was long again, though not as long as I remembered it. Despite knowing my secret identity, she seemed surprised my outfit remained the same in the Real.

"What now?"

I smiled my first genuine smile since the dreams had begun.

"You could join the Fight."

Jenn looked at the sky, dawn fighting the blackness in the east while the stars lingered above us. "No offense, but I can wait more than ten years for our next reunion."

"Fair enough."

I led her up the beach to where I'd parked my car. Water lapped at my shredded boots. The sun peeked over the hills surrounding the lake. My doom trickled away in the daylight, like any dream or nightmare. Carrie Cthulhu had claimed my fate was sealed. I was still here.

The Fight had begun long ago. Long before me. Long enough that humanity was only a blip to it, and my participation not even that. Nothing would stop my fishing for my next monster.

The Fight continued.

Treasure of the Sea

Julia Heller

MIRI FOUND THE small outlander washed in with the tide. His hair was the pale colour of sand and rippled like water; his skin was like the ivory of a sea-beast's bleached bones. His eyes were shut, but Miri imagined that if he opened them, they would be the blue-green of the sea. He was quite young, not yet in his teens. She thought he was dead until she touched his shoulder. His flesh was chilled, but alive; and he moaned.

She brought him home and wrapped him in skins by the fire. She fed him broth in his sleep and watched over him when she wasn't combing the beach. On the fourth evening she turned from loading wood on the fire to see his open eyes—not the blue-green she expected, but a grey as gentle as the morning mists.

Miri came and sat next to him. His eyes followed her, clear and unafraid. She offered him water, and he shook his head. Miri spoke.

"You have been asleep for four days. I found you on the beach. You are on the Island of Shale; none live here except the fish, the seals, the seabirds, and me. I am Miri." She inclined her head. The seashells woven into her night-dark hair clicked and thonked with the movement. Still, the boy was silent. Miri spoke once more. "Rest," she said. The boy's eyes closed gently, and he immediately fell asleep.

Miri's beachcombing took her over the entire island. The sea constantly brought forth new things, tossed and tumbled and thrown up on the shelves of shale that made up much of the island. There were only two places where the waves were gentle enough to deposit only sand, and Miri only rarely visited them. It had been lucky indeed for the boy that he had been found. This day's efforts produced a larger-than-usual load of driftwood which she stacked outside the door to dry. When it burned, she knew the flames would shine different colours.

As she leapt from rock to rock, she spied something snagged on a jut of shale in the water. It swirled and moved with the waves. She pulled it up, water sluicing off it in salty streams. It was a heavy cloak of skin, sewn with patterns of grey on grey, with a voluminous hood at one end. A huge gash marred its otherwise smooth form; the hole was ragged and wide. She rolled up the cloak and tied it to her load of firewood.

When Miri got back, the boy was sitting up, looking at the fire. Miri had left the wood outside, but carried the cloak in her hands. She shook it out with a snap, then hung it by its hood on a peg on the wall. She turned around to find the boy's eyes fixed on her, as wide as sand dollars. His pupils were huge as he looked from her to the cloak. After five days he still hadn't spoken, but Miri was in no hurry. Like the sea, she had learned to be patient. She went back outside and returned with a net bag full of mussels which she put on to cook. The savoury smell filled her home, and the boy took time to blink and give her a look of gratitude as she gave him a steaming bowl, flavoured with salt and seaweed.

Miri chewed, swallowed, and thought, her eyes resting on the boy. His gaze never faltered even as he ate; the cloak held all of his attention. When they finished, she gathered the empty bowls and washed them in the basin, then set them aside to dry. Wiping her hands, she looked at the boy. "You're interested in that, aren't you?"

The boy turned to look at her, fluid and graceful. He nodded once. Miri walked to the cloak, lifted it, turned it so he could see the rent in its surface. "It's torn." The boy's grey eyes filled with a look she couldn't identify. He made a sound deep in his throat like a hurt animal. Miri raised her eyebrows, then crossed to the table and set down the cloak. The boy had hunched and was looking down. Miri fetched out her bone needle and grey thread, as near a match as could be dreamed of to the cloak's thick material. "Let's see what we can do." She looked, saw the boy staring at her with hope bursting from his eyes. Her smile was like dawn breaking over the sea.

Miri bent to the task. Her stitches, tiny and nearly invisible, slowly began to heal the ragged edges of the rip. Behind her steady fingers the cloak smoothed out whole and neat, its patterns uninterrupted. Miri worked for two days, stopping only to add more wood to the fire and to feed herself and the boy. Her eyes burned with sleeplessness and her fingers cramped, but she worked on as steadily as the motion of the tides. On the morning of the third day, she tied the last knot, snapped off her thread neatly, and sighed. She stood, lifting the cloak. It was warm and heavy, slithering across her fingers. She turned to find the boy standing, out of bed for the first time. He was very still, but his sand-pale hair slid across his forehead, and his eyes silently asked her a question.

Miri flipped the robe open, then stepped forward and swirled it around to settle on his shoulders. She bent and kissed his forehead, cool lips to warm skin, then pulled the hood down to cover his face. The boy seemed to shrink, collapsing down to a bundle on the floor. Miri bent and lifed the seal pup in her arms.

"Come, little one," she said, smiling gently. "Let's call your family."

On the shore, Miri stood with the pup in her arms and barked hoarsely. The pup lifed his head, listening with wonder as, in the distance, the sound of barking redoubled. The sound rapidly grew louder, until finally the outcrop Miri stood on was surrounded by a pod of seals, all leaping and barking and splashing. Miri laid a hand on the seal pup's head, and he looked up at her with his huge grey eyes. She smiled at him, her own eyes glinting with tears that trembled like pearls on her lashes. "Take care," she said softly, "and grow strong, young one." Bending, she released him into the water, where he was greeted enthusiastically by his family.

Miri raised a hand in farewell, then set out along the shore, leaping from rock to rock. Her tattered robe streamed out behind her and the white shells in her black hair tinkled like wind chimes as she looked to see what new treasures the sea would bring her on this new day.

Nure-Onna

Marshall J. Moore

Kazusa, Japan. 1576.

THE DEAD FISHERMAN stared blindly up at the grey sky above, his mouth open in a last, silent scream.

"Another one," Okabe Yukiko frowned. "That makes three."

She stood, tucking her hands back into the sleeves of her kimono. A tall, knife-thin woman, she cut a striking figure as the salt wind blew her hair back from her face.

"So?" her companion asked, looking at the corpse with revulsion.

"So the killer is still active."

"What killer?" Fumiyo Mitsuhide snorted and spat into the sand. The thick glob of phlegm narrowly missed Yukiko, landing instead just beside the body lying stretched along the tideline. "This one was a fisherman, like the others. They drown sometimes."

A cool breeze rolled in from the sea. Yukiko shivered and pulled her kimono more tightly about her.

They stood on a long, narrow spit of beach beneath a cloudy sky. To the north lay a long cape of land that formed the shallow bay, its shoreline comprised of rocky cliffs and narrow, pebbly beaches. The coast was dotted by a handful of fishing villages, all under the ownership of one Kishimoto Haru, Mitsuhide's sworn overlord and Yukiko's erstwhile employer.

As a jizamurai, the lowest rank of the landholding nobility, Kishimoto held only this narrow stretch of coastline as his domain and had only Mitsuhide as his sole samurai retainer. The deaths of even two of his vassal fishermen would have a significant impact on Kishimoto's yearly tax revenue, and so he had enlisted Okabe Yukiko's service to assist Mitsuhide's investigation into the mysterious deaths.

Yukiko fixed Mitushide with a critical stare. He was a hirsute man of middle years, broad-shouldered and thick in the belly. A deep scar bisected his face from one temple to the opposite cheek, necessitating an eyepatch. His kimono was nearly as ragged as Yukiko's own, but he bore the dual swords that denoted his status as a samurai with evident pride.

"These men were not drowned," Yukiko said, reminding herself that she had been hired to assist Mitsuhide in his investigation, not the other way around.

"This one looks pretty drowned to me," Mitsuhide shrugged. "His skin's all pale and wrinkly. They get that way after some time in the water."

"True," Yukiko admitted. "But look at his eyes."

"What about them?"

"They're still there," she said. "Fish eat the eyes first."

"Maybe they weren't hungry."

"Or maybe he wasn't in the water long enough for them to start," Yukiko said. She picked up a piece of driftwood lying in the sand and used it to carefully turn the corpse's head over. "Look at his neck."

Mitsuhide looked, frowning. There were two dark puncture wounds in the dead man's neck. "Looks like a snakebite."

Yukiko nodded. "I thought so as well. But look how far apart they are spaced. Have you ever seen a snake with a mouth that wide, Mitsuhide-san?"

Mitsuhide scratched his beard. "It might have been two snakes, with one fang apiece."

Yukiko did not laugh. Instead she drew her curved tanto dagger from her obi, the sash that served as a belt. Kneeling, she drew the blade across the waterlogged corpse's arm. No blood welled from the cut.

"Tell me, Mitsuhide-san," she said, her expression grim. "Do you know of any snake that can drain all the blood from a man's body?"

Mitsuhide grimaced and shook his head.

"Then your master was right to hire me," Yukiko said, standing. She turned, the wind whipping her long dark hair from her face as she gazed out at the roiling sea. "There is a ghost preying on your people."

ONCE, OKABE YUKIKO had been a noble lady, wife to a daimyo. Her husband had been lord of a broad domain, respected by his peers and enemies alike for his honour on the battlefield and sound judgment in court.

Like most samurai marriages, their match had been arranged by their families. Yukiko had been trained as an onna-bugeisha, a female warrior, but had tried to find contentment in managing their household while her husband was away on campaign, and in raising their daughter, Izumi.

All that had ended in flames eight years ago. Such was the way of things in the Sengoku Jidai, the age of the country at war.

Alone of her family, Yukiko had escaped the destruction of her home. Now she wandered the countryside as a ronin, a masterless samurai willing to sell her sword for coin, or merely a place to sleep and a hot meal. It was a disgraceful, hardscrabble life, one most samurai would rather commit the ritual suicide of seppuku than endure.

But Yukiko had turned away from that path long ago. Her life now was one of violent struggle. For meagre pay she guarded merchant caravans, tracked down gangs of bandits, and fought in the petty wars of minor daimyo.

And on occasion, hunted ghosts.

IN FAIR WEATHER, Ishiwan might have been picturesque: a little fishing hamlet set close to the shore, bordered to north and south by rocky cliffs. A long promontory of piled rocks jutted out into the bay, buffeted on either side by the pounding waves. Beyond lay the vast blue expanse of the open ocean.

But it was not fair weather. It was late into autumn, and the wind rolled in cold and bitter from the waves. The sky above was grey and cloudy, and there was an ominous weight to the air. Though it was only late afternoon, no one stirred in Ishiwan's streets, and the doors were shut tight.

"Where is everyone?" Yukiko wondered aloud as they walked through the shuttered village.

"Working," Mitsuhide said. "The men of Ishiwan are all fishermen. They will be on their boats until just before sunset."

"And the women?"

Mitsuhide spat. "The less said of Ishiwan's women, the better."

Yukiko glanced at her companion, surprised by the vehemence in his voice. "You've been here before, I take it."

"Hai. Though last time I was here, I had two eyes." Mitsuhide tapped his eyepatch, then looked around. "I'll see if any of these hovels is clean enough for us to stay the night in. Hopefully the yokai will not come for us as we sleep, eh?"

"Hopefully not." Yukiko said, ignoring the mockery in his tone. She looked downhill towards the village's narrow beach and the crashing waves, and the long promontory of rocks. "While you do that, I will head to the shore and see if I can find any sign of our quarry."

"Hah!" Mitsuhide threw back his head and laughed. "All you'll find on that beach is rocks and saltwater, ronin."

"Maybe," Yukiko said, turning and heading towards the waves. "But foolish is the hunter who lets her guard down in her quarry's lair."

THE WIND WHISTLED in Yukiko's ears as she paced along Ishiwan's narrow beach, picking her way carefully over the stony ground. The rhythmic pounding of the surf and the bracingly cold salt air helped clear her head after so long traveling overland. As she walked, she pondered the nature of the creature she sought.

There was no doubt in Yukiko's mind that the killer was a yokai of some sort, but there were thousands of varieties of such beings, each with their own particular natures, habits, and weaknesses. Methods to hunt one yokai would be useless against another of a different breed.

Yukiko combed her hand through her long black hair as she mentally catalogued the aquatic yokai she knew of. There were the ningyo; creatures half-man, half-fish, known to bring tidal waves on coastal towns in vengeance for being caught in a hapless fisherman's net. And the victims *were* all fishermen . . .

But that would not explain the bite marks, Yukiko frowned. *And ningyo do not drink blood.*

What, then? She knew of several varieties of vampiric yokai, like the nikusui that preyed on young men, or the iso-onna, who lured travellers off of cliffs.

Cliffs like these, Yukiko frowned up at the high stone walls to her left. But iso-onna were native to Kyushu, the southernmost of Nippon's main islands. She had never heard of an iso-onna as far north as Ishiwan. Perhaps it was the iso-onna's cousin, the nure-onna . . .

A splashing sound broke through Yukiko's musings. One hand dropped to the katana tucked into her obi as she turned, half afraid that one of the nightmare creatures might have risen from the sea to attack.

Instead, Yukiko saw a small pale face bobbing up and down in the waves. Damp black hair was plastered to its brow. It stared at her with bright, curious eyes before diving back below the surface.

A ningyo? Yukiko thought. Her hand tightened around the hilt of her katana. *No; ningyo are hairless. Aren't they?*

Before she could ponder further, the face appeared again, this time much closer to shore. Throwing its head back, its nostrils flared as it let out a long, high-pitched whistle from its nose. It dove again, and this time there could be no doubt: it was heading straight towards Yukiko.

The ronin lowered herself into a fighting crouch, but did not draw her sword. Yokai were mercurial beings; some could be placated or reasoned with. If this was a yokai, it might take offense at being greeted with drawn steel.

A slender figure emerged from the waves, stepping from sea to shore with practiced ease. Saltwater dripped from a mane of dark hair down pale, naked limbs. Bright eyes looked up at her, curious and unafraid.

"Hello," he said. "What's your name?"

Yukiko exhaled and straightened from her fighting crouch. This was no yokai. It was just a little boy, five or six years old. A few years younger than her own child had been.

Izumi, Yukiko thought, and closed her eyes. When she opened them the little boy was still standing there, looking up at her with an expression of bright interest.

"Hello," she said, and smiled at him. "I am Yukiko."

"My name's Shingo," he said, taking a step forward. "Are those real swords?"

"They are."

"Can I see?"

Yukiko laughed, all tension draining from her. This child had probably never seen a samurai before. What harm could there be in satisfying his curiosity?

She knelt to his eye level, feeling the hard stones beneath her knees. Her wakizashi, the smaller of her two swords, hissed as she slid it from its sheathe.

"You can look at it," she told him, holding the sword in both hands. "But don't touch. Only a samurai can touch another's sword."

Wide-eyed, Shingo nodded solemnly. His eyes traced the finely worked steel, the delicate curve of the blade, the wrapped handle and the round tsuba guard.

A high whistle split the air, stronger and longer than the sound Shingo had made when he had surfaced.

"*Shingo!*"

The voice carried over the water, high and angry. Yukiko jerked her head up to see a woman's face floating in the waves, close to where she had first spotted Shingo. The woman ducked beneath the surface and kicked towards them, swimming faster than Yukiko had ever seen anyone move, above or below the waves.

Within seconds she stepped from the water onto the rocky beach, as easily as Shingo had. Water dripped down her bare limbs, and she had a long, broad-bladed knife in her hand.

"Back away, samurai!" she hissed, pointing the knife towards Yukiko. "Get away from him!"

"Easy," Yukiko said, looking calmly at the woman. "He's in no danger."

"Says the samurai with drawn sword," the woman snorted, her nostrils flaring. "Step away from her, Shingo."

Shingo's head turned, looking between the two women. "Okaa-san—"

"Do as I say," she said, in a voice that brooked no argument.

Shingo complied, stepping hastily behind the woman's outstretched arm.

Moving slowly and deliberately, Yukiko sheathed her wakizashi and stood. The woman kept Shingo behind her, still holding the knife towards Yukiko.

"I apologize for the misunderstanding," Yukiko said, bowing. "Your son asked me to show him my sword. I meant no offense."

The woman's gaze was direct and fearsome. She was shorter than Yukiko by almost a foot, her body dense with compact, sinewy muscle. Other than the fundoshi loincloth and a white headcloth, she was naked. There was more grey in her hair than black. She was too old to be Shingo's mother, but that was what okaa-saan meant.

"Did he send you?" she demanded, the knife trembling slightly. "Kishimoto-sama."

"He did," Yukiko said. "I am Okabe Yukiko, a humble ronin. Your lord has hired me to investigate the recent deaths in the area."

The knife lowered slightly, though the woman's gaze was still wary. "Truly?"

"Hai," Yukiko nodded. "Once again, I apologize for frightening you."

The woman looked hard at Yukiko for a long moment, then tucked the knife back into her belt and bowed from the waist. "My name is Kayo. I apologize for drawing steel on you, Okabe-sama."

"No apology is needed." Yukiko shook her head. "A devoted mother will go to any lengths to protect her child."

"Grandchild," Kayo corrected.

"As you say." Yukiko smiled at Shingo, who shyly returned the expression. "I thought he was a seal at first. I've never seen a child so at home in the water."

One corner of Kayo's mouth twisted upwards with evident pride. "He is an ama, like me."

Ama were pearl divers, renowned for their tremendous lung capacity. Tales said that they could remain submerged for up to ten minutes, and that beneath the waves they were as nimble as any fish.

"I am pleased to meet you," Yukiko said, bowing her head. She glanced at Shingo. "Pardon my ignorance, but I was under the impression that only women can be ama."

Shingo looked abashed. Kayo put an arm around her grandson's shoulders.

"That is usually true," she said. "But Shingo is a strong swimmer, and he can make the isobue as well as any woman."

"Isobue?"

"It is how we clear our lungs of air when we surface." Kayo took a deep breath, then let out a blast of air through her nose. The high keening whistle split the air again, long and strangely melodic.

"Music of the sea, they call it."

Yukiko turned to see Mitsuhide swaggering towards them along the beach, one hand resting on the hilt of his katana. Kayo moved so that she stood between Shingo and the approaching samurai.

"Hello, okaa-san," Mitsuhide nodded at Kayo.

"Mitsuhide," Kayo practically spat.

Yukiko jerked her head towards the older woman, appalled. To greet another without an honorific was a sign of intense disrespect.

There was naked hate in Kayo's eyes. The ama's hand was inching towards the knife at her hip, and Mitsuhide's was already on his sword. Yukiko had no idea what the history between them was, but if she did not act quickly there would be blood on the rocks.

And if things went very poorly, it would be Shingo's.

Yukiko knew what it was to lose a child. She would not permit it to happen here.

"Don't tell me she's your mother, too," she said to Mitsuhide.

He bared his teeth. "Hardly. All the ama call her okaa-san. She's old enough to be, anyway."

"It's a title of respect," Kayo said, staring daggers at Mitsuhide. "You are forbidden from visiting Ishiwan, Mitsuhide. What are you doing here?"

Mitsuhide tucked his thumbs into his obi, a smug look on his face. "As I'm sure Yukiko-san has mentioned, we are here on our lord's orders, which supersede my exile. Rest assured, okaa-san, I have no intention of darkening the doors of your hovel."

"Don't talk to her that way!" Shingo blurted out.

Mitsuhide's gaze snapped to the boy. An odd expression came over his face. Before Yukiko or Kayo could react, he darted forward and seized Shingo by the wrist, pulling him towards him.

"What have we here?" he said, roughly tilting Shingo's head up for a better look at the boy. "I'd no idea you could still bear children, Kayo."

"You said it yourself," Kayo said. "I am okaa-san to all the ama."

Her hand rested on her knife, but she did not draw it. Concern was etched on her face as she looked from Shingo to Mitsuhide, who continued to stare searchingly into Shingo's face. The boy gazed back at him, plainly afraid.

"Ah." Mitsuhide nodded to himself. "I see."

He released Shingo, who immediately scampered back to his grandmother.

"Keep a close eye on your boy, okaa-san," Mitsuhide said, turning back towards the village. "It would be a shame if anything were to happen to him."

Kayo hugged Shingo close to her, not taking her eyes off Mitsuhide's retreating form. Yukiko shifted uncomfortably, knowing she had intruded on something personal.

"I apologize for my fellow samurai's behaviour," she said, hoping the words did not sound as stiff as they felt. "Rest assured, I mean no threat to you or your family."

Kayo gave her a long, searching look. Finally she nodded. "I believe you, Okabe-san."

"Please, call me Yukiko."

"Yukiko-san," Kayo nodded. "You said you came here in search of the thing that's been killing the fishermen?"

"I am." She peered closely at the pearl diver. "Do you know something?"

Kayo bit her lip. She looked down at Shingo, still clinging to her leg.

"Run along, Shingo-chan," she told her grandson, giving him an affectionate push. "Go play in the waves before the sun sets."

Shingo did not need to be told twice. With a final look at Yukiko, he dashed into the surf, whooping and hollering with the joyous energy endemic to all little boys. Kayo watched him go. Only once he was far out in the bay did she turn back to Yukiko.

"We ama have heard the creature you hunt," she said. "At night she cries, lonely and grief-stricken, in a cave along the sea-cliffs."

"You are certain?" Yukiko asked, her mouth dry. "It is a yokai?"

Kayo nodded. "I saw her myself only two nights past, as I dove for pearls by moonlight. I cannot say what sort of creature it was, only that it had a long tail, like an eel or snake."

Yukiko's heart raced. "Where?"

Kayo pointed north, towards the tallest of the wave-battered cliffs. "She comes at night. Follow the sound of her crying, and you will find her."

Yukiko looked at the cliffs, then back at the village. "How long will she be there?"

"Not long," Kayo shook her head. "I hid behind a rock and watched her for a while. Perhaps an hour after moonrise she slithered into the water and swam off in search of prey."

For a moment, Yukiko hesitated. Technically, this was Mitsuhide's investigation, and she should bring Kayo's report to him as soon as possible.

But the sky overhead was already growing dark. Sunset would be hidden behind the clouds, but moonrise could not be far off. By the time she reached those cliffs it would be dark. If she delayed, the yokai might slip away, taking another fisherman victim.

"Show me," she told Kayo.

AT FIRST, YUKIKO feared that she would slip and fall as they clambered along the top of the uneven cliffs, her geta sandals clattering over the loose rock. But Kayo moved as swiftly and surely across stone as she did through the waves, never hesitating or faltering. Yukiko followed in her footsteps as swiftly as she could. Long years of hardship had given her excellent stamina, but even so she soon lagged behind Kayo's tireless strides.

They trekked along the cliffs for over an hour, past the sunset and nightfall, past moonrise. Neither spoke. Yukiko's heartbeat pounded in her chest, the thrill of the hunt singing in her veins. She was drawing close to her quarry. She could feel it.

Without warning, Kayo halted.

"This is as far as I go," she told Yukiko. She pointed toward the cliffs, where Yukiko could just make out a narrow trail leading down to the water. "There is a small beach down there. Wait a while and you will hear the yokai. Its cries will lead you to it."

"Thank you," Yukiko nodded. "Where will you go?"

"To take care of my grandson," Kayo said. "Good hunting, samurai-san."

She turned and disappeared into the night, striding surefootedly across the jagged cliffs.

Yukiko stood at the edge of the cliff and waited, listening.

Waves churned and broke against the rocks below. The breeze gusted cold and brisk from the ocean, tasting of salt and foam. Where it met the cliffs it howled and moaned and sang. Every now and again there was a cry from some distant seabird.

Yukiko listened to the world, intent for any noise that disrupted the natural harmony of sky and sea and salt.

There. Just beneath the roar and crash of the waves was a rasping sound like laboured breathing. She was not alone in the dark. Slowly, Yukiko dropped her hand to her swords.

A dark shape stumbled towards her out of the night. For half a heartbeat Yukiko thought it might be Kayo returning, but this shape was taller and broader, and moved with none of Kayo's natural grace.

Yukiko's katana hissed as she drew it from its sheathe, the blade shining bright in the silver moonlight. The dark shape staggered drunkenly, lunging towards her with one arm outstretched. The other was pressed against its neck.

Yukiko dodged out of the reach of the grasping hand. The figure stumbled, fell, and lay still.

Sword raised, Yukiko approached, her heartbeat thudding in her chest. Was this the killer yokai she sought?

The dark shape upon the ground did not move. Yukiko reached down, katana still in hand, and turned it over.

Mitsuhide's face stared back up at her, his wide eyes as sightless as those of the fisherman they had discovered on the beach only that morning. His hand was pressed against his neck, his fingers caked with blood. A long, deep cut had been carved across his throat.

Yukiko frowned. The other bodies had suffered from twin puncture wounds and drained of blood. Mitsuhide looked like someone had attacked him with a weapon, and he clearly still had plenty of blood to lose . . .

A high, wailing cry pierced her observation. Yukiko stood, katana raised in a defensive stance, but the night around her was still. She listened with bated breath, eyes scanning the darkness as her heartbeat pounded in her ears.

The wail came again, lower and hoarser this time. It sounded weirdly refracted, an echo of itself.

Kayo said the creature was in a cave, she thought. *The wailing must be coming from there.*

Yukiko bent and picked up Mitsuhide's swords, tucking them into her *obi* at her right hip with due reverence. As much as she had disliked the man, he had still been a samurai, and his weapons should be afforded respect.

Following the wailing, Yukiko crept down the cliffside to the pebbly beach below. During the day this narrow stretch of shore would be fully submerged, but now it was low tide. The waves crashed against the rocks in a constant, steady rhythm.

Another wail, closer and less distorted. Yukiko followed it to a jagged overhang of rock, beneath which a shadowy figure stood framed against the distant moon.

Fear gripped Yukiko's heart as the dark shape let loose another wail. It was a woman with long dark hair hanging in wet clumps over her face. She was bent nearly double, clutching something against her chest. Her threadbare kimono was drenched, as though she had just climbed out of the sea.

Yukiko's every sense warned her that she was in danger, that there was more to the weeping woman than she appeared. Many yokai took the appearance of a long-haired woman, after all.

But she had to be certain.

"Hello?" Yukiko called, as loudly as she dared.

The woman turned, still bent over. She was not old, Yukiko realized—in fact, the face beneath the tangled hair was young and beautiful. She held a cloth bundle to her breast, though it too was soaked through. An uneasy chill crept down Yukiko's spine.

Great sobs heaved the woman's narrow shoulders as she stumbled towards Yukiko, tearstains shining on her cheeks in the moonlight.

"Are you hurt?" Yukiko asked. The woman shook her head, sending water droplets flying.

"My baby," she said hoarsely. "My baby, he's so still, so cold . . ."

She stumbled forward, the motion oddly sinuous, and pushed the bundle into Yukiko's arms. Startled, Yukiko took the baby from her, cradling it in her right arm.

But it was no baby, just a heavy stone.

Yukiko jerked her head up. The bedraggled woman was staring at her through a curtain of damp black hair. Tears still streaked her face, but she was no longer crying. Her lips peeled back to reveal cruel, curved fangs.

Like a snake's, Yukiko thought, terror freezing her limbs. She watched in helpless fascination as the woman's eyes grew reptilian, yellow and slit-pupiled. The kimono fell from her shoulders, revealing a body scaly and serpentine, her legs fused into a long, coiling tail. Only her face and arms retained any semblance of humanity.

A nure-onna, Yukiko thought. I might have known.

The recognition shook the haze of fear from her. Yukiko reached instinctively for her sword but found she could not release the stone she carried. It must have weighed at least twenty pounds, for the motion sent her off-balance, stumbling away even as the serpentine creature reared over her to strike.

The nure-onna darted at her with blinding speed, clawed hands outstretched. Yukiko threw herself aside, biting back a cry of pain as the jagged rocks tore into her shoulder as she landed in a roll. She tried once more to draw her katana, but it was as if her hand had been frozen to the heavy round stone the yokai had pushed into her arms.

Only her right hand, though. Her left was still free, but the katana was designed to be drawn across the body, rendering her swords all but useless.

Her swords.

The nure-onna struck at her again, fangs glistening in the moonlight. This time Yukiko did not dodge away. Instead she thrust her right hand up, summoning all the strength in her wiry frame to raise the heavy stone.

The monster's jaw closed around the unyielding rock. A crack split the night as its fangs shattered. The nure-onna screeched in pain, and Yukiko felt a surge of vicious pleasure. But her manoeuvre with the stone had bought her no more than a few seconds, and she knew it.

Her free hand closed around the cloth-wrapped hilt of Mitsuhide's katana. The nure-onna was still reeling, its mouth a bloody mess. Its eyes fixed on her, full of rage and venom. A feral hiss escaped its throat as it reared back to tear Yukiko's throat out with its ruined teeth.

Mitsuhide's katana sang as it came free of its sheathe. Yukiko's draw was slow and clumsy, but the nure-onna was already striking at her. Her grip whitened on the hilt as she drove the blade up into the creature's scaly belly. Saltwater and blood poured from the wound in equal measure.

The weight of the nure-onna's body worked against it, impaling itself on the curved steel as it drove towards Yukiko. The monster's stinking bulk weighed down on her, forcing Yukiko to the ground.

The nure-onna screeched, thrashing against the stones in its death-throes. Its lashing tail struck Yukiko across the face, and her world went black.

WHEN SHE CAME to, all Yukiko could do was lie still and breathe. Her whole body felt damp with saltwater, though she could not tell whether it was sweat or the nure-onna's blood. The creature's coiling bulk lay atop her, heavy and stinking. A gargling sound came from it.

It's not dead yet, Yukiko realized. She tried to pull Mitsuhide's katana free from the monster's body, but the blade was lodged deep in the yokai's belly.

Clawed hands locked around Yukiko's face, their hard nails digging into her temples. Yellow eyes stared into Yukiko's grey ones.

"Shingo," the nure-onna rasped. Blood and saltwater dripped from her mouth. "Where is Shingo?"

"He's safe," Yukiko gasped. Her own voice sounded nearly as ragged as the yokai's. "With his grandmother."

The nure-onna's reptilian eyes widened. "Okaa-san?"

"Hai," Yukiko said. "The pearl divers' mother."

Water droplets flecked Yukiko's face as the nure-onna shook its head. "Not . . . theirs. Mine. My mother."

Understanding dawned. "You're Shingo's mother."

The nure-onna jerked its head in what might have been a nod. "My dying wish . . . she would keep him safe from his father . . ."

"His father?"

The claws around Yukiko's face tightened, drawing a faint line of blood from her temples. Instinctively, Yukiko twisted the katana still lodged deep in the monster's belly. It hissed in pain and jerked away from the blade, freeing Yukiko from beneath it.

She scrambled away, holding Mitsuhide's sword unsteadily towards the nure-onna. But the monster did not rise. It lay on the rocks besides the breaking waves, slitted eyes narrowing at Yukiko.

No, not at me. At the sword.

"Twice that blade has killed me," the nure-onna whispered. Seawater and blood leaked from between its scales.

"Mitsuhide," Yukiko breathed. "He fathered Shingo and killed you."

The nure-onna nodded weakly. "In life I was a poor ama diver. He, our lord's retainer. He got me with his child. But when he saw that it was a boy, he wanted to take him from me."

Yukiko could only stare. Samurai society prized male children over female, so it would make sense that Mitsuhide would view a son, even bastard-born, as a potential heir. But to take Shingo forcibly away from his mother? That was monstrous.

Her disgust must have shown, because a thin smile split the nure-onna's lips.

"We quarrelled, and he killed me. Now I am . . . this. Forever doomed to hunt for my child, and the lover who killed me."

"No longer," Yukiko said. Her mouth was dry, but she had found her words. She wiped clean the blade of Mitsuhide's sword, then sheathed it. "Your killer is dead, and your son is safe."

She knelt beside the nure-onna. Its monstrous visage no longer struck any fear in her, only pity. "Be at peace, lonely ghost. Leave this world and trouble these shores no more."

The nure-onna looked up at her, tears shining wet on its bloody face. It nodded once, and for the briefest moment a true, human smile crossed its features.

Then it was gone, becoming no more than so much seawater splashing onto the rocks, then draining away into the crashing waves. The spirit of Kayo's daughter was one with the bay where the ama dove for their pearls.

At least now Shingo will know his mother's embrace, Yukiko thought. *Every time he dives, she will be holding him to her breast.*

SALT STUNG YUKIKO'S lips, the wind tugging at her kimono as she picked her way carefully along the rocky promontory jutting out into the bay. The stones under her feet were slick with rain and seawater, and some shifted treacherously underfoot as her weight upset them. Seafoam surged and crashed against the rocks, sending little orange crabs scuttling across her path.

It was dawn, though the rising sun was hidden beneath thick storm clouds. The sea ahead was as grey and restless as the sky above, but Yukiko did not turn back. The answers she sought were at the end of these rocks, where the waves met the land. She would not return until she had them.

Kayo's bare back was to Yukiko as she approached. The older woman knelt on the rocks, hunched over as she worked at something with her hands. Her bare shoulders were slick with seawater, her white headcloth soaked through. *She must have just surfaced from a dive.*

"Yukiko-sama," Kayo greeted her as she drew near, raising her voice to be heard over the pounding of surf against stone. "Did you find your yōkai?"

"I did," Yukiko said, drawing level with her. Kayo was crouched over a clamshell the size of her fist, prying her diver's knife between the shell's teeth. "May I sit?"

Kayo shrugged, which was enough assent for Yukiko. She carefully gathered the folds of her kimono about her and sat on the highest, driest rock beside Kayo.

"Mitsuhide is dead," Yukiko said.

Kayo grunted, conveying neither surprise nor grief at the news. "Another victim of your yōkai?"

Yukiko did not answer. Instead she shifted her weight, watching the distant breakers churn the seafoam white.

"The yōkai was a nure-onna," Yukiko said, watching Kayo closely. "The ghost of a forsaken woman. One whose husband abandons her and their child."

Kayo's sea-slick shoulders stiffened. The knuckles of the hand that held her knife grew white, confirming Yukiko's suspicions.

Could I beat her? Yukiko wondered. If they came to blows, Yukiko's long years as a wandering swordswoman would weigh in her favour, but she had seen Kayo in action. The Ama woman was swift and strong, and her diver's lungs meant her stamina would be practically godlike.

Besides, they were in her territory. The waves themselves were Kayo's home. Fighting her here would be like trying to wrestle a shark in its lair.

"She was your daughter," Yukiko said, her voice quiet against the breaking waves.

Kayo jerked her head in a nod. "Once."

"And Mitsuhide was Shingo's father."

Kayo did not look at Yukiko. Drops of saltwater ran down her face, but she did not wipe at them. "Tama was only sixteen when he first set eyes on her." She spat into the churning waves. "He did as men do, and within the year she was pregnant. He left before Shingo was born."

"But he returned," Yukiko said.

Kayo's shoulders sagged. "Shingo was not yet two. He knew nothing of his father."

"And Tama wanted to keep it that way," Yukiko guessed. Kayo nodded.

"If their child had been a girl, Mitsuhide would have taken no notice. She would have been left to grow up as an Ama, untroubled by her father."

"But that is not how things occurred."

"No." Kayo's eyes grew hard. "Mitsuhide was only a doshin, too low-ranking to make a compelling marriage prospect with any of the samurai caste. But he knew it would take little persuasion to convince Kishimoto-sama to allow him to formally adopt his baseborn son."

"Giving himself an heir," Yukiko said. "And your daughter?"

A fierce, angry pride lit Kayo's face. "She didn't simply lie down and allow Mitsuhide to steal her son away from her. She hid Shingo away, and when Mitsuhide came to claim his son she refused to divulge where he was hidden. They came to blows."

Yukiko could not tell whether it was sea spray or tears that ran down Kayo's cheeks. "Mitsuhide's scar?"

"Tama's work," Kayo smiled bitterly. "He had his swords, she her knife. He killed her, but she left her mark."

"And where were you when this occurred?"

"With Shingo, of course." She gestured landwards, to the rocky cliffs that marked this stretch of coast. "I have lived in these waters for fifty years, Yukiko-san. There are many hidden coves and secret caves along these shores. When we emerged, the other Ama told us what had transpired."

"Mitsuhide did not take the boy with him?"

"He tried," Kayo admitted. "But the killing of a vassal is not something that goes unremarked in a domain as small as Kishimoto's. After all, that is what brought you here."

"I suppose that's true," Yukiko nodded. "So you and the rest of the Ama appealed to your lord?"

"Indeed. It put Kishimoto in an . . . awkward position. Lowly as he might be, Mitsuhide was still a samurai, and within his rights to kill a commoner. At least in theory."

"And in practice?"

Kayo smiled bitterly. "What little wealth Kishimoto-sama possesses comes from the pearl trade, not the fishermen. We threatened to cease diving unless justice was served."

"And was it?"

"No." Kayo's smile vanished, but the bitterness remained. "Mitsuhide is Kishimoto's only samurai retainer, and could not simply be dismissed over so trifling a matter. Instead he was forbidden from setting foot in our village for eight years. Kishimoto ruled that once Shingo turned ten his father would be allowed to reclaim him. Until then, he would remain with us."

"Until the deaths began," Yukiko said, the last pieces falling into place. "Mitsuhide was never truly interested in discovering their cause. He only wanted to find Shingo and take him for his own."

She unfolded her legs and stood up from the rock, her hand still resting on the hilt of her wakizashi. She was taller than Kayo by almost a foot, but out here on the rocks the older woman's lower centre of balance would be a greater advantage than Yukiko's superior reach.

"That's why you killed him."

"Hai," Kayo agreed. Slowly, carefully, she set the clamshell down on the rock beside her and stood. She faced Yukiko, her hand resting on the long, broad-bladed diving knife tucked into her fundoshi loincloth.

"To protect my grandson, I killed his father, who was his mother's killer." Kayo drew her knife and held it towards Yukiko in both hands. A cold glint of resolve was in her eyes. "Are you going to arrest me, Yukiko-san? Because if you do, only one of us will walk back to the shore from this place."

Yukiko looked down at the shorter, older woman, considering. Kishimoto had put a price on the head of the creature that had killed his fishermen; how much more then would he pay for the killer of his only retainer? Enough for Yukiko to travel comfortably and safely to the next town large enough for her to find work, certainly.

Or, she realized, shifting her weight for a better footing on the sea-slick rocks, she need not even leave. With Mitsuhide dead, Kishimoto would be in need of a *bushi* to take his place—and as a lowly jizamurai, he could not afford to turn away even a ronin like Yukiko.

Security, regular meals, a roof over her head—all the things that were denied a wandering ronin could be hers for the taking. All she needed to do was match her steel against that of this aging pearl diver.

Kayo stood before her, just outside of the reach of Yukiko's undrawn swords. Her dark eyes took in the ronin woman, alert to every shift in Yukiko's weight, reading her for the telltale signs that she might be about to draw steel. Her gaze was cold but resigned.

She has killed for her family before, Yukiko thought. *She is prepared to do so again.*

Yukiko made her choice.

She took her hand from her wakizashi, raising it with her palm facing Kayo in a gesture of peace.

"No," Yukiko said. "I will not arrest you, Kayo-san. There has been enough blood in these waters."

Slowly, Kayo lowered her knife. She still watched Yukiko warily, alert to some treachery.

"I have something for you," Yukiko said. "If you'll allow me."

She lowered herself to her knees, no longer caring if the waves and wind further soaked her wet kimono. Kneeling on the rocks was difficult, but Yukiko managed some semblance of a bow as she drew Mitsuhide's sword from her *obi*.

Kayo tensed, raising the knife in a warding gesture, but did not strike. Yukiko exhaled in relief.

"This is Mitsuhide's katana," she said, holding out the longer of the two blades, still sheathed. "With this blade he killed your daughter. I offer it to you in recompense for her death."

Kayo frowned. "It is not yours to offer, Yukiko-san."

"Perhaps not," Yukiko admitted. "But there is no one here save ourselves, the sky, and the sea. No lords or gods, so justice falls to our own hands."

Kayo's hand trembled as she reached for Mitsuhide's katana. Her fingers closed around the wooden lacquered *saya*, but she did not take it from Yukiko.

"Why?" she asked, and for the first time her voice sounded thick with unsaid feelings. "Why choose mercy, Yukiko-san?"

Yukiko looked up at the older woman. Her eyes, grey as the stormy sea, bored into Kayo's, which were as dark as the ocean's depths.

"Because," Yukiko said, her voice scarcely more than a whisper above the crashing waves, "I know what it is to have a child taken from me, Kayo-san."

Kayo bit her lip and nodded. She took the sheathed katana from Yukiko's hands slowly, almost reverentially. She stared at it for a long moment, as though testing the weight of the sword.

Then she turned and hurled it into the sea.

Yukiko watched the katana flip end over end as it tumbled through the air, landing with a noiseless splash before sinking beneath the waves. Kayo turned back to Yukiko, and this time there was no mistaking the tears that ran down her cheeks.

"There," she said, and for the first time Yukiko thought she looked her age. "May his spirit lie with it on the seabed, and trouble us no more."

Yukiko nodded, and pulled the second of Mitsuhide's swords from her obi. "And his wakizashi?"

Kayo reached for it, the same vindictive light in her eyes. Her hand wrapped around the shorter sword, but Yukiko did not release her grip.

"May I offer a suggestion?"

Kayo jerked her head in a brusque nod. "You may."

"Keep it," Yukiko said. "Hide it away in one of those caves and coves you mentioned. When Shingo comes of age, give it to him."

Kayo's grip on the wakizashi tightened. "You would have him take up his father's mantle?"

"I would have him choose his own destiny," Yukiko said. "He is a son of the Ama, a boy among women. And he is the bastard child of a samurai, born to a commoner. He will never truly belong to either world."

Kayo's gaze softened. She took the wakizashi in both hands and clasped it to her breast.

"I will do as you say," she said, her gaze shifting from Yukiko to the distant line of breakers. "A man cannot walk two paths. It should be his choice which one to follow."

"Hai." Yukiko bowed her head. "On that we are agreed."

She stood, shaking water droplets from her sleeves. She suddenly felt very tired, and in need of a warm bath.

"Wait," Kayo said, grabbing her by the arm. "I have something for you as well, Yukiko-san."

Yukiko startled at the contact, her hand dropping instinctively to her wakizashi. Kayo released her, a wry smile tightening the corner of her lips.

"A token of thanks," she said, crouching and setting Mitsuhide's wakizashi on the rocks beside her. She pulled out her knife and pried open the clamshell. A look of triumph graced the Ama woman's face as she stood and held out her hand.

Resting in her palm was a single smooth, perfectly round black pearl.

"I cannot—" Yukiko began, but before she could protest further Kayo had pressed the pearl into her hand.

"Please," she said, and a true smile crossed her face. "You have set my daughter's spirit to rest, avenged her killer, and given my grandson a future. Allow me to give you this in thanks."

Yukiko nodded, her hands closing around the pearl. "Thank you, Kayo-san."

Kayo's smile widened. "My girls call me okaa-san, Yukiko-chan."

Yukiko suddenly found it hard to speak. Was Kayo saying what she thought she was?

"There could be a place for you here," Kayo said, correctly reading the expression on Yukiko's face. "The nure-onna is not the only dark thing that lurks beneath the waves. Your blades would find work along our shore, and we are always glad to have another sister join our ranks."

"I . . ." Yukiko closed her eyes. It had been so long since she had a home. A family.

Izumi . . .

"No." She shook her head and opened her eyes, fixing her gaze on the distant shore. "I am glad I could set your daughter's spirit at peace, Kayo-san. That I could avenge her against the one who killed her."

She turned to look Kayo in the eyes. "But I cannot rest until I have done the same for my own daughter."

"I understand." Kayo nodded slowly. "Take the pearl, then. May it bring you luck in your travels. And know that wherever you go, my prayers and blessings will follow."

Yukiko nodded, unable to speak. On impulse, she leaned down and kissed the older woman on the forehead. Kayo's brow was slick and wet.

Yukiko turned and headed towards shore promontory, picking her way carefully over the rocks. Saltwater trickled down her face, and she tried to tell herself it was only the rain.

Number Hunnerd

Joel McKay

HE CALLED IT Ace of Spades Lake because it had rainbows in it as perfect as his wife Mary's thighs. I don't know about that, but then again, I never believed half of what Bert said. And I still don't believe that lake even exists. I've never seen it and I've been fishing up these parts since Bennett was calling the shots in Victoria—the first one.

Anyway, old Bertie used to say it was up in the Cariboos east of town. No, I know what you're thinking, he must've meant Jack O' Clubs Lake. Well, I never heard a jack of clubs called the finest of anything anywhere and anyway that ain't it. I've fished that damn pond a dozen times and never caught nothing worth mentioning. I think it's because of the mine waste in there, but anyway that's not what you asked about it, is it?

Ace of Spades Lake is supposed to be somewhere off the Barkerville Highway. You've got to take the 2500 Road, head up a ways, then turn at the fork onto the Dilly Dally Road and head east. I forget the rest. Don't matter, right? Ain't real anyway. Just a Bert story, and he told some whoppers in his day. I guess it makes sense he'd go out like that, come to think of it.

Anyway, old Bert took Bob Drummond with him that day. Now, before I go any further you got to know I heard this story from Gordie Jones, who heard it from Harry Tubbs, who got it straight from the mouth of Bob Drummond one night drinking down at the Billy. Way I heard it, Bert and Bob took the old twelve-footer out that way late May to catch one of them perfect trout and lord it over the guys back in town. You see, that's a good time of year to fish out that way—a week or so after the ice comes off the lake, before the water turns and gets murky. But it's bush country and hard to shore fish. You need a boat and the road is narrow, or so says Gordie who heard it from Harry who . . . well, you get the picture.

Bert and Bob played hooky from the mill and made their way out there before the sun was up. The way Gordie tells is, they were launching the boat right when the sun came up. Now, that part of the story I don't buy. I know how long it takes to get out there and the last week of May the sun is up before 5 a.m. You're telling me they left town at two thirty in the morning? Hell, Bert hardly ever got to bed that early when he was tossing a few back, which I understand to be the case on account of the bottle of rye Gina Owens down at the liquor store sold him the night before.

So sometime after sunup they hit Ace of Spades. Bob said he trolled an Adams that morning. Apparently, Bert had on a Woolly Bugger. Now, I don't know how in hell you'd be able to catch anything using those patterns at that time of year, but the way they tell it they were slaying seven- and eight-pound rainbows all day. Let me say that again. Seven. And. Eight. Pounds. In a little mountain lake. I mean, is any of this believable? Not hardly, but the best stories are that way, aren't they?

So, all morning they can't keep the fish off the fly. At lunch, midafternoon or so, they go ashore and take a break. I'm guessing that bottle of rye found its way out there because things got weird after that.

For whatever reason, they started trolling with four fly rods. Now, think about that a moment. A twelve-footer on a little mountain lake and *four* rods? How does that work? You'd be tangling things up like a polygamist on Mother's Day. But Bob says they wanted to hit the fabled "hunnerd fish" day. My guess is they were getting close because Bob says they went late that night, right into the evening. At dinner, Bert told Bob he wanted to go out for one more hour, just until dusk.

"We're at eighty-six, Bob, eighty-six!" he says. "Can't let it lie.

Got to get the number. This is the day, Bob, the day."

Bob told him to head out on his own, on account of his ass hurting like a jockey's after the Kentucky Derby from sitting in that tin can for fifteen hours. So, Bob decides to shore fish, even though really, he's just draining that bottle of rye.

Bert, meantime, heads back out and, so the story goes, he keeps fishing and the lake gave up the best of the day right at the end there. He had double-hitters, a triple-hitter, and even a quadruple-hitter. Bob says at one point he had all four rods in hand, was fighting two big rainbows, a kokanee, and a dolly. I don't know how Bob knew what kind of fish were on Bert's lines from shore, but that's the way he tells it so that's the way you gonna hear it. So, Bert's battling these four fish like a Swiss Army Knife in the canned goods aisle and calling out numbers at Bob from across Ace of Spades.

"Ninety-five! Ninety-six! Ninety-seven! Ninety-*eight*!"

He lands the fish and hollers at Bob that they're two away from an even hunnerd. Bob told Harry he got number ninety-nine just using a little green nymph from shore. I guess it was small because whenever I ask him about it, he just shrugs and keeps talking about Bert.

But anyway, he calls back to Bert, "Ninety-*nine*!"

Bert is standing in the boat at this point, all four lines drifting in the water, eyes scanning for number hunnerd. Then everything goes still. The wind stops. The birds stop chirping. The bugs stop buzzing. Even Bob stood still and kept his mouth shut, an amazing thing if you know the man. And then Bert's first rod curls over.

"Fish on!" Bert yells across the lake.

Bob cheers.

Bert picks up the rod. Then *bang*! —rod number two. He picks that one up. *Bang!* Rod three. *Bang*! Rod four. All of them curled over like a sailor's willy after shore leave.

Now, Bert was an accomplished angler. He knew the waters in these parts as good as any and could work a rod like a whore with bills to pay. But whatever he got hold of on Ace of Spades was better than him. Then the first rod snapped in two like a matchstick. Bert was jerked forward, almost falling out of the boat.

"Siddown! Siddown!" Bob's yelling at him from the shore.

Rod two—*snap!*

The boat rocks. Bert lets go and his prized four-piece five-weight is swallowed up in the drink. He almost follows it in.

"Siddown, ya' fuckin' moron!" Bob's yelling from shore.

Rod three—*snap!*

At this point, old Bert's down to his Orvis two-piece, the one he got from his dad a ways back. Now he's standing in the boat leaning back on his heels, this thing's pulling so strong, Bob says. Apparently, the fish is darting around under there so good the boat is doing figure-eights on the water, kicking up a hell of a wake too, so says Bob. Now, remember, at this point we don't know what Bert's got hold of—is it a giant rainbow? A dolly? An old mining tire? No clue, but it's snapped three rods and is jerking Bert around Ace of Spades like a five-year-old playing helicopter with a chihuahua on a twine leash.

Bert's patient though, right? He knows this thing can snap a rod so he just waits, lets it play out a bit, then reels, plays it out, then reels, like this, yeah? From shore Bob says he can start seeing this dark shadow beneath the boat as Bert's reeling in. But that never added up for me. It's dusk at this point, and you're telling me Coke-Bottle-Glasses Bob can see a shadow under the boat from two-hunnerd feet away? Nah.

Bert gives it one last yank and the water around the boat starts to bubble. The rod gives way—dunno why, Bob never said. Bert stumbles back and goes over into the drink in a splash. Bob says he's immediately worried because Bert had his big boots on and no life jacket. How do you think Mary felt when she heard that part?

But Bert pops up like a cork in a bathtub, splattering and cursing like a gull on garbage day. The boat's still floating at this point so Bob tells him to climb back in and make for shore. Bert spots the rod in the boat. Somehow it's still in that tin can and still got that fish on it. So, he claws his way into the boat from the stern, climbing up like some slippery seal, Bob says. He gets in soaking wet, practically dark at this point. He grabs that rod and presses on with the fight.

He's grunting and reeling and yanking back, giving what he needs to and then reeling and yanking again. The water starts to bubble, the boat is rocking back and forth like it's on a geyser about to erupt like a cock on Christmas morning.

Rod four—*snap*!

The damn thing snakes out of his hand and shoots across the lake like a missile, dropping in the water some seventy feet away, as Bob tells it. Bert's left standing there, stomping his feet, the boat rocking back and forth, he's cursing so loud they can hear him back in Quesnel, Harry says.

Bob's on shore hollering for him to come back in so they can get home. Bert wants number one-hunnerd though, so he's just fuming at this point. Then, just as the last of the daylight drops away, the lake starts bubbling again. I guess old Ace of Spades had one more up its sleeve, eh? Except this time the bubbling is all over, like the whole lake is at a rolling boil.

Bert sits down and starts rowing back. Bob says he's never seen him look more scared. He starts yelling at Bob from across the lake, this look of sheer terror on his face.

"I woke something up! Fuck! I woke something up!" His ropey arms work the oars like a traffic cop writing tickets at month end.

He's about halfway back, Bob says, when something starts to rise out of the water. At first it just looks like a big round rock, I'm talking a huge rock. You know the gold pan you saw on your way into town? Yeah, twice the size around as that.

Except it's not a rock, it's all purple, shiny and mottled like an octopus or something. Then it opens its eyes. Two big round orbs black as coal. It's got a stout lump for a nose and then a big fish mouth that stretches round its head like someone cut its smile wider than it should be.

Then there's big shoulders as wide as an eighteen-wheeler is long and arms thick as a Doug fir. Big pulsing gills on its neck and up and down its rib cage. No shit. I know. But this is what you asked about, yeah? This is the way Bob told it to Harry who told it to Gordie who told it to me.

Anyway, this big Fish Man rises out of Ace of Spades and stares down at old Bert in his tin boat like a randy priest at an altar boy convention. Bert keeps on rowing anyway, his eyes fixed on that Fish Man towering over him. And you know what Bob says?

I shit you not, Bob says, "Try talking to it! Tell it it's all just a big misunderstanding!"

Bert keeps rowing in spite of Bob's hollering. He's three-quarters back when the Fish Man turns its charcoal eyes on old

Ninety-Nine Fish Bert and decides number hunnerd gonna be something on top of the lake for once. Fish Man, you see, he's got hands like you and me.

No, I'm serious. That's how Bob tells it.

He raises one of these hands, makes a fist, and swings it down at Bert and that tin boat. Now, I bet you want to hear that Bert acted quick, leapt out of the way in the nick of time, and swam to shore, and he's here tonight! Gonna come out behind that bar any second and join us.

But no, that ain't the way it went. You see, Bert wasn't ever gonna leave that lake until he got number hunnerd. He'd made up his mind on that point, even if it meant fishing through the dark, which isn't strictly legal. Mind you, some guys do it on the backslide and we don't make much fuss.

Anyway, when Fish Man's fist come down on him, Bert stood up and raised his hands like he was praying to some god. Fish Man's fist slammed into the boat and crushed Bert in one go and the boat with it. Bob says neither came up.

After they went under the water, Fish Man just looked at old Bob on the shoreline and waited for him to reel in. When he had, Fish Man sat back down in that water careful as a lawyer at confessional until Ace of Spades swallowed him up again.

Bob says he passed out then, didn't wake up until morning, and then drove the whole way back by himself. Now, I ain't seen Bob in five years, and neither's Gordie or Harry or anybody else. But after the Number Hunnerd Day at Ace of Spades I heard the Mounties started looking into Bob. Damn near charged him with Bert's murder.

If you go talk to the detachment commander off the record, he'll tell you Bob was shacking up with Mary and she put him up to it. He punched a hole in that boat, knocked Bert unconscious, and then swam for shore, waited until morning when his clothes were dry, and then drove back to town with that fish story—or so the police'll say, though they never found enough evidence to charge him with it.

But you know what? And I bet this is why you're here asking me—the detachment commander is about as smart as a Frenchman in a fight. Sometime after Bert went missing, the Mounties sent up a special dive unit to go into that lake and poke around for Bert. Bob told Harry that he had to show the divers the way up to Ace of Spades because it ain't on any map. No shit, right?

When they got there, the dive team went in and scoured the lake. They didn't find Bert or the Fish Man, but they did find a boat. A twelve-foot aluminium Lund just like Bert had, except it was all busted up and bent in half like a bit of tin foil crumpled in a ball. Divers told Bob the only way that was possible was if someone had dropped that boat clear off the top of the CN Tower. Then, maybe, it would've crumpled up like that.

What do I think? Well, for starters I don't think Bert and Bob were yanking seven and eight-pound rainbows out of that lake in late May. And I ain't never heard of Ace of Spades Lake since. And the part about Bob being a murderer? Well, Bob ain't no murderer. He loved Bert like a brother. He only took up with Mary after Bert was at the bottom of that lake, and more out of guilt than anything else, I think.

Way I figure it, if that lake does exist, and that's a big *if*, then I think there was a Fish Man in it. Maybe still is. And after this many years I think I figured out what Bert was doing when he reached up toward Fish Man on Ace of Spades Lake. He wasn't praying for mercy like Bob says. No, he was trying to catch that fish. Number hunnerd. The Ace of Spades. Even better than ol' Mary's thighs.

Well, that's my story. You gonna buy me that drink now?

Amphitrite Finds A Confidante

Elizabeth R. McClellan

I wait for a foggy night, air so thick
with ocean some gills would come in handy.
I walk out on the jetty, and wait until
she elbows up on the waiting rock,

arms strong from swimming since
nearly the beginning of the world.
Draped in kelp and loose plastic,
she hides herself, and her holy beauty.

"The thing you have to understand,"
she says, tossing spray from her
waterlogged hair, "is I could never fit in.
They married mostly among themselves,

except my husband, and the spring girls."
She is not foolish; she will say no names
here at the border of her husband's fief.
"You can't compete. I couldn't compete.

Just a nymph really, the kind you knock up
and never think of again unless your wife
finds out. They make fun of him, marrying
for love, and not for greater power, stare

down their mountain-high noses at us.
I don't think they know how deep the
depths truly are, deeper than any hill
capped with snow and snobs." Under

the detritus her skin is mother of pearl,
her scales are dark opals, her hair wine
and sea. "And yes, my husband cheats;
men take liberties, since before my time.

The harvest daughter only is spared.
I cannot fix something when the queen of all
cannot even stem the tide. Still, we are happy,
among the creatures only we know and

the cracks in the ocean floor that descend
almost to Hades. He brings me every
beautiful thing, Roman bronze and stone
from India, and steel now, jewels and

lost things. The nereids do not judge
and have proper manners when they come
to dine. The orca sing symphonies for
me alone." I can see them, out of place

but reverently attending, patches of black
occasionally leaping out in the deep.
"It's never among equals. My oceanid
sisters know I married up; my husband,

who pushes continents and calves glaciers,
married down. So I talk to you, witch,
since witches live in the in between of humans."
"It is true," I say, and set a wheel of cheese,

well-waxed, to float toward her. She smiles
her fearsome smile of sharp teeth, catches it.
"Thank you. By the time we find it, it's
usually ruined. Could you live without it?"

The question surprises me. "I suppose?
If I had to." She tears a hunk of it and chews.
"There is usually a witch of the undersea,
who used to hear my discontent, between

spinning spells in the ocean dark and
bargaining with drowning sailors. The job
is open, and under my special protection:
the sea needs its witch as its gods and

he knows better than to enrage me, when
I am the calm to his storm. Would you go
and live below, like a water nymph, breathe
salt water and write by anglerfish light?"

"My parents," I say, and hate myself, but
she is smiling, all terrible teeth and joy,
twists, plucks twelve pearls from the mass
of crustaceans that encrust her tail.

"Will think you drowned, and live better
off twelve pearls than off a witch child
unlikely to marry or enchant a modern kingdom.
Is it a fair trade? Power, and pearls, every

hidden thing below the water?" I nod,
breathless, already. "Then come."
I swim out to the rock, clothes bearing
me down, until her arms pull me up,

knot the pearls in the fabrics I'm shedding
despite the cold, and push me back
into the depth, where I gulp water and
realize it will not harm me, where I see

my great body, sleek and patchy like the orca
who surround me and bear me up as
we watch our queen slide into her domain,
shedding disguise, scintillating despite

the fog obscuring the moon, and I taste air
one last time for always, feel a new power
burning in me as I follow her deeper, orca
finally leaving us, gathering a bevy

of following fish attendants, the nereids,
oceanids rising up to meet us, caressing
my changed face, draping me in jewels
and tiny crabs, twisting and knotting my

hair as we descend deeper into darkness,
hearing the sounds of whales and dolphins
and souls lost at sea, my tail powerful
and my teeth sharp as I swim for my promised place.

In the Arms of Oceana

Eric M. Bosarge

THE WAVES ROLLING ashore sounded like a man on the cusp of snoring. She lay at the high tide line where crisp, dry tendrils of seaweed formed a chain, the sun welding her to the hot sand as though she were melting to glass, becoming one with the silica and fragments of old shells and bone.

"How long will I have to stay here?" she asked, wishing it could be forever, that this summer day, this scorching sun, would last.

They scooped more wet, hot sand on her. It tickled and itched but she didn't move. "Until you become beautiful," they said, patting the sand with their shovels.

How many ancestors had been buried like this? Fish along the shore, rolling over and over in the surf, their bodies gently eroded by the friction of their scales against the seafloor and the foamy swath that pulled them deeper before tossing them ever higher. Constantly cast aside and reclaimed. Pieces of flesh torn by each interaction.

Seagulls swept overhead, causing the sun to flash and redouble its efforts to cook her skin, as though it wished to peel the flaky crust away.

She felt herself slipping into the sand with the crash of each wave, each impact on the beach a platform lowering, descending into fathomless abyss.

All of her ancestors were buried here, she realized, feeling the sea creep up from the sand, this most refined earth, to taste her skin with its salty tongue.

Grandfather told her not to slouch, and her head leaned back into the sand.

She tried to lift her legs, but the sand was too heavy. Another scoop fell onto her upper thigh. Then another. The soft pat of plastic shovels and giggles. The whistle of a Nerf football that made her think of when she was a cheerleader, how she'd spent hours teasing her hair and turning about in the mirror, memorizing and critiquing every curve of her body, the sparkle of her dress, practicing pouts and flirty smiles. Wondering if she would be what they wanted her to be, while hanging like a mist about her the question: can I ever see myself the way I want to be seen?

She remembered how all the boys at the party looked at her though, covering their faces with drinks as she passed as though to shield their fangs from view. She remembered how she had taken Charlie's hand as he led her up narrow stairs with a white wrought iron handrail that should have been unpainted and rusted somewhere outside, a church, perhaps, and how she was unsettled by its smooth surface, by the way Charlie reached inside her blouse and asked if she loved him while he squeezed her breast so hard she almost cried out in pain and pleasure. Yes, she said, the swirl of alcohol sloshing in her veins, tossing her head about as he ran his hand up the nape of her neck, pushing her hair high as his teeth caught on her lower lip. "If you love me, you'll do this for me," Charlie said, his words the only echoing sound of a night that lived in infamy.

She felt another pair of hands on her body, more touching, slipping beneath her dress, snatching pieces of her, and she was wet and they felt good and every part of her wanted to be filled up until she realized she was not steering the ship, not the captain, but a passenger, something in the cargo hold dredged up and thrown on the deck for the crew to inspect.

"I don't know," she said, shrinking lower because there was nowhere to go, the legs like pillars, like bars.

"These are my friends," Charlie said. "I want this for you. I love you."

More sand fell on her thigh and she shut her eyes tight. The sound of the waves was closer, moving like a colossus loping along the shore.

"You will make a great fish," they said, and dumped more sand on her. She thought of fish off-shore, following the tides and feeding among the flotsam and jetsam, themselves in turn being preyed upon by larger fish. Was she being buried alive, or was she a stone constantly bumping up against sharp sand, rough edges being worn smooth, perfected?

Her husband took her hand at the altar and with those fathomless oceanic eyes, deep as the great blue, as dark in the centre as a black hole, told her that he loved her. Told her she was his safe place, that he would be her biggest fan, no matter what, then cleared his throat when she opened the freezer to look at the ice cream, or heard the cellophane crinkle of a Dove Chocolate, his eyes never leaving his tablet as he swiped through the news, the stock report, whatever it was that was more important than her. At night he would search for her with his body, a soft palm at first, then fingers, probing, gripping, pulling her into him like a spider wrapping up a fly in his arms. His mouth found the soft flesh on her neck. His fingers pushed at the base of her spine as she arched her hips to him, pulling him deep, unsure of who was taking what from whom, who wanted violence, who sought collision, who took the bit of soul from the other's little death as power. Unsure until many uncomfortable days and long, uncomfortable nights of turning from side to side, feeling tossed by the hands of Charlie's friends as he gave her away, but this time the weight in her stomach forcing her to oscillate, to rotisserie, to burn with discomfort as something grew inside. And then the pain came. So sharp and hard, the weight of this *thing* that her husband had pressed into her over and over again had grown to something she was told she should already love, that she should have feelings for, that she should be enamoured with from the first flutter of ultrasonic heartbeat. She worried that there was something wrong with her, so she pushed harder when it was time, eagerly leaning into the pain because perhaps it would cleanse her, tear something from her that many men had tried to put in her soul. And then, sweet relief, she heard a cry and saw the pink flesh, the vernix like sea foam on his small, hairy head, and she laughed. It was here.

He. He was here.

Her husband held him first, smiling down with pride and joy as though it were something he did, something he suffered for, then he set him atop his bride gently, and she felt the weight of him, already rooting, looking to take something from her; milk. The life she had to give.

More sand fell, this time on her hips.

"Isn't that enough?"

"Mermaids don't have hips. Or if they do, they are under their . . . skin."

"Scales," she said in a whisper.

"Yes, you need scales," they said, dumping more sand on top of her.

She felt the long nights still, cries weighing her down, not rocking the baby so much as lifting the baby over and over; the weight made her skin sag in the mirror. Her breasts ballooned up again and again, both her boy and husband coming for her nipples with open mouths to take the life-giving milk from her. Her body wasn't her own anymore. It was something desired by everyone close to her.

"Scales," she whispered again, feeling the pain of getting on the scale and peering down over the saggy belly that had been broken into. That had been broken out of. That wouldn't become what it once was no matter how many crunches she did or how often she opened the freezer and only looked at the ice cream until her husband grunted.

The ocean whispered, breathing on her. The tide was rising. She felt it between the sand in every crevice, taking her, but not like a man. Like a woman. Like a mother, holding her close.

Small hands began to form in the sand, now the weight of long years of struggle, of sleepless nights treated by too short therapy sessions where stories she'd never thought she needed to tell tumbled from her lips like magazine clippings; dresses she'd wanted to wear and women she'd wanted be, to slip into their skin, falling to the floor about her feet.

The hands fashioned her new skin; armour.

The ocean came like a mother, searching, stretching for her, the moon dragging it further up the beach in celestial solidarity. They were here. Every ancient mother's legacy far beyond the surface, rooted as coral reef and just as sharp, as daunting, as fierce, to any foolhardy enough to think they could trespass without paying but ready to shelter all.

The seaweed wrapped itself around her wrists, shackling her in place as the water touched the edges of the sand, the weight, others had placed upon her, and washed it away.

We must leave you now, they said, and her breath caught, as the high tide found her toes and ankles, using its gentle force to soften her edges, to leave only the hardest, most worn, most beautiful parts exposed as a warning, not as ornament, and she slid into the sea.

Depth Charge

Laura VanArendonk Baugh

U-33 WAS A very busy lass, and certainly no lady. On 20 November 1940, she sank three steam trawlers off Northern Ireland: one in the morning, one in the late afternoon, and one in the early evening. By eight thirty the next morning she was shelling another trawler, the *Sulby*, sinking her in under two minutes. The *Sulby* crew had a clear view of the German commander laughing at them as they scrambled into two lifeboats and choice seats as, one hour later, the U-boat sank the *William Humphries*. That crew of thirteen shared a single lifeboat, according to the *Sulby* survivors picked up the next day. But the boat from the *William Humphries*, and the second from the *Sulby*, were never found.

Two bodies eventually washed ashore from the *William Humphries*. Neither was my bridegroom's.

I was living north of Glasgow, not far from where the *William Humphries* went down. My people were from the northeast, but I had come to the city when the war demanded more workers. I lived now in a boarding house for unattached ladies, and I worked at the shipyard.

The John Brown & Company shipyard was quite the largest fish in the Firth of Clyde. The yard had produced destroyers for the Great War and then liners such as RMS *Queen Mary* and RMS *Queen Elizabeth*, and now was building ships for the new war. Landing there was a plum for me, and life would have been fine if not for the new war. And Caelan's death.

I was called from my typewriter on a grey January day. "Someone to see you," Mr. Atcheson said. "Said he'd wait outside. In the cold, I suppose."

"Who?"

He shook his head. "Haven't the slightest. Ministry of something or other, though, by the looks of him."

The stranger looking over the firth did appear like a government man, all dark suit and low hat. He had an overcoat against the January weather and aviator glasses despite the grey overcast. He turned their smoked lenses on me as I approached. "Miss Tennent?"

"Yes?"

He didn't introduce himself. "I'd like to speak to you about something a little unusual."

I had heard worse lines in the Glasgow pubs. "Go ahead, then."

"Miss Tennent, the John Brown and Company shipyard is critical to the welfare of the United Kingdom. The confluence of the Clyde River and other waters make this an ideal building and launching site, with ships sailing away into the firth—"

"I am sure you have a good purpose in explaining the significance of this shipyard to one employed here," I interrupted, "but my tea break is short, and we're standing in the wind, and perhaps you'd better skip ahead."

For just an instant he was offended, visible in a tightening of his mouth below the impenetrable glasses, but then he nodded. "I apologize. I am accustomed to a sidelong approach for rather more resistant audiences."

That mild apology helped. "What's the unusual topic, then? What do you expect me to be resistant to?"

"We're looking for someone with special talents to recruit into a new program. That's why I came to speak with you."

I laughed aloud. "Special talents? I'm a typist in a pool, Mr.—?"

He did not offer his name. "Miss Tennent, you come from a distinguished line."

"I come from a village whose name you probably couldn't pronounce, in the hills along a sleepy loch."

"Your given name is Dierdre. Is that for the fabled Deirdre of the Sorrows?"

Oh, the arrogant ignorance of the English. I was named for Dundbhairdghall, or Dùn Deardail for less agile tongues, an Iron Age fort not far from where I was born. "Deirdre of the Sorrows was an Irish princess."

"Ah, but your family was Irish before they were Scottish."

This was true; at its narrowest the sea puts only twelve miles between the coasts, and we were hardly the only line to have crossed it. "That's so, though I'm not sure why that should—"

"Your mother was a descendant of Niall of the Nine Hostages."

That caught my attention. Niall Noígíallach wasn't a casual reference for a Sassenach. It was also true. Still, I didn't know what he was getting at.

"She came of the same descending line as Colmcille, if I'm not mistaken."

He did not say it with the possibility that he might be mistaken. And this was a disturbing amount of family knowledge, tracing my lineage to the sixth century and to a saint. "We've barely discussed it."

"Your family still lives along the loch."

"And why should we move from where we have resided for hundreds of years? Where should we be, if not there?"

He raised his hands in a gesture of peace. "I only mean to say, you inherit a considerable history."

"And a lot of good it's done me, as you can see by my place as a typist in Clydebank and my address at a boarding house."

"It could do some good for the United Kingdom." He tipped his head forward, his unseen eyes fixed on me, reaching for some connection I was not willing to offer.

I regarded him suspiciously. "If you're encouraging for the war effort, I'm already employed at a shipyard."

"Anyone can type. I've come to you for other skills."

Something stirred deep in my mind, a hereditary fear of torches and pitchforks and iron nails. For a moment, my mind ran wild with family stories and tales of tragedy.

"So, if you could see—"

"I have quite a stack of typing to do," I said abruptly, "and I'd best get back to it."

He looked at me for a moment. "I'll be staying on in Clydebank for a week or two, if you should care to hear—"

"I'm not likely to." I turned and walked back inside.

THERE WAS A new girl at the boarding house, who had come up from Bath and was struggling with the foreign culture.

"Near Inverness then?" she asked me, trying to ascertain where I was from. We were in the sitting room, near the radiator.

"No, but not too far."

"But it's Inverness that I can pronounce," she laughed. "I haven't the tongue for anything bolder. But I can manage Inverness. Inverness."

"*Inbhir Ness*, the mouth of the Ness River."

"In the Scots."

Inbhir was, yes. I did not mention that *Ness* came by way of a much older word. Many scholars thought *nesta*, the roaring one, referred to the river itself and its short descent to the sea.

Scholars.

But if the Scots have learned one thing, it's to choose their fights with the English, and so I changed the subject. "There was a man up from London today, visiting the shipyard. He didn't say he was from the government but I'm certain—"

"So have you seen the monster?"

I suppressed a sigh. A few years ago, the world went mad with Loch Ness fever, beginning with an innkeeper's report of something like a whale and then rapidly gaining steam when a couple claimed to see a dragon or prehistoric beast crossing the road in front of their automobile. That prompted a mad dash for more sightings, modern and historical, and soon all sorts of collaborating reports were discovered, modified, or created from whole cloth. Newspapers and gossipers were mad for news of the creature of Loch Ness.

"Which monster?" I asked innocently. "I don't think there was much said on the monsters of Loch Lochy, Loch Quioch, Loch Oich, Loch Sheil, Loch Arkaig, or any of the other local legends." Nor had anyone seemed to note that the sightings of 1933 had described the creatures of the new *King Kong* motion picture more nearly than local traditions.

"So many?" she gasped. "Is there a whole race of monsters, then?"

"Or a whole race of stories, at least," I said, enjoying the slow disappointment on her face. I'd had enough of tourists tramping over our roads and hills, expecting footprints and beasts and never bothering to ask if they could pay for the gate they'd knocked down trying to turn a hired car in a narrow lane. Nor was I particularly keen on questions about water monsters to be hunted.

"Dierdre, aren't you coming?" came a voice from the hall.

I leapt up from my place, embarrassed at my absent-mindedness. "I am!"

I never missed church, not Sunday service and not midweek. A soul came with obligations, and I understood the old nature better than most.

THE BANGING AT my door woke me; I hadn't been asleep long enough to be fully invulnerable. "What?" I mumbled, feeling for the light.

"There's a gentleman here for you. Says it's important, very urgent. Something to do with the shipyard."

I squinted at my alarm clock. It was only just past midnight. "What?"

"He looks important. All ministerial. And he's wearing smoked glasses at night."

That woke me fully. This was not recruitment, this was invasion of my personal life—or a threat. I rolled out of bed and drew a dressing gown around me. I opened the door to Mrs. Hedden wringing her hands but with a rabidly curious glint in her eye, and she followed me as I stalked down the stairs.

He was on the far side of the room from the radiator, examining framed pictures on the parlour wall. "Mr. Whoever you might be," I snapped, "this is my residence, not my office, and you have—"

"You'll want warm clothes," he said, turning. "It will be cold on the water."

I stared at him, caught despite myself. "And why would I be going on out the water instead of back to my warm bed?"

He looked past me, and I felt Mrs. Hedden close behind me. I stepped nearer, resentful but too well trained in cues for clandestine talk. "Well?"

"A U-boat was sighted, coming south along Islay. We expect it will be making for the firth."

"And—"

"It is the *U-33*."

For just an instant my blood was replaced with icy seawater, and siren screams rang in my ears, and then I shook my head and all was dispelled. "I don't know what you expect me to do about it."

"Just come with me. At the least, you might see vengeance done."

And there he had me. Whatever other pressures of civic duty and love of country he might try to lay upon me, they could not compete with the ancient demands of blood answered. If ever I were to meet Niall Noígíallach in some crossing of afterlife, I would need to be able to face him. Even Colmcille the saint had known the obligations of family in war.

"I'll be but a moment," I said.

He had a car and driver waiting—of course he did—and we were whisked at speed to the water, where we boarded a boat which ferried us out to the HMS *Gleaner*. I put her between 800 and 900 tons. She was a minesweeper, I soon learned, and a submarine hunter.

The sea was rough. There had been a gale all the day, undoubtedly worse out upon the Atlantic. If the *U-33* had made her way down and around Arran, she must have had a time of it.

Good.

The sailors of the *Gleaner* were not enjoying the trip, either. To be perfectly honest, I was starting to feel the effects myself. The Atlantic is a harsh mistress.

"Sir," an officer addressed my companion, "we are endeavouring to reestablish sonar contact with the target. We believe we are not far."

I went to the rail and looked out into the windy black. I was grateful for every woollen layer I'd added; the wind would eventually start to draw the warmth out of me.

We patrolled. Without task or assignment, I found a place as out of the way as anything can be on an efficient ship and huddled out of the wind.

I had not been on the firth since Caelan had. I had not been on the water at all, actually, not since we had gone out on the loch together, our last outing before I came down to Glasgow and he had taken his place on the trawler. I had dangled my feet to paddle, explaining that week's sermon, and he had rowed and made a foundered joke about living water and laughed and laughed, and we had been happy.

U-33 had taken that from us. *U-33* had taken that from hundreds of families. I hated *U-33* as a beast herself. We were called to forgive men who wronged us, but she was an entity of her own.

"Action stations!"

It was shortly before 3 a.m. The crew of the *Gleaner* scrambled with frantic precision to ready the four-inch guns and the depth charge launchers. I caught my breath, held unnaturally long in the rolling suspense.

"Lost her," someone mumbled, and the crew slumped with released tension. Now would be another long period of sweeping for a sonar signal, while below us *U-33* rolled in the deep and cowered.

Or rose to torpedo or shell us.

I shoved my gloved hands back into my pockets and went to the railing, staying out of the sailors' way. The searchlight was sweeping the surface, hoping to catch a glimpse of the submarine as it rose to air its diesel engine and recharge its battery, possibly depleted after its long run.

I closed my eyes against the glare and let the wind and spray slap my skin. It felt good to be on the water again, even if it was salt, even if it was without Caelan. It felt good to sense the depths beneath me, the wide void that was not void, the immense pressure waiting to swallow us should the *Gleaner*'s hull be breeched by a torpedo from that evil submarine, the hungry dark that might crush the *U-33* herself if a well-placed depth charge gave it the chance—

There.

I felt the beast in the way I could feel a passing whale, but this was no gentle behemoth. This was metallic, oily, wrong.

Wrong.

I caught my breath to shout—though how I would have explained my knowledge, I have no idea—but the crew of the *Gleaner* was alerted in the same moment, the sonar operator newly fixed on the target. The powerful searchlight swung according to instruction and there in the waves and spray, the light gleamed on a periscope and its curved wake.

The *Gleaner* swung to starboard in pursuit, and my heart pounded like I was swimming after her myself. The periscope vanished beneath the surface, but I felt no disappointment. A fish can flee, but a hunter can pursue.

I paid no attention to the orders given around me. I was caught in the chase, my eyes half closed against the wind, my ears hearing music in the crash of waves.

Dead on top of her.

Depth charges were released, and I counted them in succession. One. Two. Three. Four.

There was nothing.

Sonar was lost with the explosions, and my own sense was equally disrupted. For long minutes, we knew nothing.

"What do you think?"

He had come to stand beside me, bundled against the weather, a muffler pulled closed to his smoked glasses. "You might take the glasses off," I said. "I cannot imagine it is too bright for you here."

It was difficult to read his expression, all of it behind dark glasses and muffler, but after a long moment, he raised a gloved hand to pull both down. In the slanting glare of the deck lights I had a quick glimpse of hazel-orange irises with curiously narrow pupils even in the dark.

He was something like us. Not one of us, but something like us.

He replaced the concealing glasses. "What do you think of hunting for submarines?"

I could not admit that I was thrilling to the wind and wave and chase. That was only my own joy in being on the water again. "I hope we find her."

"And?"

"Well, capturing her would be a fitting succession."

I fought the deeper, darker joy that quivered far below my own surface. It was not right. Caelan had been the last, the first, to whom I had opened that secret box. We were oh, so cautious of whom we admitted to our family knowledge. Sharing it with Caelan had made him a part of me even before our marriage. Opening that box without him tore a scab from an unhealed wound and even more, felt like a second betrayal.

I could have saved him, if I had been near the *William*

Humphries.

I had hardly admitted that to myself. He had not died across the country. He had died in the same water which touched Clydebank.

And now the submarine which had killed him had returned to hunt more ships and to lay mines for when she slept safely away.

Something shifted in me, something deep and glistening, uncoiling from nascent sleep to its full reach. For the first time, I felt the draw of unbridled power, power told in stories of ships drawn beneath the water, of sailors torn from decks, of widows watching their widowing, screaming helpless from rocky shores.

The tale of St. Colmcille's rebuke of the Ness monster had never thrilled me. It was not so much to ask a cousin to stand aside. But now I felt the other side of the stories, the terrible unknown deep which rose to avenge itself on arrogant man.

I don't know what he saw in me, but the man from the unknown ministry moved his gloved hand closer to mine on the rail. "Steady."

I closed my eyes against a sudden physical craving. "Shall I go down?"

I could not see him, but I felt his weight shift beside me. "Could you—what could you do against a U-boat?"

"I could find her, for a start."

"The water is over one hundred fifty feet deep here, they tell me."

And dark and rough. I might swim in circles and eventually blunder into the *U-33*, but I could not pick her out more quickly than the *Gleaner*'s sonar. I flexed my gloved fingers on the rail and resolved to wait with the others. I further resolved not to think on what that dark temptation had been. We were to resist temptation. I tried to pray, tried to recall verses about resisting the old nature, but the words were lost in the cold spray.

A single depth charge. I waited, listened, as if I could pick out its effects with my own senses on the tossing deck. Time dragged by, viscous and thick.

Orders were given, and five more charges went down to detonate at various depths. I thought of Caelan, who had sworn to love me no matter what I might be, who told me it was an honour to marry into such an ancient line. Caelan, who had never wanted more than a rustic life, who was content to trade hard labour for simple living, who should never have been caught up in a war made by muck-stirring politicians arguing societies needed to rise above lesser contributors and lesser humans and to cast out those who were not true patriots.

I pushed dark hair from my eyes, blinked away salty spray, thought of Caelan's rich murmuring that he was honoured that I had trusted him with who I really was, that he understood why my family kept it close but that he would never think ill of something so beautiful as the life-giving water.

"There!"

More orders followed, fixing a four-inch gun on the shape picked out by the bright searchlight. I caught my breath and leaned forward, covering my ears as five shells targeted the hated submarine. She must have taken damage, to have surfaced again, and could not flee beneath the waves. I felt a thrill of vicious victory. No more mines, no more—

The searchlight showed men rushing onto the submarine's upper deck, hands high overhead in the intense light. They were shouting. *Surrender.*

We weren't near yet, but we were closing. The *Gleaner* turned, aborting a ramming course and settling for approaching parallel. Something almost like disappointment tugged at me, which was foolish. We had won. I had witnessed a victory. I did not know why the strange ministry man had brought me out here, but he had given me the gift of seeing the *U-33* surrender. I could be at rest for Caelan—

The submarine rocked, out of sync with the rolling waves, and a spray of fiery sparks leapt from the conning tower. The sailors poured off the upper deck like bowling pins.

No! Treacherous monsters! Something burst in my chest, releasing raw rage to swell through me like a rogue wave.

Beside me, the man in the dark coat and dark glasses swore and gripped the railing.

That was all the prompting I needed. Before I could think, I slid out of my overcoat and vaulted the railing. Icy water welcomed me, shocking the air from me. Water and skin wove together, blended, reformed.

Did the murderers of my Caelan and so many others think to die a quick and merciful death in the cold, heavy seas? They would never be so fortunate.

Fuath. The word burned through my bones and flesh as I shivered away the oceanic cold and dove. *Hate.* The creatures of the water which, when at last provoked, had no more mercy than the winds or waves themselves.

I kicked through the water, a torpedo of muscle targeting the men in the water. They could not be so far—

There.

I struck the first like a dolphin ramming a shark. He folded and choked, gulping seawater that filled and iced his lungs. I left him thrashing beneath the waves and went on to seek the next.

I had just killed a man. Was that what I wanted? I hated the *U-33*; I had thought of the ship as a beast, not as a collection of sailors. I had wanted the ship to die. I had not thought of killing her men, and not with my own body.

But then there was another German sailor kicking just in front of me, and his panic taunted me like a wounded fish before a shark. I swam to him, writhed around him, savoured his terror as he struggled to escape me, drew him down.

I could take them all. I could bring them all to the depths, in the waters where they had killed Caelan and all the crews of all the ships they had hunted. I could wreak upon them the same end they had given to others, not permitting them the mercy of the lifeboats the *Gleaner* was struggling to lower against the rough sea.

Fuath.

The loch was named for the river. The river was named for those who roared. The roars were ours.

I roared through the deafening deep as I spiralled down with the struggling sailor.

Something metallic pressed into my flesh, the bite of an improvised weapon. I shifted my grip and rotated to punish this resistance with fresh fury, but my fingers—what served for fingers—found the object itself. It was metal, simultaneously round and jagged, a disc with odd protrusions.

Treasure, I thought unreasonably, and I grinned.

He surrendered the object to me and thrashed away, as if he could outrun the current or me. But I did not immediately follow, turning my new possession over curiously, feeling it in the dark. It was something like a bicycle gear.

What would a sailor carry into the water with him as he fled a scuttled ship? This was no precious personal article, this was—

This was something too important to consign to a sinking ship, something the crew could not risk even a chance of capture should the *Gleaner*'s men reach the *U-33* before she went entirely down.

Treasure!

I kicked away in search of more sailors.

They were not hard to find, flailing in the chop and calling to one another. I struck them fast, and even if they could have seen me coming, they could not have escaped, not in that sea. I did not bother with killing them; Caelan would not be served with their deaths. Caelan would be served with their undoing.

I grasped a sailor, pulled him under, tore through his hands and clothing as he twisted, unable to clearly see what attacked him and frantic to surface. If I found nothing, I released him and went on to another prospect. If I felt metal, I tore it from him, felt whether it was a gear or a jackknife, kept it or discarded it.

I did not count the men I searched. It must have been a dozen. But now the *Gleaner* was picking up reluctant German sailors, and another local boat as well.

I went for my final sailor—an officer, by the feel of his uniform. I tore at his braids and writhed through his pockets. I found no gear, but as he struggled against me and I ripped at his decorations, I realized—captain. This was the man who had ordered Caelan's death.

Nothing could bring back Caelan, but I could give warning to those who might follow in these waters.

I left his body drifting near another boat—more local crews were coming to aid—and swam back to the *Gleaner*. My rage had abandoned me, leaving me breathless and shaking. I went to the far side, away from the lifeboats and the crew organizing the surrendering sailors, and I found grips to ascend the side of the ship.

The man with the smoked glasses must have been watching for me; he turned away from the action too quickly and came toward me. "Miss Tennent."

Out of the water, with normal human skin and frail human flesh, I felt keenly the January winds. I began to shake uncontrollably, and with bizarre remoteness I wondered how much was due to cold and how much to the first killings I had just committed.

Oh, God. I had killed. After generations of teaching and warning, I had surrendered control and I had killed.

He opened his coat and pulled mine from within, where he had wrapped it around his torso like an oversized muffler. "Here." He offered it on one arm.

I thought he must have meant to protect it against the spray, not leaving it on the deck to be soaked, but when I slid my arms into the woolen coat it felt like slipping into bedclothes freshly warmed. Cold as I was, the coat was far too warm for having been against a human body.

But then, mine was not always human, either.

I pulled the coat close and let the warmth sink into me. My knees weakened, and I sagged against a capstan. No, the cold water would not have affected me so much. I had to face what I had done.

"We've taken the submarine," he said in a low voice. "And if I'm not mistaken, you wanted to fight, too."

"Is that why you brought me here?"

"I hoped you could see your way to helping us."

"I hope I have." I brought out the discs. I had three, and I extended them, fanned like playing cards.

His dark glasses fixed on them. "How—how did you . . ."

"Some sailors were carrying them. I guessed that if they were too important to leave in the submarine, if they had to be consigned to the ocean individually, they must be useful."

"Indeed." He took them, gently but greedily. "Indeed, indeed."

A cry went up from one of the captured sailors, herded inside where they stripped and huddled near a stove to recover from their deadly plunge. In furious German he began to berate the others. An officer shouted back, clearly caught between wanting to preserve order in their shame and agreeing with the sailor's anger. The men of the *Gleaner* raised voices and waved arms to restore quiet in the assembly.

"Do you know what these are?" the man in the glasses asked me.

I shook my head. "But I surmise I was right about their importance."

"There is a machine the Germans use to transmit in everchanging code. These are gears from that machine."

"So—these are key to breaking the Germans' code."

He grinned. "Yes, Miss Tennent. You have been most helpful tonight."

I could not return his smile, as I thought of the men I had left beneath the waves. "I did not bring back all that I could have."

"Oh?"

"I found the captain. In the water."

He turned, looked out over the waves, blew out his breath. I thought I felt warm air brush my cheek and then it was gone. "We would need to talk about operations and procedures. If I had known you would—I did not bring you here to kill officers."

"You brought me out to hunt a submarine. How is that different?"

"It is not, and yet it is. If the captain had gone down with his ship, that would have been a tragedy to his family and an intelligence loss to us. But he scuttled the ship and attempted to escape with his life, while scattering invaluable information across the seabed. Now that he is dead, and not by his own hand, it is a senseless loss to us."

I understood. If we had recovered the coded gears from sailors, what more could we have learned from a U-boat captain?

And what could I have learned from acting on higher teachings than my own pain and fury? We had been right to hold back our worst nature.

"But, we have other officers," he said, "and nothing is sure in war. I am pleased with what treasures you have brought, and I trust you will be more—thoughtful in the future, and I hope you have reconsidered my offer."

My heart caught. "Is it an offer?"

He turned back with a wry smile. "What else could you consider the opportunity to use your talents to their fullest appreciation, in the service of your king and country?"

The crests and troughs of the last few hours rendered me a bit giddy. "And my place at the shipyard?" I raised an eyebrow. "I have a critical position at one of the key components of Great Britain's defense, the home of destroyers and great liners—"

"I'm sure we can find someone else to support the yard memoranda," he said with a chiding grin. "There's a team I hope to gather, and if you're willing to give up your typewriter, I should like you to be on it."

"Take off your glasses," I said. "I won't make deals with someone who will not look me in the eyes."

He slid them down his nose, and the glare of the deck lights barely showed the orange irises.

"I believe there is more to war than ships," I said. "And I don't want to win the war by losing myself."

"I understand."

"Then tell me about your team."

Bruno J. Lampini and the Song of the Sea

Josh Reynolds

THE ONLY TRUE villain is the sea.

A sailor of my acquaintance once said that. Granted, the judge disagreed and said sailor was summarily hung by the neck until dead. But that's neither here nor there. Bruno J. Lampini at your service. Ah, I see by your expression you've heard the name.

I came by it honestly, I assure you. No money changed hands as such, but the deed of ownership is in my possession, you might say.

No need to rush off, sir. Sit. I insist. Let me buy you a drink, there's a good fellow. Blackpool is lovely this time of year, don't you think? The lights, the music, the happy punters. But, if I might be so bold, you don't look the sort for lights and music. I'd wager you came looking for something else. Something more interesting. Like, say, a . . . mermaid?

I see I have your attention.

What? Oh yes, I saw it. Quite the thing. A once in a lifetime experience. I'd highly recommend it, if not for—well. You know. The storm and such. Oh. You hadn't heard? Blimey. Have another drink and I'll tell you all about the whole sordid business.

And it was business that brought me hence, I hasten to add. The pleasures of Blackpool, many though they are, were not foremost in my thoughts on this occasion. Rather, I was meeting a client—a seedy-looking bloke by the name of Hawser. Hawser was the proprietor of a travelling carnival which he referred to as the Illuminated Heliotropic Emporium. A tad ostentatious, but that's showbiz as they say.

Hawser was in need of a professional acquisitionist with experience in the unconventional—that is to say, myself. What? No! Lord bless me, sir. Thieves are firmly on the left hand path, while I prefer to saunter along the middle route—neither high nor low, if you will. I'm not above a bit of aggressive bargaining, but I always pay a fair price and ensure that I'm paid fairly in turn. A balanced ledger is a blessed ledger as my dear mother, God grant she lie still, often opined.

My particular line has often been what could be termed "esoterica", *id est* your cursed gemstones, your black grimoires, your possessed dollies and so forth. No dolly too haunted, I always say. It's proven a lucrative field. It has been my experience that your average toff is looking for any excuse to slap on some woad and start hunting around for virgins to stuff in the nearest wicker cage. The pull of the ineffable is hard to resist, wouldn't you say?

You take my meaning, I think. Do be a chum and stop frowning. Have another drink, there's a fellow. My story has barely begun.

Back to Hawser. Seedy little fellow, as I said, but I'm not one to make judgements. So long as a client has funds in their account, they're fine by Bruno J. Lampini. We met at dusk in a run down fish and chip shop near the Central Pier. It had begun to rain, and I was glad to be inside though the place stank of old fish and even older batter, and the less said of the chips the better. Luckily, I wasn't there for the food.

"I want a mermaid," Hawser said, by way of introduction.

"A particular one, or will any old fishwife do?" I asked.

"Was that a joke? Only I'm not paying you for japes and jests, Lampini."

"You haven't paid me at all yet." I fixed Hawser with a gimlet eye. I didn't care for his tone. He was an unprepossessing specimen, as I've previously alluded to. He had the sort of face meant for a thumping, and at that moment, I was strongly considering it.

But I refrained. Truthfully, I was in need of quick remuneration. A sudden, unforeseen debt and the renewed, not to mention unwelcome, attentions of a certain loan shark named Gorsmere had forced me to decamp from my London abode. Just until I'd managed to secure the necessary funds, you understand. And Hawser had promised payment in considerable excess of what I required. So I held my temper firmly in both hands and effected a smile.

Hawser leaned over the sticky table-top. I caught a waft of cheap pomade and clothes that were in need of a good wash. "There's a stick and rag show near the pier that's got one. A real one, not some dolly-mop dressed in fishnets and shells. Get her for me."

Now, ordinarily, the items I acquire are of the inanimate variety—or if not exactly inanimate, they certainly ain't alive in the usual sense. I said as much and Hawser sneered, further intensifying my dislike of him. "I don't need excuses. I can hire another acquisitionist, if that's your feeling on the matter."

Well, Bruno J. Lampini is not a man to be trifled with in such a manner. I gave Hawser my best stern look, trod heavily on his foot beneath the table, and he wilted swiftly enough. But pride does not a coffer fill, thus I agreed to take the commission.

We shook on it as gentlemen, and if I applied a touch more force than was necessary, well, you'll forgive me I'm sure. Suitably chastened, my new client scuttled off and left me to the hunt. *Aut vincere aut mori*, you might say, eh? Is that surprise I see on your face? I am a man of some education, though I fear no reputable *alma mater* shall clutch me to her bosom anytime soon. One can't prosper in this profession without a bit of book-learning, though I admit most of said books are of the sort no respectable sort ought to read.

Finding the sideshow in question was no trifling task, even with Hawser's directions. Blackpool is awash in such entertainments—places to idle away time and shillings alike. Street-corner starvers and sapphic dancers occupied makeshift stages and presentation halls all along the stretches leading to the piers. I passed signage advertising headless women, phrenological consultations and something called the Blackpool Beast.

The rain had not let up, but the Illuminations continued their gleaming and music spilled from open doorways. I admit, I've always had something of an affinity for such lively sprawls. The lights, the noise, the unwary punters—all of it has something of an intoxicating effect on yours truly. But not so much as to be distracting, I hasten to add. Once Bruno J. Lampini has the scent, he does not often stray from the trail.

The sideshow I was looking for occupied a smallish building that might once have been a shop of some sort. It was within sight of the Promenade, and I could hear the crash of the night ocean and taste the salt in the wind. A large sign, edged in crudely illustrated gargoyle faces, declared it Asbury's Premium Grotesquery.

As names went it seemed appropriate enough. Gaudy placards studded the exterior and a string of coloured lights had been strung across their tops. Like the others I'd passed on the way, the placards boasted lurid images advertising wonders and horrors aplenty. I recalled something a gentleman of my acquaintance had once opined about a new age of gods and monsters. Fine fellow, that Pretorius, a true grandee. Knows his gin. But I digress.

On one placard, a serpent of monstrous size coiled about a Congolese canoe, jaws set to envelope the panicked features of some would-be great white hunter. On another, a hirsute fellow of distinctly lupine countenance savaged sheep while distraught Welshmen looked on. There were dozens of these sinister snippets, but only one was of any real interest to me. I'm sure a smart fellow like you can guess which one it was.

Got it in one, chum. Bang on the bell, as they say. Yes, there she was in all her fishy, four-colour glory. The illustration put me in mind of a Waterhouse painting I'd seen once, though I doubted the flesh and blood article resembled the artist's rather nubile interpretation. Above the *belle dame sans merci* was emblazoned the legend "Atargatis".

Not a name to roll off the tongue, eh? Oh. Familiar is it, sirrah? While I myself am no connoisseur of the horrible, I know there are those whose tastes run to the monstrous. I am sure Atargatis is as infamous in her circles as I am in mine. But that is a discussion for later, I'd wager.

One could experience this cavalcade of abomination for the price of a shilling, a bargain by any man's reckoning. I ducked in out of the rain, paid my fare and insinuated myself into the queue through sharp application of elbows and the occasional glare. Suffice it to say, I have never had much in the way of patience. While your average Englishman is a placid fiend for line-standing, we Hibernians are of a more mercurial disposition.

Luckily, the only protests were of the muttered variety, and the rum sorts who ran the place paid us little attention. A barney in the queue would have put paid to my scheme before it had even begun. The rozzers tend to make a hash of these matters, and I was keen to avoid the eye of the Blackpool constabulary.

Once inside, my initial impression of the Premium Grotesquery was that it was neither. The space within had been made over into a makeshift labyrinth of canvas walls, stacks of wooden crates and the like. Lights had been strung up so as to cast deep shadows—an extra dash of theatricality, in order to hide the crude nature of the proceedings.

The exhibits were mostly the result of artifice—wax dummies, clever taxidermies and the like. The savage serpent was nothing more than a tattered strip of shed skin—admittedly large—tacked up along one wall. The bestial lycanthrope was merely a mouldering skull in a glass case, unearthed in Hexham or so the barker claimed.

The only real monster I saw was a rather sad-looking goat with a second, foetal head bouncing on its neck like a goitre. I was on the cusp of demanding my shilling back when we finally got to the star of the show—Atargatis herself. And what a star she was!

She waited at the back of the display area, hidden behind a canvas wall. The space was decorated with the accoutrements of the fisherman's trade—nets and harpoons and basket-traps and suchlike. As I passed through the flaps, I saw a large glass sphere on a metal stand. It put me in mind of a fish bowl and I almost laughed out loud. The sides of it were scummy with algae and any occupants were hidden by the resulting murk.

The barker—a bellicose Liverpudlian wearing an eye-watering plaid three-piecer—swatted the rim of the bowl with his rattan cane. "Roll up, roll up, ladies and gentlemen, here we have her ladyship, Atargatis of Syria. In her own waters, she were a queen—but here, she is naught but an object of curiosity!" He rapped the rim once more, and something stirred in the soup. Not an effigy this, oh my no. Something unworldly.

For a moment, a single moment, no more no less, I was struck dumb. It is not often that Bruno J. Lampini finds himself at a loss for words. I once kept up a conversation whilst being gnawed upon by—well, that's neither here nor there. This was a different kettle of fish entirely, if you'll pardon the expression.

First, let me say this—she was not lovely. Beautiful, perhaps, in the way a wolf is beautiful, or even a shark. An alien beauty. But not what you might call conventionally attractive. Not a wax effigy, and certainly not your standard buxom beauty of flaxen hair and milky complexion. No, from what I could see, Atargatis was as flat as a board and as sinewy as an eel—an animal with which she shared many characteristics.

"Step up, step up," the barker drawled. "Closer, my friends— come and get your shillings' worth. I assure you, sir, she is as real as you or I."

We crowded forward, and I found myself perilously close to the glass. Close enough to make out the fine details, you might say. There was a greenish pallor to her flesh, though that might have been due to the state of her bowl. Pallid scales crept along her arms and neck, along the bottom of her jaw and across her shoulders.

Her tail was more serpentine than one might have expected— a long, muscular extension dotted with fins and ending in flared half-moon of the same. It coiled about her as she floated against the side of the bowl, webbed fingers pressed to the filthy glass. She had neither nose nor lips, and her head was curiously sloped. Her hair, if it was hair, resembled lank strands of kelp that floated about her in a halo.

As I said, not your typical bathing beauty. But there was something about her eyes. Beneath those nictitating membranes, her gaze was as cold and as sharp as the waters of the North Sea. And her teeth made me think of a rusty saw blade.

She hunched herself against the filthy glass, staring out at her admiring public. Her fingers smeared the algae into strange shapes, and her lipless mouth writhed. I wondered if she were cursing . . . or perhaps pleading. Or maybe she was simply as bored by the barker's spiel as I was. He'd kept up his patter the entire time, punctuating his sentences with a tap of his cane against the glass.

"She were captured by French soldiers in the waters near Ayn al-Bayda, after a great storm what lashed the coast and cast up many a denizen of the deeps . . . a storm not unlike the one what rages outside, even as we speak. Such a storm might once again carry her home, if we were but to release her—hsst. Listen, I beg you. Listen!"

We listened, but no sound seemed forthcoming. I found myself wondering if perhaps dear old Atargatis had a touch of stage fright. Then the barker struck the glass a ringing thwack and a soft, thin trill rose from the water. It sounded like birdsong, or the clacking of an eel, or both. It swelled and outside, the storm seemed to reciprocate.

You look sceptical, my friend. I assure you, I am not a man for hyperbole. Some sonic sorcery was afoot, though I'll not pretend to understand its nature. The demimonde can have its secrets so long as I get my shillings' worth, as dear old mater—God keep her, I beg him—was often wont to say. A woman of certain wisdoms, my mother.

As the rain thudded against the roof, the mermaid rose up, causing the water to slop over the sides of her bowl. When she did so, the murk shifted, and I caught sight of something round and unsightly at the bottom of the bowl—several somethings, in fact. I do not think I have to elaborate, sir. After all, what would a creature with teeth like hers eat, save flesh?

What? Of course I'm certain. An apprenticeship with the resurrection men teaches one all sorts of useful things. Besides which—ah, but I'm getting ahead of myself.

Her song rose with the wind and I fancied I could hear the joists shivering. There was water on the floor, though whether from the bowl, brought in by the punters, or from somewhere else, I could but hazard a guess.

The performance was interrupted by the swat of a rattan cane against the bowl. Atargatis retreated, sinking back into her mire, and the echoes of her trilling song drifted into silence. Outside, the storm's fury sputtered into mild frustration.

At the barker's urgings, the crowd moved on, but without yours truly. I am a champion lurker, if I do say so myself, capable of passing unnoticed in even the most crowded of pubs. I waited until the last of them were out of sight, and then turned my attentions to the bowl and its singular occupant.

Atargatis floated in her stew, swimming in cramped, lazy circles like an oversized goldfish. I was tempted to tap on the glass, but refrained. Instead, I contemplated how best to achieve my aims with as little fuss as possible.

Even as I weighed the merits of an improvised block and tackle system, however, I heard the squelch of shoe leather on the wet floor. I turned, effecting a look of mild surprise.

"Who the fuck're you?" the newcomer demanded, without so much as a by-your-leave. He was a slight, wrinkled man, the sort who looked like a stiff breeze might send him tumbling along the pier and out to sea. He was dressed better than the barker, and by better I mean worse, in a cheap suit that strained the eye and the stomach alike.

"I might make the same inquiry," says I.

"Name's Asbury. I own this establishment."

"Then you are just the fellow I wish to see!" I exclaimed. I doffed my hat and sketched a bow. "Bruno J. Lampini at your service."

"I'll bet," he said, and sidled around me. "I saw you come in and said to myself, Asbury, there's a sharp one and no mistake. Not the usual sort of punter."

"Not a punter at all, in fact." I gave him my best fulsome grin, hat pressed to my heart. "Rather, that is to say, I am here on behalf of another."

He nodded, as if this was only to be expected. "So who sent you then? Was it that fat toad from Bournemouth? Or that spiv from Northampton? They've both tried to buy her off of me before."

Since he had obliged me with an opening, I went into my prepared spiel. "I have not had the pleasure of meeting either of the gentlemen you mentioned. No, I am here at the request of a Mr. Hawser. Like you, he is in the esoteric entertainments industry and wishes to purchase one of your attractions . . ."

"Atargatis, you mean." Asbury frowned, which made him resemble nothing so much as a melted candle. He turned towards the bowl.

"A curious name, that," I opined.

"Syrian, innit?" he said, not looking at me. He pressed his

fingers to the glass, and she mimicked him. There was nothing like affection in that gaze—just a cold hunger, like that of a shark. "Found it in an old book, I did. Some goddess or suchlike, and I thought to myself, why not? She is a goddess of sorts, ain't she?"

"*Nee divini humanive caro factum est*, you might say."

He grunted. "Don't know about that." His tone hardened. "What I do know is that she's mine. And here she'll stay, in the temple I have prepared for her." He gestured about us, indicating the confines of the Premium Grotesquery.

"Shades of the Israelites," I said.

"What?"

"The good book, Mr. Asbury. The Israelites were said to have carried Yahweh in a box for some time."

"Is that so?"

"It is indeed, and most magnificent box it is."

He peered at me. "Seen it then, have you?"

"One sees a great many things in this line of work."

He nodded, his eyes straying back to his captive. "I expect so."

There was silence for a time. Him, staring at her. Her, staring at us. And me, staring at my pocket watch. I cleared my throat. "I hate to be a bother, but the storm sounds as if it's getting worse, and I'd like to be off . . ."

"It's her song what does it," he said. "It's the song of the sea, seeping into your bones. And like a sailor, you can't bear to part with her."

"Not being of the nautical persuasion, I shall take your word for it," I said.

I see by the look in your eyes that you understand better than I. The pull of the ineffable, is it? The yearning for dark fruit, as mater always had it. Some men find the monstrous irresistible—present company excluded, I'm sure.

Regardless, I judged Asbury a lost soul—as much a prisoner as Atargatis. I am familiar enough with obsession to recognize it when I see it. Trust me when I say Asbury was obsessed good and proper with his fishy goddess—and that it most assuredly was not reciprocated. The way she looked at him—brrr. A sight to turn a fellow's blood to water.

"What was the name again—Hawser?" Asbury asked.

"The very same."

His frown deepened to such an extent that I thought his whole face might collapse in on itself. "I know that name."

"I am pleased to hear it." At this point I was envisioning an easy transaction. Folly, thy name is Bruno J. Lampini. Pleased with myself, I decided to grease the wheels a bit. "While no specific monetary amount was mentioned, I am happy to negotiate on your behalf . . ."

"You're not the first he's sent, you know."

The words came so suddenly that I faltered. "I'm afraid you have me at a loss."

"Smart fellow like you? I don't think I do." The pistol appeared in his hand as if by magic. "He worships monsters, he does. Him and them others. But she's no monster."

"No, most assuredly not." I smiled obsequiously, my eyes never straying from the pistol. While courage is certainly among my virtues, it was not present in that moment I can tell you. You smile, sir, but I'd wager if you had a pistol being waved in your face you might flinch as well. No, never mind. Here, let's have another round.

"Monsters," he went on, staring me down over the barrel of his revolver. "Bleedin' love the things, they do. Echidna this and Typhon that . . ." He continued to hold forth in similar fashion for several moments, delivering a lecture straight from the pages of a penny dreadful. I confess I paid little attention. The only thing of interest I recall was his contention that Hawser was either a member of this society of monster worshippers, or was working for them—he seemed uncertain as to which it was, and I deemed it imprudent to ask for clarification at the time.

Why, you've gone pale! White as the proverbial sheet. Was it something I said? Here, let's have another drink, it'll stiffen your giblets. We're just getting to the exciting bit.

While Asbury held forth on the myriad perfidies of his enemies, I concentrated all of my wit and guile on a quick exit. It might surprise you to know that this wasn't the first time I'd found myself on the wrong end of a firearm. Once the moment of shock had passed, my little grey cells set to work with a vengeance.

"Rest assured, sirrah, that I have no inclination to thievery," I said, as he began to wind down at last. "Bruno J. Lampini is as honest as the day is long." As I spoke, I spied Atargatis watching us. Her face was pressed to the filthy glass like that of a child outside a candy shop. She unleashed a small trill that set my back molars to itching.

Asbury glanced at her. A cunning look settled on his face. "Yes. Yes, I suppose it is time for your repast, my lady."

I recalled then the bones at the bottom of the bowl and felt my marrow curdle. "Is that how you served the others, then?" I asked. "The ones Hawser sent before me?"

"She must eat." Asbury looked at me as if I were a moon-calf.

"So she must. But I'll not be on the menu." I took a step back. On a support post behind me I'd glimpsed a lantern. An old fashioned oiler, not one of these newfangled electric jobbers. The sort that made a jolly light when you tossed it onto a hard surface.

"Don't move," Asbury snapped. I paused.

"Name your price, sir, and I assure you, Hawser will pay it. As I said, I will take it upon myself to negotiate on your behalf." He hesitated, and I tensed, readying myself to spring towards the lantern.

My plan? Simplicity itself, friend. I intended to toss the lantern, set the place ablaze and scarper. Only fate had other ideas. Fate—and one other.

You see, Atargatis had been trilling away like a waterlogged wren as we debated. The same song as before, but more urgent now, and the storm outside responded in kind. I felt a cold breeze whip through the canvas maze and heard the clatter of toppling placards.

Startled, Asbury turned—first to the exit, and then to his captive. So distracted was he, that he failed to notice my hand dart into my coat pocket, where I seized my own shooter and served him as he no doubt intended to serve me.

Eh? Did I not mention my bosom chum, the Bulldog? Why, here's the very fellow, right here in his kennel, by which I mean my pocket. The Webley revolver is sturdy and practical, much like myself. He and I have been through quite a few adventures together, such as that unfortunate occurrence in Kiev—but that is a tale for another time.

At any rate, my Bulldog's bark spooked Asbury something fierce, and the fellow gave a yelp and a hop, hand flying to his ear. He replied in kind, and I went for the lantern. I snatched it off its hook and whirled it about my head with great gusto.

Even as I let fly, Asbury's cries for aid were answered. Several roustabouts charged into the room, led by the Liverpudlian from earlier. I plugged the barker and sent the rest diving for cover.

You seem startled, sir. Or is that distaste? Rest assured, I share your revulsion. I am not normally a man of violence—love, not war, is Bruno J. Lampini's guiding philosophy—but sometimes a bit of pre-emptive defence is called for.

At any rate, at that moment the wind whipped itself into a frenzy, and the sea lashed the shore with a worsening fury. Water was spilling across the boards now, and my feet were pure soaked through. And above it all, the shrill notes of Atargatis' song cut the air, providing accompaniment to our performance. She seemed rather pleased by it all, I must say. Then, some men like to watch roosters gouge each other to death before the loser is plucked and broiled. Perhaps it is the same for mermaids.

Myself, I had other concerns at that precise moment. The lantern had done as I hoped, and shattered, spilling a wealth of burning oil across the wooden floor. It was quite damp, and the fire struggled a bit, so I shoved over a great tower of packing crates and straw to help things out. Flames whooshed up, gnawing eagerly at the canvas curtains.

Past the flames, I saw that Asbury was braced protectively against the bowl as Atargatis swum in languid circles. He shouted for his roustabouts to put out the fire, but none of them answered. One can't fault them for choosing discretion over valour. After all, who wants to risk burning for a two-headed goat and a carnivorous fish-woman?

With Asbury suitably distracted, I made my move. Two quick shots cracked the bowl and released twin geysers of green water. Atargatis' movements became frantic as the liquid level dipped. She whipped back and forth, her song becoming a shrill shriek. Even now, I cannot say with any certainty whether it was fear or anticipation that made her carry on so. In her excitement, she slammed against the sides of the bowl, causing it to judder on its stand. Full, it wouldn't have budged. But it was no longer full, and so it soon began to tip precipitously, slopping water over the rim.

Asbury was in a right state now, his pistol all but forgotten as he tried to soothe his captive. Atargatis was having none of it, however, and as her cries reached an ear-splitting volume so too did the sea vent its displeasure upon Blackpool.

I'm sure you read about it in the local fish-wrappers. Seafront property inundated, streets flooded, at least a dozen souls swept from Central Pier, etcetera and so forth. Blackpool got a battering that night, and no mistake. And at its crescendo, the bowl finally tipped. With a crash and a splash, the fire went out, and I was knocked sprawling, my Bulldog flung into some flooded corner.

Electric lights sputtered and fizzed alarmingly. In their erratic glow, I saw Asbury stagger to his feet. He still had his revolver, to my chagrin. I ceased my efforts to find my weapon as he swung his towards me, a feral grin on his wrinkled face. "She's mine," he croaked. Fitting last words, it proved.

You see, Atargatis was free. And she had not yet been fed.

What was it like? Well, have you ever had the misfortune to witness the predatory undulations of an eel? If so, imagine that but worse. The human form is not meant to bend in certain ways. Structural limitations, one could call them. Atargatis, bless her black heart, had no such limitations.

She wrapped herself about him like a lover. Her fingers bit into his skinny arms and the pistol fell from his grip. She bent forward as if to kiss him, and before my horrified eyes her jaws distended in the way of a deep sea fish—wide enough to encompass the whole of his head in a single bite. Which she subsequently did.

I trust I do not need to describe what happened next. I will say that Asbury did not pass across the Styx peacefully or gently. I hesitate to call his frenzied demise well-deserved, but, well—judge for yourself.

I did not bother looking for my pistol. There was no time, and Asbury was barely an appetizer. I spied a rusty harpoon—part of the display—and snatched it up, even as Atargatis reared up before me, gill-slits fluttering and the song of the sea rising from her throat. Perhaps she meant to thank me, rather than devour me—who can say? But I am not one to take chances in these matters. A man only has one life to lose, after all.

With one desperate heave, I threw the harpoon. At that range, I could hardly miss—and didn't. Atargatis' song crumbled into a strangled choke as she fell back, tail thrashing in a most revolting manner as she writhed in her death-throes. As ends go, it was somewhat appropriate, I think. You are free to disagree, of course.

Regardless, that, as they say, was that. After I had retrieved my pistol, I bundled her into a roll of wet canvas until I could find someplace more suitable. Thankfully, there is no lack of ice in Blackpool.

Dead? I should hope so. If not, well, I've done her a terrible disservice. It's just as well, I think. There was no place on the surface for such a creature, and I cannot imagine releasing her into our native waters. I dread to think of the mischief she might have gotten up to, especially given her decided inclination towards the carnivorous.

As for Hawser, well—he'd done a runner, of course. Once word of the imbroglio at the Premium Grotesquery had gotten around, he'd no doubt feared retribution. His absence left me high and dry, so to speak. But I am not one to lose heart—what one man wished to buy, so might another. You'll recall Asbury had mentioned a certain cult of monster worshipping loons—yes, I see that you do.

Funny that. Quite the coincidence, eh? Only I am not a man for coincidences. Nor, I think, are you. No, please, sit. I insist. We have so much to discuss after all. No sir, please do not insult me by continuing this charade. Time for all cards on the table, as they say.

Ah, there we go. Blackpool isn't the only thing that has been illuminated. Yes, I knew your lot would come looking, once Hawser turned up empty-handed. You went to some trouble to find me, though I daresay I didn't make it difficult.

Now, now, no need for such language. Do remain seated, please. That click you just heard was my Bulldog, straining at the leash. One twitch, and I shall have to let him all the way off. But I trust you'll agree that there's no need for things to become unpleasant between us. We are both men of the world.

I have something you want. Have another drink and let us talk terms, like civilized fellows. There we go. Good man.

Now then, what's a second-hand goddess worth these days?

Mano Kanaka: The Eater of Lost Souls

Liam Hogan

HE ALWAYS WAS godlike in the water. While the rest of us merely made up the numbers, Tom was the undisputed star of Larrington High's Swim Team, right from Freshman year. Gangly and awkward in the classrooms and halls, he glided effortlessly through the chlorinated waters.

It surprised all of us when he came back from the State Championships empty-handed, but finding out there was a bigger pond out there might have been the spur he needed. By Juniors he was faster than ever and starting to attract the attention of the College scouts.

As the States rolled round once again, he was constantly in the pool, training, training, training. It was his time to shine and I think he knew it.

Two weeks later he was in the local newspapers, but on the front pages, not the back.

Seeing him lying diminished in the hospital bed, monitor beeping away, wrapped in acres of bandage, I wasn't the only one who assumed he'd never swim again. He was on crutches all the way through the first term of our senior year and even after that he kept to himself, missing the Prom, opting out of the Year Book. He didn't come to any of the Swim Team meets and he pretty much drifted out of my insular little circle that final year of High School.

The grapevine hinted that whatever funds his parents had built up for university had been wiped out by his medical costs and, with the chances of a sports scholarship vanishing like blood in the water, Tom was left in academic limbo.

So it was a surprise—a welcome one, but a surprise nonetheless—to see him sporting a bright yellow T-shirt at the top of the lifeguard's chair at the municipal pool. I was home on a sanity trip; the hustle and bustle of my first term at university proving a little too unsettling. The pool was my escape from the attentions of my overly-concerned parents. With my school friends dispersed across the fifty states, I hadn't expected to see a familiar face.

"Hey, Tom!" I called up to where he sat.

He smiled. "Hey, Lucy. What you doing back?"

I shrugged, embarrassed. "Just a flying visit."

He climbed down. There was something odd about his leg but it wasn't until he was stood at the pool side and that I could compare right to left. The missing muscle mass, his right calf almost non-existent, the ragged, ugly web of scar tissue . . .

"The doc says there's still a tooth buried in there," he said, seeing my stare.

"What? Like, really? A shark's tooth?"

"Nah, I'm just messing with you. Sure feels like it though, sometimes."

I nodded, as if I could possibly know what it felt like to have a chunk of leg chewed off. Other than that, Tom looked pretty good. Relaxed in a way he'd never been at high school. Bronzed, but not obsessively. I'd not realised how handsome he was. Or maybe that first term, the pressure to fit in, to give in, had reset my compass.

"You racing?" I asked, then tried to bite it back. He gave me a look and I cursed my stupidity. Of course he wasn't. "Scratch that," I said. "Got time for a coffee after my swim?"

His attention was elsewhere, his hand half raised and fluttering. Before I could work out who if anybody he was signalling to, he launched into an angled dive that left barely a splash.

The girl couldn't have been more than about eight. It took me a moment to see her, struggling down the noisy, shallow end of the pool. I kind of assumed that whatever Tom was reacting to would be at the deep end, near where we were standing, because no-one can swim faster than they can run, can they?

Tom could and did, and somehow he made it all the way underwater through the busy pool. I saw him surface, effortlessly lifting the little girl onto his shoulders. She clung to him tightly as her arguing parents finally realised what was going on, the tight knot of them moving towards the edge of the pool.

I don't think the girl was in any major peril, but she was definitely spooked and had probably swallowed a couple of mouthfuls of pool water. Tom beckoned another lifeguard to take his place as he and the family disappeared into the cafe.

I was almost reluctant to enter the pool, but that was silly. Most of the swimmers weren't even aware there had been a scare. And it really hadn't been that serious, had it? I slipped into the pool and waited a moment for my heart to steady.

When I swim, I don't think of much at all. I let the lengths eat up the time and concentrate on my breathing, on my positioning.

If my mind dwelled on anything, it was on the sleek form of Tom diving in, a dark shape beneath the water quickly out of sight, his re-emergence at the far end a shockingly short time later. I'd always known he was fast, but I'd have expected the missing chunk of leg to slow him down some. It certainly didn't looked like it had.

When I gave up on my usual fifty lengths, tired of the midday lane swimmers who didn't know what "fast", "medium" and "slow" meant, Tom was waiting by the entrance to the showers, changed into a dry t-shirt and board shorts.

"Thought I'd take you up on that offer of coffee," he said.

I laughed. I hadn't been sure he'd heard me; thought he might have been too busy being a hero. "Give me five minutes to change. The cafe here any good?"

He lent in, lowered his voice. "Not really. But there's a Starbucks across the way?"

I nodded, sharing the conspiracy. "I'll see you there."

IT TOOK ME ten minutes in all, one of the disadvantages of having long hair and not wanting to look like a drowned cat. Tom was sitting at a little table on the sidewalk, staring across the parking lot towards the sea.

"Got you a flat white," he said, as I approached. "I'm afraid I'm back on duty at two."

"No worries," I said, though it meant he'd probably spent longer in line than he would be with me. "More swimmers to save, huh?" I pulled out the chair opposite, dropped into it, feeling comfortably warm from the exercise.

"Ah," he shrugged. "Just doing my job."

"Fast though," I pointed out. "Still got speed."

He grunted and turned away. I wasn't sure what else to say, what to talk about. With anyone else we'd be swapping University stories, but that would be one way traffic and probably not very tactful. I'd already goofed mentioning racing and he didn't seem that keen to talk about his act of heroism. It looked like it was going to be a long quarter of an hour.

In the end, it was he who spoke first, suddenly earnest. "Lucy, I wanted to thank you."

I squinted at him in the autumn sun. "What for?"

"Coming to see me in the hospital. It meant a lot."

I felt awful. It'd been well over a year since the accident and this was the longest I'd spent talking to him since he'd been discharged. Sure, we'd all been busy. But whatever he'd gone through he'd gone through alone.

It was my turn to shrug. "Didn't the whole swim team come see you?"

He nodded. "Coach's orders, I bet. But you're the only one who came twice."

I was embarrassed. "Someone had to bring you your grade papers."

"That, I *don't* thank you for," he said with a laugh.

"So, what next, Tom?" I asked, biting the bullet. "You still looking at doing a degree?"

"Maybe. Not this year, obviously." He was silent a long moment. "Having . . . what happened to me, it makes you think. Changes your priorities."

I nodded, again out of politeness rather than understanding.

"Anyway," he smiled, "enough about me. How long you in town for?"

I wondered if this was what being an adult was all about. Sitting at a table, drinking coffee, making small talk while avoiding the bloody great big elephant in the room. "Couple of days," I laughed. "I shouldn't be here at all, really. Missing classes. But university . . . it can be hard work, y'know?"

His raised eyebrows said it all.

I gulped the rest of my flat white, hiding a blush. His cardboard cup was long empty and I couldn't help notice when he glanced sideways at his watch. "Thanks for the coffee," I said, standing up. "See you around?"

"You know where I'll be," he nodding back towards the pool. "In there . . . or over there."

I followed his gaze but there wasn't anything there except a parking lot, a thin strip of gritty sand, and the ocean.

"You don't . . . you're not *still* swimming in the sea?"

He gave me an odd look. "Sometimes," he said, quietly. "At night . . ."

"Shit, Tom!"

I didn't know all that much about sharks, despite the leaflets that were thrust into our hands after Tom's accident, but weren't they more dangerous at dawn and at dusk? And for sure, there'd be no lifeguard on duty after sunset. I must have looked totally shocked, because he frowned and then started trying to reassure me. Except nothing he said did anything but make it worse.

"I don't go far," he said, "And I'm perfectly safe, really I am." He laughed. "Feels almost like home."

Either he thought lightning wouldn't strike twice or he had some sort of macabre death wish and wanted the sharks to finish the job. Whichever; it was messed up.

"Look," I said, both of us standing now, on the brink of an uneasy parting. "Come over to my folks for dinner tonight? Seven-ish?"

"You sure?" he said. "Bit short notice, isn't it?"

"It won't be anything fancy. And I'll be glad to have someone to distract my parents from tales of *their* first terms."

He nodded. "Ok. Seven it is."

MOM COMPLAINED WHEN I told her we had a guest, worried the

leftover pot roast wouldn't stretch. I helped chop extra vegetables and she quietened down quick enough. I think she was hoping Tom would be good for me. And he was, really. Instead of my parents treading on eggshells, asking tentative questions about the friends I was making on campus with veiled references to "just saying no!" to alcohol, drugs and/or sex, the conversation flowed with the light ease having a guest brings. My father seemed particularly taken by Tom, especially after I described what had happened in the pool, and it was he who encouraged the two of us to sit out on the back porch while my mother concocted some sort of last-minute dessert.

Tom was silent as we sat there, gently swaying.

"Penny for them," I quipped, half-fearful of the serious look on his face.

He grinned. "I was thinking about what you said; about applying to university. Thinking I should get an application or two in."

I nodded, timing was about right. He had the advantage of knowing his final grades, which had been decent, as far as I could remember.

"Decided where? And to study what?"

"Yeah. Thinking oceanography."

"Ocean . . . ?"

"-ography."

"Sounds geeky."

"It is. Thinking of applying to Hawaii."

"Really?" These obviously weren't decisions he'd made since that shared coffee earlier in the day. So if he'd decided anything, it was to share his plans. With me. Still, I couldn't entirely contain my surprise.

"In Hawaii," he continued, eyebrow raised, "they have stories about a shark-man, who changes shape when he's in the water. The Eater of Lost Souls. Mano Kanaka."

"You're not planning to study sharks, are you?"

"You got me," he put up his hands in mock surrender. "Figure I have some personal experience already."

I stopped my gentle kicking and the porch swing creaked to a standstill. "That doesn't sound very scientific."

"I don't suppose it is. But I guess most people make decisions about what to study based on pretty flimsy reasons."

I couldn't really argue with that. Not while doing a Sociology major.

"Hawaii got a swim team?" I asked.

"Probably," he frowned. "But I won't be in it."

"You don't think you're fast enough?"

"Oh, I'm fast enough. But that's not it. I guess the desire to compete is gone. There was a point when they didn't know if they could save my leg."

"For real?" I shivered as the evening chill penetrated the jacket I'd thrown on, Tom sitting there in short-sleeved shirt and slacks.

He nodded, but seemed distracted, staring out over the moonlit lawn, as though listening to something I couldn't hear. "Luce, thanks for this evening, it's been great. But I'm gonna split."

I wondered if I'd upset him somehow. He'd seemed on the verge of sharing something and now he was running off. "Before lemon cake?"

"Ah yes," the grin was there, but tired, perhaps even strained. "Even before your mum's lemon drizzle cake. Make my excuses to your folks, won't you?"

The hug he gave was brief and awkward, the cold skin of his exposed forearms rough to the touch. I wondered if he'd been sitting on our porch with goose bumps all the while. A typical macho move to suffer the cold in silence. "Look after yourself?" I told him.

He glanced back over his hunched shoulder as he strode powerfully across the lawn, eager to be away. "You too, Luce. You too."

I STOPPED BY the pool the next day, but Tom wasn't on duty and all I got from reception was a shrug and a "he didn't show this morning."

As I left, my eyes were drawn to the waterfront, the remnants of the morning mist merging sea and sky. I wandered over to the boardwalk between car park and beach. There weren't many people about; a couple of dog walkers, a young mother or two pushing a stroller along, the rumble of wheels over the wooden boards soothing their truculent offspring. The lifeguard tower was being boarded up, making it ready for the short winter months.

For a moment I thought one of the guys ascending the tower's steps was Tom and headed over, but as I got closer I realised my mistake. His hair was too bleached and too long. He was running a red flag up the pole and something gripped at the pit of my stomach.

"What's up?" I called. The beach at Larrington wasn't known for strong currents. Or indeed any other hazards. Except one, I suppose.

The lifeguard looked down at me, weighing his odds before nodding North. "Seal carcass washed up along the beach. Possible shark."

The casual way he spoke bit deep. He couldn't have been any older than me. Wasn't he around when Tom got attacked? Or did that not matter? Not any more? Anything short of a fatality would be quickly forgotten, ancient history after only eighteen months. Was it just me who hadn't been in the sea—in any sea—since?

Even Tom . . . and my stomach churned again. Where had he rushed to last night?

I fumbled for my mobile, hoping he still had the same number. When was the last time I'd called or texted him? I knew where he lived, assuming he was still at his parents', but it was a good forty-minute walk from the beach.

The phone rang and rang as the sea hissed behind me, and I turned in small circles on the hollow sounding boards. What was I going to say to him? But that didn't matter. I just wanted to hear his voice, to know he was okay.

An automated answer service kicked in, and I cut the message off, fingers hovering over the text button. Should I mention the red flag? Would that make it sound like I was panicking? *Was* I panicking?

As I dithered I noticed the envelope icon. A half laugh exploded out of me when it showed Tom's name.

"Hey Lucy," his text message read, "sorry for dashing off last night. I'll be in town around noon. Want to do lunch?"

It'd been sent barely five minutes earlier and I texted back a hasty yes before calling my mum to tell her I'd be home later.

"Not working today, Tom?" I asked as I joined him at the boardwalk diner.

"Ah, I was feeling a bit off this morning. Must have been something I ate."

"Not mom's pot roast, I hope?"

He looked confused for a moment. "No, not that . . . something else. Anyway. All better now. In fact I'm famished. Let's eat!"

I mentioned the red flag to him but he shrugged it off. He was in a flippant mood, conversation bright and amusing but unwilling to settle on any one topic. The lunch hour whizzed by, and despite all the chatter, he somehow still managed to bolt down two hamburgers, slathered in ketchup.

"Well," I said, standing on the sidewalk outside, "Back to university tomorrow."

He nodded and I waited for him to suggest something for that evening. The one-screen town cinema, maybe, just starting its Halloween season.

It didn't come. Just the same uncomfortable hug, his skin smoother this time, but with knots of muscle across his back and shoulders as hard as bone, as welcoming as bared teeth. And then I was on my own, in the middle of town, a blue funk descending.

Mom must have picked up on my mood because she left me pretty much alone, other than encouraging me to eat slice after slice of lemon cake—"it won't keep!"—washed down by mugs of strong tea. I took a long bath as dusk descended, and when I emerged, the full moon was just creeping above the cherry trees out back, the night clear and cold and me with it.

I packed and repacked my bag and was just going over some of my school work as a way of avoiding having to finish the last quarter of lemon cake when my phone chirped in the pocket of my hoodie. I stared at the screen. Once again it told me it was Tom, this time calling rather than texting. It was just past nine o'clock and I was more than half-tempted not to answer. Too little, too late, I thought. But by the seventh or eighth ring curiosity got the better of me. I didn't even manage to get in a nonchalant hello before he was talking.

"Lucy! Thank God . . . listen, I'm in a spot here. Any chance you can come rescue me?"

"Tom? Are you okay? What's happened? Where are you?"

"I'm fine . . . really I am. Bit cold. Very cold. Mainly embarrassed. I'm at the beach. Behind Tollys."

Tollinghams was a surfer's shack a little way along the coast, the far side of the peninsula that sheltered the town beach and made the waters so calm. It wasn't far from where Tom lived.

"O-k," I sing-songed down the line. "I'll see if I can borrow the car. Be there in about fifteen?"

"Cool! Thanks, Lucy, and . . . um, can you bring me some clothes? I'm naked!"

MOM'S RUN-AROUND was at the garage, and Dad wouldn't let me take his station wagon, but he didn't mind driving me there once he'd stopped shaking his head at the foolishness of youth. He gave me a t-shirt and a pair of sweatpants splattered with white paint; the tie-string waist would hopefully accommodate Tom's rather more athletic frame. I grabbed a voluminous beach towel as well. I wasn't sure what Tom would say when I turned up with my dad, but figured a towel might protect both our modesties.

The parking lot was unsurprisingly deserted. Dad stayed with the car, headlights bouncing off the boarded-up shack that served both hot and cold drinks as well as snacks to the surfer community, in daylight hours, at least. The moon floodlit the beach and shimmered off the black sea, slow lazy breakers foaming white. I headed to the steps that led to the sand, hesitating at the top.

I couldn't see or hear anything.

I wasn't sure whether to be worried or annoyed. I didn't think Tom would play a dumb trick on me. And if it was some elaborate ruse to get me on my own under the romantic full beam of full moon it had spectacularly backfired, what with my dad waiting less than a dozen steps away.

There was a hissed "Luce!" and I swung round, seeing the top of Tom's head appear from around the back of a chained-up dumpster.

"You got the clothes?"

I nodded, holding them aloft, but keeping a firm grip on them. "What's going on, Tom?"

He rubbed a hand ruefully over his bedraggled hair and down to his chin, glancing nervously towards the wagon's headlights. "To be honest, Lucy, I'm not entirely sure. I guess I went for a swim."

"You idiot!" I exclaimed, but he was already shaking his head.

"I hadn't meant to. I'd just gone for a walk, thinking of things, y'know? Next thing I'm here, on the beach, wet and . . . and naked, clothes who knows where, and if I hadn't stumbled across my dropped phone in the sand I'd have been totally screwed. Now . . . Could I *please* have something to wear? I'm freezing here."

I tossed the towel and clothes onto the roof of the dumpster and turned away as a pale blue arm reached to pull them back, odd shadows painted across his bare shoulders.

"That your dad?" he asked.

"Uh-huh."

"Do you mind if we say I went drunk skinny-dipping and someone stole my clothes?"

I laughed. "Less of the 'we', please. You can tell him whatever you want. Ready to go?"

He emerged, rubbing the towel across his head, scattering wet sand. I let him get into the front with Dad, who caught my eye in the rear-view as Tom laid the towel into the footwell for his still-bare feet. I shrugged and stared out of the window. What did I know?

"Where to, Tom?"

"My folks' place, if you don't mind, Mr. Peters. And thanks."

It wasn't until we pulled up outside Tom's that Dad spoke again. "You know, Tom, you should be a lot more careful."

"I know, I know, Mr. Peters, rip-tides and—"

"Not just that," Dad interrupted. "Kid over Falcon Creek way got a scare tonight. Heard it on the radio. Probably just a big fish but it brushed against him and scared the bejesus out of him. He won't be heading back into the water for a while. Seems you ought to have learnt your lesson by now."

Tom flushed bright red. "I have . . . I mean, I will. Promise."

"Ok then." Dad then turned his attention to me, still sitting quietly in the back. "You seeing Tom to the door? I can swing by and pick up you and my clothes in an hour or so?"

I flustered a yes, checking for any negative reaction on Tom's part, but he seemed glad to have a co-conspirator.

His mum was oblivious to the drama that had played out, coming into the kitchen to freshen up her drink. She smiled tiredly, not quite focussing on me.

"Hey, kids. Lucy, isn't it? Nice to see you again." She retreated back to the TV, the volume loud and the applause fake, as Tom wiped up the splash of red wine that had escaped her overfilled glass. I guessed that was why Tom hadn't called her for a lift home. There was no sign of his dad.

We sat at the kitchen table, a cup of microwaved hot chocolate apiece. "You okay?" I said.

"Sure," he smiled, his fingers laced around the warm mug. "I guess."

"You had these blackouts before?"

He frowned. "I wouldn't call them—"

"Been to see anyone about them?"

His eyes darted to the doorway where the TV blared jaunty adverts, then dropped to the wooden tabletop. "I've put them through enough already, don't you think?" he said quietly.

I reached out a hand, touched his. "See someone. Seriously. And no more nighttime swims. Not even nighttime walks along the beach, you hear?"

"Yes, ma'am." He smiled. "You okay if I take a shower before your dad returns?"

I made myself another hot chocolate as I listened to the water gurgle through the pipes, the soft snoring from the lounge, above it all the frantic sound of the TV. When the front door banged I looked up, expectant, but it was Tom's father not mine who stood frozen there, blinking myopically from behind thick lenses. "Um?"

"Lucy," I said, hopping up and shaking his calloused hand. "Tom's upstairs."

"Good to finally meet you," he said, eyebrow raised. I wondered just how often Tom had been vanishing into the night and what excuses he'd been giving. Not sure I was very happy being his alibi.

Tom came down, looking revived, the colour back into his cheeks, holding the rolled-up beach towel. "Um, thanks for the loan," he said, as a horn sounded from outside. Dad's station wagon was back.

"Hope university goes better for you," he added, following me out through the screen door. "And thanks, again."

"De nada. Speak soon, Tom. Stay safe," I said, pecking him on the cheek and trotting over to the car door my dad had already pushed open.

WHEN WE GOT back home, I threw the clothes in the wash. Except for the T-shirt. It was an old one; beer-logo emblazoned. But that wasn't what caught my attention. Down the back, the thread-bare fabric had been roughly ripped. It must have snagged on the dumpster, a victim of my underpowered throw. But as I held it out to the light, there was a moment when the abraded and torn fabric seemed to resemble a gaping mouth.

I blinked and the crazy vision vanished. No matter how I tilted it to the flickering fluorescents, it didn't reappear. Guess I was spooked. I thrust the ruined T-shirt deep to the bottom of the trash, laughing at myself. It had been a strange enough night without my imagination playing dumb tricks.

I'D BEEN BACK on campus almost a month when I picked up the message from my mum. The "Call me," didn't worry me much, but the plaintive "love you" did.

"Have you heard the news?" she asked, the volume of her voice going up and down as though she was trying not to be overheard and trying to sound normal at the same time.

Something about the way her breath caught told me that this wasn't the usual coffee morning gossip. I sat down on the edge of the small bed even before she asked me to do so, my hand gripping the iPhone with fierce intensity. "What news? Mom, what's happened?"

"It's . . . oh god, it's awful. There was another shark attack."

"In Larrington?" Tom, I thought. It could only be Tom.

"No," my mum said, voice faint, "over in Falcon Creek. A body-boarder. Half his arm torn off."

For a moment, terrible though that was, I thought everything was going to be all right. Falcon Creek was the next town along the coast, a good ten miles by road. Five as the crow flies, or I suppose as a fish swims. And Tom had never been one for surfboards and the like. It wasn't even a fatality and I began to wonder why Mom was so upset.

Then she murmured "Tom . . ." and the blood in my veins ran cold.

"Tom? What *about* Tom?"

"They sent out boats. To hunt the shark. Tom . . . I'm so sorry, Lucy; he got hit by a boat."

I stared around the little room I shared with the defiantly non-Mormon girl from Salt Lake City, the stark normality of it all. Outside, the last of the autumn leaves clung to the trees, glowing yellow against a slate sky.

"Is he . . . is he all right?"

The sob told me all I needed to know. It took her a lifetime to confirm it. "No, Lucy. He got caught . . . by the propeller."

LATER, LONG AFTER the funeral I couldn't bring myself to attend, I read the online pages of the Larrington newspaper, from the dramatic headlines to the short, unsatisfying summary: *Verdict: Misadventure.* There had been plenty to baffle the investigators. They found Tom's phone, once again not far from the dumpster at Tollinghams and shreds of his clothes washed up on the nearby beach the following morning. But Tolly's was an awfully long way from where the accident had happened. It had been a calm, moonlit night, so it was considered just about feasible for a strong swimmer to have swum that far, but why would he? Why would anyone?

I read up on the legend Tom had talked about as well, the *Mano Kanaka.* There wasn't a lot to go on, but some of the folklore talked about the man-shark, when in man form, wearing a cape, sometimes of feathers, to hide the maw of teeth between his shoulders.

The propeller blades caught Tom in the back. By all accounts, he was otherwise unscathed. But that was plenty enough. The clinical terms of the medical examiner's report—massive tissue damage, rapid blood loss, multiple organ failure—were easier to deal with than the gaping hole my mind persisted on conjuring up. A shape mirroring the one I'd imagined in that old T-shirt he'd borrowed from my dad. It was my damn fool mind that added the saw-toothed teeth.

TWO YEARS AND a change of university later, and by pure chance, I ran into the body-boarder guy on a packed Greyhound heading home for Thanksgiving. I didn't recognise his name as he introduced himself, and it was only when he proffered his left hand instead of his right that I realised what he was missing.

"You're not from Falcon's Creek are you?" I said, half disbelieving.

He grinned ruefully. "Heard about me, then? Dumb kind of fame, don't you think?"

I can't remember most of what we talked about. I do remember how much he reminded me of Tom, the way his eyes drifted to look out over the sea as the coach followed the turns of the highway along the coast.

"You must miss it," I said, at one point, "the body-boarding. The sea?"

He shrugged, looking faintly embarrassed. "Don't tell anyone, especially my folks, but I still go out."

I must have looked aghast, because he quickly did his best to reassure me. "Only on calm, moonlit nights," he said with a quiet laugh. "It might sound crazy, but it almost feels like home."

And the Wind Steal Her Vibrant Call

Mari Ness

Frankly, she would prefer to sleep. All this singing
is *exhausting,* and it's not as if
she's paid to do it, either. At least
not in cash. And the Amazons of these new days
do not believe in trade. She is tired
of gathering the bones,
of piling them up
upon the shores. She has
a thousand other things to do.
Including sleep. Or sorting through
the millennia of debris
summoned by her song.

No.

Even if
the waves are calling her,
warning of a nearby ship,

calling her to task. Even if
the salt is dancing on her skin,
pounding out a beat. Even if
she *must* sing, she *must,* even if
her bones shriek with the need.
Even if her breath
pushes fiercely against her lips,
ready to be moulded into song.
She knows—she *knows*—other ships
will come. She knows—she *knows*—
she will sing for them,
will gather their bodies on her shores.
She raises her arms to the wild wind,
turns her back against the waves,
lets the rain pound against her skin—
lets the wind steal her vibrant call.
Sleep. Yes. *Sleep*. Then song.

The Man Who Speared Octopodes

Davide Mana

THE OLD MAN called them "octopodes".

"Comes from the Greek, you know," he said the first time I met him. "Word octopus, that is. So octopodes' the correct plural."

We were on the beach, and Claire was setting up the sampling schedule, while I took a few photos. Pearl and gold sand, bright blue ocean under a hot sun.

The Old Man came out of the water, like the Creature from the Black Lagoon, in cut-offs and a wet Woodstock t-shirt, his mask and snorkel hanging around his neck, carrying a rusty speargun in one hand, and a bunch of tentacles in the other. Four or five octopuses, strung on a piece of wire. He walked towards me, grinning.

"Nice legs," he said, nodding at Clare.

"Aren't those protected?" I asked, pointing at his catch.

"Screw 'em," he grumbled. He lifted them and offered them to me. "Girlfriend's got a cat? Cats love octopodes."

I glanced at Clare. She had the sample bag ready, and was coming towards us. "She's not my girlfriend," I said. "We're

207

university. We're here to study microplastics in beach sands."

"Yeah, lotsa plastic jetsam hereabouts," he said. He looked up and down the beach. "Yesterday I speared one of these fuckers as he played with a flip-flop."

Clare frowned, coming close. "Aren't those protected?"

"I'm the one doing the protection here, miss," he chuckled. He lifted his catches again. "I mean, look at them. You know scientists say they might be from outer space? Smart little fuckers. And the eyes? They got eyes like us. And they get everywhere! So don't give me no protected bullshit. Kill 'em dead, that's what I do."

Clare and I traded a glance. She was about to speak, and I braced for impact, but the Old Man shrugged. "Well, you're not interested, I'll take them home. See ya!"

And he walked away.

"Weird chap," Clare said.

THE OLD MAN lived at the end of the beach, in a corrugated iron shack festooned with dried-out remains of octopuses.

"And yet even the seagulls stay away," Clare noted. She did not like him, the way he looked at her, and called him Aqualung, because she was into prog rock.

In the three days of our sampling campaign, we saw him often. He would come out of his shack, wave at us, and then wade into the surf with his speargun and his snorkel. We just paced the beach and collected a spoonful of sand at regular intervals. He did not offer us his catch again, but he stopped for a few words once in a while, the mask and snorkel around his neck bobbing as he ranted against the molluscs.

"I mean, this one, see?" he said, pulling at a brownish marbled tentacle. "This little bastard's a chameleon. He tried to convince me he's a rock." He rattled a long laugh. "And a few days back, one that tried to camouflage by picking up seaweeds and waving them about? But I shafted him anyway!"

Old Man Aqualung believed the octopuses were out to get him. To get us all.

"They can walk on land, you know? And they are smart! Tool-users, they are. Glass jars for houses, and all that. And there's no hole small enough where they can squeeze through. And they've got eight brains. Yessir, each tentacle has its own brain. If that's not proof they're aliens, I don't know what it is. And we all know what aliens want of us, right?"

"Steal our women?" I asked. Clare groaned. She did not like me humouring him.

But he laughed. "Well, mate, not on my watch!"

And so he patrolled the beach, two or three hours each day, swimming under the surface, carrying his speargun. We saw him sometimes, surfacing and blowing steam like a bearded dolphin in a tank top. Sometimes he broke through the surface, clenching the still-writhing remains of an octopus in a sign of triumph.

"There's sure a lot of the creatures around here," I said.

"And he's an extinction event walking on two legs."

"If he's got two legs he can't be an alien, right?"

That made her laugh.

THE SEAGULLS TIPPED us off.

Three weeks had gone by. We had come back to redo samples seven to fifteen, that had got mangled in the lab. Clare spotted them as soon as she got out of her old Suzuki. "Something's wrong."

There was a cloud of white birds, milling around the corrugated iron roof of Old Man Aqualung's shack, screaming their hearts out.

I looked at her, and she nodded. We went there, calling out. The birds ignored us and went on screeching and picking at the mummified octopuses. The door was ajar. Clare nodded me on. I went in.

The Old Man was inside, on a stuffed chair, his hands over his face. I squinted in the dusk, called him. "Sir?"

The place smelled of brine, disinfectant, and dust. Marine biology books were piled on the floor, stacks of Nature magazine, National Geographic. "Jesus Christ," Clare gasped behind me.

On a shelf, dozens of jars, each one with a different species of octopus preserved in alcohol. The seagull screams reverberated in the metal walls.

The Old Man was dead. Had been for some time. Someone had pinned his hands to his face, using two spears from his gun. Left and right. Each went through the hand and into his eye.

"Call 911."

She walked out, and I got closer. A single blade of light slashed his body in half. Wearing his dirty cut-offs and a tank top, the exposed skin was spotted like a leopard's, red sucker marks climbing up his leg and his arm, and finally wrapping around his neck, marking his cheeks.

"They can walk on land, you know?" his voice rasped in my head. "And they are smart!"

"They are coming," Clare said, startling me. And it took me a moment to realize she meant 911.

A Knot of Sea Wives

Sarah Van Goethem

A STORM HAD brewed up, spoiling the calm waters of the Atlantic and thus, the night Maeve O'Flaherty had looked forward to. It had come like a surprise guest, a knock at the door, and then rain hammered against the windows and the charcoal sky closed in, suffocating. Now, Maeve wasn't sure her husband would make it home at all.

Maeve drew her shawl tightly over her slim shoulders and paced the worn floorboards. There was something unsettling about the storm. *No,* she decided, adding more cow dung to the smoking fire in the hearth, a half-hearted attempt to ward off the chill that had overtaken her. It wasn't the storm, exactly. Or maybe, on second thought, it was. Maybe it was the churlish, caterwauling wind and the clotted grey clouds, or the creaking trees, their autumnal leaves now a swell of confetti. There was something about it that niggled at the back of her mind and drew a shiver down her spine.

Maeve had thought nothing of the lazy pitter-patter of rain on the thatched roof earlier. When the rain had begun to form puddles, she'd even let the children splash and dance until they were properly muddy. She'd only made them come in and wash and tidy themselves for bed when the air had changed, grown thicker somehow, and more still. Maeve had paid attention then; storms always made her feel irrational, wild in some way. Not quite herself. The sky had darkened, and with the first fork of lightning, Maeve's belly had twisted as if struck.

And then, the storm had broken.

It had unleashed before Padraic could make it home for the stew and bread Maeve had prepared. Before he could join her in the safety of their cottage, warm and snug, riding out the storm together.

Maeve pressed her face to the window, the tip of her nose against the cool glass. But there was nothing to be seen except one dark silhouette against another, none of which were her husband. The moon, a thin slice, was hidden behind the clouds. The ocean that Maeve loved to gaze at on a sunny day had turned savage. Black waves pounded against the rugged coast, beating like her own heartbeat in her ears.

Maeve spun away and slipped into her rocking chair. The room was dim and the fire smoked badly. Padraic had forgotten to cut any turf from the bog this summer and Maeve was already burning cow dung. She reprimanded herself yet again; Padraic was so busy, she should've done it herself. She hadn't been thinking.

She picked up her darning and attempted, with trembling hands, in the dim light of the tallow wick, to focus on the hole in Padraic's wool sock. Winter was coming, after all. There would be plenty of time for them to sit around the fire later, to reminisce about the night of the storm.

That's what the coastal people did with storms. Nattered about them later in hushed voices around fires to wide-eyed children. *Once there was this dreadful storm,* an old woman would say, her knitting needles clacking together, *it brang a wind that ripped off roofs and stole children's voices.*

I remember the time, an old grandfather would jump in, his pipe lodged in the side of his mouth, smoke curling into the air, *ahh yes, I was a wee lad back then. The storm that sunk my own father's fishing boat sure. Rained so much and so hard it filled it to the top and sunk it good. 'Twas lost forever to the ocean floor.*

The stories were told during new storms, too, in every white-washed cottage along the coast. Stories of fairy folk, of banshees and witches. And the sea folk, of course. Always the ones who dwelled underwater. If Padraic were here, maybe he'd be telling her a story himself. *Stop it now, Maeve,* she told herself sternly; Padraic never spoke of the other storms or what he knew, what he'd seen. His tongue was tied as tight as a corset. Even when he had drink in him, never a whisper of it graced his lips.

Maeve fancied she could hear them now, though, the others, spinning tales in the squally night. Murmurs in the howling wind that joined with the creak of her rocking chair. And then someone breathed the words—someone always did—*remember the night the ghost ship washed ashore?*

Maeve's hands stilled, the needle slipping from her fingers. *For the love of the sea.* That's what it was, the thing that had been bothering her. How could she have forgotten? *Because you wanted to,* her mind snapped at her. She sprang into action quite suddenly, frantically searching for the sliver of a needle on her lap. When she found it, she stuck it in her pincushion with force and rose, her throat knotted tight.

The ghost ship. How long ago had that been now?

Maeve's footsteps swept across the floor, her right hand having claimed the candle on the table, until she stood at the narrow wall, the partition to their sleeping place. It was small and dark, cast in shadows. Her boys, Conall and Seamus, lay tangled together beneath the sheets, the older one's limbs longer and slimmer than she remembered. How quickly the time passed, how rapidly the baby fat melted away and the days turned them into men. She blinked away the tears, the sadness for something she hadn't yet lost. And then Maeve turned slowly to the other corner, her free hand pressed to her thumping chest.

Maeve took a few steps closer to the girl, the girl with the golden hair, Padraic's daughter from his first marriage. *Imogen.* She lay atop the sheets, her smooth, white skin almost the shade of her cotton nightgown. Maeve held the candle higher. Was that a tinge of blue, or maybe green, some shade of aquamarine, to the girl's skin? Sometimes, in the right light, Maeve swore it was. Padraic pretended never to notice, though. It drove Maeve nearly mad—his denial. His refusal to talk, to acknowledge any of it. The child's mouth was parted slightly, a small whistle escaping her soft lips. She was sleeping now. Good. She'd wanted to go out in the storm earlier, begged Maeve to show her the swell of the water, the wee silly thing. Her chest rose and fell, her hands splayed on either side of her.

Those hands. Maeve shuddered. Webbed between each tiny finger, same as her exposed toes.

Her watermark.

Maeve did the math to be sure, horror circling in her belly. *Yes, the child was nine years old.* They'd held her upside down at her last birthday festivity, not so long ago, and bumped her head on the floor (gently of course) nine times. And one extra, for luck in the upcoming year.

Nine bumps.

Nine years.

The amount of time before Marina, her merrow mother, had threatened to come back.

MAEVE KNEW ABOUT Marina from the midwife, Brigid Sweeney. Maeve's births hadn't been easy, the big, sturdy boys reluctant to fold themselves nicely and slip smoothly out of Maeve. No, instead, Maeve had spent too many daylit hours with Brigid each time, the midwife cooing and pressing on her belly, prodding the places only Padraic had ventured. Hours for Maeve to wheedle it out of Brigid, in between the piercing pains that clawed at her belly and back. With the second birth, Seamus, Maeve had been relentless. By then, she'd spent enough years with her husband to know he wasn't going to tell her himself. That everywhere Maeve went, shadows followed her. Ghosts of Padraic's first and most beautiful wife, and everyone knowing except Maeve. Every time the pains had become sharper, so had Maeve's tongue. *Tell me about her*, Maeve had begged, and then, more fiercely, *I have a right to know about the child.*

She did, didn't she? Have a right? After all, she was the one who cared for the child, fed her and plaited her hair and washed the dirt off of her bluish-tinted skin.

Finally, she'd broken Brigid down.

Yes, I was there the night Imogen was born. The midwife had admitted to this with a furrow of her brow and a twisting together of her fingers. She'd then left Maeve's side to scurry about the small cottage, to check on Conall and Imogen, the two of them playing with pebbles in the yard. She'd drawn the thin curtains against the too-bright sun and shut the door as if she were afraid someone was listening. She'd returned just as Maeve's body was racked with another pain.

Still, it didn't stop Maeve; she'd scrabbled for the midwife's arm as her body convulsed, tearing flesh where her nails dug in. *Tell me,* she'd begged again, sensing she was close. Close to the story, close to the birth.

And then Brigid's words had sliced into her, quick and fast, even as the woman tugged Maeve into a squatting position. *This is just between me and you, and if anyone asks, I didn't breathe a word of it, you understand?*

Maeve had nodded, of course she had. Anything to pry the story from the woman's chapped lips. Then, she'd pushed, involuntarily, her body a traitor when she'd rather have sat quietly with a cup of tea, absorbing the story she'd longed to hear.

The stories are all true, Brigid had confessed. *'Twas only a short time she was here, on this land. I know how that sounds, but there's something to it, and you know it, and that's why you're asking.* Brigid hadn't looked at Maeve, only poked about inside Maeve with her bony fingers and declared it was time. *Now go on push,* she'd said to Maeve, but in her next breath she was talking about the first wife again. *The child just slipped out of her, it did, like it'd barely been inside at all. I never checked her, never even had her spread her legs.*

Legs? Maeve had thought vaguely, because she'd heard snatches of the story before, uttered behind her back. She just wanted someone to say it, to say it all.

Out loud.

Did the woman have legs?

It was storming, of course, the midwife had gone on quickly. *You'd remember the night. Everyone does. The night the ghost ship washed ashore. But that was after the fact, after she'd gone. They blamed the ship on her kind, the men. They are hideously ugly you know, and bitter because of it. It's said they stole the sailors and drowned them all far beneath, on the ocean floor, and then the ship washed ashore. What? Of course, I've gotten away from myself. The birth, right. Marina, the sea maid. So, where was I? Oh yes, the storm. Lightning struck outside and I turned to see the flash, and next thing I knew, the babe was on the floor, all blue and quiet, with tangles of wet hair. So much hair, God Almighty, and when I reached down and cleaned out her nose and mouth, little bits of seaweed so.*

Seaweed. Maeve had repeated the word, dumbly, then grunted with another push. How she hated the woman, the first and most beautiful wife, whose child slithered out with no help at all, with barely the bat of an eyelash. *What does that mean?* Maeve had asked, even as her body arched, writhing in pain. *The seaweed?* She needed Brigid to say it, to speak the words aloud.

Let me see, let me see, Brigid had said, her tongue wetting the cracks of her lips, *come on now, push harder. There we go now.* Maeve had pushed. Her legs had been shaking. Her face had burned with the strain. Brigid's voice had dropped so low, Maeve could barely hear. *She was a merrow. That's what it means.*

Yes. There it was.

A merrow.

It was gratifying somehow, knowing the truth. Knowing it wasn't all in her head. It might've been enough, to know just that, but the midwife kept going, and Maeve couldn't stop her; the pain was unbearable now, and took all her focus.

Brigid's words had drifted through the haze of Maeve's pain. *Story has it he found her on the shore, in distress, her tail floundering in the sand. I'm sure you've heard, about their glistening scales, their exquisite singing. He meant to give her back, you see, to return her to the waves. But she was the most beautiful thing he'd ever seen, and him a young man . . . well you know how it is with first love. Consuming, intense, almost unbearable.*

Maeve had known. That's how she loved Padraic then, with every part of her being. She had since the first day she'd seen him.

She was striking, story has it. Bewitched him from the first.

The words had echoed in Maeve's ears, like something far away and yet too close. She'd grit her teeth together and mustered a glare at Brigid. Did the midwife know how her words hurt? Stung worse than the pain of labour, if that was possible. Maeve would forget the labour, she knew it would dull with time, but these words . . . she could not unhear them.

And yet. Perversely. She had to know the rest. *What then?* she'd groaned. Oh God, what then. She'd already hated that she'd asked.

And Brigid, so eager to tell her, eyes glassy and wide in the dark, still room. *He stole her little red cap, right off her head. Her cohuleen druit. That's how they live in the ocean you know, how they go from tails to legs. He snatched her cap and she was at his mercy. Ahhh, there we go now, dearie. There's the head so.*

Maeve had been splitting apart. Her body, her heart. Still, Brigid went on. Like she'd waited all this time to spill the story, and now her tongue had run away from her, unable to stop even if she'd wanted it to.

The night Imogen was born, that night he brang the cap back. He'd hid it all that time, but he went and got it that night, pulled it from his secret hiding spot. He cried, he did. Sobbed. A grown man weeping over his lovely wife and his beautiful new daughter, and I think, you know, I think he thought if he gave it back to her, she would choose him and the baby.

Brigid had shaken her head with the tragedy, and Maeve could see in that moment the midwife had slid into the past, again in this very room with the sea fairy wife, and the great, wild love the sailor had bestowed on her.

Laughter had bubbled in Maeve's throat, a sick thing. Padraic hadn't been there that afternoon, the day Seamus was born. Not with Conall either. But he had been there when Imogen was born. Of course, he had.

Maeve had bore down with all her might. All she'd ever wanted was for Padraic to love her that much. She'd recognized that in that moment. But he couldn't, not the way he'd loved his first wife. There could never be another first. She could give him five more sons and still he wouldn't, couldn't, love her as much. *She didn't choose him,* Maeve had spat out, and although she thought the fact would console her, it didn't. Not at all.

No, they always choose the sea, Brigid had muttered, and it had occurred to Maeve the midwife had seemed not quite herself. Her hands too jerky, her words too quick. Like the story had made her slightly mad. *They become homesick. She took the cap and fled, but he wouldn't give her the child. In the end, she left without the girl baby, but she said she'd be back, in nine years time.*

Nine years. Such a long time, or so it seemed when you were young. *Back for what?* Maeve had asked. *The child?*

Their eyes had locked then, for a split second. Blue on brown. Water meeting land. Brigid hadn't answered, but Maeve had known. She'd read it in the pinch of Brigid's forehead, the tightness of her shoulders.

Marina would return to reclaim Padraic, her human husband who had held her captive.

Maeve gave one last startling push.

Seamus was born, slowly and agonizingly, while Maeve thought about a little red cap, hidden away somewhere in this very cottage, and her husband, deceptive and cunning, keeping it from his merrow-wife.

Of course, Marina would come back, return the favour.

And then, Maeve was tucked back into bed, weary, her new baby suckling greedily at her breast, the story fading away like the labour pains. Leaking into the slats of the floorboards and cracks of the walls, joining with the story of the first wife, like a knot tied together. Maeve at one end, Marina at the other.

But Marina wasn't here and Maeve was. Maeve was the one who had claim on Padraic now. She drew her finger over the new baby's soft cheek. He was hers, same with the first boy, and all of them belonging to Padraic.

But there, when Maeve had looked up, at the door, with her wide green eyes and her mass of yellow hair, had been Imogen. So solemn. So thoughtful. Webbed fingers wrapped around the door jam. Oh God, she was his too. *How much had she heard?*

The child had already been five years old then. Old enough to listen, to absorb a story.

Maeve had begun to tremble.

Sometimes that happens after a birth, Brigid had fussed, back to her usual self. *It shouldn't last long.*

NINE YEARS WAS gone, just like that, like a snap of the fingers. And now, this—Marina coming back. Maeve doubled over the kitchen table, just barely setting the candle down safely. The thought of her dropping it crossed her mind, of the cottage suddenly consumed in flames, an orange glow in the black night. Fire—the opposite of water. Everything burning. The chairs with their handwoven rush seats, the table, the kitchen utensils. The oat straw. The small pile of potatoes. All of Padraic's ropes hanging from nails on the walls, his pastime with the children, teaching them to tie knot after knot. And on into the bedroom the fire would spread, to char her one beautiful and deceitful item, her stolen gilt brush and mirror set. And then, oh yes then, her beloved carved rocker. *No,* she corrected herself. *Marina's rocker.* It had been hers, first, hadn't it? Maeve could see that now, quite clearly. How they'd shared a cottage, a rocker, a husband.

Thunder rumbled outside and Maeve's knees nearly buckled. She slapped her palms to the wooden table, bile rising in her throat. Would Padraic come running up from the ocean, if there was a fire? Would he save them? Or would he only make it there too late? To kick the ashes about and clutch at his hat and shake his head. Not nearly as sad as he'd been when Marina had gone.

Stop it, Maeve told herself sternly, straightening. *You're being ridiculous.* This was the thing that had been driving her and Padraic apart, wasn't it? Her imagining these things in her head, her own worst enemy.

So what if Padraic didn't say much? Didn't want to speak of his past? Not everyone was like Maeve, ready to divulge every last shred of themselves. And Padraic spending every waking moment by the water? That was his job, wasn't it? As Keeper of the Cape Clear Lighthouse. She should be glad he'd given up his sailor days; he'd be here even less in that case. Swallowed by the ocean for long lengths of time.

He hadn't been able to make it back tonight on account of the storm. That was all. He'd still make it in, just later. It couldn't be helped if his dinner had gone cold on him. Or he'd come tomorrow, when the ocean had calmed itself, turned placid and smooth. Maeve would relax then, too, and feel foolish for her thoughts tonight. They'd enjoy his week off together. *Yes,* Maeve consoled herself. *That's what will happen.*

And yet.

Maeve couldn't help herself. She crossed to the door, flung it wide open. Let the rain lash at her face, and the sounds of the raging ocean assault her ears.

Such a bittersweet love she had. Marina the merrow wasn't the only one with a love of the water.

MAEVE HAD LOVED it with her whole heart once—the ocean. She'd been born in a lighthouse. Sole daughter of Killian MacNamara, Keeper of Blacksod Lighthouse. It had been a magical childhood with the beam of the light sweeping through her bedroom window at night. She'd climbed the great steps of the lighthouse as soon as she could walk, guided by her father's gentle hand, turning on the light that would stretch across the water, searching, searching, always searching.

Had Maeve seen something once? Something truly magical? Yes, in the black waters, where she searched her fuzzy memories. Was it real? The image of the tail, of the hank of hair dipping back below water, or had she only imagined that, too? Moulded and created it in her mind to fit cleanly into her life now. To explain her own husband in a way that made sense?

How was her father's lighthouse-keeping, her childhood, so enchanted in her mind, like a charming painted picture, a soft dream, whereas her husband's latched on like a nightmare?

Blacksod had been land-based, maybe that was it. It had kept Maeve's parents together, bound in salt and skies of blue. Unlike Cape Clear, which was offshore, a column of cast iron protruding from jagged rock, and kept the mam and children (her and her sons and Imogen) in their squalid shore dwelling. Put another divide between her and Padraic, as if there weren't enough already.

Maeve hated that, too. How her love of the lighthouses could become soured, hardened like the crust of bread she'd left for Padraic on the table.

Someone was singing in the dark. Maeve strained her ears, her face wet, wondering for a split second how she'd come to be standing outside in the storm. How she'd become mother of three children, only two born of her body.

But yes, there, in the distance. A song, dragging her back into the present (how easy it was to get lost in the past!). A voice, not quite lost in the roar and crash of the surf. Exquisite.

No.

Maeve leaned against the door, dizzy.

Nine years, Brigid's voice echoed. *She said she'd be back in nine years' time.*

Something icy hot snaked through Maeve, quite suddenly, and she wondered vaguely if it'd always been there, simmering beneath the fear. Whatever it was, this devouring anger, it was easier to chew on, easier to swallow. It felt better than being afraid. Her fists curled, nails digging into her palms. She was sick of it. So sick of it all. Of living in the shadow of the sea fairy. Years of festering, swept just under the floorboards, so.

Maeve burst back into the cottage, blinking in the smoky room. The candle burned low on the table, the stew cold and congealed, uneaten by the husband who should've been here. The wind hissed through the door, fluttering the threadbare curtains and flickering the flame.

And then the flame snuffed out. There was only Maeve and the gloom and her own thoughts, wild and terrifying.

She was filled up, consumed with the thought of a red cap. She knew where Padraic had hidden it, too. Without a doubt. The loose stone in the fireplace. It was pointless to look now, wasn't it? Still, Maeve rushed over and scraped at the stone with her fingers in the firelight, desperately and meticulously working it free. The stones were crude, the seams uneven. Still, it was a fine fireplace, if anything in this cottage could be considered fine. It made a perfect hiding spot.

Aha, Maeve thought, comforted by the thought that she knew something Marina hadn't. So what if Padraic hadn't specifically showed Maeve? Did it really matter that he'd thought her asleep any time he'd removed the stone himself?

Details.

The stone was high on the inner wall, above the bar with the hanging pot where Maeve boiled potatoes, and below that, the lower iron kettle where she baked the bread. Hot to the touch, but not too hot. It wouldn't have mattered. Maeve would've blistered her roughened fingers, burnt them clean off to remove the wretched stone.

Finally, it fell away. Slipped from her clutch. Landed on the hearth with a thud. Maeve thrust her hand inside the gaping hole.

There was no red cap inside, not now. No piece of fabric to lend something solid to the story, an ounce of truth. Of course, there wasn't. Only some old copper coins and a few silver tenpence tokens. Money Maeve could've used to buy peat. Even now, her eyes burned, her throat tight with the cow-dung smoke.

Maeve's rage grew, like the storm outside. It clouded her vision and solidified her heart. And the haunting voice, the singing that filtered beneath the door and tapped against the small windowpane, the voice she'd imagined a thousand times over, it made her forget everything except the storm and her disloyal husband and the merrow wife who'd returned. It drew her toward the child with the webbed fingers and toes, little Imogen, the reminder. The girl who had asked to go out in the storm. The child barely stirred as Maeve plucked her out of bed and glided out of the cottage, onward toward the water.

THE GHOST SHIP had run aground the same night Marina had birthed Imogen, though Maeve hadn't known that at the time. No, she'd only been a lass back then, innocent and naive, and tucked yet within Blacksod Lighthouse, in her parents' care.

It'd been her father who'd seen it first. He'd later described the large cargo vessel as angling itself into the rocks below quite gently, as if it'd simply decided it'd had enough of the sea. Maeve had climbed down with her Mam the next morning to gawk at the hulking steel while the seagulls circled, squawking overhead. Maeve had taken inventory. No mast collapse. No hull damage. No captain, no one at the helm. No one aboard.

Just a lonely ship, washed ashore.

Other folks had come, too. Clawed their way over the rocks like crabs, to stand silent and still, observing the abandoned ship. *Where it had come from?* they wondered. *Had it drifted about for some time, perhaps up from Africa and past Spain? Where was the crew?*

A search had revealed cargo aboard: chandeliers, optical instruments, mirrors and dining sets. What treasure! Looting had begun quickly, the taking of riches by people who'd never seen such delights.

Maeve's mam had traipsed aboard herself, snatching a gilt mirror and brush set for Maeve, setting it atop a lace runner that night. Laid out on the dresser for Maeve like a gift.

But the riches had become reminders. Polished, gold-plated baubles that inspired stories and legends and ocean lore. And a few months later, when Padraic O'Flaherty had ventured forth with his new daughter, with her webbed fingers and toes, and no mother so-to-speak, the story of Marina the Merrow had been woven.

Marina had always been odd, hadn't she? a plain-faced young woman had asked, her shrewd eyes on Padraic.

Yes, yes. Different somehow, her friend assured her. *But now she's gone.*

And besides, what human mother would leave her child?

another, more suitable mother, had commented. *And what coincidence, the same night as a ghost ship washes up? Unlikely the two were not connected.*

No, no, an old man had agreed, arms crossed. *Terribly suspect.*

And then another, the local midwife. *'Twas the merrow men, of course. They are hideously ugly you know, and bitter because of it. They stole the sailors and drowned them all and then the ship washed ashore.*

Yes, the ghost ship had washed ashore and Marina, the merrow, had disappeared, once again. Lost to the water.

Maeve hadn't heard the stories, not then. Not holed up in the lighthouse, secluded from other folks. This was the way she'd pieced it together, the way she'd imagined it happened.

She'd only met Padraic when he'd come to see her father, when he'd given up his life as a sailor and wanted to learn the ropes, to know everything Killian MacNamara knew about being a lighthouse keeper.

Padraic O'Flaherty, with the freckles over his nose and his flaming hair, the shade of the setting sun, and his watery-blue eyes, full of melancholy and depth, a place for Maeve to get lost in. A place that spoke of secrets. Maeve had loved him from the start. And the tiny baby in his arms, well, it only made Maeve love him more.

The poor man, the widower. Left all alone with a tiny little girl.

That's what Maeve had thought.

That the first wife was gone forever. Only a memory.

And there was Maeve, eligible and eager. Ready to be a wife. Ready to save him from himself.

Maeve had flipped over the gilt mirror that first night, the night after Padraic had left her father's lighthouse. *What had Padraic seen when he looked at her?* she wondered. *Was she enough?* It was the first time she'd wondered such a thing, considered her own adequacy. She still shuddered to think of it now. Her own lack of self-assurance. And the other part, of course.

Over her shoulder, past her own dull reflection, she'd sworn she'd seen a flick of yellow hair. The greenest of eyes.

She'd still swear it now, to this day.

MARINA THE MERROW had been taking over Maeve's life, slowly but surely, for far too long. Maeve could taste it on her tongue, the resentment, the bitterness, maybe her own regret. She licked her lips, let the salty sea spray overpower the other flavours.

The child was squirrely in her arms now, having woken in the cold, in the dark. "Where are we going?" she asked, twisting her head to see the water, and her clear voice made Maeve seethe inwardly. She knew her boys, in the same situation, would be whimpering, snivelling and crying and pressing their faces to her chest. This girl child had no fear. Always solemn and pensive, too clever. "Has Da come in?"

Maeve didn't answer. Only kept going, slithering her way down the path cut into the rocky hillside. The child was heavy, too heavy for carrying, but Maeve didn't set her down. Maeve had a super-human strength, something born of the storm and years of unsaid words. She only stopped for a moment to readjust the child. And the child, full of trust, wrapped her legs around Maeve's waist, and her arms around Maeve's neck.

The child's body was warm and Maeve hesitated, but only for a second; the child cocked her head to the side, listening.

"You hear it?" Maeve asked, her words caught in her throat. And she knew, she knew this would be it, the determining factor.

The child nodded solemnly, her eyes wide and white in the dark. *Yes, she heard the singing.*

"Right then. There we go now." Maeve moved forward again, over the slippery rocks, toward the voice. The child's mother, the sea fairy. Calling her back.

Children should be with their mothers, Maeve thought. She'd reunite them, bring them together. Offer the child as a consolation. Perhaps Marina would forget about Padraic then. Maeve swallowed past the guilt in her throat, the screaming in her head. *Would you forget him?* she asked herself. *Would you trade your husband for your children?*

"You're hurting me," the child murmured, and Maeve stopped as she reached the bottom of the cliff and loosened her arms, sucked in breaths of salty air as if she were the one being squeezed.

"Sorry," Maeve whispered, surprised at her apology, surprised to find her bare feet cut and bloodied, devoid of pain. Surprised she hadn't thought of this sooner, sacrificing the child. "There, there, don't be scared," Maeve cooed, though the child didn't seem fearful in the least; Maeve had brought them to the beach many times, almost daily. Even at night, to lay in the sand and count the stars.

But there were no stars tonight; they were all blotted out. Only a leaden sky, and leftover raindrops. But the ocean was still riled up, kicking up angry waves that rushed onto the shore, licking at Maeve's feet.

Maeve scanned the stormy water, blinded by the thoughts in her head, deaf to everything save the song that skittered about, tossed on the waves. It was everywhere all at once, in every whitecap and froth, in every day on the bleak, obscured horizon that promised Maeve more of the same. More of her withdrawn husband and his reminder of a child. The wind was so strong it nearly knocked Maeve over and she dug her feet into the sand, anchored herself firmly, and wondered, *if I let go of the child, is the wind strong enough to carry her into the briny waves?*

Another wave rolled in then, in response, stronger, swelling over Maeve's feet. She gasped with the cold, her fury rising again. There was no mercy tonight, no grace in the water, and Maeve knew how it felt. Her life had become this string of moments, all leading up to this, right now.

The child was struggling, sensing something now, unnerved by Maeve, but Maeve only tightened her grip again, holding the shaking child close. "Look," she said, "you wanted to see the water," and she nodded toward the ocean where she could see them all now, the other storms from the stories of the past. There was the one that filled the rowboat up with water and sank it, and the one that ripped the roofs off and stole the children's voices. She even saw the ghost ship, jostling its way onto the rocks, lodging itself in Maeve's very bones. Ever so gently.

And then, she saw red.

There, bobbing about amidst the choppy water. The thing that had haunted Maeve's dreams and every waking moment.

The red cap.

Maeve pressed forward, leaving footprints that were just as quickly washed away. No one would know what she'd done. Her ankles were submerged, then her knees, her skirt grew heavier, saturated. Clinging to her legs, tugging her back.

The child was flailing, hands pushing against Maeve's chest, legs thrashing. And the song, so loud, so very loud in Maeve's ears, a chant without words. A shrieking in the night. Maeve caught something in the corner of her eye and jerked right. Just as quickly, something flashed to the left, and Maeve spun about. Back and forth, back and forth, until she was dizzy. And the child, wailing, drowning out the song.

And then. Her name called.

"Maeve!"

The child fell silent. Maeve stilled, her chest heaving, her limbs frozen with cold and fright and the sound of his voice.

Padraic.

He'd come after all.

"Da," the child called, reaching out her arms, out and around Maeve, as if Maeve didn't exist.

Another wave rolled into Maeve, and her arms, numb and trembling, gave out. The child fell into the water, tumbling underneath. Her nightgown, white and smooth, billowed out like a sail.

Behind Maeve, Padraic called and called, cursed and screamed, his footsteps pounding on the rocks and sand, and suddenly Maeve was present again, terribly and horribly present and aware. The moon slipped out from behind a cloud, and there, dragged some feet away, further out, was the child. The child Maeve had reared since birth, petted and snuggled and tucked into bed. The child with her webbed hands now slapping against the water, hair silver and floating in the moonlight. Mouth round and open, sputtering water.

Water that was not for her.

Oh God. She was only a child.

Maeve dove in, swam for the girl. What had she done? What had possessed her? *Imogen.*

The child was hers as much as she was Padraic's, as much as Marina's. How could Maeve have not seen it before? Maeve grabbed for her nightgown, screaming and screaming the child's name, her voice raw, but the child was scared, kicking and elbowing about, and then another wave swept her away. Fabric slipped through Maeve's fingers.

Padraic yelled again, his voice closer, and though Maeve couldn't hear his words, she knew he was begging her, *save my daughter.*

Maeve plunged forward.

Water splashed behind her and Maeve twisted about, frantic to find the child, frantic to latch onto Padraic. But Padraic was several feet to the side of her, his arms outstretched for Imogen as well. Of course, he should save her first. Maeve reached out, too, tried to work with the water, to become part of it, rising and falling, but her clothing was so heavy, so very heavy. And then she couldn't touch any longer, the ocean floor gave away. Something connected with her jaw (the child's foot?) and another great wave rolled over them, dragging Maeve under.

IT WAS QUIET beneath the water. Not what Maeve expected. The crashing and roaring of the surf, the grumbling of the sky, the frantic calling of Padraic's voice—all of it was gone. There was only a faint hum, a silent lapping of the water.

And a song. A luring song. *Bloody hell, that song.*

Maeve felt a brush of fingertips, a caress of silky soft hair. And the slick, somewhat slimy feel of fish, of scales, of a tail, against Maeve's legs.

Marina. The two of them at last, entwined in an underwater dance.

A knot of sea wives.

Maeve didn't fight, didn't writhe about. She only held her breath, blinking in the dark, searching for the red cap, and wondered vaguely, *is this what Marina expected?* Did the merrow-wife expect to find Maeve here, fighting for Padraic, and now Imogen? Did she expect anyone to want what she'd left behind? To want it so badly that they'd risk it all?

Maeve could only wonder so long; her breath was leaving her, her lungs bursting. She kicked her feet, propelled herself toward the surface. But she was no longer sure what was up from down, and panic set in.

She widened her eyes, searched, searched, searched in the dark, like the beam of a lighthouse, the thing she knew. There was a flash of red, a flick of yellow hair, and Maeve snatched something in her hand. The last thing she saw was emerald green eyes.

MAEVE CAME TO on the beach at daybreak. *Alive,* she marvelled.

I'm alive. The ocean, the water, had spit her out. Even it didn't want her.

Maeve rolled over, her limbs stiff and heavy, her hair matted to her face. The sun was warm on her skin, the morning a quiet hush. The only sound was bird song and it was peaceful in a way Maeve hadn't known in a long time.

Until she heard her name called, once again.

"Maeve!"

Padraic.

But Maeve could not call back, the storm had stolen her voice. Just like in the story. She pushed herself up, knees pulled to her chest. And then Padraic was coming towards her with Imogen in tow, the two of them scrabbling down the rocks. Maeve's shoulders slumped in relief; Imogen was okay, perfectly fine. It had all come to naught.

But just as quickly Maeve wondered, *what will Padraic think? What has the child said?* The night was murky in Maeve's mind, filled with apprehension. And now, on this beach, on the shingle, she suddenly pictured how Padraic had found Marina, the sea fairy wife, all washed up like Maeve was now.

The start of everything.

What a strange circle. What a tightly-tied knot.

Padraic stopped a few feet from her while Imogen hung back, and she could tell he was thinking the same thing. He blinked several times, before his mouth turned up at the sides (oh how she'd longed to see him smile!) and then he let out a rush of air. "Oh God," he said, trembling, blinking over and over, shocked to see her alive.

Maeve ran a hand over her damp dress, the material clinging and wrapped about her legs. She remembered when she was a child and would wrap herself just so, to make a tail. To pretend she was a merrow, a product of the sea. *That's what he's seeing,* she thought, *me with a tail.* A laugh crawled up her throat at the absurdity, then erupted, and she clapped a hand over her mouth.

Padraic inched closer and fell to his knees beside her and she realized he was laughing, too. It was a strange sound, one that didn't belong to them, or this relationship. But just as quickly his laugh turned to tears and he reached for her, uncertainly, as if he'd only just discovered her in the flesh and blood, his real human wife, almost lost to the water, too, and tenderly lifted her onto his lap. It was everything she'd wanted for so long it nearly broke her heart. "Imogen says you went to watch the storm, you wee silly things," he said, choking on his words.

Maeve looked up, met Imogen's eyes. A staggering green, like the ones underwater, and Maeve's hand fluttered to her throat as she remembered the feeling, the push that had guided her to the surface before all went dark.

Marina.

She hadn't taken Maeve, or Imogen. Not even Padraic, and now an awful and most treacherous thought plagued Maeve, *did she decide he wasn't worth it?* Maeve looked again at her husband in the new morning light. He was observing her, too, his eyes softer than before.

The child displayed a foot, interrupting their thoughts, webbed toes drawing circles in the sand. "It's my fault," she told her father, eyelashes brushing against her bluish-tinted cheek (how glaringly obvious it was in the morning light!). "You know how I like the water during storms."

Padraic nodded, his lips pursed together, acknowledging something about his daughter for the first time. "I do," he said, and that was all, but it was enough for Maeve. She was glad her voice had left her; she wouldn't know what to say. She swallowed her unsaid words, her nerves taught. *It's true,* she thought, twisting the story to convince even herself, *Imogen always liked storms.*

Padraic stretched out an arm, welcoming Imogen into their circle. "Yes, but you know how Da likes the two of you." And he seemed to mean what he said. That he liked Maeve, too.

Maeve could nearly cry at how differently this morning could be. How different the dark night was from the day. How different the ocean was now, the water a sheen of glass.

Maeve tentatively reached out as well, rubbed her hand over the child's arm. She wondered for a split second, *does Imogen know?* Did she truly know what Maeve had intended? But yes, just there, in the steady green gaze she bestowed on Maeve, the slow blink of her eyes. She knew, and she was covering. Protecting Maeve, but why?

"What have you got there?" Imogen asked, prying open Maeve's fingers. Maeve hadn't realized she'd still been clenching her fists. But there, in her palm, was a tangle of seaweed (not hair?) and a scrap of red fabric. Just a morsel, a part of something bigger.

Padraic sucked in a breath and Maeve felt his arms stiffen around her. How delicate they all were this morning, dancing around each other.

The child took the fabric, her brows scrunching together. "Pretty," she said. "May I have it?" It wasn't really a question, Maeve could tell by the way the child's mouth quirked up just so, just at the corner. Maeve's lungs squeezed, her throat tight, and she thought she may drown on the land, baked in the sunlight, and she knew, in that single moment, how Marina had felt when her cap, her power, was stolen. And Maeve could say nothing, not a single word. The keeper of her secret, her happiness, was now the child of Marina, the merrow-wife.

And just like that, with a tug of the rope, the knot was secured again.

The child stuffed the scrap in her pinafore pocket with a twinkle in her eye, and set off to dance where the water lapped against the shore.

Going Home

Valerie Hunter

EACH TIME REUBEN Wallace surfaces from the haze of morphine, a nurse explains what happened again. Each time, he can't quite believe her.

"You were on the *Sultana*, do you remember?" the woman asks. She has eyes that are tired but kind.

Reuben nods even though it makes his head throb. He remembers that terrible boat, how they were crammed in like livestock. He remembers how he panicked, how Landy pressed his shoulder against his, a firm reminder that they would be all right, that it was over now and they'd survived.

But now he's here in this hospital with this fiery pain, with Landy nowhere in sight, with the nurse hovering over him saying, "The boiler exploded. A terrible accident. You were found six days later, washed up on shore. It's a miracle you survived so long, when so many others . . ."

He hears her words, thinks he knows how her sentence ends, and yet he can't believe it. The *Sultana* can't have blown up, not after everything else. And if it had, surely he would remember. Why doesn't he remember anything between Landy's shoulder and now? How can he trust anything at all with this gaping hole in his memory?

He asks the nurse about Landy, and she says she'll check but then never mentions him again. He thinks he's asked more than once, but each time she acts like it's a new request. Or maybe the question has never actually left his mouth at all, because he's too scared of the answer.

He's able to stay awake a little longer each day, to see, through the eye that isn't bandaged, the way the doctor peers at him like he's a curiosity. To see the other patients around him, no one he knows but most of them recognizable as prison camp survivors just like him. This must be a nightmare. If he can only wake up . . .

The nurse continues to remind him of what happened each time he asks, treating him like glass that might shatter at the slightest pressure. Reuben feels close to shattering, but still resents her tone.

The steward who helps him use the chamber pot is more forthright. When Reuben asks him how bad the wreck of the *Sultana* was, he says, "Terrible," straight out. "Over a thousand dead. Drowned, mainly. You must have been a strong swimmer."

Reuben doesn't tell the steward that he can't swim, that he's always been terrified of water. That every time he closes his eyes he can feel the cold water swallowing him. He might welcome this as a sign he hasn't completely forgotten his ordeal, but he's been having these nightmares for as long as he can remember.

"They found you washed up naked as a jaybird fifteen miles upriver," the steward goes on. "At that point they were only finding corpses, so you were quite a shock. People thought maybe you were a victim of the sea monster at first. Lucky you had that scar on your shoulder, or we wouldn't have known who you were with the state your face was in. But your mate recognized the scar and the stump, and told us your name."

"Who?" Reuben asks, no longer wondering about the nakedness or the sea monster reference or anything else. Landy is here, Landy is—

"Red-headed fellow. Dickinson, I think his name was?"

Reuben's elation drains away. Still, maybe Dicky knows where Landy is. "Is he still here?"

"Nah. He's long gone. Wasn't hurt near as bad as you."

The doctor explains Reuben's injuries the next time he comes around. A badly broken arm. Broken ribs. Burns and gashes on his face and chest. A concussion.

"No idea how you lived," the doctor says, shaking his head.

"The other survivors clung to wreckage and tree limbs, were at the mercy of the currents, but with your injuries, I'd be shocked if you managed to stay conscious, let along hold onto anything or swim. You really don't remember anything?"

"Nothing," he says. The memories of the past three years claw and bite at him, but whatever happened when that boiler exploded stays hidden. He looks at the old scar on his arm and wonders at how his mind works.

He passes many weeks in the hospital. Gradually, the nurse can change the bandages on his face without him passing out from the pain. Gradually, it hurts less to draw a breath. Gradually, he's able to sit up for longer stretches, and convince the steward to bring him some newspapers.

The headlines scream of tragedy, using sensational language to turn the wreck of the *Sultana* into a dime-store novel. The fact that the articles are side by side with reports of a sea monster sighted in the Mississippi makes it all the more ridiculous. The words swim, and he puts the newspapers aside, lays back, tries to breathe. He reminds himself he's still alive, that he's been in far worse places, that all he has to do is get through the next second, and then the one after that, and then—

His mind riots, bombarding him with memories, and he tries to set them in order to keep from drowning in them. Maybe if he looks at it all in a methodical way, he'll remember what happened with the *Sultana*.

His earliest memory is being at the orphanage and telling Billy Hinks that he was seven years old. Billy said he must be lying, because Billy was seven himself and much bigger than Reuben. He hit Reuben again and again, but Reuben kept insisting he was seven, because it was the only thing he knew for sure besides his name. Everything from before the orphanage was and still is a dark shadow.

He remembers all the long years at the cold, grey orphanage in Indiana, though each memory is as dull and colourless as the next, and accompanied by a terrible ache. Surely every orphan dreams of a home, but for Reuben it seemed all-consuming, as though somewhere out there a home existed and wanted him back, if only he knew where to look.

When he finally left the orphanage at the age of eighteen, he emerged into a world in its second year of war. He enlisted because he had nowhere else to go, and the army seemed as good a place as any. Later he wondered about the other choices he could've made, and how they might have turned out for him. What it might have been like to live a life where fear didn't constantly boil in the pit of his stomach, threatening to spill out of every orifice.

He was a good soldier, though. The orphanage might not have taught him courage, but it taught him obedience. He knew how to follow orders without comment, to eat without worrying about the taste, to ignore his feelings and fears because no one else considered them worthwhile.

He got along until June of '64, when he entered a battle and then found himself buried in muck, his wrist and his chest both pumping out blood. The memory is hazy, a swirl of pain and panic, but it's there. He reminds himself of this now. He's capable of hanging onto some tragedies, so why not others?

He was captured and taken to a prison hospital where a harried doctor made haphazard rounds. Reuben resigned himself to dying, but it turned out the wound on his chest was only a graze, and though he'd lost his left hand, the arm didn't putrefy. For awhile he lay there in the narrow, flea-ridden bed and attempted to build up his strength, and then he was deemed fit to move and crammed on a train with hundreds of other prisoners bound for Andersonville.

He heard talk of this open-air Reb prison while he was in the hospital, but nothing prepared him for the reality, the stench of thousands of unwashed bodies roasting in the summer sun, the sight of all those starving prisoners pressing against the newcomers like angry ghosts. Reuben felt sure he was about to be crushed to death, but he also never felt more alone.

The other newcomers were forming squads, attempting to find a little patch to set up shelter. Many of them had been captured together and were already friends. Reuben had no one. Hands kept groping at him, demanding to know what he had brought with him, what news he had of the war, and he was unable to answer or wrench away. He wished they would pull him apart so he wouldn't have to spend another instant in this wretched place.

And then someone took him firmly by the arm. "Come with me. We've got room in our shebang for another, and you look like just the man. I'm Gillanders MacPherson, and I've been here two months and seventeen days already. It takes getting used to, but it's survivable if you don't lose your head."

At first Reuben concentrated only on putting one foot in front of the other and holding onto Gillanders MacPherson's voice in the same way Gillanders MacPherson was holding onto his arm. In a moment, though, once they passed through the worst of the crush of bodies, Reuben looked at his rescuer, a slight young man with a wild blond beard, a tattered uniform, and eyes the colour of clouds just before a thunderstorm.

"Here we are. Home sweet home," Gillanders said, grinning as he stopped in front of a primitive structure constructed from sticks and blankets.

And Reuben, who had never known a home in his life, found himself grinning back.

The next nine months were the longest Reuben had known in many ways. Andersonville lacked adequate food, water, and hygiene, and the very air seemed to choke him. They were a camp full of lice-ridden skeletons waiting for death.

When Reuben arrived there were five other people in the shebang, all of them captured together, but he learned there had originally been seven. As the months passed they lost three more, though they took in some new men, too. Reuben was an old-timer by then, dressed in patchwork scavenged from the dead, living most days one second at a time because it wouldn't do to think of the future. Rumours of paroles and prisoner exchanges no longer excited him, and even when they were evacuated for a time in November, it didn't surprise him at all that they wound up right back where they'd started. Hope didn't exist at Andersonville.

But a person couldn't live that way, not really. He was convinced he would have died like so many others if it hadn't been for Landy and the home he'd created in the midst of this hell. It wasn't the pathetic shebang, but rather the people within it, with Landy at the helm keeping their spirits up. Landy encouraged all of them to find industrious tasks to fill their days and potentially their bellies, whether it was volunteering to dig graves or helping out at the camp laundry in exchange for a little extra food. In the evening he organized entertainment, from never-ending card games with the dog-eared deck he'd procured to lice popping contests to sing-alongs where they all tried to create the most off-colour lyrics to the Rebs' favourite anthems.

In short, Landy kept all their spirits up, and that gave them a chance at surviving.

Reuben knew the whole shebang depended on Landy, but as time passed the two of them developed the closest friendship. To everyone else Reuben was Wally, the quiet kid without the hand, but to Landy he was Rue, someone worth talking to and listening to in the dark night outside the shebang when everyone else had fallen asleep. Similarly, everyone else called Landy Mac and looked to him for all the answers, but Rue called him Landy and let him be human, listening to his doubts and fears. It should have been demoralizing, hearing Landy worry, but instead it made Reuben feel strong. They were equals, partners, able to get through anything if they had each other. And someday there would be an afterwards, and they would have a home together then, a real home with walls and a roof not made of blankets, a home where they could sleep with full stomachs and no fears.

During the days, Reuben could never picture that home, could never see more than a second ahead, but at night when he listened to Landy's voice, felt his hand on top of his as they made plans together, it was crystal clear. They might be surrounded by thousands of people, but for those few moments in the darkness, they were the only two people in the world.

By the time the war ended, it was just Landy and him and Dicky and Mills left of their makeshift squad, all of them more bone than flesh, all of them haunted by a slew of ghosts. But they still celebrated as best they could, talking of the future in voices that shone with something like confidence for the first time. They'd survived. They weren't prisoners anymore, or even soldiers. They were just men, and could do as they pleased.

The first choice they faced was how to get home. The government would pay their steamboat passage, and despite his lifelong fear of water and his Andersonville-acquired aversion to crowds, Reuben insisted this was the best way. He squirms now, remembering that insistence and Landy's equal assertion that they find another way.

"The both of us hate water, Rue," he said. "What's the use of going by boat when we'll be miserable?"

"What's a little misery if we can just get home?" he countered, because they'd already travelled by train and foot just to get to the Mississippi, and it had been terrible. "We survived Andersonville; surely we're brave enough for a few days on a boat."

At last Landy reluctantly agreed. They boarded the *Sultana*, and it was Reuben who immediately regretted the decision because the boat was crammed fuller than seemed possible. They mostly stayed on the deck because at least there was a little air there, but panic made it hard to breathe, all those bodies packed around them and the furiously rushing water of the Mississippi beyond that. For two days, the only thing keeping him breathing was feeling Landy's shoulder pressed into his, never leaving his side.

Eventually they reached Memphis, and disembarked for a few hours while the boat unloaded some cargo. Reuben's legs trembled the entire time. He told himself it was just because he wasn't used to being on solid ground, but he knew it was really the fear and dread of having to get back on that boat.

Landy must have known, too, because he said, "We could just stay here."

Reuben forced himself to smile. "Nah. We need to get home." He put all his hopes and dreams and happiness into that last word, and Landy smiled back. Reuben made his legs carry him back onto that boat, pulled every bit of strength he could from Landy's shoulder nestled against his.

And then—

But no, his memory is still a void, a great dark stretch until he woke up in this bed with the nurse's gentle voice and the doctor's curious eyes and no Landy. The newspaper might try to fill in the blanks, but it could only give him details too terrible to imagine. How could fate be so cruel as to kill a boat full of survivors?

Reuben doesn't feel like a survivor, even though he's here. He doesn't feel like anything without Landy.

The hospital releases him towards the end of summer, once the plaster cast comes off his arm. He walks by the river even though it terrifies him, the water rushing with a seemingly demonic force. He feels a coldness gripping him, pulling at him, and he wants to run far away, but he stays because this is the last place he had Landy with him. Even though he knows the river isn't going to give Landy back, he keeps staring, hoping.

He walks the street that he and Landy walked together when

they disembarked, and pretends he agreed to stay. That the two of them heard of the wreck of the *Sultana* after the fact, and thanked their lucky stars they hadn't been a part of it. His throbbing arm and face and ribs don't allow him to pretend for long, though.

He turns his eyes back to the river. At the very least he wants to see the sea monster everyone's talking about, come face to face with something more monstrous than him. He notices the way people's eyes slide around him, how they try to look anywhere but at his mess of a face.

But the sea monster is gone, if it was ever here at all. Reuben never believed in monsters before, but now he isn't sure about anything.

He spends a week walking near the river. The first few days he has to sit and rest often, but gradually he builds up his strength, can go a little farther each day before he turns back, as though this extra distance might make some kind of difference.

Of course it doesn't. The wreck of the *Sultana* happened months ago, and everyone has moved on but him.

It's time to go. Memphis isn't home. He thinks about taking another boat, but in the end he can't bring himself to. He takes a series of trains instead, heading north. He starts out for Indiana, but that has never felt like home, so he switches course and decides on Maine instead.

Landy was from Maine originally, even though he left, mustering into the army in Indiana just like Reuben. Landy never talked of his childhood much, but he mentioned the name of the town he came from, Jenkins Cove, and how it overlooked the ocean.

"You were raised by the ocean, but you're scared of water?" Reuben asked.

"Yes," Landy said shortly, in a tone that didn't encourage further questions.

Reuben decided that fearing water when you'd grown up near it probably made more sense than fearing it when you lived nowhere near it, and left it at that. But months later he awoke from a particular terrible nightmare and went outside the shebang to collect himself. Landy followed, putting his arms around him tight there in the dark with no one to see, and Reuben whispered the sparse details of his dream. So much water all around him and a sharp pain and darkness. It didn't sound like much, and he should have been ashamed, but Landy whispered in his ear before he could be.

"I have nightmares like that."

Somehow, the thought of a shared nightmare made him shiver less.

"Why do you think we have them?" he asked.

"I don't know about you," Landy said after a long pause, "but when I was younger, I watched my mother walk into the ocean and never come back."

The words dropped like stones, and Reuben tried to snake his arm around Landy, because surely his friend was more deserving of comfort than he was. But Landy shook him off and slipped back into the shebang, and by the next morning Reuben wondered if their conversation had just been an extension of his dream.

Still, he remembers Jenkins Cove. Landy mentioned a sister a few times; hopefully she still lives there, and Reuben can tell her what happened to her brother. That's what friends do for each other's families, isn't it? He tells himself it's his duty and doesn't think beyond that. If he tries to imagine a whole long life without Landy, it becomes hard to breathe. So he does what he did in Andersonville, and just focuses on a moment at a time.

When he reaches the coast of Maine, the smell of the sea is everywhere. It hits him the moment he gets off the train, not only the smell but the familiarity of it. The realization that he knows this smell is a taunt from that stretch of years before the orphanage, that period he can never remember.

He feels like puking but he doesn't, just goes to the Jenkins Cove General Store, where he enquires about the MacPherson family. The clerk keeps his gaze on the counter, but gives Reuben clear directions to a little house overlooking the ocean.

Reuben knocks on the door, but no one answers, so he sits a little ways off, staring down at the beach and, beyond that, the sea. It seems to call to him, but he stays where he is, certain it means to entice him in and then drown him. The day is overcast and the water pale, an endless barrage of waves licking at the shore. On the horizon he can see a large mass moving about, an occasional splash of tail. A whale? Whatever it is, it's big enough to be terrifying.

A woman with a pronounced limp walks just out of reach of the water, and Reuben keeps his eyes on her because staring at the water for too long gives him a sick, dizzy feeling. At long last the woman finishes her circuit of the beach and makes her way up the dune, hesitating when she reaches him. "Can I help you?"

She has blue eyes and caramel-coloured hair, but there's something about her face and the curve of her mouth that reminds him of Landy. "Are you Miss MacPherson?"

Her eyebrows go up. "Yes. Do I know you?" She looks at him hard, like she's trying to recognize the face beneath the scars.

"No," he says, ducking his head. "I knew your brother. Lan— Gillanders, that is."

"Gilly?"

The nickname comes out full of love, and he forces himself to look back at her. She's smiling brightly—Landy's smile, so wide and elastic—and he feels terrible, afraid she hasn't caught the past tense in his words. "I . . . that is, he . . ."

"I know he's dead," she supplies. "Over a year now. I read his name in the newspaper. Isn't that a horrible way to find out? I crumpled it up and threw it in the fire I was so upset. And then I nearly managed to convince myself it hadn't been true, that I'd just imagined seeing it. But half the town told me they saw it, too, so it must have been true."

It's his turn to stare. "No, miss. That wasn't true. He was taken prisoner. That's where I met him. At Andersonville." He sees her eyes start to fill with hope, and spits out the rest to stop it in its tracks. "He's dead now, though. Did you hear about the *Sultana*?"

Reuben watches her eyes widen with anguish, but it fades surprisingly quickly, replaced by something else that he can't place.

"You saw the body?" she asks, and there's a strangeness in her tone, too.

"No. Some of the bodies were too battered to identify, and some were never found."

She nods, and he can practically hear cogs turning in her head, as though she's on the verge of solving a tricky equation.

Then she shakes herself like a wet dog and attempts a smile. "Where are my manners? Let's go inside. Would you like some refreshment? Goodness, I don't even know your name."

"Reuben Wallace," he says, and reaches to shake with the

hand that's not there.

She squeezes his left hand instead. "I'm Marceline. Our mother liked grand names, but Gilly always called me Leenie."

Gilly and Leenie. He can picture them, two children playing on the shore, keeping away from the tide.

Inside, she puts the kettle on and cuts him a slice of gingerbread. His stomach still isn't right after so many months of starvation, but the gingerbread is the most glorious thing he's ever tasted, and he eats it slowly, savouring it.

"Would you tell me about it?" she asks as she pours their tea. "About the prison camp? About Gilly?"

He does, because she is someone who can mourn with him. He starts slowly, telling her about Andersonville in the broadest strokes, not wanting her to know anything of the true horrors. But gradually they creep in, because for her to know how wonderful her brother was, he has to show her all that they were up against.

"He's the reason I survived," he ends with, and sips his tea to keep from saying the rest of what he's thinking—that he's the reason Landy's dead.

"You love him, don't you?" Marceline asks, and he's not entirely sure how she means it, but he nods anyway. However she means it, it's true.

"Then perhaps I should—" She cuts off mid-sentence, frowning, then tries again. "You'll think I'm foolish."

He doesn't say anything because he doesn't have any idea what she's talking about. He waits, instead, hoping she'll go on.

"I'm surprised he went on a boat," she says finally.

Reuben takes a deep breath. "It was my idea. We were both scared of water, but I insisted because it was fastest . . . And then I was the one who could barely breathe the whole trip, and he was the one . . ."

He can't get words out anymore, he's back on the boat, breathless and panicking, but this time there's no steadying shoulder pressed against his.

Marceline reaches across the table and takes his hand. "Don't blame yourself."

"I . . . if I had . . ."

She squeezes his hand. "Did he tell you why he was afraid of water?"

"He mentioned his . . . your . . . mother. How she walked into the sea and never came back . . . I figured . . ."

"That's part of it, yes." She withdraws her hand and fiddles with her empty teacup.

"And the other part?"

"Our family has . . . certain ties to the sea. To water." She gives a strange smile. "Our mother didn't go into the sea to die, like you're probably thinking. She just . . . returned to herself. Went home, you might say."

Reuben stares at her.

"It's hard to explain. And I know you'll never believe me. But our family—we—that is—" She seems to run out of words, and gets up instead, going to a shelf and bringing back a book, handing it to him like it will explain everything.

He opens it, sees drawings, some sparse and others detailed. Newspaper clippings, yellowed and crumbling. Snatches of handwriting in a variety of styles. His vision spins, but he takes enough of it in to realize it's all about creatures in the water. Sea monsters.

He keeps turning pages so he doesn't have to look at Marceline. He focuses on the pictures, beasts with thick and scaly tails, muscular arms, curved horns. Faces that are more demon than human, the jaws jutting forward and the teeth oversized and sharp. He keeps turning the pages until he reaches the last entry, an article about the monster spotted in the Mississippi.

He finally looks up. "I don't understand."

She nods. "I'm going to tell it to you like my mother told me, all right? Like a story. You can believe it or not. I didn't at first.

"My mother was a MacPherson. We never knew our father, we just knew Ma was a MacPherson, had always been a MacPherson. And MacPhersons were special. They heard the call of the sea, but they could never answer it. Because if they did, if they ever submerged themselves completely in water, they became . . . that." She motions to the journal.

A laugh escapes Reuben's mouth; he can't help it. "You mean you're sea monsters?"

"As I said, it's just a story. But one we've documented well. Plenty have seen it happen."

He pushes the journal away because surely it's the ravings of madmen and women. "And once they transform, it's forever?" he asks, unsure whether the question comes from curiosity or an attempt to seem polite.

She shakes her head. "The opposite can reverse it. Submerge us in water, and we become sea monsters. Beach us on land, and we're back to being human. But the sea monster never wants to return to land. The few times it's happened, it's been an accident or by force. And the person who comes back never remembers their time in the sea." She looks out the window, rubbing absently at her thigh.

"And you think that's what happened to Landy?" Reuben asks, unable to keep the disdain out of his voice. "He's out there in the water, and all we have to do is drag him back?"

"He'd be far too strong for the likes of us to drag back," she says, as though this is the only thing wrong with his supposition.

Reuben shakes his head.

Marceline gets up and refills their teacups. "I scoffed, too, when my mother first told me this story. I scoffed until I watched her walk into the ocean, and saw the monster emerge."

Reuben knows the mind is a fragile thing. He saw some break in Andersonville, and those were grown men. A girl watching her mother disappear into the ocean might imagine all manner of nonsense and think it was real. He can't judge, not when his own mind has erased so much. Maybe everyone's mind just has cracks and holes that have to be gotten around.

Marceline sits down again, and over their second cups of tea she tells him stories from her childhood, ones that seem normal and true and free of monsters, ones in which Landy is both prevalent and heroic. It's clear Marceline adored her brother, and Reuben lets the stories wash over him, smiling and nodding and not wanting them to end because as long as she keeps talking, Landy is alive in the room.

She talks and talks, and then she makes supper, insisting he stay not only for the meal but also for the night. When he attempts to decline, to hint that her neighbours may find it unseemly, she won't hear of it. "You're as good as family."

Over supper they talk of the war. For Marceline it was far away and had more or less ended when she thought Landy died. "We're so isolated here, it's easy to pretend the rest of the world's problems don't exist. Cowardly, I know."

Reuben shakes his head. If he could have ignored the war, he would have.

"It just felt so terrible, knowing Gilly was never coming back. That I could never thank him."

"Thank him?"

She turns her eyes to the window again. "He did something for me, years ago. I was very ungrateful about it. Downright rude, even. And then he left. We wrote to one another occasionally, but it wasn't the same. I never apologized. I never thanked him."

He knows he should say something soothing, like he's sure Landy knew she was sorry, but it seems wrong to put words in his friend's mouth. Instead he asks, "What did he do?"

"You'll scoff again."

More sea monsters. He composes his face carefully even though she still isn't looking at him, and says, "I promise I won't."

"Our mother taught us to fear the water, like I said, yet she warned us that it would always have a pull on us that we had to learn to resist."

"Why didn't you move away?" he asks when she doesn't go on. "Live somewhere land-locked?"

"She said it wouldn't help. That the farther away it got, the worse the ache would be."

"But Landy left."

"Maybe our ma lied. Or maybe Gilly was just good at enduring the ache. He never said in his letters. I think he would have mentioned if Ma had lied, but maybe not. I was too proud to ask.

"Anyhow, one day our ma gave into it. Ran right into the water and became . . . something else. Gilly and I were on the dune, and all we could do was watch in horror. She'd trained us well. We didn't dare go after her.

"I was eleven when she did it. Gilly was fifteen. We were all alone after that, except for each other. Gilly got himself a job at the depot, and eventually I started taking in laundry, and together we made do. He was a good brother, and I never wanted for anything. But as the years went by, the water kept calling to me, unrelenting. I tried to tell Gilly, but he insisted I just had to ignore it. Maybe he didn't understand, maybe the call wasn't as strong in him. Or maybe he was stronger than it, and I wasn't.

"Regardless, I gave in. When I was sixteen, I went into the ocean just like our mother had."

Reuben waits for her to say that nothing happened, or that

Landy had to fish her out before she drowned.

"I don't remember after that," she says finally. "Gilly said I was gone—transformed—for a week. That I stayed in the cove the first few days, but then I ventured farther and farther out. So Gilly went after me, in a friend's boat. It took both of them the better part of two days to get me back. They tried a net at first, but I was too strong, so then they used a harpoon, too. I struggled so much that they nearly capsized several times. And of course if that had happened, Gilly would have transformed as well. Yet he persisted in rescuing me because that's the kind of man he is."

She rubs at her thigh again. "All I remember is waking up in bed, with my leg bandaged up and the pull of the water as powerful as ever. I told Gilly he shouldn't have bothered rescuing me, that the sea was where I belonged. Of course I didn't know that for sure. I didn't remember a thing. Maybe when I was in the sea, I was miserable there, too. But I don't think so. That journal is full of stories of MacPhersons who went into the water. None of them ever came back to land voluntarily.

"Anyhow, Gilly ended up leaving not long after, once I was back on my feet. Said my life was my own and I could do as I pleased, but he couldn't bear to watch it."

"But you didn't go back in the water," Reuben says.

"No. Every time I think about doing it, I see Gilly's disappointed eyes, and I can't quite bring myself to go."

"Even once you thought he'd died?"

"Especially then." She pauses. "I know you don't believe me."

"I . . ." He doesn't want to make her feel bad, doesn't want to lie.

She stands, hikes up her skirt, peels down her stocking. "You can see the scar," she says, displaying her bare leg. "Where the harpoon went in."

He wants to look away, but his eyes lock on the long scar running up her leg which ends in a puckered starburst on her thigh, and suddenly the room is spinning, the world has stopped, because he knows that scar.

That's his scar.

"Are you all right?" Marceline asks, her voice seeming to come from very far away. She pulls her skirt back down. "I didn't figure you for a prude."

"I'm fine." He forces his lips to form the words, even though he isn't. How can he be, when everything she said sounded crazy and yet it makes sudden, perfect sense?

"You don't look fine. You've gone a funny colour."

"I'm just tired," he insists.

She bustles him to a little bedroom and then thankfully leaves him so he can fall apart in private.

He unbuttons his shirt with trembling fingers. His right arm has always been weak due to the long-ago wound in his shoulder, and breaking it hasn't helped any. But it's the only hand he has, so he takes a deep breath and forces himself to keep trying until he fumbles open every button.

He stares at his naked shoulder in the little mirror above the bureau, as though the scar might have changed or disappeared. It hasn't. A long line up his arm ending in a starburst pucker on his shoulder. Nearly identical to Marceline's.

Of course there are any number of ways a person can get a scar. And even if he was harpooned as a child, that doesn't make him a monster. It's ridiculous to even consider.

Still, he can't stop thinking about it.

He paces the small room, which he gathers used to be Landy's. Reuben shuts his eyes and tries to pretend his friend is here now instead of dead at the bottom of the Mississippi.

He remembers the first time Landy saw the scar on his shoulder. He'd taken his pathetic rag of a shirt off to try to mend it when he noticed Landy staring at him intently.

"Sorry," Landy said when he saw him looking back. "Is that from the war, too?" There was a strangeness to his tone, a feigned nonchalance.

Reuben shook his head. "From when I was young."

"Too young to remember?" Landy suggested in that same tone.

"Yes."

Landy looked away, and Reuben went back to his mending. It was a tricky task to do one-handed, especially when the fabric was all but disintegrating, but he was still aware that Landy kept sneaking looks at him.

"You're making me nervous," he finally said.

"Sorry. I didn't mean to—I wasn't—" He shook his head and then took the shirt from Reuben. "Let me do that." Once his head was bent over the sewing, he said in a low voice, "Scars are something to be proud of, you know. They're reminders that you're tough enough to survive."

Reuben snorted. "More like reminders that you were unlucky enough to get hurt."

He stares at his scars now, the newer ones. His face isn't his anymore. He feels like he doesn't know himself at all, but he knows he's not tough, has never been tough.

He paces and waits and tries not to think. Once it's late enough that he figures Marceline has gone to bed, he sneaks into the main room and takes the journal and a lamp. Back in Landy's bedroom, he sits on the edge of the bed and reads.

The light is flickery and he only has the one good eye, but he perseveres. He starts at the end and works his way backwards, reading an account of Marceline's rescue that he realizes must have been written by Landy, every word filled with anguish.

It ends with, *I thought I was doing the right thing, but I'm no longer sure. I've crippled my sister, and all I can think is that she may have been happier in the sea.*

Reuben keeps paging. The drawings vary greatly; some of the creatures look fearsome, others majestic. They have many labels: merrow, mermaid, sea-devil, creature.

The newspaper articles are all sensational and meant to inspire fear, so he stops reading them and focuses on the handwritten accounts because these are written by MacPhersons, or men or women married to MacPhersons. People with a vested interest, people who know.

There is an account of another woman rescued with a harpoon, which must have been where Landy got the idea. Her father and uncle did the rescuing, but the uncle got pulled overboard and couldn't be rescued himself. *A terrible loss*, the father wrote, but under it, in a different hand, someone added, *He was lucky.*

There is a family tree towards the front which has clearly been added to over the years till it has become sprawling and overgrown. Lots and lots of MacPhersons, of course, but other last names, too, united to the family by marriage. The ones farthest back are faded and cramped, but Reuben deciphers each one until he finds a Jonathan Wallace married to an Annabelle MacPherson.

The branch withers away. Perhaps they never had children.

He tells himself that, tells himself Wallace is a common enough surname, but he feels a growing wave of something ready to engulf him. He's drowning in information, history, and it's getting hard to breathe.

He reads accounts of MacPhersons who left the coast, moved far away from any water. Some of them went mad, and some came back. There's one letter from a man named Cedric who wrote of living in Pennsylvania. *I think I can manage to stay. It's not such a bad place, and I love my new bride, but there's a place inside of me that feels as though it will be forever hollow, and I ache for a home I can never have.*

Reuben blinks, aware that this man who is probably long dead—the letter is dated 1803—has summed up the way he himself has always felt.

When he finally reaches the first page, his vision is swimming. Still, he manages to read the story despite its faded ink. How Alasdair and Elspeth MacPherson, newly wed and deeply in love, crossed the ocean to the new world. How the ship met with a storm and wrecked off the Massachusetts coast, drowning nearly all on board. How the MacPhersons never realized the curse they both bore, transforming into something else the moment they submerged. How they might have lived like this forever, except Alasdair, even in his monstrous form, had a burning desire to rescue his injured wife and the child in her belly, and pushed her to shore. She lived, but they were separated forever, she on land, he in the sea. And their curse lived in every generation since, the ultimate choice of who to be, of who to leave behind.

It's a myth, of course. Reuben puts the journal aside, blows out the lamp, and shuts his eyes. He's filled his head with nonsense, but he just needs to sleep. When he wakes up, the world will be set right again.

But he knows it won't. The world will never be right again without Landy, and Landy is either dead in the Mississippi or a sea monster in the cove.

He can see it now, behind his closed eyelids. Is it an actual memory, or everything he's just read filling in the gaps? He can't tell, but he can see it clear as day, and feel it, too. The enormous explosion on the boat. The water, so much water, and his body transforming. It hurt, everything hurt terribly, but he was all right because he had Landy.

Landy was with him the entire time in that terrible rushing water. Landy's arm wrapped around him, pulling him along because he couldn't manage on his own, not with a broken arm, broken ribs, a broken head.

And when it became apparent that he couldn't go on, was getting worse, not better, Landy was the one who pushed him onto the shore where he could be human again, where he could get help.

Reuben opens his eyes. It feels real, even though it seems impossible.

He gets up, slips from the room, slips from the house. He walks down to the beach in the dark, feeling the water pull at him even as it terrifies him.

He knows he doesn't know anything, not for certain. He may look monstrous, but is he actually a monster? Is Landy? Even if that is Landy out there, suppose he's waiting for Reuben and Marceline to find a harpoon and a net and rescue him?

Reuben reaches the edge of the water, lets the waves lap his toes. He imagines himself drowning, because this is probably what will happen if he walks into the water. The thought makes him sick, and he tells himself to run to the depot, take a train all the way back to Indiana.

But Indiana has never been home. The waves wash up to his ankles, and he sees the shadow of a tail near the horizon.

Exhaustion buzzes through his blood. He should go back to the house, get some sleep. In the morning he can talk to Marceline. Tell her he believes her. Ask her what they might do to save Landy.

But he knows that once he sleeps there's a good chance he'll no longer believe in any of this. His good sense will return, and he'll believe without a doubt that Landy died and there are no such thing as monsters.

This thought terrifies him far more than the water.

He knows what he has to do. This is the only future he can imagine, the only home he wants. One with Landy. However slim the chance.

He takes a step, and then another, and lets himself be submerged.

He goes home.

Love is a Locked Box
and the Ocean on Her Lips

Kelly Sandoval

THE WOMAN ON the Virginia Street Bridge had been standing there for almost an hour, slipping her wedding ring on and off and dangling it over the summer-low waters of the Truckee River. Evelyn had watched the same scene play out dozens of times, but had only seen three women let go. It was one thing to pretend to be Ava Gardner, tossing away a diamond, and another thing entirely to do it. A decent ring could fetch fifty dollars or more at a pawn shop. For most of Reno's divorce tourists, that was too high a price for whimsy. Still, it did happen, and Evelyn could use the fifty bucks. So, she waited.

At last, the woman looked away from the water and slipped the ring on to stay. She walked past Evelyn and down to the bank where, with a casual disregard for the pedestrians passing above her, she stepped out of her shoes and into the river. Even at its mid-point, the Truckee was no more than a foot deep. The woman could have made it across without ruining more than her stockings. But once she reached the middle, she knelt, the water soaking her skirt, then stretched out, floating on her back.

A gasp, a giggle, a few long whistles. The woman's eyes were closed; she didn't react to the sounds.

Evelyn swallowed an exclamation of her own. "Ma'am? Hey, Ma'am?"

No answer. The woman rolled over. Floating on her stomach, her dark curls haloing her head, she looked drowned.

Evelyn glanced around but no one else was doing anything but gawking.

"Lady!" she called, wading in without even bothering with her boots, the water soaking through the leather and climbing up her jeans. Despite the warm day, the river was cold enough to raise gooseflesh on her arms.

The river rocks were rounded and slick and Evelyn had to slow down, picking her way to the woman's side. She made no visible attempts to turn or breathe. Reaching down, Evelyn got her arms under the woman's and hauled her upward. She weighed more than Evelyn expected but didn't struggle, and after a bit of awkward handling, they were both dripping but upright.

"You okay?" Evelyn asked, keeping a grip on the woman's shoulders.

The woman laughed: a low, sobbing chuckle. Her eyes were so dark Evelyn couldn't distinguish between iris and pupil. "Now isn't that a silly question?"

"Guess so," Evelyn admitted. She took the woman by the elbow and led her out of the water. "What's your name?"

"Meara," the woman said. Her voice was low and breathy; it felt intimate, like she was telling a secret. "And I guess you're Lancelot?"

"Evelyn, actually." She'd come to enjoy catching people's surprised reassessment, even savouring the inevitable disapproval. She courted it, with her military haircut and oversized leather jacket.

Meara hmmed, taking Evelyn in with a glance that started at her boots and traced upward until their eyes met. She smiled, but the expression seemed more a performance than a display of emotion. "Of course. Evelyn."

"So, you often get a sudden urge for swimming?"

"Maybe. Does it count as a sudden urge if you have it all the time?"

"There are pools, you know." Evelyn let go of Meara's arm and ran to fetch her shoes. "Here."

Meara took her arm, using it for balance as she stood first on one foot, then the other. "It doesn't matter. Nothing helps."

Evelyn caught Meara's hand, turning it so her ring, a diamond circled by chips of sapphire, caught the light. "This got anything to do with why you were practicing drowning?"

It did happen. How could it not? Reno was full of women from states where divorce took years and evidence. Women who'd married their G.I. sweethearts in fits of patriotism, only to face the truth of them when the troops came marching home. Women whose husbands had once promised to take care of them, who didn't have the skills to be a secretary or typist. Women who found ropes or rivers.

Meara didn't pull her hand away. She didn't smile, either. "That has everything to do with everything." She squeezed, then straightened the collar of her jacket, as if it mattered with her whole outfit dripping. "It was nice to meet you, Evelyn."

"You'll be okay?"

"Week five," she said. "I hear when it's all over, I'll be just fine."

Evelyn didn't know the words to make that true. "Pawn the ring. You might need the money."

"It doesn't matter," Meara said. "Money won't change anything."

Evelyn couldn't think of much in her life money wouldn't change, but she let the comment pass. Her wet clothes clung to her body, sticky and uncomfortable. If she wanted to bring in a little cash, she'd need to stop mooning over suicidal tourists and get changed.

CLIFF HAD SPENT five months arguing with Meara before agreeing to the trip to Reno. In the end, it seemed better to spend six weeks in Nevada than have her go in front of a judge back in Maine and make up reasons. He'd never strayed, never hit her. She had no right. They both knew it.

He'd imagined Reno like the movies: bright lights, horses, beautiful women falling back in love. He had imagined winning it big and showering Meara in gifts, until she was once again the woman who loved him.

The glamour wore off in the first week. Reno was as sparse

and claustrophobic as the rooms they rented by the week, and every time he breathed the air coated his tongue in dust. He was terrible at poker, and even if he'd been better, Meara would rather stare at the half-dry river than spend time in the casinos with him.

The door opened, and he glanced up from his newspaper. Meara stood in the entryway, her hair damp, her clothes stained. She smiled at him with the same mournful sweetness he remembered from when they'd met, four years ago. He hadn't known then, that she was anything but human. He'd believed her smile. He still did. He couldn't help it.

"Hello, darling," she said. "Did you win me anything?"

"What did you do this time?" he asked, grabbing a towel from the bathroom and draping it over her mostly dry shoulders.

"I met someone," she said, flipping her hair and towelling it dry.

"Who? This town is nothing but swindlers and cowboys." There'd been a time when he'd have pulled her to him, would have kissed the river from her lips. "A lady isn't safe on the streets."

"So? What's left for me to lose?" She threw the towel at him and walked to the window. Gaudy at night, by day Reno was simply ugly, the neon signs shoddy and pathetic without darkness to illuminate. "I hate this place."

He touched her shoulder and pretended not to notice how she flinched. "We don't have to do this. We can go home."

"You can," she said it without malice; he always wished she would scream at him.

"I'll give the skin back," he said. "Once we have a family. If you'd just settle, I'd give it back. I love you. I want you to be happy."

"Once we're married. Once you've found us a nice house. Once we have a family." She pressed her forehead against the window; her breath fogged the glass, shrouding the city in false mist. "Once upon a time, Cliff. I know this story. My mother knew it. She warned me, you know. Humans are all the same."

"I'm not," he said.

"Go away," she said. "I can't have this conversation anymore. It's been five weeks. Do you really think I don't mean it? We're getting this divorce."

"Leave me, and I'll never give it back." The skin was a part of her to have. And didn't the stories say she couldn't leave him, while he had it? Wasn't that the point of marrying a selkie?

"I don't care anymore. At least you won't own all of me."

He stood behind her, wrapped his arms around her waist and rested his chin on her shoulder. He could feel the dampness of her clothes and how stiff she was beneath the gentle yielding of her curves. "But that's what love is," he said.

She laughed, the low music of her voice ruined by a bitter edge. "Then how can I possibly love you?"

THE NUGGET JUST before midnight was Evelyn's favourite place in the city, whether or not she was working. The red leather seats, the gold lined mirrors, the waitresses with their short black dresses and trays of free drinks, all created an illusion of luxury the tourists were only too happy to believe. She was a small predator, pecking at crumbs. The casino didn't even have to hunt. It put out a plate and people lined up to be picked clean.

She did a few rounds of the floor before settling on an open slot machine next to a man who kept his overflowing cup of nickels on the floor. She placed her more modest cup beside his and fed his coins into her machine. He was too busy watching the cocktail waitresses and cigarette girls to notice. Evelyn lost his money for long enough to get a shot of scotch, then, scooping up her meagre winnings, took his cup and disappeared back into the crowd.

Skimming wouldn't make rent but, as a way to enjoy the atmosphere, it served just fine.

"I guess you're not Lancelot." Meara's laughing voice came from a slot machine one aisle over. She wore a long grey dress that hugged her full figure and held a glass of red wine. "It's not nice to take things that don't belong to you."

Evelyn considered worrying, but Meara's expression showed no hint of real disapproval. "That's what we do here. It's what Reno's for."

"I had noticed that." Meara looked down into her wine glass, swirling the liquid without tasting it. "My husband seems taken enough by it."

"He's here?" Most men looking for a divorce had their wives handle the residency requirement, while they worked or spent time with the mistress they had lined up as a replacement.

"Oh yes. Darling Cliff does hate it when I wander off alone." Meara started walking toward the tables, where the black-vested dealers presided over their green-felt empire. "He'll be waiting for me, by now."

"But he'll sign the paperwork?"

"I think so. Yes, if it comes to that. He thinks I'll come back anyway, no matter what I get the courts to say." She drained her wine.

"You don't have to."

"Buy me a drink, won't you?" Meara handed Evelyn her empty wine glass and her fingers lingered on Evelyn's skin for a second longer than necessary. "This desert of yours. I feel like I'm drinking ash."

"You don't mind profiting from my bad habits?" Evelyn asked, leading the way to one of the Nugget's quieter bars.

"Maybe it's about time I was on the taking side of things."

The bar, all cherry wood and lights that highlighted the darkness instead of illuminating it, was busier than Evelyn expected. The bartender, Joel, was trying to extract his arm from the petting affections of a pretty blonde, but he met Evelyn's gaze and grinned. Joel always had a smile and a drink for a fellow pervert. She waved him over, looking frantic and irritable enough to give him the excuse he needed.

"Not exactly the place to be bringing a lady friend, Ev," he said, after pouring Meara's wine. "Why don't you take her to Tomi's?"

"Meara's just a tourist. I'm showing her the sights."

"Guess you can get away with it, tonight. Though people might wonder why she brought her little brother to the bar. Can I get you a glass of milk?"

"Oh, shut up. I think your girlfriend's waiting for you." She turned back to Meara, who smirked at her over the rim of her glass.

"Nice place."

"Joel's not so bad. Feel better?"

"Not really." Meara rested one arm on the bar, cupping her chin in her hand. "You ever seen the ocean, Evelyn?"

"Never been out of Reno."

"Good. Don't go. Sometimes it's better not to know what you're losing." Meara ran her thumb over her wedding ring. "You know, I thought he was the one I was losing, once. Thought I had to prove that he could keep me. And I did."

"What's he got on you? Kids?"

"No. I listened to my mother on that one, at least." She finished her second glass of wine, drinking it like water. "I gave him something of mine. Something valuable. If I had it, I could start another life. Without it, well, you know how it is, for a woman alone."

"Something you could sell?"

"More like an heirloom. I can't see my family without it."

Evelyn pictured her father's face, closed like a fist as he threw her out. And what if some lost present could make him forgive her? Would she even want that? She liked to pretend she wouldn't.

"Can't you just tell them he has it?"

"It doesn't work that way. And he keeps it locked up." Meara slipped off her bar stool. "Thanks for the drink."

"You need me to walk you home?" Evelyn wanted to lead her down Virginia Street, see her dark curls highlighted with neon, maybe duck into Tomi's for some dancing.

Meara glanced at her watch. "He's at the tables, waiting. Goodnight, Evelyn."

She did look back and her eyes, dark and full of hunger, left Evelyn aching for an ocean she'd never seen.

Cliff frowned as Meara pressed her lips to the pillar on the courthouse steps, leaving a pink stain on the white stone.

"Come on, Darling. There's one more thing we're supposed to do."

Cliff let her take his arm, let her lean against him like it was four years ago and they were courting again. Her smile was no warmer for the papers signed, and she still wore his ring.

"What will you do now?" He'd been asking the question for six weeks.

"What can I do?" She was warm and soft, and he hated her a little for humiliating him in that courthouse and still making him want her. "I guess I could learn to type. Earn a salary."

"You're not cut out for work, Meara," he said. "You'd get halfway through your first day and wander out for a rainstorm." In truth, she didn't even make a particularly good wife. She burned toast and didn't notice when the carpets needed cleaning.

"Right now, I just want to get out of this desert."

The river was coming into view ahead of them, the same trickle of water Meara pilgrimaged to every day.

"Let me take you home," Cliff said. "All this, it's just a silly whim of yours. You know you can't leave me."

"True." She looked at the river like he'd always wanted her to look at him. "But I can hurt you. It passes the time."

He swallowed, choking down anger and dust. "You'd be happy, if you just let yourself."

Meara let go of his arm and knelt beside the water, drinking from cupped hands.

"It tastes like the mountains," she said.

"Meara, people are staring."

"I should have drowned you," she said. "I should have called you into the waves and kissed your breath away."

"I wouldn't have come."

"I know." She took his arm and stood. "But just imagine how happy we would have been."

He could imagine it; a love so brief she never learned to hate him. But he needed so much more of her than that. They walked together up to the bridge; her fingers briefly intertwining with his.

"I like this bit," she said, twisting off her wedding ring. "Here, give me yours too."

He curled his fingers inward and reached to grab her wrist. She jerked away, holding her hand out above the water.

"Don't be silly, Meara."

He remembered how she'd kissed him when he'd slipped it on her finger, the two of them sitting with their feet in the waves, her skin folded beside her.

"I can do what I like with it," she said. "What does it matter?"

"Let me keep it for you, until you're ready to wear it again."

Her laughter, usually low and soft, rose higher and higher becoming something very like a shriek. "That's just what you said last time."

He tried to grab her again, but her fingers opened and the ring fell, a sparkling flash of gold and diamond disappearing among the rocks.

"Dammit, Meara!"

"Hate me yet?" she asked.

He did. He was so tired of her, of every day putting up with her stupid, selfish madness. The hurt of her, the way she wore her wounds like badges. He remembered being happy before she came into his life.

She leaned into him, pressing her lips against his ear. "Then let me go."

He kissed her, tasting the river, and beneath it, the salty hint of ocean that was purely Meara. "I'll get you another ring."

THE AIR IN Tomi's was thick with smoke and Sinatra's new one played on the jukebox, sounding tinny and strained. Evelyn sat at the bar, drinking a beer that tasted like ditch water and pretending not to notice the redhead waiting to be bought a drink. She'd thought she wanted the distraction of company. Now she wanted silence, to walk into the desert until she disappeared.

She glanced up at the sound of the door opening, the usual paranoia. Meara wore grey again and her hair was pulled up into a bun, little wisps of curl escaping to frame her face. Evelyn caught a few others eyeing her. New faces were rare, and everyone was hungry for a little novelty.

"Meara!" she called, lifting her hand. Their gazes met and Meara nodded, making her way to Evelyn's side.

"This isn't an easy place to find," Meara said, settling on the stool next to her. "I was afraid I wouldn't see you before we left."

Meara's left hand rested on the bar, her fingers bare.

"We?"

"We." She took a sip of Evelyn's beer, frowned, and set it down again. "I thought, maybe, after this, he wouldn't want me. But I should have known."

"You could stay here," Evelyn wasn't sure why she said it, except that she hated the hollow spaces behind Meara's words. "I could look after you, until you got on your feet."

"Could you?"

On a good month, Evelyn just about made rent. Her last girlfriend, pretty and charming in her pearls and little gold earrings, had worked as a waitress and supported them both. She'd left months ago. Evelyn had tried, for a few weeks, to find a real job. It hadn't gone well, and she'd been glad of the failure.

"Sure," she said. "We could make it work."

"You're that good a thief?"

She wasn't. "I make do."

Meara reached into her purse and set a key on the bar between them. "The heirloom of mine, do you think you could get it?"

"Can't you?"

"No. I can't touch it. Can't even touch the box it's in. Look, it's complicated. There are rules. But he's gambling now, won't be back for hours. I'm supposed to join him."

Evelyn picked up the key. The number 317 was etched into the metal. "What is it?"

"Me."

"I don't understand."

"It's a skin. A seal skin. Can you get it?"

Evelyn had learned how to pick locks, but that sort of thing was a lot more likely to get a person arrested than just slipping a wallet out of some guy's coat. She wondered if she still remembered how.

"It's not a good idea," she said.

"No, I guess not." Meara held out her hand, palm up. "It was nice to have met you."

Evelyn met her gaze and saw a still form in the darkness there. A body, face down in the Truckee. She closed her hand around the key.

"I can try."

Meara brushed her fingertips along Evelyn's chin, tracing the line of her jaw. "Sweet girl."

Evelyn leaned into the touch, "Maybe I still want to be your Lancelot."

Meara closed the space between them; her lips tasted like tears. "Be my Robin Hood."

A FULL HOUSE, tens over twos, finished out Cliff's night, leaving him $125 richer and more than a little drunk. Meara always said it wasn't about the money, but she didn't flinch when he put his arm around her. They walked together through the carnival brightness of Reno after midnight, and he drank in colours, felt them shining through his skin.

"Let's go to the river," he said, stopping in the middle of the sidewalk. Other tourists, less lucky, glared, but Cliff didn't care. Some you won, some you lost, and he was a winner for once. "I'll find your ring. We'll get married again. We'll start over."

"Just like that?"

He pulled her against him, nuzzled her neck. She laughed and didn't push him away.

"Just like that. I forgive you, for everything."

"Oh, Cliff." She pulled back but not out of his grasp. "Don't make it easy for me."

"I will," he said. "I'll make everything easy for you. My father will give me a promotion when we get back. We'll move back to the beach. Have a little boy. You can teach him to swim."

"And my skin?"

"I've told you. As soon as there's a baby." He turned, leading her back toward the river. "Let me find it for you. I'm lucky tonight."

"Have I ever showed you how long I can hold my breath?" she asked.

He laughed, patient, willing to put up with her eccentricities. "Forever, I think. That's your thing, isn't it?"

"Not quite," she said. "Not quite that long. What about you, could you hold your breath forever? Would you show me?"

"Meara, you're being silly. We're talking about your ring."

"Yes," she said. "About the ring and the river. It's been so long since you've stood in the waves with me."

"You loved me then. When I called you out of the water."

She smiled, meltingly sweet. "Yes. Then. When it could still have been the other way."

"It doesn't have to be like this." He kissed her bare finger. "Let's go to the river. I'll make things right."

She glanced at her watch. "We've been out long enough."

"Tired?"

"Oh, very. But not so tired as that. Not anymore. Come on, back to the hotel." She spun out of his arms and started walking.

"Tomorrow, then." He hurried to catch-up with her, his steps weaving a little. "Before the plane."

"That sounds nice," she said. "Before I get on a plane with you, we'll go down to the river, together."

"And find the ring."

"And make things right."

EVELYN FOUND THE trunk without difficulty, shoved into the

closet next to a perfectly secure hotel safe. Well, who was she to complain? If he'd used the safe, she would have been out of luck. And, at first, she thought her initial amusement might turn out to be hubris. The padlock on the trunk was better than it looked, and it'd been a long time since she'd practiced. It finally gave, and there was the skin. Stiff and sleek, not as soft as she'd imagined. She was just stepping out, the skin draped over her arm, when she heard the front door opening. She didn't freeze, but slipped deeper into the shadows of the closet, sliding the door closed behind her.

Meara and her ex-husband lingered in the front of the suite. She could hear voices without meaning, laughter, ice in a glass. The smell of the seal skin, musty and animal, filled the small closet. The slick feel of it, the odd warmth and weight, made her oddly uneasy. She held it anyway, trying to imagine what such a thing could mean to a woman like Meara. Some great-grandfather of hers must have killed the seal, dragged it to land and kept its skin, wrapped his first born warm in the folds of it. And Meara needed it back because, well, that bit was still hazy. She needed it. Evelyn had it. That was the part that mattered.

The bedroom door open. The laughter was the husband's, drunk and too confident. He didn't seem to realize Meara had left him; his words were slurred but affectionate.

"Come to bed," he said.

"We're not married," Meara answered. The closet opened, light pouring in and there was Meara, silhouetted. Evelyn winked, but Meara's expression was obscured by shadow. The door closed.

"What does it matter? You're still mine."

"What kind of woman do you think I am?" Meara asked, her voice warming with laughter.

"You're not a woman at all."

"And that's why you can keep me."

"Exactly."

There wasn't much conversation after that, and Evelyn did her best not to hear the other sounds. Her hands fisted tighter and tighter into the skin, her fingers growing stiff and painful. By the time the room went silent, she could barely feel them at all.

She counted to a thousand twice, hoping to hear snoring. Silence, and the smell of the skin, suffocating her.

The closet door opened a second time, the shadowed shape of Meara beckoning. Evelyn glanced to the bed, saw the husband sprawled naked, his arms circling a shape that wasn't there. Aching from the enforced stillness, she crept from the closet and followed Meara out of the bedroom.

Meara wore a thin silk robe that did nothing but accentuate the bareness of her skin and still, she kept walking, until they stood outside, the front door locked behind them. Evelyn shrugged out of her jacket and draped it over Meara's shoulders, a minimal effort at coverage.

"Did you drive?" Meara asked.

"Yeah."

The Henry J had been ugly when she bought it, lacking the chrome and hard angles of a Chevy or Mustang. Now, five years out, it was almost drivable. They'd stopped making them, she'd heard, in '54. And she didn't wonder way. But if Meara was disappointed with the state of the thing, she didn't show it.

"You all right?" Evelyn asked, handing over the skin and starting the car.

Meara didn't answer, just buried her face in the skin. With the help of the streetlights, Evelyn could make out the colour of it, the same deep grey as Evelyn's dress had been. The robe she wore now was orange with white lace. Strange as it was, the skin suited her better.

"You're okay?"

"Yes," Meara said. "Thank you. I will be."

"We can go back to my place. Tomorrow, we'll talk about what's next."

"I need to get back to the ocean," Meara's voice shook, and Evelyn didn't know what with. "I need to get back now. Will you take me?"

Evelyn had never been out of Reno. She knew San Francisco was about five hours away, but couldn't imagine driving that far, leaving the desert and the lights for waves that went on forever.

"Let's talk about it in the morning," she said.

Meara nodded, her face still half hidden by the skin. "Fine," she murmured. "Just, soon."

Evelyn's apartment was little more than a converted bedroom, standing in the middle, she could stretch out her arms and brush both walls with her fingertips. Most the girls she brought home at least commented, but Meara's eyes were glazed and distant. She walked straight to the window and stood looking out at where the shadows of mountains cut stars from the sky.

"I've never been to the Pacific," she said.

"Me either." Evelyn walked over and put her hand on Meara's arm. "You should go to bed."

"I need a bath. Water. Anything." Meara still smelled like smoke and sweat and her husband.

"I'll get you something to sleep in." Evelyn had one set of pyjamas and no second towel. But she offered what she had, all the same, and Meara didn't seem to mind. She took them without letting go of the skin and locked the bathroom door behind her.

Evelyn poured herself a beer, lit a cigarette, and went to the window, trying to see what Meara had seen. San Francisco. The ocean. And what would she do there that she couldn't do in Reno?

After awhile, Meara came to stand beside her. The pyjamas were too long and indecently tight, the buttons straining. She had the skin wrapped around her shoulders like a blanket, the seal's head flopping down her arm.

"Better?" Evelyn asked.

"It's a start." Meara nuzzled against her, slipping under Evelyn's arm and pressing her head against Evelyn's shirt, moisture from her curls soaking through the wet fabric. "Why did you give it back?"

"The skin? You asked for it."

"You could have kept it." Meara's tone was odd, somewhere between teasing and accusation. "Kept me."

"You're welcome to stay." She squeezed Meara's arm, trying to offer comfort without quite understanding why.

"That's not the same thing. I thought you liked me." Flirtatious now, but still with that edge underneath.

"I like you fine." Evelyn spoke carefully. She didn't trust this sudden shift in mood. Meara had been through too much, too recently. "But I don't think you like being kept."

"Don't I?" Meara's barked a laugh. "I don't know. It's what I do. What we've always done. 'Kill them fast, or they'll kill you slow,' that's what my mother always said. And I'd rather not kill you. Of course, that's what I thought about him."

"Well, neither of you are dead." The metaphor was over Evelyn's head, now.

"Her point stands, I think," Meara murmured.

Desperate to change the subject, Evelyn nodded to the parking lot below, "We can leave for San Francisco in the morning."

"Just like that? You'll let me go? Toss me in the ocean?" Meara was staring out the window again, and there was, in that look, a hunger that made Evelyn nervous.

"Maybe not toss, but I'll get you there."

Meara turned from the window, her dark eyes still full of the same aching want. "Will you go in with me? Let me take you out under the waves?"

"I never learned to swim," Evelyn lied.

"Smart girl." Meara put her fingers on the back of Evelyn's neck, pulling her down and kissing her, a greedy, taking sort of kiss. "I guess you're the one who gets away."

"You too," Evelyn said.

"Yeah." Meara drew the word out, almost made a question of it. "I guess, me too."

Biographies

Rhonda Parrish
Editor

Rhonda Parrish's favourite place to be is in water and she does more work there than you'd expect. She's the editor of many anthologies and author of plenty of books, stories and poems. She lives with her husband and two cats in Edmonton, Alberta, and she can often be found there playing Dungeons and Dragons, making blankets or cheering on the Oilers.

Her website, updated regularly, is at rhondaparrish.com and her Patreon, updated even more regularly, is at patreon.com/RhondaParrish.

Catherine MacLeod
The Diviner

Nova Scotia writer Catherine MacLeod's publications include short fiction in *Nightmare*, *Black Static*, *On Spec*, Tor.com, and several anthologies, including *Fearful Symmetries* and *Playground of Lost Toys*. Her story "Hide and Seek" won the inaugural Sunburst Award for Short Story. Catherine's astrological sign is Scorpio—a water sign.

Kevin Cockle
Hidden Depths

Kevin Cockle is a speculative-fiction author credited with over thirty short stories appearing in a variety of anthologies and magazines. His novel *Spawning Ground* is narrowly believed to have invented the micro-genre of "occult game theory". In 2019, Kevin alongside co-writer Mike Peterson won AMPIA's Rosie award for the feature-film screenplay *Knuckleball*, breaking a persistent streak of long-list nominations, honourable mention citations, and other close-but-no-cigar metrics. While there is no need to read *Moby Dick* in order to fathom the story "Hidden Depths", the author notes that the two works do share the same cosmological ocean.

Greta Starling
Creatures of Water and Salt

Greta Starling is a teen poet and writer from Massachusetts. You can find her other work in *Blue Marble Review* and *Capulet Magazine*, or on Instagram @greta_writes. If she's not working on her superheroic novel right now, it might be because she has seal flippers, but you didn't read that here.

Elise Forier Edie
After Ariel

Elise Forier Edie is an award-winning author, playwright and screenwriter based in Los Angeles. You can find her fantasy short stories in anthologies edited by Rhonda Parrish, Ellen Datlow, and Kate Wolford, and in online magazines such as *Mysterion*, *Metaphorosis* and *Disturbed Digest*. Visit her website eliseforieredie.com to find out the latest news about her writing.

Kate Shannon
in the bog where we are walking cautiously

Kate Shannon is a farmer, suspected kraken, and editor from the mountains of Upstate NY, where she lives with too many arcane secrets. Her work explores queerness, feminism, politics, and trauma through a speculative lens. Her publication history includes *The Mithila Review*, *The Metaworker*, *Anti-Heroin Chic*, *High Shelf Press*, and *The Blue Nib*.

Particularly unfortunate souls might find her lurking about on Instagram, @chronosynclastic_.

Sara Rauch
Blazing Stars

Sara Rauch is the author of *What Shines from It: Stories*, which won the Electric Book Award. Her fiction and autobiographical nonfiction have appeared in several publications, including *Meetinghouse, Autofocus, Split Lip, So to Speak, Hobart*, and *Paper Darts*. Though she is fascinated by all things oceanic, she's not much of swimmer—getting her feet wet and turning up sea treasures is her idea of the perfect beach day. She lives in Massachusetts (USA) with her family. www.sararauch.com

Katie Marie
There's Something in the Water

Katie Marie is a horror writer from Norfolk, England.

She has been published in several anthologies and magazines, including *The Horrorzines Book of Ghost Stories* which recently won Best Anthology in the 23rd Annual Critters Readers' Poll.

Katie is a fan of Lovecraftian horror which inspired her story "There's Something in the Water."

www.katiemariewriter.co.uk

Rebecca Brae
The Witch's Diary: Adventures in Hut-sitting

Rebecca Brae lives in Alberta, Canada with her partner, daughter, and growing pack of animal companions. She is an artist, lover of diversity, fog enthusiast, and proud geek who aspires to one day live in a cave by the ocean (with wifi, of course). Rebecca has co-authored two urban fantasy novels, *Chaos Bound* and *Curse Bound*, published a fantasy novel, *The Witch's Diary*, with Tyche Books, and has short stories in two Rhonda Parrish anthologies: *Swashbuckling Cats: Nine lives on the Seven Seas* and *Water: Selkies, Sirens and Sea Monsters*. Connect with her on Twitter @RebeccaBrae and at www.braevitae.com

Colleen Anderson
Siren's Song

Colleen Anderson has a BFA in writing and was nominated for the Aurora, Rhysling and Dwarf Stars Awards in poetry, and longlisted for the Stoker Award in fiction. As a freelance editor, she has co-edited *Tesseracts 17* and Aurora-nominated *Playground of Lost Toys*. She edited *Alice Unbound: Beyond Wonderland* and guest edited *Eye to the Telescope*. She has served on both Stoker Award and British Fantasy Award juries, and received BC Arts Council and Canada Council grants for her writing. Her works have seen print in numerous venues, including *Polu Texni, The Pulp Horror Book of Phobias, The HWA Poetry Showcases*, and *Cemetery Dance*. Her fiction collection, *A Body of Work* was published by Black Shuck Books, UK, and her poetry collection will be published in 2021. When not writing, reading and drinking wine, she keeps an eye out for mould monsters and mermaids. Colleen can be found at www.colleenanderson.wordpress.com

L.T. Waterson
Sarah McKensie

L.T. Waterson lives in a house full of books, halfway up a hill in Southampton, England. As well as the books, her home is also full of boys, three sons and a husband, meaning that finding a quiet spot to write is quite the task! Finding the real world a little mundane, her favourite genre for reading and writing is fantasy, so writing a story about a selkie was almost as easy as making a cup of tea. In the past she has been both a journalist and an archaeologist, and has an abiding interest in history. She has written many short stories which have been published by Clarendon House Publications and Zombie Pirate Publishing, to name just two. She is currently working on the first draft of a fantasy novel.

Chadwick Ginther
Midnight Man versus Carrie Cthulhu

Chadwick Ginther grew up playing in Dead Horse Creek, learned to swim in a murky, artificial lake, and after watching *Jaws* too young, was briefly concerned that sharks might live in waterbeds. The initial inspiration for "Midnight Man versus Carrie Cthulhu" came from seeing artist Nyco Rudolph post pictures of the rusting hulk of the MS Lord Selkirk II on social media. While Chadwick never attended a riverboat grad cruise, he did take to the water in university for a party where everyone was drinking rye & coke by the pitcher as if it was the end of the world. To the best of his recollection, no monsters showed up that night. Chadwick lives in Winnipeg where he writes stories full of skeletons, giants, and dragons.

Julia Heller
Treasure of the Sea

Julia Heller was never far from water where she grew up in Minnesota. Water, and the mysterious creatures that live in and around it, have always fascinated her. Previously published as Julia Christianson in *Through a Glass Darkly: A Collection of Fantasy, Poetry, and Science Fiction*, as well as in several different poetry collections, she writes and edits professionally. Her writers group, made up of friends she met at church, is an invaluable resource for feedback, encouragement, and inspiration. She loves swimming and tubing almost as much as she loves long walks and reading, and has two wonderful dogs, one amazing husband, and an endless delight in fantasy, poetry, and science fiction. Visit her website at juliachristianson.com.

Marshall J. Moore
Nure-Onna

Marshall J. Moore is a writer, filmmaker, and martial artist who was born and raised on Kwajalein, a tiny Pacific island. His childhood was spent diving with sharks, snorkelling with manta rays, and feeding sea turtles. He has travelled to nearly thirty countries, once sold a thousand dollars' worth of teapots to Jackie Chan, and on one occasion was tracked down by a bounty hunter for owing $300 in overdue fees to the Los Angeles Public Library. He lives in Atlanta, Georgia, with his wife Megan and their two cats.

Joel McKay
Number Hunnerd

Joel McKay is a Prince George, B.C.-based writer, avid fly fisherman, and passionate northerner. "Number Hunnerd" is his first published work of fiction. Although, technically, it is not a true story, "Number Hunnerd" is based on Joel's countless adventures into Northern B.C.'s remote wilderness lakes in search of trophy fish. He scratched out the first draft of the story while, you guessed it, staying at a cabin during a fishing trip. Joel is a father to two daughters, an economic development practitioner for small towns by day, and an award-winning former journalist.

Elizabeth R. McClellan
Amphitrite Finds a Confidante

Elizabeth R. McClellan is a domestic and sexual violence attorney by day and a poet in the margins. They are a disabled gender/queer demisexual poet writing on unceded Quapaw and Chikashsha Yaki land. Their work has appeared in the *Air* anthology in this series as well as *Strange Horizons*, *Illumen Magazine*, *Apex Magazine*, *Girls Who Love Monsters*, and many others. They may be most easily found on Twitter @popelizbet

Eric M. Bosarge
In the Arms of Oceana

Eric M. Bosarge believes there is never a bad time to go for a swim, so long as you can warm-up after. He has written two novels, over a dozen short stories, and is the winner of the Maine Literary Award for speculative fiction. When not obsessing about his own writing, he's busy as an editor at Vernacular Books. Learn more at www.vernacularbooks.com

Laura VanArendonk Baugh
Depth Charge

Laura VanArendonk Baugh writes fantasy in a variety of flavours (epic, urban, and historical) as well as non-fiction and a smattering of other genres. She did not realize when she set her Fire story in WW2 London that she was committing to a complete set of elements and UK countries, but here she is, and she'll plan ahead next time. (Narrator: She won't.) Laura did have a delightful time researching this story and fitting it around the historical *U-33* and the capture of the Enigma wheels. She lives in Indianapolis with a husband, two dogs, a stash of fair trade dark chocolate, and a stockpile of disused words which need new homes in fiction. Find more stories and downloads at LauraVAB.com.

Josh Reynolds
Bruno J. Lampini and the Song of the Sea

Josh Reynolds has been a professional author since 2007. He has over thirty novels to his name, as well as numerous short stories, novellas and audio scripts. Much of his work has been for Games Workshop's Black Library, as well as Asmodee's Aconyte Books. Born and raised in South Carolina, he crossed the ocean and now resides in Sheffield with his wife and daughter, as well as a highly excitable dog and something he hopes is a cat.

Liam Hogan
Mano Kanaka: The Eater of Lost Souls

Liam Hogan is an award winning short story writer, with stories in *Best of British Science Fiction 2016 & 2019*, and *Best of British Fantasy 2018* (NewCon Press). He's been published by *Analog*, *Daily Science Fiction*, and Flame Tree Press, among others. He helps host Liars' League London, volunteers at the creative writing charity Ministry of Stories, and lives and avoids work in London. He once fainted in a garden swimming pool and had to be rescued, and is disappointed (but not terribly surprised) he didn't return to consciousness with some sort of aquatic superpower.

More details at happyendingnotguaranteed.blogspot.co.uk

Mari Ness
And the Wind Steal Her Vibrant Call

Mari Ness lives in central Florida, where she often watches alligators slowly make their way across freshwater lakes. Her fiction and poetry have appeared in multiple places, watery and less so, including Tor.com, *Clarkesworld*, *Lightspeed*, *Nightmare*, *Uncanny*, *Fireside* and *Apex*. For more, follow her on Twitter at @mari_ness.

Davide Mana
The Man Who Speared Octopodes

Davide Mana was born and raised in Turin, Italy, with brief stints in London, Bonn and Urbino, where he studied palaeontology (with a specialization in marine plankton) and geology. He currently lives in the wine hills of southern Piedmont, where he is a writer, translator and game designer. In his spare time, he cooks and listens to music (mostly jazz, these days), takes photographs of the local feral cats, and collects old books. He has a blog called Karavansara, and co-hosts a podcast (in Italian) about horror movies, called Paura & Delirio.

Sarah Van Goethem
A Knot of Sea Wives

Sarah Van Goethem is a Canadian Author who resides in southwestern Ontario. Her novels have been in PitchWars and longlisted for both The Bath Children's Novel Award (twice!) and CANSCAIP'S Writing for Children Competition.

Sarah also writes short stories, one of which was nominated for a Pushcart Prize, all of which can be found on her website at SarahVanGoethem.com

Sarah is a nature lover, and a wanderer of dark forests. Born under Pisces and ruled by water, Sarah has been known to live up to the reputation of being a dreamer.

Valerie Hunter
Going Home

Valerie Hunter teaches high school English and has an MFA in writing for children and young adults from Vermont College of Fine Arts. Her stories and poems have appeared in publications including *Cicada, Storyteller, Edison Literary Review, Other Voices, Room,* and *Wizards in Space.* "Going Home" is the second short story she's written about a survivor of the wreck of the Sultana, but the first involving sea monsters.

Kelly Sandoval
Love is a Locked Box and the Ocean on Her Lips

Kelly Sandoval grew up chasing lizards in Reno, and her stories still take her back to those desert hills. She now lives in

Seattle, where the weather is always happy to make staying in and writing seem like a good idea. She shares her home with her patient husband, chaos tornado toddler, and increasingly irate cat. You can find her online at kellysandovalfiction.com.